Rochdale,
United Kingdom

Kandahar, Afghanistan

Karachi, Pakistan

W9-BSR-857

# GUANTANAMO BOY

## ANNA PERERA

ALBERT WHITMAN & COMPANY
CHICAGO, ILLINOIS

Library of Congress Cataloging-in-Publication Data

Perera, Anna.
Guantanamo boy / by Anna Perera.
p. cm.
Summary: Six months after the events of September 11, 2001, Khalid,
a Muslim fifteen-year-old boy from England is kidnapped during a
family trip to Pakistan and imprisoned in Guantanamo Bay, Cuba,
where he is held for two years suffering interrogations, water-boarding,
isolation, and more for reasons unknown to him.
ISBN 978-0-8075-3077-1 (hardcover)
1. Guantánamo Bay Detention Camp—Juvenile fiction.
[1. Guantánamo Bay Detention Camp—Fiction. 2. Prisoners—Fiction.
3. Prejudices—Fiction. 4. Torture—Fiction. 5. Cousins—Fiction.
6. Muslims—Fiction.] I. Title.
PZ7.P42489Gu 2011
[Fic]—dc22
2010048016

Text copyright © 2009 by Anna Perera.
First published in Great Britain by Puffin Books.
Published in 2011 by Albert Whitman & Company.

For more information about Albert Whitman & Company,
visit our web site at www.albertwhitman.com.

*For JLK, with love*

*Guantanamo Boy*
**Advanced Praise for the US Edition**

"Teen readers need and deserve stories that open windows to worlds they cannot and do not inhabit. *Guantanamo Boy* opens wide a window that casts a bright light on the ethics of interrogation. Like Cory Doctorow's *Little Brother*, it should raise questions for which there are no easy answers."
—*Teri S. Lesesne, Professor of Library Science, Sam Houston State University, Huntsville, TX*

"*Guantanamo Boy* is one of those rare reads that bridges a fictitious story to that of a real time, place and event making the story so vividly real in its telling. Khalid is a normal fifteen-year-old English boy, who loves soccer, computer games and has a crush on a girl at school. Soon after 9/11, on a trip to visit Pakistan to visit family Khalid finds himself kidnapped, tortured and eventually incarcerated at the Guantanamo Bay prison for terrorists. Terrorism and its consequences on the innocent are brought into such focus that you are shocked beyond belief with the sheer reading of this story. This is a must-read for young adult readers and a great crossover for adults. A book that will stay with you a very long while; a book you'll want to tell others about, discuss and ruminate over."—*Becky Anderson, Anderson's Book Shops*

"All I could think about while reading *Guantanamo Boy* was this could happen to one of my friends! I'm a sixteen-year-old sophomore and Khalid the main character is only fifteen, an innocent, when he is kidnapped and eventually thrown into prison at Guantanamo Bay. What kept going through my mind was the injustice, the pain, the loneliness, the anger, the tears, and the hopelessness. What a read—it really opened my eyes to the hysteria that terrorism causes in our world."
—*Hallie, age sixteen*

"A chilling and horrifying story of an innocent fifteen-year-old London-born Pakistani boy who is captured by the US government, taken to Guantanamo prison and tortured until he collapses. The novel will raise important questions related to government profiling, human rights, and the use of 'torture.' This may well become one of the most important teen novels about social justice of the new century. It will be chewed up, debated, and hopefully digested."—*Pat Scales, librarian, author, and member, National Coalition Against Censorship Council of Advisors*

"Anna Perera has written a book for young people, but it is a real world book, with lessons for adults as well."
—*Clive Stafford Smith, Founder and Director, Reprieve*

## Praise for the UK Edition

"This powerful and humane book shows that hatred is never an answer, and proves the pointlessness of torture and the danger of thinking of anyone as 'other.'"—*Sunday Times "Children's Book of the Week"*

"One of her greatest achievements is to make the frightening monotony of the two years [Khalid] suffers so full of suspense." —*The Observer*

"An excellent novel . . . superb."—*The Times*

"Exteremely powerful, and the descriptions of torture are genuinely harrowing."—*The Guardian*

"Timely, gritty fiction."—*Times Review*

"Could it happen? It has happened. That's why teenagers should read this book."—*The Irish Times*

# Author's Note

I would have preferred not to write this story, but it wouldn't leave me alone.

The idea came to me after I attended a benefit for a charity called Reprieve, which fights for the rights of prisoners around the world. When Clive Stafford Smith, Reprieve's founder, said that children have been abducted, abused and held without charge in Guantanamo Bay, I was so shocked and appalled that I felt driven to write this book. The title came to me immediately.

Many people have asked how I managed to spend months poring over such a harrowing subject. All I can say is: I felt the story had to be written. To be honest, I asked myself the same question several times but at no point did I want to give up. I like Khalid and his family and friends, and I rooted for him, and for justice—though the justice system has been ripped apart and abandoned to the four winds. I struggled daily with the issues I had to examine, and at night I was kept awake imagining the consequences if I didn't hit the right note—the right combination of pressure and sensitivity—in telling this story. Above all, I was determined to enable you, the reader, to find—through the pages of one boy's fictional experience—some way to understand the stories behind the news.

Once the character of Khalid formed in my brain, I needed to get him to Guantanamo. This turned out to be easier than anticipated: Through my daily research of newspapers and Internet articles I saw that the paranoia, hypocrisy, and fear that led to the creation and maintenance of this prison also provided endless opportunities for Khalid to become an innocent victim of the "War on Terror."

Two books that I turned to while writing mine were *Bad Men: Guantanamo Bay and the Secret Prisons* by Clive Stafford Smith and *Enemy Combatant: My Imprisonment at Guantanamo, Bagram, and Kandahar* by Moazzam Begg. Both provided valuable facts and insights. The British film *The Road To Guantanamo* was useful in providing visual details, as were many news items. I purposely had no contact with anyone who had firsthand experience of the prison because I didn't want to steal or be influenced by another's ordeal.

Telling this story was an ordinary act of compassion. It is a plea for another vision in an increasingly war-torn world because, as we know, there really is no "them," no "they"—there is only us—and more of us.

—Anna Perera

An eye for an eye and the whole world will soon be blind.

—Mahatma Gandhi

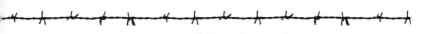

# GAME

*Sometimes*, Khalid thinks as he drags himself home after another boring day at school, *I'd rather be anywhere but here.* The thought of having to explain to his dad what happened yesterday is making his guts turn over and he hopes and prays the letter from school complaining about his behavior in the science lab won't be there waiting for him. But as soon as he unlocks the door to 9 Oswestry Road, the envelope catches the corner of the mat.

*Great.* Khalid shakes his head at the sight of the school crest of Rochdale High on the back of the white envelope. Picking it up, he dumps his bag at his feet, throws his school blazer at the hook on the wall and, breathing in the smell of last night's curry, hurries to the kitchen, where there's more light.

For a moment, Khalid spaces out looking round the open-plan kitchenette. At the knives in the correct slots of the wooden knife holder. At the blue striped dishcloth, folded neatly on the metal drainer, and bar of pink soap in the see-through plastic dish between the shiny taps. Everything's clean and bright, nice and neat, and nothing like the mess and terrible panic he feels at the thought of his dad reading this letter from his science teacher. He slumps down on a chair and listens to the hum of distant traffic. Checks the clock, ticking steadily on the wall, counting down the seconds until the front door clicks open. For the last three days Dad hasn't left the Vegetarian First restaurant in Manchester, where he's been working for ten years as a lunch chef, until around six o'clock and it's only three forty-five now. It could be hours before he gets home.

The sweet smell of polish is coming from the small wooden table pushed up against the yellow wall beside Khalid. He lifts his feet up to rest them on the table. With the letter from school in his hand, he waits patiently for his sisters, six-year-old Aadab and four-year-old Gul, to charge down the hall, followed by Mum rustling bags of shopping.

"Sadly, Khalid, you cannot be trusted to behave sensibly in the science lab," Mr. Hanwood had said. "I'm going to write to your parents about this."

Thanks a lot.

"I never liked him," Khalid says out loud. Yesterday wasn't even his fault. His mate Nico was angry with Devy, who owed him money, and when he asked for it Devy told him where to go and Nico reached for his collar and Devy went crazy and tried attacking Nico with his science book. But Nico ducked and he hit Khalid in the face instead. Naturally Khalid threw his school bag at him, which knocked most of the lab equipment off the bench, sending everything flying. And the only thing Mr. Hanwood saw as he came through the door was Khalid flinging his bag.

Oh well, it's too late now. Unless he gets rid of the letter . . . Things get lost in the mail all the time, don't they? But a moment later the front door bashes open and he hears Aadab and Gul squealing.

"Ouch! Mum, Gul's pinching me," Aadab complains loudly.

"Khalid, how many times have I told you not to leave your bag on the mat and your jacket on the floor?" Mum shouts, ignoring the girls' bickering.

"I didn't!" Khalid shouts back, taking his feet off the table and stuffing the letter quickly into his pants pocket. "I put my jacket on the hook. It must have fallen off."

"Yes, because you didn't hang it up properly," Mum says, suddenly there beside him with a white plastic shopping bag cutting into each arm. Behind her Aadab and Gul thunder up the stairs to change out of their school clothes.

"Sorry." Khalid jumps up to take the heavy bags from her. "What time's Dad home tonight?"

"Any minute now," Mum says. "He'd better not be late again or I'll be having words with that boss of his. He works too hard, your father, and never complains."

Khalid stares at his mum. She's frowning, always worried about something or other, which is probably why her thick, shiny hair is starting to turn gray. Her eagle eyes are all over the place, looking for anything out of order that she might need to put right. Of course he could give her the letter, but she looks tired out and is too busy unpacking groceries, and anyway, she'll just tell Khalid to wait until his dad's back.

Trying to act normal, Khalid wanders into the living room and switches on the TV. There's a news item about Guantanamo

Bay, the prison in Cuba that Mr. Tagg was telling them about in history yesterday. A picture flashes up of a group of soldiers pointing guns at men in orange prison suits bent double on the ground, surrounded by high wire fences with a couple of nasty-looking dogs to one side.

"The camp is being expanded to house more Taliban prisoners," the newsreader says.

*Poor guys*, Khalid thinks.

"Six months after 9/11 and the world is getting madder by the day," Dad says, suddenly behind him.

"Oh, hi, Dad. Didn't hear you come in. How's it going?" Khalid's heart is pounding faster and faster as he tries to sound calm.

"My feet are killing me," Dad mutters, not noticing anything odd as he shuffles away.

Half an hour later, Dad is sitting beside Khalid at the table, telling them all about his day. How much lentil khoresh was wasted. How many half-eaten naan breads were thrown out. He goes full tilt through the contents of the restaurant bins with pain on his face. Aadab and Gul frown along with him, trying not to giggle during his long pauses, and wait patiently for him to unwrap the tin foil from the slices of nutmeg cake he keeps in his pocket for dessert.

Khalid worries and fidgets, not daring to fish the letter from his pocket.

"Things will get worse before they get better," Dad says. "A man came into the restaurant today, pointed his finger at the waiter and said, 'You better watch your step round here,

4

mate.' Can you believe it? The boy hasn't done anything wrong. Nothing except wear the shalwar kameez. That's it."

"The table is not the place to discuss world events," Mum says. "Food goes down badly if you are concerned at all." She doesn't like sitting on the floor to eat either, like her brother's family. "We are living in England," she says. "Not Turkey or Pakistan, and English floors are cold, with or without cushions."

Khalid always does the dishes after tea. It's something Dad taught him to do when he was six years old. "Helping your mum shows her respect," he says, and Khalid's glad to do it, because Mum works hard in the office at the local primary school and is always tired when she gets home.

Today, Khalid dries while Mum washes, picking up the cutlery with the tea towel in one swoop to save time. Quickly arranging the red tumblers in a line on the shelf, anxious to get it over with, because he has plans to meet his Pakistani cousin online at six o'clock. Tariq's in Lahore, so this time works out OK for both of them.

Mum spots him checking the clock. "Tariq isn't a bad boy." She smiles, reading Khalid's mind. "But he can't settle to anything, Uncle says."

"Can't settle? He's learning Arabic, isn't he?" Dad laughs, unfolding his newspaper. "That's not something I ever managed to do. Tariq speaks English, Urdu, Punjabi—now Arabic. He's going places, that young man! You'll see."

Khalid glances at his mother, but there's no smile on her face.

"Why don't you like Tariq, Mum?"

"He's having too big an influence on you. All the time you are Tariq this, Tariq that, as if he's someone very important." Mum folds her arms and raises her eyes to heaven. "Even Dad says this." She glances at Dad's blank, innocent face with disbelief. "Yes. Yes, you do!"

Dad smiles secretively at Khalid, as if to say, *Let it go*. But Mum can't let it go, insisting on staring at the computer in the corner as if it's an evil monster.

"My brother tells me Tariq spends too much time on the computer and he doesn't listen," she continues. "What kind of young man lives like this? A very bad way to behave, and don't argue."

"I wasn't going to!" Khalid protests, while remembering it was Mum who encouraged their friendship in the first place. For a long time, because of her, he's hero-worshipped his older cousin. Sending his first e-mail to him almost two years ago, when he heard the news from Mum that Radhwa, the two-year-old sister Tariq adored, had died. Died slowly after a long illness. Mum explained that Tariq went totally crazy, refusing to believe she was gone, and had nightmares for weeks on end. At the time Tariq was fifteen, Khalid only thirteen, and though the whole family was brokenhearted, no one took Radhwa's death harder than Tariq.

"Write to him, your cousin," Mum had ordered. "Say something to help him get better." So he did, e-mailing him the hottest Web links for his home town, Rochdale, and their football club. It was strange at first, e-mailing someone he didn't really know, but bit by bit they became friends who chatted mostly about the stuff they had in common.

Computers, video games, football, movies, the usual things that everyone likes whether they live in Rochdale or Lahore.

If Mum ever found out that Khalid sneaked downstairs to talk to Tariq for hours on end, in the middle of the night when everyone was asleep, she'd have a fit. But if she knew how much he was learning from his cousin, not that he was ever going to tell her, then perhaps she wouldn't worry so much. He could talk to Tariq about stuff that his friends wouldn't care about. They were probably all going to stay in Rochdale their whole lives, but Khalid wanted to see the world. He didn't want to end up like his dad, working hard for someone else all his life. Khalid was always telling his dad to set up a restaurant of his own, but he wouldn't listen.

"There's nothing I haven't seen," Tariq writes in his e-mails to Khalid. "I've been to Turkey, to Medina, seen the first mosque at al-Quba. You wouldn't believe how green the dome is."

Khalid tries to imagine a green that's brighter and greener than any other green, but he can't. Green is just another color to him.

Tariq tells him about the sacred places of Islam, especially Medina, where the Prophet Muhammad is buried. But they are places Khalid finds it hard to care about. His curiosity sometimes closes down when he reaches these bits of Tariq's e-mails. The places that interest Khalid are cold and isolated, like remote parts of Iceland and the Arctic. Countries with few people and loads of floating icebergs would suit him. He hates being hot. Greenland, for example, he'd love to go there.

Plus he hates being preached to. It annoys him because it

makes him feel he's back in school, not at home chatting to his cousin. Tariq's only two years older than him, yet sometimes he treats him like a little kid. For a start, Khalid doesn't know where any of these places are. He's only been to Pakistan once, and that was eleven years ago, to see Uncle, his mother's brother, who moved there from Turkey. He hadn't met Tariq, who was staying with his grandmother at the time. All Khalid could remember was the heat and the dusty roads, plus the curved gold sword on the wall in Uncle's living room. It's not much of a memory.

He's never been to Karachi to visit Dad's sisters. But he imagines it to be just as boring as the small town near Lahore where Tariq and his family still live.

The bits of Tariq's e-mails that really interest Khalid are about computer games, and now that Tariq has invented a game of his own, Khalid can't get enough of their online sessions.

"Khalid's actually touch-typing now. You should see him," Dad boasts to anyone who'll listen. Mostly, that person is Mac, their Scottish neighbor from number 11, with daughters the same age as Khalid's sisters. "He types faster than the wind." Mac pats Khalid on the head whenever he pops round, which makes everyone laugh. Then Dad and Mac wander outside to talk about petrol gauges, drive shafts, tuning, or something else that the rest of them don't care about.

Mum hurries Aadab and Gul to get in the bath and the kitchen falls silent. Always the best time of day for Khalid.

The barrage of words from Tariq begins the moment the kitchen door closes and Khalid is at last alone in front of the computer, which takes up all the space on the smaller corner table.

"Hi, cuz," the e-mail starts. "I haven't had time to look at Rochdale Football Club's results for Saturday. How did they do?"

"It was a draw—a bit of a tough game," Khalid fills him in.

"Which means they have to win the next match or they'll be in danger of being relegated, yeah?" Tariq types.

"Looks that way." Khalid sighs as he waits for Tariq's response.

"What a shame for Rochdale. The only real lesson I learned today is that no matter how much you learn there is always more to find out. Reading many books has shown me how little I know about anything! And I thought that match was going to be a sure-fire thing. For something happy I will tell you what I have been doing today . . ."

Khalid rushes through the news about Tariq's Arabic lessons. Scrolling quickly down the page to the bit he wants. Leaning forward, elbows on the table, to grab every detail.

From the very first sentence, "Latest game news," Khalid hangs on every word of his cousin's ideas and plans, whether he understands them or not.

"I haven't decided what to call it yet," Tariq begins, "but I think six characters placed in different countries would be the best. Then we can have multiple players online at the same time dissing each other. What do you think?"

"Yeah, six would be brilliant," Khalid types quickly. "It's gotta have a real cool name, though!!!!"

Khalid doesn't notice time passing as he reads about the

complexity required to implement the programming language. Plus the goals, rules, mathematical framework Tariq's been working on to put the game together make it sound as if his invention is going to be even better than *Counter Strike*. Khalid loves *Counter Strike*, a war-based shooting game that he plays at Nico's place on his console. One team are the terrorists and the other are the Special Forces who have to sneak in and defuse the bomb. Tariq and Khalid both love playing *Grand Theft Auto* too, getting an adrenaline rush from blowing stuff up and stealing cars. *Starcraft*, the online strategy game set in space, is their favorite at the moment, but they chat about loads of other games while Tariq finishes off his own invention, which doesn't have a name yet. It's going to be basic, but it's much more fun knowing that it's their own private game.

These e-mails make Khalid feel so much better that he forgets about giving Dad the letter from school. Then the door opens and Mum silently crosses the kitchen to pluck something from the fruit bowl.

"It's half past seven. Get off the computer, Khalid!"

It's always the same. There's never enough time to talk to Tariq. Reluctantly, Khalid quickly types, "Later, cuz!" and then closes the computer down.

"Nations around the world are strengthening their anti-terrorism laws. Pakistan is providing America with more military bases and airports to use for its attack on the Taliban," the newsreader states from the TV in the living room.

"Haven't you got any homework to do?" Mum sighs.

"I can't work with the TV on in there," Khalid says.

"Oh, that's a good one." Mum refuses to be taken in by his excuse for a moment, then gives him an only-kidding smile before heading back to the living room and shutting the door behind her.

Dragging his school bag to the table, Khalid is soon absorbed in Galileo.

Galileo, the genius who knew everything about astronomy and mathematics. He even managed to improve the telescope. Khalid sits back and folds his arms. How did Galileo know the telescope needed improving? Thinking about this makes his mind go fuzzy. There's so much to take in and most of it Khalid has to read twice before it makes any sense at all. One thing Khalid's sure of, though, is that Galileo is way cool. Everyone throughout history knew that. He even took on the Catholic Church.

"We're all part of this misery." Dad pops his head round the door to get a glass of water. Khalid doesn't know what he means or what he's talking about. Nor does he ask. But he thinks about it for a moment. That's Dad all over. He says things you can't pin down, which is a major part of the problem between them. How exactly is Dad going to react when he hands him the letter? He just doesn't know.

The thought flashes through Khalid's mind that his friends, if they were here, might think Dad was a bit weird saying something like that out of the blue. But then his family aren't what people suppose they are. Mum has never worn the veil and neither did her mother in Turkey, where she was brought up. Maybe Dad was referring to the fact there has been more hostility in the neighborhood lately towards Muslims. Though

Khalid hasn't been called any names, or been punched or anything, a couple of the Muslim guys at school said they felt totally unsafe being out at night now, while before 9/11 they had felt fine.

OK, they sometimes say Friday prayers and usually eat halal food, but that's as far as the Muslim religion goes in Khalid's family. Dad was brought up in Karachi, Pakistan. His father, who is now dead, owned a furniture shop there and Dad was the last child born to his mother, when she was thirty-nine years old. His three sisters are much older than him and only the oldest is married, so the others live with her and her husband.

"Those whispering ninnies!" Dad calls them. He doesn't like them much and hardly ever mentions them.

"Your dad's just like my grandpa," Nico says. "Always telling you to straighten your shirt and comb your hair before you leave the house. As if anyone cares about that stuff any more!"

Whenever Khalid sees Nico on the street, he's wearing a black T-shirt and blue low-riders, eating a bag of chips. Always grinning like a lunatic, as if he's just seen something mad. Nico's a mate but he's also the main supplier of alcohol to kids in the area. Being lucky enough to have an eighteen-year-old brother, Pete, who looks just like him, Nico only has to flag up his brother's ID at the local store to buy crates of beer, which he then sells at inflated prices. Why he spends so much on chips, Khalid can't understand. But then Nico always has an answer.

"Eating chips, drinking beer and nailing those steroid heads in the park, how's that for a brilliant life, eh, mate?" His deep laugh sounds more like a barking dog than a fifteen-year-old boy, which makes Khalid laugh too. Nico's never mentioned nailing Muslims and Khalid doubts he ever will. He's not that kind of kid. None of his mates are. They don't see color, race or religion, any stuff like that. And the kids they call the steroid heads are a bunch of eleven- and twelve-year-olds with shaved heads who live on the estate behind the school and get their kicks from acting hard and bullying old ladies.

"You finished your homework?" Mum's back in the kitchen and watching Khalid out of the corner of her eye as she makes a cup of mint tea.

"Yeah. Think I'll go round Nico's for a bit to talk about the match tomorrow."

Mum's mouth twitches as she sits down at the table with a magazine. "Ask Dad first, Khalid. I don't like that cocky boy!"

"Mum! Nico's top of the class in math and his brother's at Manchester Uni doing electrical engineering. Dad says you don't get much cleverer than that."

"All the same, there's something strange about him. I don't care what you say."

"Yeah, yeah, whatever!" Khalid kisses her on the cheek, pretending to be interested for a moment in her *World of Cross-Stitching* magazine. The sudden smell of her jasmine perfume catches him before, quick as a flash, he grabs his cool blue cap and dashes out.

"Wait a minute, son!" Dad lifts his head from under the hood of Mac's old Ford Fiesta as Khalid scoots past. "You can't go out in your school clothes. You'll wreck them."

Khalid puts on his innocent face. "I'm only going to Nico's to check some math—a few equations and that."

For some reason this makes Mac laugh.

"When I was your age we didn't go round bothering our heads about math and footie when the streets were packed with girls."

Dad sighs. He hates Mac passing on advice like this to Khalid. But at fifty-four Mac is always that bit out of touch, so Dad doesn't need to worry that Khalid is listening to him properly. Khalid tries to imagine what it would be like for Mac to hang round with his mates in the park, see what life is really like now.

"Aye, you couldn't move for hotties round our way!" Mac laughs to himself.

"Yeah? Cool!" Khalid grins, wandering off. "See you later."

At the end of the road, Khalid rolls back his shirt cuffs, pulls his school trousers low until they sag, turns right, then second left and cuts through the cul-de-sac to the park. Once there, he runs past the swings. Straight to the spot by the oak trees where everyone hangs out on the broken benches.

"Eya, Kal! Whassup?" Tony Banda grins. "Nothing's like going on here, mate."

They were all there: Nico, Mikael, Holgy, Tony, a few other random kids from school, all making their own entertainment. Rough-readying each other with fake punches, dirty jokes, cigarettes and the odd can of lager. Fighting each other for the last of the Pringles.

"Idiot face! Give it back!" Holgy tries grabbing the green tube from Tony.

"Nah, you ate all mine last week!" Tony whacks him over

the head with it. Then Holgy, thick brown hair in his eyes, elbows Tony until he drops the Pringles. Nose-diving the tube as he runs backwards, pouring crumbling crisps down his throat. Everyone laughing because, let's face it, Holgy's a nutter.

"Goal. Goal, yay!" Mikael shouts out the picture flashing at the front of his mind, which makes Khalid smile. The main thing they have in common apart from school is the fact they're on the same five-a-side football team on Thursday evenings. How their little team is doing is never far from anyone's mind, especially Mikael's.

"We need a game plan for tomorrow's match." Tony Banda looks at Nico.

"Let's just try and win for once." Nico drags on a cigarette. "How about that for a change?"

"Yeah, we were a bit sluggish last week," Khalid adds.

"A bit sluggish?" Holgy roars with laughter. "We haven't scored a goal in ages and, Tony, try not to get another card from the referee for spitting tomorrow, eh?" A nifty goalie with big calf muscles, Holgy croaks like a sea lion with every spectacular save he makes. He's the best player of the lot.

"Leave it out," Tony says. "That wasn't my fault."

Tony's a great attacker, Khalid thinks. He pushes forward like no one else. But no matter how long Tony's played football, he still can't keep to the rules. It's a shame his mind is usually somewhere else.

"Where's Lexy tonight, Tony?" Mikael asks. The mention of Lexy makes Tony go all gooey. In fact, with her blonde hair, big blue eyes and a great figure, she makes them all go gooey.

Standing there on the sidelines at every match, dressed in a pink duffel coat whatever the weather, she runs up to Tony in her high-heel black boots when he's sent off (which happens every other game) and throws her arms round him as if he's just scored a goal.

"Dunno," Tony says. "She'll turn up, I expect." And, just like that, there she is, tripping towards them in her high heels.

"What does she see in you, Tony?" Nico shakes his head in disbelief as she comes across the park.

"Lexy needs her eyes tested," Mikael states, and they all laugh.

"Too right she does," agrees Khalid. Lexy is fit, but he really fancies this Irish girl from school, Niamh. *Why am I too shy to do anything about it, though?* he asks himself, falling back in the damp grass to stretch out. There's a sudden chill in the darkening clouds, which adds to his nervousness as he finally rips the envelope from his pocket.

"Whoa!" says Nico, whooping with laughter as he spies the school's crest.

"Go on, Hanwood, do your worst," Khalid announces. Holding the envelope to the sky, he tears it open and begins reading in a teacher-like voice for everyone to enjoy:

"Dear Mr Ahmed,

Your name was mentioned at the committee meeting today for the school fête, which is being held next term on July second. We wondered if it would be at all possible for you to set up another curry stall as you did so successfully last year? *Blah, blah, blah*."

Khalid kills himself laughing at the wasted hours he's spent worrying over nothing. "Hanwood said he was going to write a letter about my behavior in the lab."

"He's said that to me a million times. School fête? It's still only March," Nico says.

"So you've learned the months of the year, have ya, Nico?" Holgy grins.

"Januwaree," Mikael joins in. "Febooraree."

"Shut up!" Nico kicks him.

Then, beyond the dissing, a spiraling warmth breaks out between them. These lads of the same age who share the same streets and school. The same teachers. Same gelled spiky hair. The same stupid jokes and sometimes the same dreams that just might, one day, come true.

# BLOOD'S THICKER THAN WATER

The next evening, Gul and Aadab are chattering away in the warm, cozy kitchen, bathed in the glare of the red shade hanging from the ceiling. The whole family sits at the table, finishing off a delicious plate of chapattis, curry and vegetable fried rice. The room smells of fried onions, tomatoes and garlic, Khalid's favorite smell, and he's happy about more than the delicious smell of food today because Mr. Tagg gave him a B plus for his essay plan on the Spanish Inquisition. Not that it changes anything once Mum tells everyone what's happening.

"We're going to Karachi next week for the Easter school holidays," she says casually, as if announcing they've just run out of salt.

Khalid sits bolt upright. For a moment he's too stunned to speak. "What? That sucks!" he moans. But Mum just frowns at him, as if to say, *Don't try that. Don't start that.* But surely this can't be right? "There'll be nothing to do there. If we have to go, why can't we stay with your brother near Lahore instead? I'd rather see Tariq than those whispering ninnies you're always complaining about, Dad. You can all go, but

I'm staying here with my mates." He slumps down, exhausted by this sudden shower of protests.

"That's enough from you!" Shocked by his outburst, Mum shakes her finger at him, while Dad lowers his eyes. "Dad hasn't seen his sisters since before you were born and, well, maybe you'll think twice when you know your grandmother has just died and that's why we're going."

"What?" Khalid looks from one to the other, suddenly ashamed. It's typical of Dad to hide his news and get Mum to tell them what's happening. It's also annoying to Khalid that he's shot his mouth off so quickly and ended up embarrassing himself.

"Of course the funeral happened within twenty-four hours, so we're too late for that," Mum adds.

No one speaks for what seems like a very long time, though it's probably no more than a couple of minutes. Then Mum gets up. Gul and Aadab follow to help her clear the table, making faces at Khalid for being in the wrong, leaving him and Dad sitting there in deathly silence. No mention of the pieces of nutmeg cake in his pocket they always fight over after dinner. No mention of the half-eaten potatoes and chickpeas thrown in the bin during Dad's time at the restaurant today. No mention of the grandmother Khalid's never met who's just died.

Khalid wonders why he hadn't noticed Dad's lack of conversation earlier this evening. Why he hadn't guessed something was wrong. Perhaps because he was too pleased with himself over his B plus? Enjoying the family's praise too much to notice Dad's serious face. Now he feels ashamed and too embarrassed to apologize or ask for his father's forgiveness.

Aadab clatters dishes in the sink one after the other, while Gul runs around for no reason. In the end Mum ushers them out of the kitchen. And Khalid sits and sits, fiddling with the stainless-steel salt cellar. Moving it up and down, around and about, waiting for the lecture from Dad to begin. He doesn't dare leave the table before him, but Dad doesn't say anything at first, just looks at him for a long time in a way that makes him feel bad. Then he gets up, pushes the pine chair back and pauses for a second. Khalid feels the hesitation bearing down on him and twists in his seat.

A moment passes before Dad turns and quickly walks away. Khalid bites his lip to stop himself from saying something silly to lighten the mood.

That's how it's been lately between them. Pretty distant. Both of them have been suffering from strong emotions that are too complicated to find words for. Even harder to share. Nico's right: he's more like a grandfather than a dad. Old-fashioned. He's nothing like his mates' fathers, who swear and have a pint like other people. Khalid wishes he could talk to his dad about the things that matter to him, like Tariq's computer game for example, but even imagining doing that flashes up a picture of Dad tutting and frowning. "Games are not what life's about," he'd say.

If only he'd come down the park just once to see Khalid play football. If only he'd ask about his mates. Dad's never horrible about anyone, not ever, but he seems to live in his own world and sometimes Khalid thinks he might as well not be here. Plus he's so irritating these days, where once Khalid had thought him funny and basically a nice guy.

For instance, Nico's dad always wears baggy jeans and T-shirts and has recently had his head shaved and a five-centimeter tattoo put on his neck which says "Defend Her." "That's awesome," his mates say. "So cool for a guy his age!" While Khalid's dad wears a white shirt and black trousers every day, as if he's a kid going to school. Black hair neatly combed with a side parting makes him totally boring too, but in actual fact he's far better-looking than Nico's dad. Everyone can see that. If only he'd get a nice haircut or do something different apart from cook at the restaurant, then come home, clean his shoes and watch TV. Or chat to Mac next door about cars.

Khalid tidies the spectacular mess of salt he's made with his fingers on the table and is scooping it into his cupped hand when Mum appears at the door.

"I can see you've been thinking about your rude behavior," she says.

"Nah, I haven't been thinking about anything, actually," Khalid says with a slight tone of irritation in his voice.

"I see. Khalid, please don't be the way you are around these friends you're always with. Understand family is the only way to live. Family is thicker than friends."

"Blood's thicker than water, Mum!" Khalid smiles, his irritation gone.

"That's what I said." Mum's expecting Khalid to argue some more, but instead he bites his lip.

"I didn't know she died, did I?" he tries explaining.

"Submission to your parents shows respect. You know that, Khalid."

"Only said that ten thousand times before, Mum. Will you really not let me see Tariq if we're going to Pakistan anyway?"

Mum sighs. "Lahore is too far from Karachi. Going there would only add to the cost." She starts playing with her hair in a childlike way, her big brown eyes staring into space as her mind races elsewhere. Then she rushes to get the notepad and pencil from beside the phone. Quickly, she makes a list of things she must take to Pakistan for Khalid's aunties. Once she starts writing, she can't stop.

Khalid slowly, very slowly, gives up hope of a nice Easter holiday hanging out with his mates as he glances at Mum's boring list:

1. Shampoo
2. Soap
3. Hairbrushes
4. Toothpaste and toothbrushes
5. Nail files
6. Hand cream
7. Moisturizing cream
8. Pencils
9. Paper
10. Books

The list goes on and on, the only interesting item being "21. DVDs." Khalid smiles. *Oh no*. Surely Mum isn't going to bring them her favorite film, *The Sound of Music*?

Soon he drifts off to the computer on the table in the corner to google Karachi. It's a place he knows nothing about. The first page tells him it has a population of fifteen million and lots of international restaurants and high-rise office buildings, as well as a beach called Sandspit, which makes him laugh. He learns that 69 percent of people in Pakistan don't have access to running water or a flush toilet. There is massive unemployment and water pollution, as well as a high rate of illiteracy, which turns him off the whole subject. Helps him switch his search to the Spanish Inquisition, before Mum says, "Run to that new shop on the main road for chilli powder and tamarind paste, Khalid, please. We're totally out." She hands him some money.

"Do I have to?" Khalid moans.

One look from Mum sends him running to the door, jamming his school shoes on without a backward glance. When Mum narrows her eyes in fury like that she usually just shouts for Dad.

"Hiya, Kal," voices call from behind as Khalid reaches the shiny, bright shops. It's Holgy and Tony, lounging about outside Rashid's Electricals. Khalid hoped to run into them at the park on the way back. Not here at the shops.

"There's been a right punch-up at the park. Some nerd's in the hospital. Don't bother going down there later, because they've locked the gates early." Tony jumps off his swish bike, chewing gum madly. Black hoodie pulled low over his round, innocent-looking face. Dance music twittering in his earplugs.

"Yeah? What's gone on?" There are always fights round here after dark. Khalid hopes it's no one he knows. Holgy pulls a face. Tony shrugs. Neither of them care much, knowing bad news always travels fast. If it was a mate or someone close they would have heard by now.

"By the way," Holgy says, laughing, "Mikael's parents are bunking off somewhere on Saturday so he's having a party."

Khalid's about to get the details, as he's never been to Mikael's before, when a commotion starts up outside the fish-and-chip shop a few doors down. A slim woman in a gray tracksuit and gym shoes, about thirty years old, is arguing with the steroid heads from school.

A slightly tubby kid swigs from a bottle of beer. Behaving like an idiot, he starts jumping up and down as if bouncing on a trampoline, while the others surround the woman, grabbing her chips and flinging them in the air. "There goes another one—wooeee!"

Taunting her with a blizzard of daft hand movements, they pump her space with their shoulders so one of them can dip his hand in her tracksuit pocket to steal her mobile.

*They're at it again*, thinks Khalid. "Hey!" he screams at the top of his voice. Being the kind of kid who likes a beer now and then, has stolen a couple of things from the stalls down the market for a bet, he often finds himself pretending to be wilder, more confident and stronger than he really is to prove he can hold his own with some of the older kids. But today resentment at the steroid heads' stupid behavior rises in him like never before.

Holgy and Tony laugh their heads off as Khalid angrily runs over to push the kids aside. "Give it here!" He knocks the mobile out of the little fair-haired one's hand, then grabs the bag of chips from the tubby one, who now has them.

"Sorry," Khalid tells the woman as he hands back the phone. "They're a bunch of losers."

She thanks him briefly with a nod and refuses the remaining chips with a sour expression. Gives him the feeling she doesn't want his help, then strides off proudly, swishing her ponytail as if she was never in any danger in the first place.

"Whaddya do that for?" One of the kids frowns. "We were only having a bit of fun."

"Push off, you jerk!" Khalid says. "Do that again and I'll thump you."

When he turns back to Holgy and Tony, they are still killing themselves laughing.

"What are you like? Fess up, Kal. Didn't you see—ha-ha-ha—how pale she went—ha-ha—when you screamed at them?" Holgy says. "I mean, you're pretty tall, Kal. She was more scared of you than—ha-ha—of that lot."

"If you had a beard, you'd be a dead ringer for Bin Laden, mate," Tony adds, and both of them crack up again.

"Yeah?" Suddenly it dawns on Khalid that the woman maybe thought he was a terrorist or something. "These are dangerous times for Muslims," his dad said the other day. And he was right. That much he does know.

It's pouring with rain by the time Khalid turns the corner to the new Indian grocery shop. A teenager from school, Matt Garwell, shouts to him from the pavement opposite. He does a mental dance to show how wet he is, his brown, stringy hair falling like worms over his pug face.

"Hiya, Kal. I'm freakin' soaked." As Matt runs off, Khalid

reads the message written in large black words on his flapping white T-shirt: SMALL-MINDED FLAG-WAVING XENOPHOBE. Eh? Khalid stops for a second to wonder at the meaning of the word "xenophobe."

Hands tucked deep in his pockets, Khalid stands under the green canvas of the shop, staring at the display of grapefruits, cabbages, tomatoes, peppers, ginger and garlic, suddenly unable to remember why he's there. Unable to remember anything but the look of contempt on the slim woman's face and Tony's words, which he knows were supposed to be a joke, but even so . . . It's the first time world events and George Bush's so-called "War on Terror" really come home to him.

A sudden shiver rises up his spine. A damp, fearful chill spreads over him, sinking deep inside, until a weird kind of paralysis sets in. He'd run out of the house in his open-necked school shirt and trousers, thinking he'd be back home in ten minutes. But in that time one event has changed his life. Being resented and feared for what? For having brown skin and black hair? For being a Muslim? A bitter, nasty feeling opens up inside, making him angry with himself for helping a woman who can't look beyond the surface and see he was only trying to help.

In the end, the owner of the shop pushes the door open and waits stock-still, hands on hips, gazing out at the passing traffic, pretending not to notice Khalid, who's been staring at a pile of plump grapefruits for quite a while.

Finally, their dark eyes meet.

"It's not like I'm doing anything wrong," Khalid says crossly.

"No." The man stares at him, stroking his modest gray beard. "I can see that."

"Sorry!" Khalid is cross with himself now. There's no need to take it out on this old guy just because that woman made him feel like a lump of dirt.

"I've got an old fleece jacket upstairs if you want it," the man says.

"Nah, I'm cool. Thanks, mate." Khalid gives him a quick grin. "I do need some chilli powder and tamarind paste, though."

Pleased he's all right, the man nods him into the brightly lit shop and insists on getting him some hot tea. Disappearing behind a blue striped curtain to fetch Khalid's drink, he beckons him to sit on the wooden stool beside the till. The counter is crammed with chocolate, soft mints, chewing gum and scratch cards. There's a smell of ginger mixed with carpet cleaner, which adds to the strangeness of it all.

"Kindness is the quickest path to heaven," the shopkeeper says when he returns, as though Khalid's thoughts were written all over his face. Then he tells him his name's Nasir and he's been in England for twenty-five years but here in Rochdale for only three weeks. "I always wanted to be my own boss. Now I have a shop."

Khalid snaps out of his trance. Wishes his dad could be more like that.

The youngest of six children, Nasir grew up in a mountain village in Pakistan, where his elderly mother still lives, growing her own vegetables and keeping chickens, just as she's always done.

"Does she live far from Karachi?" Khalid says.

"About fifty miles," Nasir answers. "Why?"

"We're going there for Easter to see my aunties." Khalid half smiles.

"I'm thinking you must be careful, lad. My wife's family have plenty of friends who live there and they say the Americans are paying people big bucks to report anyone suspicious to them. US soldiers came with guns in the night and kidnapped two brothers who were in Karachi for two weeks from Saudi to set up a business selling cooking oil.

"Neighbor saw soldiers dragging the brothers from the house. Nice boys, she said they were. Not a bit suspicious-looking. The next day she heard that another neighbor had been paid a lot of money for reporting them to the American authorities. Remember, most people have so little money in Pakistan. The Americans are offering more than five years' wages for these reports."

"That's stupid," Khalid says. "Once they find out the brothers are innocent, they'll want their money back."

"The brothers never returned." Nasir shakes his head. "The rich neighbor has bought a car and rented a big house with the money the Americans gave him and now his friends want to cash in too. They are on the lookout for anyone new in town."

Khalid can't believe it. "That sounds like bounty hunters like back in the Wild West!"

"Yes, exactly the same lawlessness is there now," Nasir says, nodding.

"Why don't they pick up some real terrorists?" Khalid asks.

"Like George Bush?" Nasir laughs, raising his gray eyebrows.

"But we're from England. We speak English," Khalid says. "Surely we're safe?"

"Were you born in England?" Nasir frowns.

"Yeah, I was. Turkey's where my mum comes from. My dad's from Pakistan, but he's lived here for twenty years."

"Ah! But still you have to watch your step if you're going there," he warns.

"Our whole family's more British than anything else, to be honest," Khalid says. "Anyway, I've only just turned fifteen."

"That might not be young enough." Nasir looks concerned. "Five thousand dollars is a lot of money to get for a foreign Taliban."

Hints of a dangerous trip begin gathering in Khalid's mind as he swigs the last of the tea. The sound of a vacuum cleaner suddenly humming behind the curtain makes him think Nasir wants to lock up, so he shifts from the stool.

"I bet they let the brothers go in the end," Khalid says, nodding goodbye and wandering home with the chilli powder and tamarind paste safely stowed in a blue plastic bag under his arm. All the time puzzling how anyone can sell lies about people they don't know for money.

Then he starts questioning the truth of Nasir's words. *Surely the brothers were released when their story was checked by the Americans and they legged it home to Saudi?* Khalid is itching to find out more. He unlocks the back door, deciding not to mention anything to Dad about Nasir in case he rubbishes him. Tells him not to speak to Nasir again.

Luckily, Dad's standing with his back to him by the sink, busy laying out sheets of newspaper so he can polish his black shoes, which gives Khalid the chance to switch on the computer in the opposite corner before he can object. Cleaning shoes is a job Dad takes great care over. Unlacing them before lining up two brushes and a soft cloth and flipping open a tin of black Kiwi polish, he brushes the shoes methodically from toe to heel to remove the dirt while Khalid frantically types a message to Tariq.

"Hey, cuz, do you know anyone in al-Qaeda?" he asks.

"Don't ask questions like that, Khalid, you dorkhead, unless you want to get yourself killed," Tariq instantly replies. Which strikes Khalid as slightly over the top. Who on earth would suspect him of anything dodgy?

"OK, sorry, calm down. I just heard the Americans are paying stacks of money to Pakistanis to shop anyone suspicious to them—is that true?"

"Cuz, it's a paranoid hellhole here. That's only one of the terrible things that are happening. Now, tell me how Aadab and Gul are doing."

What? It's the last thing Tariq always asks before he signs off. And he's not just being polite either. No, sisters are a subject they never talk about, because of what happened to Radhwa. But still he asks. Maybe to show he's all right about it now.

Khalid replies in the same way he always does: "Annoying as usual!" But it doesn't register because the screen fades. Crashes. Leaving Khalid staring at the black square in a temper as he reboots, while Dad smiles at his black, highly polished shoes, which he proudly thrusts at the ceiling light.

"See the shine on that? Look!"

"Can't miss it, Dad!" Khalid nods, taking out his mobile

to text Mikael for the address of the party on Saturday night while the computer boots up.

With Khalid there are two types of friends: those who like football and those who don't. Mikael is one of the former. Small for his age and quieter than the rest of them, he's a great defender. Fast on his feet like Khalid, who's solid at the back, Mikael's always the first to praise a teammate and never lets unexpected injuries, bad weather or no-shows dampen his enthusiasm. Khalid laughs at the picture in his head of Mikael charging down the field like a rocket in lift-off while the others skid in the mud after him.

Khalid wishes their team was doing better. They've had a lot of bad luck this season and now he realizes he's going to miss a couple of important matches because of the trip to Karachi. The dream of being promoted to a higher league depends on those games.

"48 Mandela hse c u l8r," Mikael texts back.

Khalid thinks maybe he shouldn't go to the party. He'd be chancing his arm to stay out past ten thirty. Then he glances up to see Dad staring at him with worried eyes. Obviously a bit put out.

"What's the matter, Dad?"

"Your school shoes are a disgrace, Khalid. When did they last see a jot of polish?"

"What's the point in cleaning them? They'll only get messed up again as soon as I go out."

By the look on Dad's face, Khalid knows it's time to give up and shuts the computer down. Tariq isn't back online now anyway. Under Dad's watchful eyes, he cleans his damp, scuffed shoes, hoping it will partly make up for his earlier outburst.

"Point the toe away from you. That's it!" Dad frowns with concern at the half-hearted job Khalid's making of it. "Shoe polish has a habit of getting on white shirts," he says, grinning widely. Their dark eyes meet with a lightness of touch that says past arguments are forgotten for the moment. Dad laughs at himself for once, instead of listing all the things that drive him mad. Things like Khalid's shirt collar being up on his neck instead of neat and flat like his. Forever pointing out how he slouches all the time and why his eye-rolling and abrupt answers to everything stop him from making the best of himself. The list goes on and on, but for now there's peace between them and it feels nice.

"They say car-jackings, armed robberies and murders are happening every day in Karachi, Dad."

"That's also why we must go, son. To pay respect to my mother and make arrangements for my sisters. You know Fatima, the oldest one? Her husband is very ill, cannot work at all. This might be the last chance we will have to see him. I must bring money and things for them. Perhaps move them to another part of the city. We'll be safe there, don't worry. It will be good for you to see Pakistan again and remember where you come from. Gul and Aadab have never met their aunties before, so it's a treat for them also. Plus I need you to take care of your mother while I see to everything. Do you think you can do that for me?"

Khalid realizes how selfish he's been. "Course I will, Dad. But how come we can afford the plane tickets? They must cost a fortune." He blows the last specks of dust from his shoes, then snaps the lid awkwardly on the Kiwi tin.

"All my life I've been saving, you know that, son. Every penny I put away for the future. For your future. For your sisters' future. Every day not to waste anything. But I also save for this moment. This I must do with family in a faraway place like Pakistan." Dad carefully replaces the brushes and soft cloth in the cardboard box under the sink. Then takes a satisfying last glance at the tidy box before closing the cupboard with a firm, quiet click.

Khalid watches him shuffle off in his gray socks to watch one of the travel programs he likes so much on television. A sunny smile on his face and the smell of shoe polish lingering in the air.

# 3

## KARACHI

Scrunching balls of waste paper and empty crisp packets into the plane's seat pocket, Khalid shifts sideways towards the window to take in the sight of the tall buildings of Karachi twinkling brightly below him. The last of the strong black-coffee smells drift from the man to his left, disappearing the instant he pops some chewing gum in his mouth.

Feeling relaxed and unworried himself, Khalid is excited to be here at last. The man to his right, who looks like someone you'd meet in a church, was the most boring man in the world. A pale creature who read his book the whole way, speaking to no one. While Khalid watched three movies and listened to his MP3 player, trying to ignore the streams of mums, dads and kids going up and down the aisles to the loos.

Finally Khalid can stretch his arms and legs when the boring man leaves his seat.

Mum, Gul and Aadab are on the opposite side of the plane, while Dad spends the flight at the back. He swapped his seat at check-in when an elderly man at the next desk began complaining about the lack of sleep he'd suffer in a seat next to the toilets. Khalid thought of offering him his seat to impress Dad, but then Dad swapped his own. Always quick to help anyone old—it's an important part of his showing-respect thing.

"I'll be able to rest all the way without Gul and Aadab bothering me," Dad said, not entirely unselfishly. "There're plenty of people who will never afford this journey at all," he reminded Khalid. Aware his son was slightly miffed that the man didn't thank him.

Shifting uncomfortably in the seat, staring at the video screen in front of him, his mind drifts back to Mikael's party on the weekend and the chat he nearly had with Niamh. Suddenly he remembers the almond scent of her dark wavy hair swishing from her shoulders when she brushed past him.

"Grand party, eh, Kal?" Niamh winked. "Shame that old gas fire isn't giving out a bit of heat!"

Khalid nodded, embarrassed. She has the kind of voice you get lost in, so he can't help being dumbstruck around her. The rest of the girls behave like stars in their own movies, jiggling their hips for an invisible camera, unlike Niamh, who's real. No cutesy pouts and head-waggling for her. No, just a little shrug and a look that says, *Here we go*.

Plus, she likes art and books. She always comes in the top three in English exams and Khalid is impressed by that. In fact she looks like someone interesting just by the way she dresses. While the other girls were squashed into tiny shorts and stretchy T-shirts that left nothing to the imagination, Niamh was dressed in that nice, white, long skirt that swung around her dainty ankles when she walked. Plus she had a baggy shirt on with a multicolored belt and loads of silver tinkly bracelets.

That's all she said to him the whole evening. Yet the way she smiled, nodded her head, rolled her big green eyes—they set his heart on fire. To him, she's the most beautiful girl in the world. Not that he'd ask her out. Well, maybe one day he will.

He watched her crack open another beer and sit on the floor in front of the gas fire, chatting to Nico about his new MP3 player. Then a whole bunch of losers turned up, determined to get blasted, and Khalid walked out in a huff. He didn't like the way Niamh's best friend, Gilly, took over the moment she arrived. Linking arms and making her sit with them. Her glittery eye make-up was all over the place when she took the pink band from her claggy hair and glared at Khalid. Wildly blinking and posing as always.

Gilly was wrecked by the time he left. Everyone was, and though he'd had a couple of cans too, he wasn't prepared to make a fool of himself in front of Niamh, who was sadly going the same way. Anyhow, Khalid doesn't like the muzzy feeling he gets in his head when he drinks too much beer.

Besides, he has to take great care to hide the fact he's been drinking or Mum and Dad will go ballistic. Two beers are the limit before his eyes start glazing over and he slurs his words.

Khalid tucks the picture of Niamh curled up on the floor to the back of his mind as the plane descends into Karachi.

Now they are here at last, everyone feeling fine, although the tiredness of the long flight shows clearly in Khalid's drooping eyelids. In a swarm, they hurry through the small, bustling terminal that looks nothing like the orderly airport in Manchester they left behind.

It's mayhem here, with men and women in leather sandals

and shalwar kameez in every shade of brown, heaving cases, crates and boxes from one of only two carousels. Everyone's busy rescuing other things too: loads tied with string, some the size of boats, while their young, sweet, smiling children tug at knotted carpets, boxes and baskets, eager to help.

Outside, the evening feels strangely muggy to Khalid. He'd expected Karachi to be cool at night.

"Yes, cool at night in winter," Dad explains. "But from now on it's hot all the time."

So hot, Khalid wipes sweat from his forehead as they pile into an old brown taxi, catching sight of a pair of mini boxing gloves made from tiny Pakistani flags that are swinging from the driver's mirror. At the wheel is a man with striking black eyes. He glances in the mirror at Khalid. A look of kindness on his face.

Dad warns them, "I'm afraid this will be a roundabout journey, because you know I have parcels, letters and money to deliver for my friend from the restaurant who has family in Karachi. But you will see something of the city, anyhow."

So they set off. Gul and Aadab, who are squashed up in the back, instantly fall asleep on Mum and Khalid. Dad in the front proudly points out the city he grew up in.

"Look, the shop where I bought my first book," he sighs. "That's the same furniture shop on Club Road I told you about before."

Their car quickly overtakes a yellow bus decorated like a birthday present in bright reds and greens with tassels and ribbons. Khalid glimpses a huge market crammed with fruits: tangerines, pomegranates, bananas. Coconuts piled high. Then

Agha's Paradise, the one-stop supermarket selling imported Western foods, which excites Mum for a moment. Then they drive along a very different road, littered with rubbish. Old cans. Open bin bags smelling of rotten fish.

Khalid is disappointed not to see any signs of a car-jacking or gang feud.

"Only the rich have deep enough pockets to eat here," Dad says as the taxi turns down a posh road filled with a wide choice of restaurants: Chinese, Japanese, Turkish and French. Past streets with low, brown buildings. Then dark streets. Empty of people.

A rare car parked outside.

The lamps inside highlight black metal grilles fixed to windows and doors, giving Khalid the feeling there's lots of crime here. Two stops later, the parcels safely delivered, the taxi pulls up outside a plain, two-story gray building.

A concrete box with windows. *What a dump*, Khalid thinks, instantly fed up.

The door opens and three elderly ladies, Fatima, Rehana and Roshan, in dark shalwar kameez, rush out as one to greet them. Babbling warmly with toothy grins. Their eyes take in every inch of Khalid, giving him no escape from their loving welcome and out-of-control squeals of joy that seem to go on forever.

"I'm tired, Mum," Gul says at last, while Aadab crossly rubs a hand over her nose. Both seem confused by all the fuss and noise.

At least modesty stops the aunts from kissing and hugging, or even touching them.

"Well, we got here," Khalid says, shrugging. Immediately,

he wonders how to say no to the glass cups of hot black liquid smelling of sugary cabbage that are thrust in his face the moment he sits on the long, soft sofa with a wooden ceiling fan whirring overhead.

Eventually giving in, Khalid swallows the whole lot in one go and wipes the remains from his mouth with the back of his hand. Only to see his angelic auntie Roshan fill the dainty glass again. Everyone begins talking at once. This time Khalid slides the drink behind a tall fern, hoping for the best. Gul pulls a face as she tips hers into Aadab's glass. Aadab seems to like the taste, drinking it up as if she can't wait for more of the disgusting stuff. Dad frowns at Gul to remind her of her manners, while Mum pretends not to notice. Khalid dares his sister Aadab with a long, hard stare to please get rid of his hidden drink when she's finished hers, but it doesn't work.

After tea, the fuss dies down a bit. Gifts are given and politely put to one side for unwrapping later. Bored to tears, Khalid stares at the complicated oriental carpet under his feet until Fatima, the oldest aunt, takes pity on him.

"Come. Come." She points to the door and walks him a few paces down the hall to a small back room done up with red carpet, gold curtains and a big gilded mirror.

In the corner is a wooden bed with an old scarecrow of a man asleep in a pale green Pakistan cricket shirt. Thin black trousers tapering at the ankle. This, Khalid learns, is Fatima's husband, his uncle Amir. And a sight far harder to digest than the oriental carpet from before.

Fatima mumbles something to him, then leads Khalid to another door with a Pakistan International Airlines Boeing

777 sticker on it. Fatima points to it proudly, as if Khalid might be pleased by the photo of a plane that looks a hundred years old.

"I have to go to the loo," Khalid says, thinking this is all getting a bit much.

"No. No. No." Fatima seems to be on a mission to bore Khalid to death. Or drive him nuts. Or both. She refuses to let him pass. Insists on opening the sticker door wide. Steps aside to make him peer into a black space slightly bigger than the airing cupboard at home.

"Wow! You've got a computer!" Khalid freezes with surprise, scarcely believing his luck.

"Have. Have." Fatima grins and points at the screen, trying hard to tell him he can use it whenever he wants. There's nothing more he wants to hear. His big smile warms Fatima's heart, almost bringing tears to her eyes. But before Khalid can begin to enjoy it he races back to the living room to say goodnight to everyone and be polite for a while. Waiting until the house goes quiet before he returns to the cupboard to start the game for the first time.

After half an hour or so, Khalid gets the hang of how to use the computer without being able to read the language. It gets better when he logs on to his e-mail and discovers that Tariq's game—*Bomber One*—is ready. A whizz-kid friend of his in Lahore has helped to finish the program and download it. Tariq's sent him instructions on how to set up his profile so they can all play together soon. Khalid tests it out several times before getting too jet-lag flaky to carry on.

He sends off an excited reply before he shuts down the

computer. Going deathly weird with tiredness the moment the screen goes black. Then he wanders into the front room trying to remember where Mum said he's supposed to sleep. His mind was on the computer at the time. Did she say the room next to the bathroom? Or was that his sisters' bedroom? Either way, Khalid doesn't want to disturb anyone by wandering into the wrong room so he wobbles for a bit before kicking off his sneakers and falling on the musty-smelling sofa in a heap. Still wearing the jeans and blue hoodie he's had on since yesterday morning.

Within a couple of days, Khalid settles into a pleasant routine. Morning starts with breakfast in the far corner of the dining room, which is marked out by comfy cushions and rugs surrounded by large windows on two sides. Fresh fruits, juice, curry, rice and bread set him up for the two hours he has to spend watching over Uncle Amir until Fatima comes back from doing her marketing and relieves him. Giving him a chance to chat with the visitors who are always calling by, before playing and reading with Gul and Aadab to give Mum a break.

If it wasn't for all the news and talk about the earthquake in northern Afghanistan and the pictures of people freezing to death outside flattened houses, Khalid might feel worse about missing his team's football games back in Rochdale. He knows he can't complain when homeless people without proper shoes or blankets are shown on TV wandering snow-covered hills in their search for food.

One of the visitors, a man called Abdullah, who is twenty-six, with a bushy black beard and cloth round his head, strikes Khalid as odd. He never mentions the earthquake, only Islam. A book-keeper with hard staring eyes and a scar on his cheek, he's in the habit of popping in every day to try to persuade Dad to come to the mosque with him. But Dad doesn't like him. Says he's too serious, even for him.

Abdullah's staring eyes bother Khalid. But it seems the feeling is mutual and they mostly leave each other alone.

Although Khalid likes the fact that this house is busier than his house in Rochdale, he's surprised at how different things are for people in Karachi. For a start everyone's much more polite and friendly than they are at home. Khalid can't imagine what happened outside the chip shop happening here. Instead they talk a lot about prices shooting up and about dwindling services and the lack of decent plumbing, complaining most when the taps run dry, which they usually do in the middle of the afternoon. Not that Khalid speaks Urdu. For some reason, Abdullah translates everything without ever being asked.

In the afternoon, the aunties like taking naps, which suits Khalid just fine. It gives him the opportunity to catch up on lost sleep after a night spent gaming with Tariq.

Dad's often out—checking on cheaper houses for the aunties to move to. Then he sometimes helps with the street collections to send stuff to the earthquake region. So on the fourth day after they arrived, Khalid makes a decision to stay up all night playing *Bomber One*. No one in the house seems to mind what he does later, as long as he's helpful during the day. Probably thinking he hits his snug bed in the tiny room next to the bathroom some time after midnight. Never guessing it's nearer five in the morning, depending on what Tariq's plans are for the next day.

At the moment, Tariq's busy studying for some accountancy exams, or so he says. Khalid thinks they sound more like A levels, but anyway Tariq always takes a break from his studies by playing a game or two, whatever the time is.

Now there are more players: two in Egypt, one in Iraq, one in Australia and another in America. The game is really heating up. A secret group of fighters have to get together to plan the annihilation of an imaginary town called Arch Parkway. All of them enjoy going head to head at the same time and dreaming up mad strategies for winning, but really they're all on the same side.

It's still a bit basic and not as good as *Counter Strike* or anything, but then this game's home-made and, who knows, one day Tariq might be able to sell it and make a ton of money and he might even give some to Khalid for helping him out with the names.

"Could be a bestseller some day, with kids all over the world paying to play," the American says.

"It's far better than anything out there," Khalid lies, suddenly yawning his head off. Secretly wishing he could play *Starcraft* instead for a while—as he moves the mouse over the high buildings so the twinkling lights of *Bomber One* come on again.

# MISSING

Khalid leans back from the computer when the call to prayer begins echoing around the city, realizing it's five o'clock. Almost morning.

For a moment, he wonders if it's worth going to bed at all. Or maybe he should answer Nico's e-mail from Rochdale before making coffee to keep himself awake. It's hardly worth taking a nap because he'll need to get up for breakfast by nine at the latest.

Why is Nico talking about Niamh? Does he like her too?

The thought worries him for a second before the sounds of Karachi waking up and of prayers fading away bring him back to the tiny, dark computer room.

He starts googling the latest information on various computer games and after a while glances at Nico's e-mail again: "Hiya, Kal. Niamh says hello. I saw her at the shops last night and she says to tell you you should have stayed at the party, it was so way better later on, man."

Wondering what to say back, Khalid wants to ask Nico if Niamh's seeing anyone. She didn't get off with anyone at the party as far as he knows. But if he does ask, everyone will know he likes her. And if Nico likes her too, then there's nothing he can do, because everyone knows he's nearly 4,000 miles away in Pakistan. In the end, he decides to keep it cool by not replying.

He quickly closes the computer down when he hears Mum's footsteps clattering on the stairs. Running from room to room.

"What is it, Mum?" Khalid hurries to find out.

"Dad. Where is he?" Mum's in a state, her hair spread out over her shoulders and still in her blue nightie.

"What do you mean?"

"Dad! He's missing, that's what. He went to see a flat yesterday evening after dinner and he hasn't come back."

"Mum, he probably fell asleep."

"Fell asleep? Where? In the street? Sometimes you know what's happened in your heart, Khalid. I'm telling you it's bad."

"Sit down, Mum. I'll get some coffee. We'll sort it."

Mum's eyes suddenly narrow at the flickering computer screen in the corner. "I hope you haven't been on that stupid thing all night," she says crossly.

"I haven't, honest," Khalid protests. "I just couldn't sleep."

This time she shakes her head with disbelief. "Don't try that rubbish on me!"

"I'm on holiday. I don't see what the problem is."

"Not now, you. I'm too worried for nonsense. You must go to find it, this place. The address, he wrote it down somewhere. Go wash your face. Brush your hair."

After two cups of strong, evil-smelling coffee and a quick

45

shower, Khalid grabs a pinch of yesterday's naan bread to eat while Mum works out where exactly in the city Dad went. This takes some time as she doesn't know the city and most of the street names are unfamiliar. Plus, she's in such a panic she has to sit back every now and then to pat her chest and calm herself.

"Perhaps we should wait until one of the aunties gets up? Or one of the neighbors comes?" she says at last.

"Then we'll still be sitting here at nine. It's gone seven now. I'll find it, don't worry, Mum." Khalid folds the tourist street map of Karachi away in his pocket. Knowing if he turns to his right outside the house and keeps going left he should arrive in the right area eventually and hopefully someone can direct him from there. He checks the address scrawled in pencil on a scrap of paper again and heads towards the door.

It's hot now. There's a feeling of promise in the lightening sky as the sun peeps through the spaces between the tall buildings in the distance. Khalid takes a deep breath. He hasn't been out of the house much, and never on his own, and he feels scared stiff of being mugged or beaten up or getting lost in a city he doesn't know and hasn't explored. Chickens squawk from a nearby yard. The street is empty apart from several bags of rubbish propped up in a doorway, an old Coca-Cola bottle and dented can of turpentine beside a rusting car.

A huge truck trundles past crammed with men huddled together like sacks of flour and wrapped in scarves that give little protection from the dust the tires are blowing down the street. Their faces are miserably thin. Hands folded in front. Heads down.

46

*Workers*, Khalid thinks. His heart is beating faster than his hurrying steps.

Turning the first corner, Khalid sees a crowd gathering up ahead. A crowd he wishes he could avoid, but the narrow side alleys are also filling with men coming this way, running to catch up. There's a feeling of fear in the air. Or is it just him?

Then the shouting starts. Some man on a platform begins yelling with his arms in the air. Others join in. Fisting the air violently. Young men push past dressed in exactly the same brown shalwar kameez that Aunt Fatima gave him. One of them shouts something that Khalid doesn't understand.

The throng of men is growing by the second. Khalid stops. Turns to go back and find another route to avoid this chaos. But he gets caught in a sudden wave of men surging from a side alley. Pulling him forward in a lawless mass of anger that reminds him of getting caught in the rivers of fans coming out of Old Trafford after Manchester United have lost a game. The same feeling of suffocation and frenzy cuts into Khalid. The same fear of falling. Being trodden on. The only difference is the shocking sweet smell of coconut and musk drifting from their hot skin and hair.

With a mad degree of nudging and side-stepping, Khalid manages to work his way from the middle of the crowd to the area just past the yelling man on the wooden platform. The sun beats down on his bare head as he pulls up his sleeves, finding it easier to move through the crowd if he screams and punches the air like the rest of them. Soon Khalid's jumping backwards to his heart's content. Drifting across slowly until he arrives at the edge of the road, laughing. Clouds of dust billow around him and he starts to enjoy the ongoing joke of being a newly arrived foreigner and not really one of them, all the way to the end of the road, where he pauses to get his breath before turning down a quiet side street.

No road sign to guide him, Khalid stops to pull the crumpled tourist map from his pocket. Sand everywhere. A corner of his eye flames red from grit, making it impossible for him to read.

He stumbles down the dusty road, pressing hard on his eyelids to remove the dirt caught in his eye, but his sandy fingers are making it worse. He trips down a tunnel-like passage filled with shoppers hurrying with baskets towards the bazaar. Red-eyed, he gradually makes out the blur of a man in a doorway selling carved inscriptions on slabs of stone. Another trader points to turquoise beads and cinnamon sticks on a wooden tray that he lifts to Khalid's face. Khalid bends his head to tug at several lashes in a final attempt to dislodge the grit and blinks and blinks until he can focus on the old bead-seller standing beside him, too close for comfort.

Khalid shows him the address of the flat, but it's obvious he can't read English, leading Khalid to the conclusion that he might have to retrace his steps or get even more lost. Then a broad-shouldered, pasty-faced white man in a white cap appears out of nowhere and says something to the bead-seller in Urdu, nodding to Khalid to show him the address.

"You lost?" he says in a broad Liverpool accent. Khalid is shocked. The man winks. "I know how you feel, mate. This place is a madhouse. Me name's Jim."

"Khalid. Hi." He blinks, surprised. "How come you speak Urdu?"

"I'm studying Eastern languages in London. Plus I'm a genius, like all Liverpudlians. Can't you tell?" Jim laughs and Khalid immediately warms to his friendly smile.

"Yeah, mate, whatever you say," Khalid jokes in reply.

Relieved to find someone who can help him, Khalid wanders with him through the bazaar as it fills with people and Jim tells him about his trip to Pakistan with two mates who are also students in London.

"My friend Mohammed invited me here for the holidays and I thought, *Why not?* At any rate, it gives us a chance to speak the language. Know what I mean? You're a bit bleary-eyed, mate. You OK?"

"I got some dirt in my eye." Khalid explains about the demonstration, his dad not coming home, plus the fact he's never been into the city until now. "That's why I've got this address, although I have no idea where the place is."

"You're looking for your dad? What are you going to do if you don't find him?"

"Dunno." The same question had occurred to Khalid when he left the house.

"Look, I can take you to this flat. But I suggest if he's not there you scarper home and wait for news. If you want some good advice, don't go near the police without a group of male friends and then always cooperate with them fully. Answer any questions. Do ya hear?"

Khalid nods. "Can't I trust the police, then?"

"Let's just say there's loads of backhanders going round this city." Jim frowns. "Drug-trafficking and the like and plenty of CIA blokes paying out for supposed al-Qaeda suspects."

"Just like my nearest city, Manchester, then?" Khalid laughs.

Jim grins but his smile quickly fades. "They're obsessed with finding dirty bombs," he explains. "Men are disappearing all over the place."

Khalid thinks back to his conversations with Nasir and Tariq. "Not my dad, though. He's a Westernized Pakistani. He doesn't even like it here—only wants to help his sisters move house."

Jim shakes his head. "Everybody from a Muslim country is seen as a threat to the USA right now."

Something about the way he says this makes Khalid feel suddenly more anxious than ever. If only he can find his dad and get back to Rochdale and their normal lives.

After ten minutes, they come to a small block of flats. Jim leads the way up narrow concrete stairs to the top floor. With a firm hand he bangs on the door of Flat 26, looking round for signs of life. Then he peers into a small window hardly bigger than an envelope while Khalid waits anxiously for his dad to answer the door.

There's nothing but silence and a moldy apple core on the dusty concrete floor at Khalid's feet.

"Doesn't look good," Jim says before shouting in Urdu at the top of his voice. The door to Flat 25 next door opens in slow motion. Locks and bolts click and slide before an elderly man peers out an inch. He eyes them suspiciously.

"*Salaam!*" Jim rushes to greet him while he has the chance. Quickly explaining about Khalid's dad. Pointing to Flat 26.

The watchful old man takes his time to reply, as if not certain that Jim's telling the truth. A feeling of dread spreads over Khalid as the man looks them up and down, then spits. He stares hard with suspicious eyes, even as Jim speaks to him in the local dialect. Finally he answers quickly, then shuts the door. Bolting and locking it as fast as he can. His footsteps hurry down the creaking floor as if he can't wait to get away from them.

Jim turns to Khalid and holds up his hands. "Sorry, mate. I tried. He said there's no one at the flat. Some rich bloke owns it, wants to rent it out. He thinks someone might have banged on the door last night but he's not sure."

Khalid closes his eyes and breathes out. Like he's been holding his breath the whole time. Without saying anything, he peers in the small window of the flat to see nothing but a small hall with red tiles and a pile of unopened mail on the coir mat. "I guess he's not here, then," he says eventually.

They walk back together, Khalid in silence with a heavy heart and Jim talking non-stop about a girl he likes called Carla, an archaeology student he's madly in love with. Trying in his own way to make Khalid feel better by distracting him from the disappointment.

"You know how it is when you like a girl, you can't get her out of your mind," Jim says, smiling. He leads Khalid down a side street to avoid the market and the demonstration, which has grown even larger. But the rhythm of men chanting and yelling, and a car screeching to a halt nearby, fire rockets of unimaginable fear and panic through Khalid with every step.

*Dad? Dad?* Terrified he'll never see him again, a sudden smell of woodsmoke overwhelms Khalid. His thoughts, his feelings and senses are out of his control. Unless Dad's at home when he gets there, his life will be turned upside down.

A strange numbness sets in as Khalid walks the dusty road, drifting between noise and silence. Jim's voice takes him to the edge of a cliff and then back again, the pointless chatter sounding as if it's coming from the bottom of a deep cave somewhere.

"She's amazing. Know what I mean?" Jim says.

"Yeah." Khalid hasn't got the energy to smile. The words *She's amazing—amazing—Yeah* zip past in a circle above his head, while the terrible thought his dad might be dead squeezes a clamp around his heart. They walk in silence for a few moments and for some reason Khalid's mind shoots back to a day last September, when he and Niamh were sitting together under an oak tree in the park. And even though Holgy was pulling faces at him all the while and Nico was throwing sticks at the bench, Niamh told him about her plans to become a lawyer and live in New York. About how she was going to get out of Rochdale the moment she could, because her mum was driving her crazy after the divorce.

"Will you have to marry a Muslim girl?" Niamh asked.

"I can marry who I like," he'd said. Not wanting to get into this. Thinking, *Should I tell her if she isn't a Muslim she can convert? Loads do.*

"Mum says it's better if I marry a Catholic. Hah, she had to marry one—and look where that got her. Anyway, we're past all that now, aren't we, Kal, us? Thanks for listening." Jumping up when the ice-cream van sounded its silly tune at the park gates.

"Are you in the mood for an ice cream?"

"Er—no. Yeah, OK!" Khalid remembers how he grinned. Sitting there like a lost puppy until she came back with two double whips. Silently praying she'd sit next to him again, which she never did.

Five days after the party, when he last saw her, he already felt bad. They went to Karachi, and now Dad's gone missing he feels even worse. Perhaps he should have warned him about the kidnappings and stuff that Nasir, the shopkeeper, had told him about.

Jim stops suddenly. "That's your aunties' road, yeah? Didn't you say it was this street?"

"Yeah. Yeah. They live at 74A." Khalid nods.

Jim stares at him. "Are you OK? Do you want me to come and speak to your family with you?"

Khalid shakes his head, knowing that a stranger in the house will just make things worse when he gets home without Dad.

"OK, well, see you, then. Bet your dad's already home," Jim says with little confidence. "Here's my mobile number if you need anything. Look after yourself, OK?"

"Thanks a lot," Khalid says finally. He wants to say more, like how he couldn't have found the flat without him, or spoken to the old man in the next-door flat, but he's worried if he talks too much he'll start crying or something. Jim understands and just grins a show of affection as Khalid turns and heads down his street. Raising a hand to wave goodbye in a half-hearted way.

As soon as Jim's out of sight something snaps inside Khalid and he runs as fast as his legs will carry him, arriving at the house in a gasping, dusty, hot heap. Adrenaline makes his head swim with a thousand awful pictures of Dad hurt, bleeding, kidnapped, shot, and he becomes convinced the instant he opens the door that Dad isn't back.

When the sound of a passing, rumbling truck dies down, Khalid prepares himself by taking a deep breath of fried garlic and cumin.

# 5

## EASTER

There's an oasis of silence and peace inside the house as the door closes. The dark wall-hangings create a sense of cave-like gloom. Though his temporary home is familiar, it provides no comfort to Khalid as he pauses to gaze through the open door of the dark back room to see Uncle Amir curled up, asleep as usual, in the far corner.

Everyone else, he can tell, is in the other room, listening hard. Knowing it's Khalid by the way he kicks off his sandals before he heads towards them with hesitant steps.

Looking round at the sea of questioning faces, Khalid thinks that the whole neighborhood seems to have crammed itself into the living room. There's barely space on the small tables for another bowl of sugar cubes or cup of half-drunk coffee. He suddenly has no idea where to start. All at once, hundreds of inquiring voices fire questions at him in Urdu and Punjabi, neighbors and distant relatives crowding round him. The aunties wring their hands, sobbing. Mum stands in the corner, wailing. Gul and Aadab, pale and shaken, are close to screaming.

"I dunno where Dad is," Khalid says when everyone

eventually falls silent. He goes over the chain of events as quickly as possible, not bothering to mention the demonstration and the hordes of angry men he'd come across.

The moment Khalid finishes, leaving people none the wiser, everyone begins sounding off with their own ideas and gesturing to heaven for help. A stream of desperate prayers begins to flow from their downturned mouths. No one notices Khalid slip away to grab a glass of water, wash his dusty face and hands and flop on the kitchen floor. At last, he gets to sit on his own in a state of total disbelief at his useless, wasted search.

He is tired out of his mind, head spinning from too many hours without rest. The wooden ceiling fan seems to loom over him as he builds a nest of red cushions on the floor, their gold tassels swinging as he lies down. Soon falling under the gentle hypnosis of the fan's whirring and faint clicks, he enjoys a moment's peace until people begin coming and going, stepping over him. Clattering cups, brewing coffee, whispering, trying not to be noisy, even though they can see he's not asleep.

In the end their constant interruptions force Khalid to get up again. He pads back to the living room, where Gul and Aadab stare from one sad face to another, wondering if anyone will notice if they eat the rest of the sugar cubes in the green glass bowl. Gul reaches to grab a handful and pass some to Aadab. Both try hard to enjoy the cloying sweetness while pretending not to be eating anything and, along with Khalid, gaze sadly at Mum. Fatima and Roshan stand with their backs to them at the window, looking out. Aunt Rehana listens blank-faced to a neighbor who's brought a pot of honey and some walnuts to cheer them up.

Everyone is in the same state of lonely grief, only half here in this room, their minds overloaded with stories they've read in the papers about people who've gone missing and are later found dead from bomb blasts, accidents, murders. It's easy to think the worst here.

Later, after a few hours tossing and turning in bed, Khalid gets up. He moves quickly, pulling on his jeans, hurrying to hear what's happened. Peeping into the living room, he sees the same faces, feels the same hopelessness, and steps back. Rushing instead to the computer cupboard, where he half expects an e-mail from someone, anyone, who might be able to tell him what's happened to Dad.

He opens the door and is amazed to find Abdullah on the computer. "What are you doing here?"

"What do you mean?" Abdullah clicks on the corner of the page he's looking at so it disappears. Quickly turns to face Khalid with a calm, unsurprised smile.

"That's our computer," Khalid stutters.

"I have permission from the family to use this, but I have finished with it now so you may continue your game," Abdullah says in his annoying formal English and scrapes the chair back.

The thought flashes through Khalid's mind that he's never told him about Tariq's game, but then anyone could see what he's been doing online because he didn't log off the last time he used the computer. From now on, he'll log off each time and shut it down properly.

"Don't worry. I am not interested in what you are doing on the World Wide Web. I am not a spy," Abdullah says, reading his mind. "Myself, I am only reading the newspapers, as I have always done. My brother and my sister's husband, they come here to do the same. We have not been doing this for some days because your family are here. I was looking to see if there was any news of your father." He stands up and walks off, leaving Khalid standing there, unable to say anything back.

He feels guilty for a moment, but quickly forgets as he checks his e-mails. There are three: one from Tariq, suggesting the time to play *Bomber One* tonight; one from Nico, rambling on about how he's downloaded a bunch of songs for free on his MP3 player; plus one from a kid at school called Jamie, who's doing his history coursework on Galileo too.

"He could have had a stroke," someone says from the hall, their thoughts clashing with the lovely smell of curry that's building in the air.

After a while Khalid closes the computer down and steps out of the dark cupboard, surprised to see Abdullah is back again with his wife. They are smiling at everyone and their arms are loaded with dishes of steaming food.

"Bottle gourd curry and chapattis. Chickpeas too for you!" Abdullah says.

Someone bangs on the door, too calmly for it to be urgent news about Dad. *Another neighbor*, Khalid thinks, heading down the hallway and opening the door to a familiar face.

"Hiya, how's it going?" Jim smiles. "Just thought I'd pop in on my way to the airport. Everything OK?"

Khalid shakes his head. "Nah, Dad's not here." Mum and the aunties disappear from the hall after seeing it isn't anyone with important news.

"We still, like, don't know what happened," Khalid says, hogging the doorway. Hearing Abdullah and his wife offer to put the food out in the kitchen, all of a sudden Khalid's stomach twitches with hunger.

"Have you checked the hospitals?" Jim asks.

"The neighbors have." Khalid nods, all of a sudden wanting to talk about something else in case he gets worked up again. "We're just about to have some food. Do you want to join us? One more mouth won't make a difference round here."

"Nah, I've gotta go. Thanks, though. Just wanted to see how things were going. Wish it was better news." Jim sighs. "Well, best of luck, mate. Hope you enjoy the rest of your Easter holiday."

"Thanks." Khalid closes the door as Jim jumps back in his taxi. Remembering Easter at home, a picture of his town, Rochdale, flashes through Khalid's mind. Suddenly he's walking with his mates down a pretty cobbled street—York Street. The shops are crammed with chocolate Easter eggs as they make their way to the shopping arcade. He feels such a strong connection to the lovely old mill town that for the first time in his life he realizes he loves it there. Then Abdullah's suddenly behind him with a suspicious look on his face.

"Yeah, what?" Khalid asks, feeling annoyed again.

"Who's that man?" he says, expecting an answer immediately.

"Just some bloke." Khalid's tempted to tell him he's a grenade thrower, but stops himself, not trusting Abdullah to take it as a joke. "I met him in the market. He's a student in London and he helped me find the address of the flat Dad went to."

"What else?"

"Nothing else. What do you mean?" says Khalid, thinking, *None of your business.*

"What things did he tell you?" Abdullah asks.

"Things? What do you mean? Nothing. He's from Liverpool. He's English. Look, I'm starving. I haven't eaten anything proper since yesterday." With that, Khalid wanders off. He suspects Abdullah knows more about his dad's disappearance than he's letting on. That suspicious look on his scarred face isn't right and the sick feeling Khalid has in his stomach won't go away. Luckily, when Abdullah comes to get some food he doesn't mention anything about Jim in front of the others.

Later in the evening, when the neighbors have gone home and the aunties and Mum have finally been persuaded to go to bed, the house falls silent once more. The latest decision is to go to the police in the morning. A group of male neighbors are preparing a list of questions to ask.

There were some questions Khalid wanted to ask Abdullah, but Mum stopped him by putting a finger to her mouth. She warned him not to speak out of turn, even though the knot in Khalid's stomach is still there. All this is on his mind as he switches on the computer. The familiar ping is the best sound he's heard all day.

"Hiya, cuz." Tariq's already there waiting for him with a message.

"My dad's disappeared," Khalid types immediately. Tells him the whole story without quite believing it himself.

"I heard from my father," Tariq replies. "Everyone is so worried. They're saying the War on Terror is getting worse each day." Tariq sends Khalid some links to online articles written in English, knowing he hasn't seen any newspapers he can read since he's been here.

"Why my dad, though? He's no one," Khalid questions after scanning the reports.

"He's a man, isn't he, you dorkhead?" Tariq types. "That's good enough reason for them."

"I don't get it," Khalid answers wearily, worried sick again.

"Come on. Log on to *Bomber One*. Your dad might be back by the time we finish this game," Tariq says. "The others are ready and waiting."

Khalid eventually clicks through to the game, hoping for a simple distraction. The other players quickly line up their soldiers, moving them to the target points to start. The fighter planes shift into view. All the points from the last game are quickly calculated to the highest fraction before the battle begins.

Losing himself in the desire to win, Khalid types wildly. His fingers start tapping to the beat of the pictures on the screen until the keyboard appears to be playing the game on its own. Spontaneously battering every plane in sight. Using up bombs to bust the targets with effortless ease. Blasting the enemy's boats out of the water, power surges through Khalid with every explosion. Finally he's not thinking about anything else but the game and suddenly his mind feels lighter, despite the complicated scoring system.

At last, coming up for air, Khalid pauses to dash to the loo. Hurrying, jeans half zipped, he's determined to get back to the computer before it's his turn to man the rockets, when the front door swings open. Immediately excited and distracted, Khalid rushes back down the dark hall to the door. Surely only his dad could be coming through the door without knocking at this time of night?

But he's badly mistaken. Blocking the hallway is a gang of fierce-looking men dressed in dark shalwar kameez. Black cloths wrapped around their heads. Black gloves on their hands. Two angry blue eyes, the rest brown, burn into Khalid as the figures move towards him like cartoon gangsters with square bodies. Confused by the image, he staggers, bumping backwards into the wall. Arms up to stop them getting nearer. Too shocked and terrified to react as they shoulder him to the kitchen and close the door before pushing him to his knees and waving a gun at him as if he's a violent criminal. Then vice-like hands clamp his mouth tight until they plaster it with duct tape. No chance to wonder what the hell is going on, let alone scream out loud.

Stunned and shaking, Khalid feels his world slow down to a second-by-second terrible nightmare as they grab at his ankles and arms, handcuffing them tight before dropping a rag of a hood over his head. Then, without missing a beat, someone kicks him in the back, ramming his body flat on the floor. A heavy boot lands firmly on his spine, forcing Khalid to moan with muffled pain, while dust from the rug works its way inside his nose, making him sneeze uncontrollably through the threadbare hood. This simple reaction makes the strangers add a sharp thrum of boots to his side and a fiery agony explodes over Khalid's body as, stunned and shaken, he snorts desperately, trying to get air in through the tape stuck fast across his mouth.

*Dad. Dad*, Khalid pleads silently. This must be what happened to him. Khalid twists and turns, unable to breathe or scream or stop his heart from thumping. He recoils in terror as they lift him like a crate, hot fists on his legs and shoulders, and silently carry him out. Dumped in the back of an open truck, he groans as his face and body smash hard against the floor. The sudden movement of the truck jolts him from side to side as it drives off, the men breathing heavily and crowding over him with their smells of warm flesh and tobacco.

Paralyzed by fear, Khalid wonders desperately where they are taking him. Who are they? Why him? What for? Questions he can't even speak out loud.

The sounds of the city die away as the truck speeds along a potholed road that sends Khalid rolling across the truck in agony. He breathes in oil stains and the stench of animals, knocking his head on the uneven metal floor. A hefty boot kicks him back to the center each time he slides their way. Pictures of his kidnapping flash quickly, one after the other, through his mind, building to an overwhelming fear that he's going to be dumped at the side of the road any second and left there to die.

# POWER

As the truck rumbles over another pothole, Khalid's cloth-covered face is pressed into the spreading dirt and dust flying across the hot, hard floor. Head pounding, arms tied back and aching like mad, eventually all he can think is, *Why put a gun to my head? Is this really what happened to Dad?* The situation is so way beyond Khalid's everyday reality, he can't take it in. Things like this don't happen in his world. Things like this can't happen to him. It's more like a movie or a computer game. Again and again he thinks back to Abdullah always hanging round the house. About what Nasir and Tariq told him about people lying for money. Are these men US soldiers? But why would they be interested in a British kid like him? There must be a mistake. If they've got his dad, then they'll work that out soon enough.

Khalid rolls to one side when the truck turns a corner and a big boot nudges him away. One of the men at the edge of the truck shouts angrily, which makes Khalid want to scream. His mum, his sisters, his aunties, they'll go out of their minds when they find him missing. First Dad and now him.

After a while the truck stops. Two men lift Khalid out to

carry him across a concrete forecourt with footsteps and cars nearby.

Inside the building the cloth hood is whipped off. A bright ceiling light dazzles Khalid for a moment as he tries to make out the faces of his kidnappers hidden behind tightly wound black cloths. Only their angry eyes and rough fists give a small clue that the blue-eyed one might be a Westerner, with his freckly pink hands. Without warning someone behind Khalid rips the duct tape from his mouth, slashing his lips and skin to bits, tearing wisps of hair from his face, making him feel he's been stung by epic-sized bees. He screams in pain as his eyes flood with water. Clenching his jaw as they leave the hand-and ankle-cuffs where they are.

Now out of his mind with fear, pain and anger, Khalid gazes down at the state of his jeans, covered in dust, totally wrecked, and feels so weak and dizzy he can barely breathe or utter a sound. What the hell are they up to? No one will believe this—it's too crazy for words. He almost smiles with delirium at the thought of what Holgy or Nico would say if he tried to convince them.

"Who are you?" he asks desperately, almost whispering, but no one speaks.

They all sit there until a podgy-looking Pakistani with immaculate hair and neatly pressed shalwar kameez, a huge gold ring on his right hand, appears from nowhere and shuffles him into a gray room, which he locks the second they're inside. The man looks him over for a second with a shocked expression that proves Khalid's face is badly swollen and bruised. He can taste the blood from his lips as it dribbles into the corners of his mouth. The throbbing under his eye is so painful Khalid has to squint to take in the gray room, which smells of dog biscuits. It's empty apart from two chairs, a rug and small black table with a wodge of loose papers on top.

The man points Khalid to one of the chairs, then bends down to unclick Khalid's ankle-cuffs, which he kicks across the room. He gives the impression that Khalid's ordeal might soon be over. But then he takes a moment to twist the chrome watch that Dad gave Khalid for Christmas from his wrist and it becomes clear that it won't. The man squirrels the watch away in his pocket before sitting down opposite him.

"Name and address," he says in perfect English, pen poised.

He speaks so beautifully, Khalid begins to doubt the man's from Pakistan at all.

"Give me back my watch," Khalid croaks.

"You'll get it later," the man answers.

"Is this a police station or what? Why did those idiots beat me up?"

"Just answer the questions," the man says sourly. "What are you doing in Pakistan?"

"Doing in Pakistan? I'm here with my family on holiday. Then I'm going back to school in England, where I come from. My name's Khalid Ahmed. You've just been to my aunties' house. You know my address." He can't believe this is for real.

"England? University school? Your name's Khalid Ahmed?"

"I'm at a school for kids. Teenagers. I just said my name." Khalid sighs. "Who are you? Let me out of here."

The man tilts his head to one side to get a better look at him. "Where have you been since you arrived in Karachi?" he says, as if he knows something Khalid doesn't.

"Nowhere. What are you on about?" Khalid's even more confused when he takes a small photo from his back pocket.

"Who is this man?" He points angrily to a blurred photo of someone in a brown shalwar kameez jumping in the air with arms outstretched, surrounded by hundreds of similar-looking men. This guy could be anyone.

"Dunno. How would I know?"

"What's his name?"

"I don't know him, mate. But do you know where my dad is? What's all this for? Why am I here? And give me my watch back."

The man stares at him, uninterested. Clearly this is a one-way conversation and Khalid gets angry. He's seen enough kids round his way being stopped and searched by the police to know what his rights are.

"I'm saying nothing until I get a lawyer. That watch cost my dad thirty-five pounds. Give it back."

"This is Karachi, not England," the man says. "You don't have any legal rights here. Tell us what you know and you can go home."

"I've told you the truth. Get me someone from the British Embassy. They'll help me out. I haven't committed any crime."

"You don't understand. You are wanted. We can't intervene. I'm sorry." For a moment the man does seem genuinely sorry, which surprises Khalid.

"Someone wants me? Come on. I haven't done anything. Are you crazy?" Confused and nervous in equal measure, Khalid quickly tells him about himself, about his family and

Dad going missing. Everything about Jim and looking for the flat. "I'm only just fifteen," he adds.

"We are living in terrible times," is all the man says. As if his hands are tied and the truth's unimportant. "You look much older than fifteen. It's late. I'll see you in the morning." He gets up to leave.

"You can't leave me handcuffed like this!" Khalid shouts. "My arms hurt!" The door slams. "You stole my watch!" The lock snaps.

Baffled and shocked, Khalid's no closer to understanding the reason for being kidnapped, beaten up and brought here, and the more this goes on, the weirder and sicker he feels. The thought of how Mum will cope when they find him gone in the morning crushes him. He feels guilty even though none of this is his fault. All of it on top of Dad disappearing is too strange and mad to take in. How can something of this sort happen to an ordinary family like his?

Now there's a horrible pain in his side which makes him think they've shattered one of his ribs, and what with his aching arms and shoulder, the throbbing pains in his chest and legs, his stinging face and sore eye, he's so tired and weirded out he can hardly think.

Too messed up to sleep, Khalid shouts out a list of vile swearwords as he walks around the room. Magnifying them in his mind as he yells. Stabbing the air with them. Angry beyond belief with himself for not keeping his mobile phone in his pocket, even though they would have taken that too. Picturing it beside the computer in the cupboard where he left it, he wonders whether it's worth trying to kick the door in with his bare feet before he lies down on the cool, concrete floor. Within minutes, he's asleep.

A while later he wakes suddenly, due to the unbearable aches and pains throbbing in every part of his body. The ceiling light is blazing down on his eyes. He turns to face the door, gazing at the bleak shadows of the table and chairs, and cries his heart out.

In the morning, still half asleep, Khalid settles into an upright position, determined to stay clear-headed enough to get himself out of here. Believing these people, whoever they are, must know by now they've got the wrong person. Khalid Ahmed isn't such an unusual name, he reassures himself.

Listening to footsteps approach the door, Khalid decides to do as Jim advised him, to cooperate as much as possible. He knows he was reasonable last night, but things might go better today if he's more helpful. Calling the podgy guy "Uncle" will show respect. Khalid smiles, now feeling confident he'll be out of here within hours.

When the lock turns in the door, Khalid's ready and smiling. But instead of the guy from last night another younger Pakistani comes in with tea and flat bread to tempt him.

"Where's the other man?" Silence. Khalid tries being friendly. "What's your name?" Silence. Then the man leaves without saying a word, clearly unable to speak English, taking the tea and bread with him.

"Bye," Khalid calls. No response. The door clicks shut.

A few minutes later, a woman with straight brown hair, about thirty-five, in a gray suit and white shirt, comes in with a clipboard. Two men in navy trousers with blue and white pinstriped shirts accompany her. Standing at the door, they say nothing while she pulls up the other chair. Then another guy in a black suit slips in behind them.

"Hi, Khalid," she says in a friendly American accent, as if she's going to help him. "I'm Angela and this is Bruce." She points to the man in the suit. The other men she doesn't bother introducing. "Now, what exactly were you doing in Afghanistan last week?"

Khalid's mind is scrambled again. "My name's pronounced *Haleed*," he says, surprised at himself for mentioning it, something he gave up doing years ago in infant school. "I've never been to that country!"

Angela smiles sweetly at him. "Come on now. We know you were there. We have your passport."

This was getting ridiculous.

"That can't be true. My dad keeps all our passports. How come you've got mine? Have you got my dad?"

"Your father? Why do you keep talking about him?"

"What? I told that other guy—he's missing."

"Your father works for al-Qaeda?"

"What? No! He's a chef in Manchester. Don't be daft. You can phone the restaurant. They'll tell you. Ask my aunties, my mum."

"You have no idea where your father is?" Angela frowns.

"Don't you?" Now Khalid's getting really confused.

"Why would we?" Angela leans back in her chair, exchanging glances with the men at the door as if to say, *This might take a while.*

Khalid is totally baffled. "I'm only fifteen," he says. "You can't do this. I haven't done anything. Where's my watch?"

One guy butts in. "My name's James. I'm from MI5." The silent one nods briefly, staring at Khalid with a stern expression.

"Then get me out of here!" Khalid yells.

"I'm afraid we can't do that," James says.

"You have to! I'm only a kid!"

"It's best to cooperate with the Americans and tell them what you were doing in Afghanistan and why you were at the demonstration."

"What demonstration? That thing the other morning? I just pushed through the crowd on my way to look for my dad. You've mixed me up with someone else." If the British guys won't help him, who will? Khalid finally crumbles. "Please!" he begs, tears springing into his eyes. But the men are expressionless, unmoved.

Soon the door opens and the men leave. Angela's joined by another guy who is about forty years old with a round, smiling face. Getting Khalid's hopes up for a second. But after whispering to the woman, all he says is, "We've got the others."

"What others? Have you kidnapped my mum and sisters?"

If only they'd tell him what they suspect him of doing, he could put them right, but they turn away whenever he glances at them. Talking quietly to each other out of earshot.

"WHAT OTHERS?" Khalid yells.

Then the round-faced guy begins tapping his foot. At this, Angela gets up and two Pakistani guards grab Khalid by his handcuffs.

"Am I going home? Where are you taking me?" Khalid shouts as they walk him to the door, then down the mildew-smelling corridor and outside into blazing sunshine towards a dusty brown truck parked right outside. This time they don't bother with the cloth hood. They know he has no idea where he is and there's nowhere to run.

It's then that Khalid first begins to think they won't be taking him home. Shoved in the back, pushed face down again, he can just about make out four more men in shalwar kameez as they climb in to sit on the edges of the truck. Holding on with their hands, they lean over Khalid in case he decides to escape. Their tobacco-smelling breath makes him want to heave but there's no room to move, their sandals and hairy toes are right in his face. Nobody speaks. The driver speeds off down a wide, busy highway, jolting Khalid again on the uneven metal floor. Dirt in his face. In his eyes and mouth. He bumps around like an empty brown bottle, trying to avoid another jolt to his ears and bruised head.

Suddenly the truck brakes sharply and Khalid's quickly bundled out of the back, sweaty men on either side of him. They push him towards a tall building with high windows and shove him through a black shiny door to the poshest place he's ever seen. Full of gilt-framed pictures, luxurious red and gold chairs, the marble hall smells of silver polish. If it wasn't for the men beside him with their hands on his shoulders, Khalid might think this was the home of a famous Pakistani cricketer.

Two men from the truck disappear inside one of the rooms. The others stay close to Khalid as they push him into a smaller room at the far end of the hall.

Once inside, the door closes quickly behind him and the key turns in the lock with a loud double clunk, giving him the feeling it won't be opened again any time soon. Khalid runs to the window to see if he can escape. But there's another two men outside in a parked car and, in any case, the window's bolted. Down the wide street, there are other tall buildings, some with black gates in front of them. Across from him is a park-like open space, marked out with narrow railings. It looks nice out there. Safe. Rich. The kind of area Khalid goes out of his way to avoid at home in case someone thinks he's a burglar or up to no good. The kind of road that makes him feel poor and scruffy. Out of place. Uncomfortable.

Why didn't they just ask him to come with them? Why kidnap him with a gun and beat him senseless? Why the stupid hood and cuffs if all they are going to do in the end is bring him to a flash place like this?

With little idea what to do or think, Khalid sits on the dark yellow sofa with his feet on a small coffee table, rubbing his sore wrists against his T-shirt behind his back in an attempt to shift the cuffs farther up his arms. His aching shoulder hurts worse than ever. The pain in his side forces him to sit leaning forward, almost doubled up, staring at the ornate rugs on the wooden floor while wondering what on earth they are going to do with him next.

He doesn't have long to wait before two men in jeans and blue shirts creak open the door. Khalid quickly drops his feet from the coffee table and sits up straight, trying his best not to look scared. More Americans, they introduce themselves as Dan and Bobby. Like last time, no surnames.

"We're here to help you," Dan says unconvincingly as he lounges in the chair opposite with his big hands clasped in his lap. The gentler-faced Bobby nods several times as he holds out a blown-up photo of Khalid jumping high, arms in the air, at the demonstration in Karachi.

"Is this you?"

Khalid nods, surprised to see the photo. Do they have photos of everyone at the demonstration? Was it an al-Qaeda event or what? Or have they been following him?

The two men look at each other. "Right," says Dan. "Good. Now, tell us what you are doing here and we'll let you go."

"I told you! I got caught up in that, trying to look for my dad. I didn't even know what it was!"

"What were you doing at the demonstration?"

"Who was the guy in the skullcap next to you?"

"What's the name of the man to your right?"

"Why did you return to Karachi from Afghanistan?"

"Who did you meet in Afghanistan?"

"What did you bring with you?"

"Why did you go to the demonstration?"

This was beginning to feel like a scene from *Groundhog Day*. The same questions going round forever. With the same answers being ignored because they don't fit the answers the Americans want. Dan's and Bobby's freshly shaved faces and neatly combed hair, together with their wide, toothy smiles and stupid questions, force Khalid to suspect they are completely out there, on drugs or something.

He does his best to hold his temper. Patiently telling them again and again who he is and why he's in this photo they have.

Reminding them he's never been anywhere near Afghanistan. Wondering if he's going to lose his mind if this carries on much longer.

"I'm fifteen," Khalid says for the millionth time. "I'm still at school."

This time Dan leans back on the chair, shaking his head impatiently. "Come on! Answer the questions."

"Admit you're twenty-two and a member of al-Qaeda. Go on," Bobby says with the kind of smile that's worse than nasty.

"What? No way. How come you think that?" Khalid pleads.

Dan finally looks like he's given up. "OK, Kandahar for you," he says smugly, flicking a finger at Bobby, who rushes to the door. "You're wasting our time!" he adds with a smirk.

"What do you mean 'Kandahar'?" Khalid shouts, a part of him thanking his dad for making him learn the map of Asia when he was young. "That's in Afghanistan! I told you I haven't been there and now you want to *take me there*? Are you crazy? I want to see my family. Where's my mum? Someone's made up lies about me—I know what goes on here. Don't pay them. Was it Abdullah, that maniac?'

"You should have trusted me!" Dan heads for the door, ignoring his outburst.

Five seconds later, the guard reappears and Khalid jumps up, ready to fight, though there's little he can do with his hands cuffed behind his back. But all that happens is the guard roughly pushes him away, then waits beside the door as Dan and Bobby leave the room and quickly follows them to ram the key in the lock.

Once Khalid is alone on the dark yellow sofa once again,

the thought slowly dawns on him that they really are going to take him to Kandahar. His mind races back through their questions in a desperate attempt to figure out who they think he might be.

"Do I look like a terrorist?" he says aloud, totally confused by the whole thing. His thoughts scatter to consider every possibility. *Is it because of Dad? Did he do something bad? Was the demonstration about al-Qaeda? What do they think I've done? Why do they keep talking about Afghanistan?*

All he knows is that something's gone terribly wrong, and, with his dad not around, it's probably going to get a whole lot worse.

An armed Pakistani guard comes in with a bottle of water. His movements and face are gentle, unlike those of the last one. Khalid gets the sense he can talk to this guy and gestures to him that he needs the loo. The guard uncuffs him. At last Khalid can see the damage the truck journey has done to his arms, which are covered in red marks, cuts and bruises and ache with a sudden, dragging pain as they fall to his side.

The guard eyes Khalid's arms, then frowns to himself. He leads him outside, where another guard throws a white towel over Khalid's head to prevent him from seeing where he's going. The first guard clutches his elbow, walking him slowly to the toilets at the other end of the corridor.

A murmuring sound inside one of the two cubicles tells Khalid he's not alone as the towel's removed. The door locks quickly behind him as he gazes at the dark, damp toilets that look like something out of a horror film. No windows. Only one dripping tap and two stained porcelain urinals. Such a flash house and these smelly toilets are ten times worse than the ones at school.

"Hello?" Khalid whispers to the closed, gray cubicle, aware the guard's listening outside. The murmuring suddenly stops. The door opens and an alarming-looking Indian man with dazed eyes and a vacant expression pushes past without seeing him.

"Hey, man!" Khalid whispers.

Shocked by the greeting, the man bangs anxiously on the door to be let out. In a second he's gone, leaving Khalid even more bewildered. How many others are there like him here? Is this posh house a disguise for a prison? Who owns this place? The door opens again for Khalid soon after. He is handcuffed once more, the towel is thrown over his head and he's led up some stairs and down another corridor to another room, where the towel's removed again.

Khalid can't bear it any longer. "I need help." A weird sound like that of a wounded animal escapes his mouth. "Please! Please!" His teary eyes meet the guard's flat, cow-pat eyes. A look of hopeless recognition that they're both out of their depth passes between them. The gentle-faced guard lowers his head to gaze at the floor while Khalid begs for help.

"I haven't done anything wrong. I'm a schoolkid. Please get me out of here!" Knowing this might be his last chance of escape.

"I cannot." The guard sighs.

"Why are you helping them, not me? At least go to my aunties' house and tell them where I am. Please. Please. If you can't help me, help my mum."

"We have rules not to aid," he answers, clearly upset.

"Who'll know? I won't tell anyone! Please. My poor mum."

Suffering from a roller-coaster of emotions, Khalid thinks maybe kicking him before running for the stairs is worth the chance of getting shot in the back. Anything's better than being held here. This time the guard stays quiet. A look of guilt passes over his worried face as he hurries out. Quickly the lock turns, clicks then clunks, followed by the kind of silence that feels as if it might go on forever.

Khalid turns from the door with a tightness in his throat and tension in every muscle of his aching body that threatens to bring him to his knees at any moment. For some reason the room this time is smaller, far less luxurious, containing six hard wooden chairs, a polished table and several rugs. The window is covered with black tape. *A dining room*, Khalid thinks. Suddenly aware of the sound of a hammer drill starting up in a building close by, the rhythm of rapid gunfire adds to the strange feeling of being holed up in someone else's nightmare. He's trapped, finished, with no one to help him and no way out.

Khalid's never felt special. Nothing but an ordinary kid from Rochdale. He's OK at football. If he works hard he gets decent grades at school. He isn't bad-looking, but none of his features are amazing. Not like his mate Tony Banda, who looks like a film star and has gorgeous Lexy for a girlfriend. Not like Holgy, who's a brilliant goalkeeper. Not like Nico, who's famous for being the top alcohol trader in the area. Not like Mikael, who's clever and great at football too. And aside from Khalid's close friends, it's easy to go through all the kids he knows and pick out something about them that makes them stand out. While him, he's no one—nothing. Nobody. That's what makes this whole thing worse than embarrassing. Everyone's going to laugh their heads off when they hear Khalid Ahmed's been kidnapped.

He sits on one of the hard wooden chairs, staring at the five empty ones that surround him. Who uses this room? It doesn't feel used. Why him? Why's he sitting here with his arms cuffed behind his back, feeling totally crushed and aching all over?

A short while later, Khalid sees the nice guard for the last time when he opens the door to fling a thin, brown blanket at him, which smells of mice. His bedding for the night. Another guard brings a cold dinner of chicken curry, which, after uncuffing his wrists, he watches him eat. Only to grab Khalid's elbow the moment he finishes popping the last fingerful of rice in his mouth. This time he kindly attaches the cuffs a little looser, Khalid guesses, to make the night more comfortable for him.

He must have been held here for over twenty-four hours now without reason. Why? Khalid curls up under the smelly blanket on the red oriental rug. Pausing for a second to wonder how the carpet-makers manage to weave such intricate geometric patterns, he lets his mind drift off to imagine a weaver alone in a small dark room, deciding where to put the diamonds and crosses, the bold border with red flowers.

A few years ago, Dad insisted on taking him to the oriental rug sale in Rochdale Town Hall. Khalid moaned all the way, while Dad was as excited as a child. Rubbing his hands at the thought of the beautiful carpets they were going to see.

"Oriental carpet patterns always please the eye," he told Khalid. "No matter how different the pattern, the effect is always the same, beautiful. Do you hear? A kind of magic is there. Many patterns, but one carpet. Unity, that's what they are showing here."

Of course they couldn't afford to buy a rug. The cheapest was several hundred pounds. Not that Khalid cared. Bored out of his skull, he didn't really take in any of this stuff at the time. Even when they arrived at the town hall, which was crammed with people wanting to buy, rug after rug held up by the auctioneer as if they were the crown jewels, Khalid didn't get it.

"A carpet's a carpet, Dad! It goes on the floor." Now Khalid wishes he hadn't said that. He feels guilty, worrying that Dad must have been disappointed by his lack of enthusiasm even though he didn't say anything at the time. But when he did speak he said something Khalid never forgot.

"Giving thanks for something beautiful is the best way to find peace."

Now the more Khalid examines the rug he's lying on, the deeper and more satisfying the patterns appear to be. How peculiar is this? Sitting up suddenly, he can see himself handcuffed, on this strange floor, scared to death, and all he can do is stare at this rug. But the longer he looks, the more perfect the repeated diamond shapes seem to be. A strong black line here and there turns the pattern on its head for no reason, breaking the set order in a strange, surprising way. Which forces him to wonder why the shapes suddenly reverse and then sometimes continue as before. In a flash, he suddenly understands why Dad took him to see the carpets.

Before long, Khalid can't help giving quiet thanks to the thousands of weavers who are, right now, hard at work making something as beautiful as this out of wool, cotton or silk. Not guessing that it could mean so much to a fifteen-year-old boy who's usually playing computer games and larking about with his mates.

It's true, saying thanks does make Khalid feel better for a moment—even a bit more peaceful, like Dad said. In a second, Dad's wide smile comes back to him and that quick laugh he has whenever he spots something special. Silly things like a stone in the shape of an egg.

"The whole world's in this kind of surprise," Dad once told him.

The idea that Dad might also be staring at a carpet in some other room, somewhere in Karachi, feels like a real possibility suddenly. But the truth is, the rug he's lying on is the only link he has to him right now. Khalid's mind is desperately grabbing at something to stop himself from going completely crazy, tugging at the shapes and colors of the rug like a baby pulling apart a favorite blanket.

He lifts his head from the rug to stare at the ceiling, wishing the yellow glow from the bare light bulb above him would spin into the shape of a genie. A fat, laughing genie or jinn, like the one in the story of Aladdin's lamp. The jinn, an immortal in human form, is coming to carry him away from here. He can see him, right there, right now, carrying him home on a magic carpet, back to his mum. His mum.

"Your wish is my command," the jinn says, and Khalid's heart locks on to the image of being returned to the computer cupboard, switching off the machine this time. Seeing himself pick up his mobile, put it safely away in his denim pocket, the chrome watch back on his wrist, and walk up the stairs to bed. Waking a few minutes later to the smell of steaming hot tea and Mum standing over him with a wide smile, saying, "Dad's still asleep."

But the jinn has gone. No one comes and after a while the light bulb flickers off and Khalid's thoughts change course to the hopeless feeling he'll never get over this. Lying on his side, he listens to the night-time noises of the big creaking house, occasional footsteps and the murmur of a passing car outside. His eyes on the beautiful rugs reaching out to the dark hidden corners of the room which smells of mold and wax polish. The only light a streak of yellow coming in under the door.

# 7

## BREAD

In the morning another armed guard, with a drooping face and a curling beard, brings Khalid tea and bread. Uncuffing him like last time, the guard stands over him until he finishes eating. Footsteps hurry past the door while Khalid sips the hot, sweet tea, and the sound of banging and angry shouting from the room above keeps him company as he hungrily snaps up the flat bread. Scoffing it in three eager mouthfuls. The smell of stale white flour on his fingers.

"Any chance of a shower?" Khalid says without much hope. Finally losing it when the guard turns away to gaze vacantly at the blank wall. In one fell swoop, the tea and plate crash to the floor as Khalid leaps at him. His hands close tightly round the soft skin of the guard's warm neck and the anger rises so fast Khalid's fingers tingle as the guard struggles to pull them off, punching him like a boxer as he wildly yells for help through the stranglehold.

Four guards charge in, pointing their guns at Khalid's head. Standing feet apart like a firing squad, ready to kill him the second he releases the guard's neck. But, exhausted by the power of his own nervous fury, Khalid drops his hands and sinks in a heap on the floor, head hanging low. Thick black hair falls over his forehead and he begins to sweat as an out-of-body feeling of sheer hopelessness drains him of every molecule of energy.

Now he's down, a boot jams into his side, knocking him flat. His arms are twisted back, he's handcuffed tight. Another boot lands on his shoulder. Boots come down on his stomach until there's nowhere for Khalid to turn to get out of their way. He doubles up in pain until blood runs from his nose and he vomits.

He lies there for what seems like hours until eventually he falls asleep. Waking up to find the room dark again. The moment he remembers what's happened, he panics. His stomach hurts. Arms hurt. Face hurts. There's hardly a part of him that isn't in pain. Despite the tears welling in his eyes, Khalid stares into his invisible future and sees nothing worth living for, just a small horrible world with nasty people who don't give a damn about anyone.

At that point, the door opens and a square of fluorescent light floods the room. Khalid squirms to focus on the shapes at the door, unable to make out the shadowy faces. A man says something that might be in Urdu. Khalid picks out a word that sounds familiar.

Then one of them says, "Only English him speak."

"Up from there!" another quieter voice commands. With the shadow of a gun on the wooden floor beside his feet, Khalid struggles to stand, a piercing pain in his ankle causing his foot to suddenly fold, making it hard to balance. But he tries and tries—knowing if he stumbles they'll start kicking him again.

Two rugged-looking men on either side of him elbow him to the door and out of the room. There's enjoyment on their faces as they rush him down the corridor to yet another room. A room with a ceiling light, a small desk and two black plastic chairs.

*What kind of weird game are they playing with me?* Khalid wonders. *Are they moving me around so I won't remember where I've been?*

Three of the men hurry away, leaving only one man with a kind face. Khalid sees he looks ashamed when he meets his gaze. He quickly lowers his eyes before sneakily attaching one of Khalid's handcuffs to the chair. The other arm is left to hang limply in his lap. Then he stands back while Khalid examines the extent of the yellow and purple bruises on his brown skin. Plus his filthy hand, which is smeared with dirt, dusty and bloody, with a few carpet threads attached. His fingernails look as if they've been dipped in ink. Khalid raises his arm for the guard to see his injuries, pointing his finger firmly at him as if he's responsible for the state he's in. But the guard doesn't seem to care. He leaves, only to return a couple of minutes later, grinning for the first time with tatty, wonky teeth while he cracks open a bottle of water.

"Thank you." Khalid's suspicious of his sudden smile, not wanting or trusting the kindness he's showing by giving him a measly bottle of water. Khalid would rather he scowled at him. Then maybe this jailer–prisoner relationship might have a vague chance of being an honest one. Khalid glances down, avoiding his gaze.

He drains the last drops of water and thrusts the empty

bottle back at the guard. Watching him closely while he talks rapidly to the other man waiting at the door. In the end, the man rushes off. He gives a final gesture of irritation by flinging his hands in the air before slamming the door.

"Yeah, and good riddance," Khalid says out loud, then wonders if his rude remark has seen off his chance of breakfast. But no, soon the door opens again and another, much harder-looking man hands him a piece of thin warm bread that Khalid stuffs quickly in his mouth. Making a mental bet with himself that this is the last bit of food he'll see today, he's anxious to swallow the lot before the guard makes it back to the door. Just to shock him. Show him how hungry he is. How nasty they all are.

Now what? Feeling somehow crushed the moment the door closes without the guard even glancing at him. Some things you get over and some things you don't. Khalid knows this will stay with him for the rest of his life.

With each slam of the door, followed by the sound of hurriedly retreating footsteps, Khalid feels such self-pity it makes him want to faint. Waiting and waiting in this room smelling of grime, that's bad enough, but the thing that hurts the most is not understanding anything.

# 8

## MASUD

The ear-splitting noise of screeching furniture being dragged across the ceiling wakes Khalid up. For some reason the maroon velvet curtains are open. The strange sight of sunshine flooding the room takes a few seconds to reach his brain. Someone must have come in while he was sleeping and pulled the curtains back.

Nothing else about the room has changed. The small desk is in the same position in the middle of the floor. Two black plastic chairs on either side of it. Bare bulb hanging from the ceiling. The now-familiar smell of filth on the walls.

It's then he realizes that two pieces of tape fixed to the window have come undone. The curtains are in the same place.

Now he remembers the guard with the wonky teeth coming in last night, fixing him with a sorry look and trying to rouse him as he lolled in the chair, half falling off. The guard uncuffed Khalid from the seat, then gently recuffed his wrists behind his back so he could lie down on the rough coir matting that covers most of the wooden floor. He threw Khalid a smelly blanket from the doorway before shutting out the yellow light from the corridor—he remembers that.

Khalid wonders if it's possible to pull all the tape off. If the window opens he might somehow be able to get out. The thought makes his arms begin to ache. In whatever position he tried to sleep, he had to compensate for the unnatural place his shackled wrists found themselves. The best was when he lay on his stomach. Only then did the pain in his shoulders ease a little.

For some reason, the sight of the clear blue sky brings a feeling of expectation to Khalid. Perhaps today's the day he'll be going home, though by his reckoning this is the fifth day since he was captured and nothing's happened to give him any hope.

With a sudden burst of energy, Khalid jumps up, runs to the window and, with his back to it, begins scratching at the tape stuck fast to the frame. Eventually, one corner comes away. Threads of tape peel off like string, leaving the main strip behind, which irritates him into getting down on his knees to attack it with his teeth. He soon realizes he's achieving nothing but getting the odd stringy thread in his mouth—they tear off like cotton.

Then the door opens and yet another new guard smiles at him. Speaking in hesitant English.

"You want go toilet. Yes?"

Khalid nods, getting up slowly from the floor and angrily spitting out masking tape. "Tell me what I'm doing here."

"Americans they you want." The guard gives him a concerned grin.

"That's crap," Khalid responds. "I haven't done anything to them. What did I do?"

This time the guard widens his eyes and shrugs, giving the impression after this question that he has no choice but to ignore him. His smile quickly disappears.

Like before, Khalid's led to the toilet with a cloth covering his eyes. Like before, he's back inside the plain room in a couple of minutes. Again, the door snapping shut on him feels like some kind of insult. Like a thump in the back.

"How dare you?" Khalid pounds it with cuffed wrists, then switches round to kick the door until it opens again. "You can't leave me here on my own!" he yells at the same guard, who's quickly joined by another man.

They both look at him for a second, then agree something between them with a shared look and a few whispers. Instantly, the cloth is thrown over his head again and he's led down the same corridor as before.

Soon a door opens and he's pushed inside. The towel is whipped off his head as the door closes on another bleak, gray room with an old desk and two chairs, and the strange sight of a scruffy handcuffed man sitting cross-legged on the bare concrete floor. His small face is swollen and covered in bruises. His ruffled, graying hair and beard are matted with dirt but there's a strange, calm dignity in his expression.

"I am Masud Al-Dossadi," he says proudly. "And you?"

"They kidnapped me. Beat me up. Stole my bloody watch, the gangsters," Khalid gasps.

Masud nods wearily. "You have a name?"

"Khalid Ahmed. I'm English, from Rochdale near Manchester. You know it?"

"Rochdale?" For a moment, Masud searches his mind for such a place before shaking his head.

"I'm fifteen. That's all," Khalid says. "They can't do this to me."

"Me—forty-eight years."

They both half smile and Khalid tries to find a comfortable position to rest his bruised body as he sinks to the rough floor. The pain in his side starts up again the second he straightens his spine but, anxious to hear Masud's story, he ignores the discomfort, leaning in to catch every word.

"What happened to your face?" Khalid asks.

Masud sighs. "First they make resolution, I very dangerous person. Beat me with big pipe. Then they are preventing me from sleep. Make standing all night. Hit hard on head when I start to fall. Then use pipe again all over body."

"Who? Who did it?" Khalid asks, horrified.

"The Pakistan security men, they doing it under American orders," Masud says. "Who do you think?"

Khalid goes cold. Shivers race up his spine. "Why?"

"I am Egyptian man," Masud explains. "They collect me up at Afghanistan border with 2,000 dollars I got in my pocket for not buy many things because village gone. They putting bomb there, now is being my fault."

"Because of the money?" Khalid suddenly understands why they might have been suspicious.

"For five years I'm buying many goods from there to sell in the shop I got in Cairo. Turquoise necklaces, blue ceramic bowls, woodwork. Birdcages are very, very good to buy at Afghanistan. Anything, I bringing it back." He smiles. "I am

90

knowing this country long time. Plenty things good to see. Nice people invite me eat—all time. Good people, not like you think."

"But why did you go there when you knew there was a war on?" Khalid thinks he's friendly, a sweet man without the slightest hint of malice in his face, but he still can't understand why he went to Afghanistan when everyone knew it was dangerous.

Head high with peeping eyes, bruised and swollen, Masud begins his tale. "You asking me why? The roads are bad and some of the towns they not really towns, just little ramshackle house, but Afghanistan is wonderful country. Mistake I making this time was go from bombed mountain village to visit Kabul with good friend. We are wanting to see what happening."

Pausing to catch his breath, Masud twists round to make himself more comfortable before continuing.

"Americans looking everywhere, all time for Bin Laden—it ruin my business. Kabul is very sad there. Bombing every day. Women, children, dying in streets. Explosions going all time. I'm trying leave. But thousands of refugees in same position, going also."

Khalid remembers the pictures of truckloads of men on the news. Broken men with sand-colored cloths wound tightly around their heads. Staring at the cameras along the dusty road. Dad saying, "Do they look like terrorists? Or refugees?" But the newsreader said they were members of the Taliban and maybe they were. Either way, how could they tell? And at the time Khalid thought, *Who cares?* They had nothing to do with him—until now.

"Then I'm having moment of typhoid," Masud says. "Lucky for me, my friend is looking after me until I well enough cross the border for Pakistan. When they looking at my passport they ask why I'm always going Cairo to Afghanistan? Why I stay Kabul for months? Why I having much money in pocket? I am telling them about my business, but no believe, and I'm having no birdcages, just necklaces in pocket."

"What about your friend?" Khalid asks. "What happened to him?"

"They say he have no visa. What happening to him? I'm not knowing this. Then they say my passport out of date. I telling them I got typhoid. Very ill I being for months, but they not hearing."

"Maybe they just wanted your money?" Khalid says. "They stole my watch."

"This is possible." Masud sighs. "But now they got money, you think they free me? They say Americans wanting me. They accuse me of being enemy combatant."

"An incompetent? Why?" Khalid knows that word well. Remembering Mr. Tagg calling Nico an incompetent when he handed in his essay outline on the Spanish Inquisition with only three words on the page and plenty of space in between: *beginning, middle, end.*

Masud looks a lot cleverer than Nico to him. It doesn't make sense.

"Combatant. Enemy combatant." Exhausted, Masud closes his eyes.

"Oh, right. Sorry!" Khalid nods.

"Look at me!" Masud shakes his head.

"I'm looking," Khalid says. Hoping for more.

"They are thinking I fighting against them. Against America. But I have no gun. No bullets. No knife. Only turquoise necklaces and money in pocket."

"They can't keep you here forever," Khalid says quietly, trying to comfort him.

"No, they telling me in morning I'm going Kandahar in Afghanistan for processing. Why they bringing me all way here first, I'm not knowing." For a second, silence overtakes Masud.

"Kandahar." Repeating it, Khalid rests his head on his chest. Reminded of what the guy Dan said—is he still going there too? The memory of his abduction comes back to haunt him, speeding round and round inside his head. Why didn't he try and stop them? Why didn't he fight or try to run away? Why didn't he scream? Do something? And though he and Masud are in the same situation now, they have nothing in common. Two weeks ago he was playing football in the park in Rochdale. Rochdale, for heaven's sake—nowhere near any war zones or dangerous borders, any bombing or kidnapping. Masud is a grown-up who was found with a bunch of money in his pocket in a dangerous city, while he—he was just returning from the loo to the computer at his aunties' house. Somebody sold Khalid to the authorities, made up lies about him, he's certain now that's what happened. It's the reason no one listens to him. It must be. But what can he do to change their minds and convince them he's innocent?

The faint tapping of footsteps resonates down the corridor. Khalid glances at the door, still half expecting someone to come and tell him there's been a mistake.

"In the name of Allah . . ." Masud responds to the call of prayer coming from a nearby mosque.

Khalid mumbles something about being tired, blushing slightly, but he has no desire to join in. The one thing he wishes he could change right now is the religion he was born into.

# 9

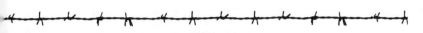

## TO KANDAHAR

Inspired by Masud's calm dignity, Khalid finds plenty to think about when they take him back to his room and he lies down—but he can't sleep. There's a car outside that keeps honking its horn and there's no comfort to be found on this hard floor and itchy mat. So there are others here who have lost not only their families—Masud had a wife and four children in Cairo—but their businesses too. Masud has lost everything. What's going on in the world that this can happen? Khalid cannot get his head around any of these crazy facts and each day he feels weirder than the day before.

Not until the first glimmers of daylight begin to peep through the gap in the window and he spreads flat on his stomach does Khalid finally fall asleep.

Waking up hours later to another quivering bolt of blue sky at the top of the window doesn't rid him of the feeling of impending doom. The shooting pains down his arms, caused by trying to sleep with his wrists cuffed behind his back, are so severe now he feels sick and light-headed. Worse than ever.

He curls into a ball on the floor and cries. He'd always thought of himself as strong, but he realizes now that this was because he had his mum and dad to pick up the pieces whenever anything went wrong. And what went wrong in the past—letters from school and underage drinking and stuff— was nothing like this. Now there's no one to make his aching arms better. He can't even touch the sore skin under his eye to feel if the swelling's going down. Has to ask permission to go to the toilet, like he's at primary school.

Five minutes of suffering the rough bristles of the mat on his wet face is enough, though. Khalid stops crying and turns on his side, only to endure the sudden pressure of the hard floor on his shoulder. He sits up, groaning in agony. Letting his head fall, he moves it slowly round to stretch his stiff neck, but it doesn't help ease the pain.

He never wanted to come to Karachi. Why didn't he argue with Dad? He could have stayed with Mac next door, or Nico, or one of Dad's friends from the restaurant. He doesn't like Pakistan. He's totally British, so why did he smile politely when Auntie gave him the shalwar kameez to wear? It was so uncool and a horrible sand color, and if he hadn't worn it that day when he was trying to get past the demonstration maybe he wouldn't be here now.

Panicked and frightened, locked inside this unending pain, Khalid begins to imagine he's still in England, waving his family goodbye at the airport—off they go to Karachi without him. Great. He feels better for a moment, until the door clicks open and the ordeal of breakfast starts again. Two unsmiling guards. Warm water. One thin piece of bread. Watchful dark eyes on him. Guilty downward glances as he eats and drinks. But then the routine changes. He's cuffed more tightly and, after being taken to the toilet, led from the house. The only sound is the faint rustle of his denim jeans as he walks barefoot between the guards, tears falling.

They push him into a car that smells of grease and petrol. One guard on either side. Khalid doesn't bother to wonder if they are taking him home to his aunties' house. In these handcuffs it doesn't seem likely. At least this time there's no hood and, despite the hot, sticky air, he can vaguely see tall buildings through the grimy window as they turn the corner and merge with the traffic on a wide highway.

The scruffy driver keeps his deep-set shadowy eyes on the busy road ahead. The serious man beside him speaks only to give what sound like directions in short, angry bursts. In the seat next to Khalid the heavily covered man keeps his head down the whole way, veined hands in his lap, so Khalid doesn't get the chance to see what he looks like. He doesn't dare challenge him or reach for the door handle to try and escape. The tense, clammy atmosphere in the car is so unbelievably bad he knows they will happily kill him if he moves a limb.

After about an hour, worried sick, Khalid senses an airport as the car turns off the main road. He can hear the sound of planes overhead. Engines whirring. As they draw nearer, he sees lines of men in shalwar kameez, heads bent, handcuffed like him, being led up the ramp of a cargo plane. He scans them quickly for anyone who might be Masud. Other men in army uniform yell orders with an American accent. Then a few men shout in Urdu or another language he's never heard, perhaps Arabic. The same harsh tone to their voices causes his skin to creep with fear. A fear Khalid fails to master as they lead him trembling from the car up the ramp of the plane. An aggressive soldier screams abuse, kicks Khalid up the backside to hurry him inside the door. A suffocating feeling of unbearable heat lays into him like a branding iron the moment he steps into the entrance of the dark plane. A plane crammed with men. They push Khalid down the lines to join the middle row, where he squashes into the aisle, grateful for a bit of space to one side—until another man crashes down on the floor next to him.

As the plane taxis to the end of the runway, there's no doubt in his mind he's going to Kandahar. The sound of the sudden powerful rush of the engine tears into his heart, scooting him back to that day, which now seems so long ago, when he sat down in the comfy seat to fly to Karachi. Packet of crisps and fizzy drink safely stowed in the seat pocket. Then a terrible noise starts up that makes Khalid feel he's inside a tumble dryer as the plane roars off with its cargo of prisoners, squashed together like sardines in a tin.

All of a sudden an insane panic builds up at the realization that he's leaving his family behind. How will they find him now? The chaos, the craziness—it feels like he's being stunned with charges of high-voltage electricity, destroying his ability to think clearly.

Strips of sunshine from the plane windows light up the bent shapes huddled on the ground as Khalid breathes in the foul smell of hopeless desperation.

# PROCESSING

Some time later, in a vile, sticky heat, the plane lands with a thump on the runway, screeching to a halt as a soldier yells, "Welcome to Kandahar, folks!" The loud voice has a ring of satisfaction to it that crushes Khalid as well as confirming where he is.

He's squashed between two much larger handcuffed men who've spent the whole journey praying. Their bobbing heads and closed eyes are now impossible to ignore as men nearby join in. Each in turn, including Khalid, is hauled up, pushed towards the wide ramp and led stumbling from the plane to an area of dusty ground and the noise of engines, generators and mad barking dogs.

Khalid sinks to his knees after a thump on the back. A plastic hood is shoved over his head while he sniffs the spreading dust. Then he's thrown down on his face to wait.

A man begins wailing, pleading for help nearby. A man Khalid hopes isn't Masud. Within minutes, Khalid's bundled towards what sounds like a big echoing building. A building teeming with yelling soldiers and the sound of men crying and groaning as they're herded and kicked into line with hard boots.

A soldier trips Khalid, crashing him to the concrete floor with a violent yell. A familiar pain rips through his side, giving him the sensation his arms are splintering from their sockets. He bangs his head so hard he blacks out for a second and teeters on the edge of consciousness. Coming round only when they start stamping on his aching spine to hold him down before buzzing a metal-cutter through the tough handcuffs, allowing his arms to flop to the ground like rags.

Then they begin ripping off his T-shirt and jeans and pull him to his feet totally naked. Surrounding him, one pulls off the hood. Khalid squints at the extraordinary sight of soldiers screaming abuse at naked men lined up against the white walls of a massive hangar-like, metal-ceilinged building. The prisoners' heads are bowed in shame like something out of a horror movie as another man photographs each one in turn.

Men with gloves start searching Khalid's body. Touching him all over. Others scream in pain at the intrusive violence of the searches. The worst embarrassment of their lives. Humiliated at every turn by the soldiers' ugly taunts, the naked men are taken to one side and photographed again. When it comes to Khalid's turn, he refuses to move forward. Standing proudly, no matter what they intend doing to him. With a swift punch, he's knocked into line.

Several photos are taken of his face, front on as well as in profile. After that a barber shaves his adolescent face stubble, then his head, with the same tenderness as a sheep shearer with a thousand fleeces to go. Then another photo's taken of Khalid with his head shaved.

"OK, move it. You're done!" The photographer dismisses

him. Swearing harshly at the next man in line to hurry up. The middle-aged, soft-faced man, naked, vulnerable, with tears in his eyes, glances at Khalid as if to say the experience means his life is over. It ignites a terrible anger in Khalid, who knows the shaving of the man's beard—an important part of his Muslim identity—is the final insult for him.

The naked man sits and weeps while his face is being shaved. The barber carries on, while the sight of grown men crying and yelling like babies as they're routinely humiliated gnaws at Khalid's heart. The two nearest him, naked as the day they were born, close their eyes and silently pray. It's then that Khalid spots two kids younger than him: one skinny boy about thirteen years old who's acting brain-damaged, with his tongue hanging out and rolling eyes, and another scared-looking boy at the back of the line who's so small he could be eleven or younger. He cranes his neck to see them better, but they disappear from view when, one by one, men are taken into a nearby concrete building.

Shielded by a soldier on either side, Khalid is shoved into a small room where more American soldiers take his fingerprints, then swab saliva from his mouth before herding him through another door where two men in jeans and white shirts sit behind a green plastic desk.

The biggest American smiles. Holding out his hand as if welcoming the shivering, naked Khalid to Afghanistan.

"Hi, I'm Anthony. This is Sam. We're CIA." Khalid doesn't know whether to laugh or cry. Standing there waiting to hear his fate, he's not sure if he's supposed to say hi back to them or not.

With a poker-like expression on his pink face, Sam asks, "When did you join al-Qaeda?"

Not this again! "Listen to me—I've never joined them. I don't know anyone in al-Qaeda," Khalid says breathlessly. Scared of the thoughts going on behind Sam's sharp voice, he's not sure what else to say.

Then Anthony raises his eyebrows. "You speak good English!"

"I *am* English!"

"Oh yeah? Where you from?"

"Rochdale." Khalid watches Anthony lose interest, not having any idea where Rochdale is. "It's near Manchester!" But the queue behind him is getting longer and the Americans keep looking past him to check it out, giving him the impression these questions are just a formality.

"When did you last see Osama Bin Laden?" Sam pipes up.

"What?" Khalid frowns. "I've seen him on telly if that's what you mean. I've never met him. You lot can't even find him, so how am I supposed to know where he is? Just let me go. I haven't done anything."

"Tell me about your links to terrorist cells in England."

"*What?*" Khalid's too puzzled to answer.

"You communicated by code on the computer with other terrorists."

"No way. Who said that?" Khalid says. "What computer?"

"But you know Al-Jaber?" Anthony asks.

"Who's he? What computer are you talking about?"

Sam clasps his fingers together on the green desk. "As usual, another time-waster!" He nods to the soldiers to take Khalid away. Making space for the next naked man to be asked the same questions.

They lead Khalid off to one side and hand him a large white T-shirt and navy-blue plastic-feeling trousers with an elasticated waist. They don't bother with underwear, taking him as soon as he's dressed to another room, where a different man asks his name and address, and whether he's married or not. The names of his children.

"I'M FIFTEEN!" Khalid screams for England. "DON'T YOU GET IT?"

That's when he loses consciousness. Blacking out from the thump to his back. Waking up later on a cold earth floor in a makeshift wire cell. One of many cells dividing a long, low building into ugly compartments. The prisoners are dressed in the same blue trousers, some in Afghan-style white caps. The grinding sound of a nearby generator interrupts everyone's thoughts with the same constancy as a road digger and there's a faint smell of urine in the air. Then a whiff of cooking oil.

"No talking while you're here," the military policeman warns him as he patrols the space between the cells.

Khalid gazes around him, through the dazzling spotlights shining from either end of the row. Eyeing the bucket in the corner with disbelief. A bottle of water to one side. Blanket folded on the floor next to a thin mat. Woollen shawl on top.

A man with big cheeks and bushy eyebrows in the next cell watches him closely, sympathy in his eyes as he waggles his head from side to side, as if to say, *Keep quiet. Take no notice. You'll be OK.*

Beside the open doors at either end of the building, soldiers with huge rifles, machine or hand guns laugh and joke among themselves. Their eyes move down the lines every few seconds to check nothing's changed. As if any of them have the smallest chance of escaping when they can't even leave their cells to go to the toilet without asking permission.

It's not really a surprise to Khalid when the nearest man covers his lower body with a shawl to go to the loo in the metal bucket, but surely they have toilets here for all these men? What kind of place is this? In desperation, Khalid scans the cages for Masud, for Dad, for any familiar face in the midst of this madness—or even for more boys who look his own age. As he gazes from cell to cell, face after face stares back at him with the same look of miserable resignation. Utter defeat in their dark eyes. Angry, afraid, lost and forgotten—just like him.

One man kneels to pray, hands clasped to his chest. The hum of his words gradually spreads round the cages until many adopt the same position. The volume of their voices increases to such a pitch, it adds a strange echo to the noises outside of planes and barking dogs.

Khalid sits back against the wire wall, full of compassion for their devotion but angry at the same time. Angry at the Americans for seeing them as just that: Muslims. Dangerous foreigners who they can't even tell apart. Angry too at the Muslim religion for getting him into this mess. He once heard a newsreader say it was the fastest-growing religion in the world. Khalid remembers wishing the media wouldn't say stuff like that. People don't want to hear those facts, and he doesn't particularly want to be lumped together with loads of people he doesn't know, Muslim or not. And Muslims aren't all the same, just like Christians aren't all the same. He's Khalid—himself, not a result of any religion. He hasn't even done anything with his life yet.

Time drags. Not being allowed to talk makes the hours go by slowly. There's nothing to do but watch the soldier with the machine gun walk up and down, staring into each wire cage as if there's a chance something might happen.

The soldiers at either end of the row chat idly to each other. Laughing. Coming and going after coffee breaks and lunches. Performing high-fives after only ten minutes apart, as if they haven't seen each other for years. Acting as if they're guarding a warehouse of baked beans instead of forty kidnapped men with no access to a lawyer and no way to reach their families.

Khalid realizes that the only stuff he knows about prisons is from films. American films. Exciting ones where the hero wins the respect of the most hardcore prisoners before breaking out. But then he remembers they have the death penalty in America too.

Death Row—yeah, people are electrocuted there all the time. Khalid remembers a news item about some guy who spent twenty years on Death Row before they found him innocent. Plus that film, what was it called? He'd watched it on Nico's computer after he'd downloaded it from the Internet. They watched loads of films like that when there was nothing else going on. Usually lounging around on the beds and floor with the rest of the gang in Nico's older brother's bedroom until Pete came in and screamed at them: "Get off my bed!"

And everyone would scramble as if they'd committed a crime by just sitting there.

Holgy was always the first to straighten Pete's stripy duvet, plump up the pillow and apologize: "Sorry, mate."

"Don't sit there again!" Pete would yell, while Khalid and the others kept their eyes focused on the computer, annoyed by his interruption but unwilling to react. They all know Pete is a mess—a bad-tempered bloke all round. The complete opposite to Nico, who rarely has anything but a smile on his face.

Suddenly realizing there's nothing to relieve the boredom but remembering his mates and small incidents like this, Khalid wonders if perhaps little fox-faced Holgy had been right when he said, "We're all holograms, you know?" He'd made the mistake of saying this when they were in the first year, all about eleven years old. Repeating the fact to everyone whenever he got the chance. So much so, they gave him the nickname Holgy, even though his real name, Eshan, is so much nicer. Being short for hologram, it was the obvious choice. Invented by Nico, who else?

"Your real life is happening on another planet," Holgy argues whenever he gets the chance. "You are just a stupid gonzo reflection."

"No, YOU are," Mikael puts him right. He's the brainbox, after all.

"Shut up about holograms," Tony would add. "I'm a deathless star."

Then the conversation would spin quickly to include Darth Vader, possible life on Mars and whether Lyn Howser has better legs than Jancy King. Yeah, awesome Lyn Howser and the new tattoo of a butterfly on her right ankle that makes them all drool.

In fact, Khalid was the only one who liked talking to Holgy about holograms. Holgy forced him to think about things that were far beyond his imagination, and the idea of reality being nothing but a projected 3D perception made him feel weird. Almost like electrodes were sparking fires in his brain.

Trouble is, there's no one here to talk to about anything. There are no computers. Nothing to read. Nothing to do but think. All they have is one copy of the Qur'an between them. The guards pass it on when someone's finished with it. The problem, though, is it's written in another language and, after glancing at the pages for a while, Khalid gives up trying to make sense of the holy book.

Holgy, what would he do if he was stuck here? Khalid guesses he'd sit there just like him. Legs crossed. Staring across at the sleeping man next to him. Thinking a mixture of things. Same as him.

Khalid's mind directs itself to the ongoing problem of his history coursework, however unimportant that seems right now. Like all his mates, schoolwork is something he worries about non-stop, simply because the teachers and his parents never let up. Most of them pretend not to do homework or care about school, but they all do.

"What are you going to do with your life if you don't get any qualifications?" Dad always says.

"Er—become a chef like you?" Khalid once smirked.

"Not like me," Dad said. "These kids now, they got college

degrees in catering to cook. To be electrician these days you must have papers. Everybody want certificates."

Khalid knows he's right. Most of his mates—well, Nico and Mikael along with him—are in the top set for most of their subjects, expected to get As and Bs in seven or more GCSEs, and the pressure is constant. Escaping some of that by being here is no relief, because weirdly all Khalid can think about is if this goes on for much longer he won't have time to look at any of his coursework over the holidays. Unless he gets out before term starts he'll fall behind. Will the teachers take something like this into account? Khalid doubts they'll care. None of the "official" people here care what happens to him, so why should they?

What if he never gets out and fails all his GCSEs? He'll become the class loser. They might even make him redo everything and put him down a year to repeat the work he's almost finished. What a fool he'll look then. Sat in the year below's class. Probably behind that idiot Derek Slater and the bunch of stupid toads who follow him round like he's God. Despite his growing fear, Khalid decides he's not going to allow that to happen. Nothing will make him suffer the shame of being a year older than the rest of his class.

If worst comes to worst, he'll refuse to go to school ever again. He'll ask Mac, their neighbor, to get him work in the supermarket where he's a cashier, stacking shelves or something—part-time. Anything to make some money to pay for the bus fare to the sixth-form college on the other side of town. He read in the local paper that they do GCSE courses in the evenings with loads of good subjects.

Now Khalid has a plan, he feels slightly better. More prepared. They can punch him, keep him awake, treat him like a criminal, but they can't ruin his chances of a better life when he gets out of here. And that's *when* he gets out, not if.

"No one's ever going to do that to me, man!" Khalid says out loud without thinking. Embarrassed, the moment the words leave his mouth.

The soldier halfway down the line turns to look at him. The man two cages down quietly puts down his bottle of water and whispers something. Something that sounds like English but Khalid can't be sure.

Khalid shuts his eyes to blank everything out while he goes over the plan again. Mumbling to himself so the approaching soldier will think he's crazy. It works. The soldier passes by, his brown desert boots pausing in front of Khalid's cell for a moment before moving on.

Khalid conjures up an image of himself in baggy jeans and a white, long-sleeved T-shirt, hair slickly gelled, waiting at the bus stop for the number 23 that will take him to college. Stamping the picture at the front of his mind, a weird feeling spreads over him that his real life is happening somewhere else. Perhaps Holgy's right. We are all holograms.

Imagining he's waiting for the bus right now instead of sitting in a wire cage in Afghanistan sparks a picture of Niamh in the weird red-and-brown knitted Peruvian hat with side bobbles she sometimes wears. She's waiting, arms folded, for the bus.

"Hiya, Kal. You all right?" Smiling at him with glossy pink lips.

"Not bad," he says.

"Your hair's looking great," she says.

"Yeah? Thanks. I, um, great hat." No, no! This isn't working. Khalid can't tell her he likes that mad hat. She'll have to take it off. That's better.

Niamh's still smiling at him in 3D moving color, as real to him as the wire that surrounds him. She only disappears when voices at the end of the row bring Khalid back to the present time.

The noise of creaking wheels forces him to glance at two men in white aprons wheeling a food trolley into the building. A few men stand up to grasp the wire fence in anticipation, carefully watching the guards take cardboard boxes from the trolley and dish them out by throwing them over the tops of the cages.

"Nice curry lunch!" one of the trolley men shouts in a strange, not-quite-right American accent. "Here you go!"

Imitating feeding time at the zoo, Khalid quickly grabs it but finds the tightly folded box hard to open with his fingers, and has no choice but to bite into one corner. Pulling back damp cardboard with his teeth until specks of white rice and a runny curry are revealed.

The curry is like nothing Khalid's ever seen or tasted before. The small squares of stringy meat, which he hopes is chicken, not pork, are surrounded by yellowy broccoli spears and raisins. Raisins? Who puts raisins in curry?

Whoever made the sticky white rice should give up trying to cook. His mum would have a fit if she saw him eating like this with no spoon, knife, fork, pepper, salt or anything else.

They never ate with their hands at home, because she insisted on them being British first, while when they were in Karachi with the aunties, they scooped up their rice with their hands like everyone else. Here, Khalid has no choice but to drop his head in the slop like a dog. The man next to him is licking his food hungrily. Another sucks the contents up from a hole he's made in the middle. Everyone improvises the best way they can to get the runny food down their throats as quickly as possible. Worse than the glue they call curry that's dished up in the school canteen, this stuff smells and tastes of rotting lettuce.

Then plastic containers of crackers and cheese are flung at them. Wrapped tightly like airplane food, they take an effort to get into. Unfortunately, Khalid's crackers land in his toilet bucket in the corner of the cell and, since it hasn't been emptied yet from this morning, he decides to go without. After lunch, the soldiers appoint a couple of them to empty the buckets. The first two refuse. In the end, they ask for volunteers and three men from the other end of the row are let out of their cells.

The volunteers stretch their arms and legs for a moment. One man, who looks a bit like a Muslim Tony Blair, with the same grinning face, nudges the smaller man beside him, nodding as if to say, *Anything's better than being stuck in there all day*.

After watching them closely, Khalid half changes his mind. Perhaps he should have volunteered, though he can't get his brain past the horrible job they are doing. But there are clear benefits: for a start, the soldiers keep well away from them as they enter each cell to collect the bucket. Meaning each one has the chance to exchange a few words with the occupant and find out something about who they are and what has happened to them. They even get the opportunity to whisper to each other as they head towards the end of the building to hand the buckets over.

When the Tony Blair lookalike gets to Khalid, he's ready for him.

"I'm only fifteen. English. I'm innocent," he pleads quickly.

The man smiles. Saying something kind in a language that sounds like Pashtu, which confuses Khalid. Then he disappears into the next cell. Khalid watches closely as his neighbor reaches out to greet him like a long-lost son. Shutting Khalid out. There's no one here he can talk to. He's not like any of these men. He'd have a better conversation with the guards.

Increasingly frustrated, it's the final nail in his coffin. Not only has he been kidnapped and taken to this joke of a place, but he can't speak to anyone and he appears to be the youngest person in this building. Some look like they might be in their twenties, but none of them look as young as him. Where are the two kids he saw when he arrived?

He's not even that comfortable talking to people older than him. The respect-for-elders thing has been drummed into him for so long, he finds it difficult to be natural about it. Remembering how some of his class had an easy, jokey relationship with the teachers, while he blushed when attempting to say something friendly to them. Even to Mr. Tagg, who's the best of the lot.

His mind spirals out of control. Are those two boys being held somewhere else? Given special treatment because of their age? It didn't look like they were at the time, but perhaps things have changed now.

Khalid's thoughts exhaust him. Totally alone, out of place and forgotten, he lies down on his mat to cry. Hiding his head in his arms so no one can see.

## RED CROSS

When a solid, overbearing heat descends on the building, the sound of plane engines whirr into action, interrupting Khalid's fitful sleep. In an attempt to stop the noise from fully waking him up, he turns over and dreams of chips and Cheddar cheese being spread on the football field at home in Rochdale. Then he opens his eyes, quickly calms himself down and tries to go back to sleep, but he picks up the dream at exactly the point where he left it, going through the whole nightmare again of trying to stop the mess ruining the field.

The noisy trucks, the shouting men and the incessant hum of the electricity generator annoy him as he sits cross-legged on the mat for a moment to bring himself round. All the time wondering about the men nearby—blue and white shapes he can barely make out through the layers of wire. Who are they?

It takes a while before Khalid gets to know the man to one side of him.

"*As-salaamu alaikum*," he greets him each morning.

Soon Khalid answers him with the words, "*Wa alaikum as-salaam*," as if he's an old friend.

One day he surprises Khalid. "My name is Abdul Al-

Farran," he says.

"You speak English," Khalid gasps. He can't believe the man hasn't spoken to him until now—he must have heard him shouting at the guards. But he doesn't want to waste the opportunity by getting annoyed.

Abdul turns out to be the most random guy he's ever met. Pressing his face against the wire, Khalid sees he's slightly overweight, with a downturned mouth and miserably fat cheeks. His bushy eyebrows have a life of their own, rising and falling like curling caterpillars whenever he speaks.

Having decided to trust him, Abdul tells Khalid he was born in Lebanon. He moved to Pakistan, where his brother lives, some years ago to get a job teaching math. His English is quite good too, which helps.

"Mistake for me was travel all places, all time. I'm look— for wife. When I return Islamabad, I meet very bad man. Big fight. He make lie. Tell police I making bomb factory in house. My wife tell me run away, so I go Afghanistan. Wrong time I go that place." Khalid finds it difficult to follow Abdul. He has the annoying tendency of jumping from one subject to another without pausing and Khalid can't always understand what he's getting at. Plus there's the problem of his jumping eyebrows making it hard to concentrate, but he likes having him to talk to—it finally makes him feel a part of the group.

"How old are you?" Khalid interrupts, moving closer to their shared wire wall.

Abdul smiles and holds up his fingers, quickly flashing three tens and a five for him to count.

"Thirty-five?"

"Yes," Abdul says, sighing.

"I'm only fifteen!"

"Fifteen! Bring you here for why?" Abdul's shocked.

"I dunno. Who knows? I should be at school."

"Then you must take chance to learn. I will teach everything I know for you." Abdul grins. "Hezbollah, you know, means party of God!"

"Party of God?" Khalid blinks with surprise. From news reports he'd heard at home, Hezbollah were a dangerous group of some kind. Didn't they go round kidnapping Westerners? But maybe Abdul is right. Maybe the actual meaning of the word is far more simple. Even so, he looks round to make sure no one's listening. He's scared, in case the word will be held against him in some way, thinking it really means terrorist— or something far worse—and Abdul Al-Farran's having him on.

But then, "Fakir means poor man," Abdul Al-Farran says without a hint of concern for the easy way he'd mentioned Hezbollah.

"Yeah? Cool." Khalid makes an effort to calm down. Not really able to decide who Abdul really is. Maybe the word Hezbollah is a secret signal of some kind.

"Hmm." Thoroughly enjoying being a teacher again, Abdul's face crumples into a huge smile. His eyebrows suddenly part. "Imam means leader. Many English words they come from Arabic words. Yes. Genie—spirit. Sofa. Mattress. Checkmate—the king is dead. Algebra. Orange. Monsoon. Cotton. Zero. All Arabic."

There's no stopping him. Now Abdul has an audience,

Khalid must wait and listen. Trouble is, his mind keeps wandering. It's not his fault that Abdul reminds him of his geography teacher, Mr. Giles, who speaks in the same dull tone of voice, which sends the whole class to sleep even though what he's saying is interesting.

"The word syrup, this is also Arabic!" Abdul smiles. "Sultan too."

"Really?" Khalid mutters, without much hope he'll ever stop bending his ear with endless information, certain Abdul Al-Farran has spent his life reading the dictionary.

"Ah, of course! I finish now." Obviously slightly hurt by Khalid turning his head away from the wire, Abdul finally stops talking, drawing his bushy eyebrows down for the last time. For today anyway.

A military policeman wanders past. Not bothering to tell them off for spending the last half-hour talking. It seems that as long as they whisper for no more than a couple of minutes at a time no one will say anything. At least not on his shift. The later shift consists of two nasty soldiers who seem to enjoy making their lives miserable, but these two—one of whom is called Wade and comes from Atlanta—are almost human in the way they treat them.

Khalid feels a gut-wrenching shame for insulting Abdul Al-Farran. Especially after he's dreamed of having someone to talk to.

"I just can't take it all in," he tries explaining later. But the midday call to prayer starts up from the other end and Abdul is happy to move from the wire to face Mecca.

Prayers fill the rusty hangar, rising to bounce off the roof and echo in the humid air like exotic birdsong. They transform the ordinary sounds of the building into a pure connection to the divine.

In time, Khalid's eyes adjust to the dense wire separating the cells. In time, he can focus his eyes to see Abdul quite clearly without getting up from his mat. While the door wire is thin enough to see the soldiers walking up and down every few minutes, Khalid has no desire to look at them.

Wade, the friendly soldier, walks past again. This time he stops in front of Khalid to adjust the machine gun hanging on his chest.

"Don't you like praying?" he says with a cheesy, fake grin.

"Not right now," Khalid says.

"But you're Muslim!"

"Yeah, but we don't all pray all the time," Khalid says crossly. Not seeing any reason to explain why he's not able to let go just yet.

"Perhaps you'll make a better Christian than a Muslim. I can bring you some pamphlets Mom sent me from Atlanta, so you guys can learn about Jesus."

So that was it. The reason for Wade's friendly manner. They were lost souls in need of saving. Mom in Atlanta was worried about them.

"It's all right, thanks." Khalid sees him off with a weak smile. Hiding his anger and frustration by clenching his fists behind his back.

Some time later, three sterner-looking soldiers, the first two with guns pointed at everyone, come down the line. The biggest one begins unlocking every other fence in turn. While the last soldier follows with an armful of shackles. Soon men are handcuffed and pushed out. Tied together with a long rope and led away. Khalid cranes his neck to see where they're going and before long his question is answered when they return with water dripping down their dazed faces and soaking-wet hair. Plus big damp patches on their clean white T-shirts.

"Shower?" Khalid gasps in anticipation. The soldier nods, cuffing him tight. The thought of gushing water and sweet-smelling soap dominates Khalid's mind as he's tied to ten other men. Soldiers double up beside the line, all eyes and guns.

Twinkling hot sunshine hits Khalid's face as he lowers his lids and steps from the gray hangar into an empty forecourt. Everyone is soon pulled through a block of cool shadow and a short walk takes them to the nearby doorway of a building with a wet, cold concrete floor. Inside the gray walls is a miserable place smelling of toilets, with rusty stains dribbling down the walls from the shower heads and a sound of running water. A sound with no feeling of pleasure attached.

The fear of communal washing is too much for the man behind him and he begins screaming, shaking his head in fear. Two more join in, yelling objections, while Khalid meekly allows himself to be untied, then uncuffed. He steps quickly to one side to undress, hard eyes bearing down on him, a gun a few centimeters from his forehead. The crying men are pushed to one side and stripped. Their clothes flung on a heap. One of the naked men stumbles, then falls to his knees. Head in his hands. They soon haul him up and throw him under the shower.

In a state of shock, Khalid faces the wall and squeezes the small soap brick which smells of taps, a hair's breadth away from kicking out at something. For a moment he tries to relax into the water and enjoy the sensation. But the sound of crying cancels out any pleasure. It's OK for Khalid, he's used to showering with his mates after school sports and football matches. He's not embarrassed to be seen naked. But for these men this is worse than death.

By the time Khalid's back in his cell, his mind flipping in and out of the abuse he just witnessed, he's in no mood to talk to the fair-haired man in jeans and red bomber jacket who's wandering down the hangar with a bulging white plastic bag under his arm. Accompanied by one of the military policemen, this guy is a picture of happiness. Greeting each prisoner in turn with an Arabic phrase or two, he's giving out paper and pens and a small plastic cup with a red cross on the side. When he gets to Khalid's cage, he gives him a proper smile before saying with a posh-sounding American accent, "I'm with the Red Cross. Do you want to write a letter to anyone?"

"A letter?" It's the first time Khalid's thought about it. "Just one letter? Can't I do more?"

"However many you want!" The soldier opens the cell and hands Khalid three pieces of paper and a black pen. Plus a cup which holds a card with a number. His is 256.

"I'll be back later," the guy says, smiling.

"Wait a minute." Khalid grabs the door of the cage as it's being locked again. "I shouldn't be here. They've made a mistake. I'm a schoolkid."

The man looks at him for a while. "OK, I guess you don't

look so old," he says after giving him the once-over. "But you're not a prisoner of war now—the term is 'enemy combatant' as the military like to say. I'm afraid that's the situation at the moment." He nods.

The last drop of hope drains from Khalid the second the man's comforting smile disappears.

"The letters won't get there, will they?" Khalid shouts after him, watching him quickly move on to speak to Abdul in Arabic.

"What was the point of that?" Khalid whispers to his friend when the man's gone.

"Doing job." Abdul shakes his head. "Red Cross—they have power to do nothing. America making all rules. Finish for us."

"Enemy combatant! Me?" Khalid laughs. "How mad can they get?" Nevertheless, he sits in the corner, paper on his lap, to write a letter to Mum and Dad. Even though he doesn't know for sure where they are, it's worth trying to reach them. He half suspects Mum won't return to England without her husband and son. But then, neither will Dad if he's turned up at the aunties' somehow. He won't leave Karachi without knowing what's happened to Khalid. Or maybe he's here in Kandahar, somewhere in another building. Who knows where he is?

Either way, it's hard to decide where to send the letter. A letter that probably won't arrive anyway, because the Red Cross will most likely hand it over to the Americans. Then Khalid has an idea to write to Mr. Tagg. And maybe Mac, his neighbor. The Red Cross man has given him three pieces of paper. One of them might get to his family. If not, there's a chance someone out there might read the truth.

"So this is how it happened when I went missing," Khalid writes. Describing his abduction in Karachi, before quickly adding details about the trip he made to the flat, looking for his dad. Finding once he starts remembering, the words stream out.

A feeling of being someone else watching his own life overtakes Khalid as he scribbles as fast as he can. The first page fills up before he says anything about Kandahar, leaving him no choice but to draw an arrow pointing over the page, with the words STORY CONTINUES written along the edge.

Sadly, the blue airmail paper is too thin to take the strong black ink of the pen he's been given and the words on the other side jumble into those on the first page. So much so, Khalid gives up after adding quick kisses for Aadab and Gul.

Going over the final words, "How can this happen? I didn't do anything wrong!!!!!", he sits back to read what he's written. Just how well he's described his situation, he doesn't care. This is urgent.

There's a sudden feeling of panic in his chest as he realizes he's left no space for the address. Unless it'll fit along the bottom of the first page under the arrow he's drawn. He sucks his bottom lip and frowns as he tries to squeeze the address in and, weirdly, the words "9 Oswestry Road, Rochdale, Lancashire, UK" fit perfectly at the bottom of the page. He worries they might not notice the address down there, so he goes over it several times with the pen to make it stand out. Then does the number 9 again in case someone thinks it's a zero.

Khalid's tempted to quit worrying and start again on the next page. But he's only got three pieces of paper and he might not be given any more. Trying all the while not to wind himself up by fretting that the letter won't reach them. But when it comes to what to say to Mr. Tagg, the tip of the pen hovers over the blank page like a fly.

Mr. Tagg's a teacher, after all, so he's going to notice the bad sentences and misspellings, isn't he? All this worrying cramps Khalid's style. After several crossings-out, he decides to give it a rest for a while and go back to the letter when he's clearer about exactly what he wants to say.

Glancing down the cages, he watches one man toss his cup in the toilet bucket, while another jumps on his. The cup feels and smells like the foam they stuff boxes with, but Khalid keeps it anyway.

When the Red Cross man finally comes to collect the letters, Khalid still hasn't got round to deciding what to say to Mr. Tagg and Mac. Instead, he gives him the letter for his family. A horrible feeling inside warns him it'll never get there and a split-second picture in his mind of Mum crying her eyes out at the kitchen table, Gul's arms around her neck, brings tears to his eyes.

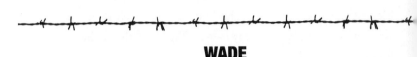

# WADE

The boiling-hot days fold into each other, passing by without notice. Once a week, Khalid's taken for a shower. Once a week he writes another letter and hands it to a soldier to give to the Red Cross guy, and one by one the months pass by.

"September 2002," he recently heard a guard shout in answer to one of the men's questions, and still there's no sign Khalid will ever go home. The familiar sounds of trucks and whirring engines, squeaking leather boots and the humming generator settle at the back of his mind, like a TV permanently left on in another room. Today the smell of petrol mixed with a whiff of vegetable soup reminds him he's woken up in the wrong place again.

Now and again, one of them is taken away for questioning. The same routine each time. First the military policemen call out a number so that person knows it's his turn. Then the soldiers drop by with an armful of shackles to bind him to himself.

Today it's Abdul Al-Farran's turn.

"Good luck," Khalid whispers. The poker-faced soldier forces Abdul to get down on his knees, legs crossed, hands behind his back while he applies the shackles. Abdul quietly prays the whole time he's being clanked and locked into the chains.

Two hours later and he still hasn't come back. Lunchtime and more boxes of food are thrown at them. Fish-paste sandwiches in foil wrapping and a packet of salted peanuts. The calorie content is written clearly on the side. Information telling him the peanuts come from Texas.

The squares of daylight at either end of the building begin turning a rich navy blue. The noise of the planes and trucks outside at last begins to die down. Only the annoying drone of the electricity generator fills the night air when they bring Abdul back. He's bent double, head almost on his chest, as they lead him down the aisle between the cages. Khalid kicks the wire fence, making it wobble noisily. Anxiously, he watches his friend's slow progress. Feeling cross because he can't see Abdul's face properly until he's pushed inside and the soldiers finish undoing the restraints and leave.

Once the desert boots have marched angrily away, Khalid creeps to his side of their adjoining fence. Abdul's in the same position they left him in—on the floor, knees bent, legs crossed, hands on his head. He looks up, meets Khalid's gaze as if he's a stranger and not someone he's spent hours talking to. The tears rolling down his face make Khalid back off.

It's way past dinnertime but a box of food is thrown at Abdul and lands in his lap. He gingerly picks it up, looking at it from every angle as if he doesn't recognize the box. Khalid watches him eye everything written on the side before opening it with his teeth. Then Khalid turns away, trying to give his friend some privacy as he chews on tuna, cold pasta and beans. Eventually he stops crying. But it still takes an hour or two before he leans in to the shared wire wall to whisper to Khalid.

"They say I do spy. They take me interrogate. One man—he say, 'Admit you be a spy. You spy. Say you spy.' This happening me—not right. They say me, I looking secrets. How they know this?"

There's nothing Khalid can do but shake his head. Abdul can't stop repeating himself. Going over and over the accusation because he cannot believe anyone would think he's a spy. Words of sympathy escape Khalid. What do you say to someone who looks so broken he can barely lift his head from his chest?

A knot of fury forms in Khalid's stomach as he starts walking round his cell. Endlessly walking to prevent his friend's words from touching his heart. Moving in small, trance-like steps to rid himself of the horrible certainty that he and Abdul will die here.

After a few minutes of mindless trudging round and round the wire fence, the same military policeman stops again outside Khalid's cell. Catching sight of Abdul sitting cross-legged, head in his hands in the next cell, murmuring to himself, he seems upset and gazes at him with concern.

At this point, Abdul becomes aware of the guy standing there and smiling down at him. He lifts his head, his face a mess of conflicting emotions, and straightens his back. Then something breaks in him and he leaps up to batter the fence, yelling, "Death to America!"

*Good for him*, Khalid thinks at first.

A gang of angry voices soon join in. The sound of rattling fences begins to take hold all the way down the building. Lengths of wire pop with bulging fists. A chorus of "Death to America!" grows louder and louder.

Khalid's tempted to join in, but then he thinks, *How can you kill a whole country? And why do they hate America? It should be George Bush and his mates they're angry with, not the country whose action films, rap music, TV programs and sneakers they all like.*

Wade races up from the side. For all his niceness, he's actually trembling a little. Hands slightly shaking as he points his machine gun at Abdul. Suddenly Wade's surrounded by a horde of soldiers who stare anxiously at the rippling fences as if they're about to crash to the ground.

It's then that Khalid realizes Wade's just another human being. They all are. Khalid lets go of the fence and retreats to the far end of the cell to sit on his mat. He places the shawl over his head to block out the nervousness on Wade's face. Then he hears Abdul being dragged screaming from his cell.

A soldier yells, "Shut up!"

Eventually the banging and shouting stop. Fingers uncurl from the cool wire fences and the hum of the electricity generator dominates the building once more.


The next morning, Wade stops by again with another soldier. A tall guy of about twenty who smiles shyly.

"This is my buddy, Michael!"

"Where's Abdul?" Khalid asks, uninterested.

"He's OK. He'll be back soon when he's calmed down," Wade says.

"How can you do this?" Khalid questions Michael. "He hasn't been found guilty of anything."

"Hey, man, I'm a part-time soldier. A reservist," Michael says. "They gave me a few months' training a while back, that's all. I only serve for six weekends and a couple of weeks a year. I thought it would be fun this time, I'd get to see Germany or somewhere in my two weeks, you know?"

"You're here for two weeks?" Khalid can hardly believe what he's hearing. "They put you in charge of us lot? Aren't we supposed to be evil terrorists?"

"I had no idea I was coming here," Michael says, sharing his disbelief. Shrugging at Khalid to show this isn't his idea of fun either. Then his radio bleeps and he turns away to answer it. Talking in number-speak, which confuses Khalid.

"Eighty-four, two-one—in five. OK, Bob. I got that. Sun, right." Wade turns to Khalid to explain. "It's time for a trip outside."

"Why?" The look on Michael's face suggests the trip is a good thing, but Khalid has no reason to trust this weekend soldier and, when he doesn't answer, Khalid's sure "sun" is some kind of code to take him for interrogation, like Abdul Al-Farran.

Then someone starts shouting from the other end. Footsteps rattle down the row and, much to his surprise, Khalid watches a chain gang lining up in the middle of the row. Hearing the reason why from another soldier nearby.

"Y'all need to stop ya complaining about no sunshine."

Khalid is amazed that anyone has bothered to complain and even more shocked that something's happening as a result.

Suddenly excited by the simple thought of seeing the sky, he wonders if Wade had anything to do with the fact he's been included. Reminding himself to thank him the next time he sees him—because "y'all" aren't actually going outside, only about twelve of them are being shackled and attached to a joining rope that smells of cats.

It's a sad scene to witness in the twenty-first century: prisoners standing in a line, roped one behind the other. Heads bowed. Ready to be led away to work on a railway?

Following the long drawn-out procedure, the line finally crawls outside. It's the first time Khalid has been allowed to enjoy fresh air since he arrived here six months ago. Apart from being hurried through cool shadows at the side of the building to the showers and then the barber's, he's never been allowed to just stand in the sun. For some reason the excitement of going outside reminds him of a digital photo Tariq once sent of himself sitting on a rock in his garden in Lahore. The picture was so bright, the window of the concrete house behind him sparkled like water and had a kind of inner power that looked odd. Tariq loved that photo. He said the glass had become a river of energy because of the power of the midday sun. Khalid smiles at the memory of the picture in his mind. Tariq? Where is he? Was he kidnapped from his computer too? Is he being led from a prison cell into the sunshine—like him, right now? Khalid gazes at the sky as if for the first time and the sudden, searing light makes him feel drunk as anything. It's so wonderful and perfect, Khalid can nearly taste the feeling of infinity it brings. Everyone else shuffles from chained foot to chained foot, blinking hard with half-closed bleary eyes at the brown trucks and concrete buildings, as well as at the caged men in the barn opposite. It seems to Khalid that only he can see the thin streak of cloud with a petal shape at one end. Only he can hear the distant bird flapping its wings and singing to itself.

Standing here doddering around is all very well, but the blazing-hot sun on Khalid's head for the first time since it's been shaved is making his skin prickle. The growing stubble demands to be scratched and he can't move his hands. In Khalid's mind, his bare conk looks like a turkey's head and the ugly picture destroys the nice feeling he had when gazing at the sky.

The odd sensation soon passes when a voice shouts, "Move on!" bringing Khalid back to the shuffling chain gang, which is slowly being led back to the building after the smallest, shortest glimpse of fresh air and sunshine known to any modern prisoner. He can't believe they've gone to all that trouble to shackle and tie them up just to give them about four and a half minutes outside.

Next day, when the soldier asks, "Anyone for a trip out?" Khalid firmly shakes his head. All that stupid effort for what? No thanks. He'd rather sit here and be eaten by maggots than go through all that crap again.

Abdul Al-Farran still hasn't returned. Much as Khalid questions Wade, he never gets a straight answer. He's gone forever, Khalid can feel it in his bones, knowing the truth for certain when they bring another man into his cell.

His new neighbor is puny and wiry, with nervous eyes that dart here and there as if he expects to see a gap in the fence. Just once he pauses to stare at Khalid for a moment before falling on the mat to pray. Something he does incessantly. It drives Khalid mad. Mostly because his voice is a whining, unpleasant one, but truthfully because he wishes he was Abdul, or even Masud from Karachi, whom he'd hoped to meet here, or someone, anyone, he can pass the time of day with. Maybe someone like the man a few cells down, who, he's just noticed, the military seem to respect more than the others.

Khalid doesn't know his name, but he appears to speak several languages, including English. They look at him differently. Giving him bananas and occasionally a carton of orange juice, which none of the others have received.

Khalid never finds out who he is, because the next day Wade announces, "You better come up with the goods, dude, or your name will be added to the list for Cuba."

"What's in Cuba?" Khalid panics.

Wade looks at him strangely. "Kandahar is a way station, a holding place, midway point before Guantanamo Bay. Camp X-Ray's now closed and the new facility there, where you'd be going, is Camp Delta."

He hands him a piece of unwrapped spearmint chewing gum. "I'm on leave—going home. Good luck."

Khalid's still absorbing the information as he mumbles a thanks. *Guantanamo Bay?* They can't send an innocent person like him there, surely. He puts the gum in his mouth and chews slowly. The familiar taste is a nice surprise. So nice, he keeps chewing away at it until it resembles a piece of leather and all thoughts of being sent to Cuba are stored in a no-go part of his brain.

Later, after a revolting dinner of gray meat and sloppy potatoes, Khalid slips into a place he's never been before. Begins singing to himself in a language he doesn't know. A language no one knows. The same babbling nonsense babies conjure up.

"Wooeee, chucka, chucka," Khalid yells to the three soldiers who come for him in the middle of the night. "Doody, doody. Fish eyes doody! The three doody boys. Dude one. Dude two and fish dude, head of dudes, number three, doody boy."

"Shut up, moron!" one of them screams. "You're going straight to hell!"

"On your knees!" another guard yells. "Hands on your head."

What are they going to do with him now? *Why can't they wait until morning?* is all Khalid thinks as they shackle his wrists. Forcing him to bend double as they walk him out of the barn and across the concourse—not towards a plane, but towards a concrete building where he's been several times before for questioning.

An unimaginably bright spotlight blinds Khalid for a few seconds before he's led inside. This time he's taken to a steel room with a wavy crack running across the concrete floor.

It's a room Khalid gets to know well, because every single half-hour over the next three days the soldiers barge in to wake him. He fades in and out of the most disturbed sleep ever conceived as his mind wanders to thoughts and images he had no idea were even stored there.

# 13

## LIGHTS

The lights are on . . .

. . . Apart from a blue mat, there's nothing else in the cell, which is the size of the bathroom back in Rochdale.

Nothing,

except a steel toilet in one corner.

No window.
Only gray walls and the smell of burning, dust and sweat . . .

. . . They drag him out—they throw him back.

Now he's staring at the air conditioner again.

Breathing in the smell of his own flesh.

On his own.

For


how


long


this


time . . . ?

. . . If
he can close
his brain down for a bit,
then maybe he can forget?
Perhaps if the guards stay away, he
can fall into a long, timeless sleep instead
of the half-hour here and there before another bitter
wake-up . . .

. . . Khalid turns over

on the mat

to lie on his back,

listening

to his

beating heart.

Vaguely wondering

if he's got

the energy

to          pull          himself                    up

and          take          a                    leak.

Can he be bothered?

141

Not

really


Not really

Now, this is the third day in a row they've disturbed him:
...
more ... This is the third day in a row they've disturbed

h         l         m         .

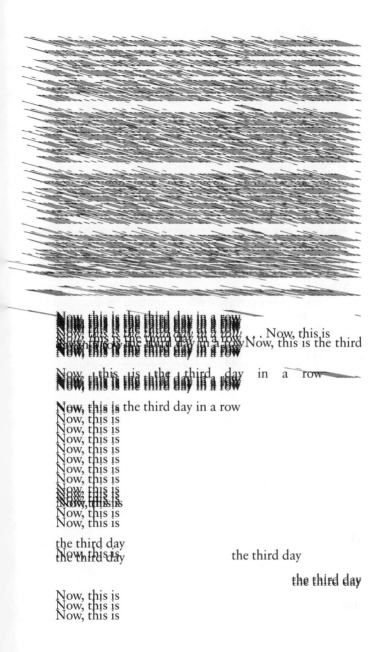

Now, this is the third day in a row
Now, this is the third day in a row  . Now, this is
Now, this is the third day in a row Now, this is the third

Now, this is the third day     in     a     row

Now, this is the third day in a row

Now, this is the third day in a row
Now, this is
Now, this is
Now, this is
Now, this is
Now, this is
Now, this is
Now, this is
Now, this is
Now, this is
Now, this is
Now, this is

the third day
the third day                              the third day

                                    the third day

Now, this is
Now, this is
Now, this is

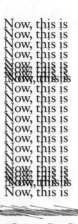

Now, this is
Now, this is
Now, this is
Now, this is
Now, this is
Now, this is
Now, this is
Now, this is
Now, this is
Now, this is
Now, this is
Now, this is
Now, this is
Now, this is
Now, this is
Now, this is
Now, this is

Now, this is the third day in a row they've disturbed him. Aware he might never sleep again, Khalid decides not to try again. Especially as he's done everything to numb the light. Pulling the mat over his head. Burying his face in his arms—in the wall. Nothing works. Even trying to sleep with his hands on his face only makes his eyes itch more . . .

This is the third day in a row they've disturbed him.

He'll never sleep again, why try? Especially as he's done everything to numb the light. Pulling the mat over his head. Burying his face in his arms. Nothing works. Even trying to sleep with his hands on his eyes only makes his eyelids HURT . . . Pulling the mat over his head again and again. Once more burying his face in the wall.

iiiiiiiiI

IN
T
H     E

WWWWWWWWWWWWWWWWWWWWWWWWWWWWWWWWWWWWWWWWW
WWWWWWWWWWWWWWWWWWWWWWWWWWWWWWWWWALL
WWWWWWWWWWWWWWWHis face in the wall

Seeing only his own hands over his own eyes.

Red fingers on fingers.
Smelling of sweat.

                        Footsteps down the corridor sound
inside a mind of shadows so dark, he can hardly remember
what day it is anymore . . .

# WATER TRICKS

Finally they unlock the adjoining room next door, taking him into a smaller room with a black table and large spotlight. Three chairs.

The same two interrogators from before march in to question him. The same dull angry faces bear down on him. One flashes up photo after photo of the victims of 9/11. A blazing spotlight on Khalid's weak, defeated face.

"You see this woman? Her four children are now orphans. See this man jumping from the flames? His mother died the day before and now his daughter is suffering from cancer. See this girl—she was the cleaner. Only her second day there. See this guy? See him . . .?"

The blazing light is left on here too and Khalid is completely delirious. His mind wanders back through his life. His memories change shape the more he looks at the photos. Expanding, shrinking, merging into story forms, adding scenes from films and episodes from football games. Until every detail of the life he once knew becomes too painful to relive.

Khalid's heart slowly gives up on him at the sight of so

much pain. So much heartache. These ordinary people. Dead. Their lives cruelly cut short. By the time Khalid's dragged back to the cell next door, all he can think about are the things he's done wrong in his life. The pain he's caused. Like the time he stole those black jeans from that little Polish guy down the market. Galloping off like a maniac, jeans under his arm. Nico running behind, roaring with laughter. They thought they were so clever. So cool.

He remembers all the people he's hurt and betrayed. Like when he collected money in the street for Bosnia and, instead of handing it in, emptied the tin with a knife, putting the pound coins in his pocket and leaving only the small change behind. Thinking back to the day he and Tony Banda bunked off school to go to Renzo's house to smoke cigarettes and swig his dad's gin. Telling his teacher his mum would write a letter to explain his absence, then writing it himself. That time in the high street he ran away when he saw Dad walking towards him, ashamed of the sight of him in his old-fashioned clothes. And Mum, he'd snapped at her so many times just because she wouldn't let him go on the computer until he'd done his homework.

The list goes on and on as they drag him back to his cell, adding to the awful pictures flashing through his mind. That poor woman. Her poor kids. Now they've got no one.

The next day, hell starts with the dull thudding of footsteps down the corridor. On the mat, Khalid turns from the wall to lie on his back, staring at the green light of the air-conditioning unit until it starts blinking on and off again. An uncomfortable smell of feet hovers over him all of a sudden, while he clocks the same twisting ache of disappointment and loneliness that he felt yesterday, the day before and the day before that.

After yet another endless night without sleep, he can't even be bothered to wonder what questions they're going to ask him today. The lack of sleep tears his dreams to shreds. The piercing shouts of the guards waking him up time and time again during the night scramble his brain. Barging in to steal sleep from him every time he grows close to losing himself, sharply pulling him back to these four walls. By the time they come for him, Khalid's barely conscious.

The sudden ache of being tightly chained and dragged from the room makes him scream like a tiny baby.

*Not to worry*, the thought flashes through him. *They interrogated me yesterday and then left me on the floor to freeze, but I slept for three hours straight.*

When they push him into a dark room, so cold that even the man in the black suit in the corner is hugging himself for warmth, Khalid knows something's up. The room's so dark and gloomy, he can barely locate the slanting plank behind him, an old cloth slung on top, let alone the tap on the wall.

The suited man glances at Khalid as if he's scum. Khalid raises his head to stare back but his eyes soon close, his mouth runs dry and he can't stop shivering. Then a burning sensation starts up in his stomach. *What the hell are they going to try now?*

The sound of gurgling water from the tap echoes round the room. On the floor, a dirty glass jug stands beside a stinking drain. They've run out of toilet buckets, Khalid guesses.

*Get on with it*, he thinks, as they rip off the shackles and tear off his crumpled T-shirt and navy trousers, stripping him naked. The full force of the freezing temperature throws him into such a shivering fit, he can hardly cover himself with his hands.

Suddenly wide awake, Khalid's shocked by the steely gaze of the suited man, who clearly means business of some awful kind.

"You spoke in a secret code when online?" he says.

"No, it was normal computer chat," Khalid says. "We were playing a stupid game."

"Ah, so you did communicate by code?"

His mind is so scrambled his words come out slowly and exaggerated. "We all talked in text lingo. Don't, please stop. I can't take it." Khalid shudders, remembering so many past conversations just like this. "Please." He stares up at the man, his eyes red raw from lack of sleep.

"Who's 'we all'?" the man says, ignoring his pleas.

"Us gamers," Khalid stutters. "Let. Me. Go. Please. *Please.*"

"You insist on dragging this out," the man says, casting a shadow over his ugly face with a fat hand. "Unless you start talking now, we have no choice but to take stricter measures to loosen your tongue!"

"Help me," Khalid whimpers.

Three guards shuffle closer to Khalid. In this state he can barely stand up, but he knows the guards are baiting him in the hope he'll lash out and they can have some fun "restraining" him. The sudden whiff of body odor makes Khalid want to heave, while something worse than fear lodges in his chest.

Quickening his heart. Crushing him. Emptying his mind, while his teeth chatter noisily on and on.

"Don't. Don't."

All it takes is a nod and the guards reach for him. Their sudden warm breath prickles the hairs on Khalid's neck as they shove him towards the plank, which they straighten with a kick. Then remove the cloth. Taking either end of him, they lift him up and hold him down until his feet, neck and hands are straight.

Gasping, Khalid cries out, "What are you doing? Don't hurt me. Don't . . ." A smiling guard slaps his face with the back of his hand.

They don't need to use the ropes to keep him on the plank thanks to the built-in straps underneath. They unfasten them like leather belts before throwing them over his body to bind his forehead, chest and feet with clamp-like force.

When they tip the plank back, Khalid's thrown upside down with a sickening thump. Blood rushes to his head, cold feet in the air.

"This is your last chance," the man says, standing over him, holding his ankles. "Tell us what you know and we'll let you go home."

"Please. There's nothing . . . Don't."

Eyes closed, their hands pressing down on his shoulders, Khalid hears the jug being filled with water at high velocity. A cloth lands on his face. More hands hold it down, so that he breathes in the smell of gauze bandages, and at the same time a trickle of cold water pours through the cloth and down his nose and mouth.

At first, Khalid coughs and splutters, gags, sucks the cloth into his nose and mouth, which suffocates him. Struggling, his hands jerk and tremble to get away from the straps and he tries to vomit. Groaning. But the rough hands clamp him down more. A split-second memory of Dad's ghostly face passes through his dying mind as water floods his face.

*Dad, help me, help me. Don't let them kill me.*

A flicker of breath sits there—just that bit out of reach. His mouth opens to grab it, battle for it. Spitting. Gurgling the pouring water, but his neck goes rigid with the effort to breathe—with the effort to cough. A slush of water hits his ears.

"Tell us what you know!" the mad man shouts.

*Dad, they're killing me. Help me.* And still the water comes. Drowning him in slow motion. Choking him. Suffocating him. His swelling, bursting lungs force his neck muscles to go limp and he swallows and swallows.

"Are you ready to admit your involvement with al-Qaeda? That you and others planned to bomb London?" The man's voice sounds a million miles away.

With a clack, the plank straightens. The water stops and Khalid spews violently, coughing up his guts, spluttering for breath, opening his sore, bleary eyes. Through the gauze, he sees the suited man standing over him.

He leans down right into his face, his stinking warm breath washing all over Khalid. "Admit your part in the plot and we'll let you go."

Khalid yelps, choking violently. Mumbling a watery something even he can't understand, because he's soon tipped back, gagging for breath under the cloth again, and even though Dad's face is there in his mind he can't reach him.

A few seconds pass before the next wave of water bubbles down Khalid's nose and rushes down his throat. Blocking air. Mouth closed until he splutters. Choking. Gagging wildly before he loses consciousness with the smell of open drains drifting up from the floor as they kick the plank straight with a thud. The shock of a sharp elbow in his stomach makes him vomit again.

"Are you ready yet?"

The stupid question is worth nothing more in response than a thin, gray, watery stream of sick from Khalid's mouth and nose and a violent ache in his belly. Gulping for breath, grabbing for air, trying to store oxygen to breathe, he groans and coughs, watching over himself as he chokes to death while time stands still and they tower above him.

The sound of a dog barking outside loops round the dark room as they force Khalid down again. He's shivering worse than ever as they tip the plank up—feet in the air. Sending the blood to his head in another sickening rush.

"This procedure will continue until you confess your part in the worldwide bombing campaign you planned with known accomplices," the man says firmly.

The ice-cold water floods Khalid's face again. The slow-motion drowning starts again. But he's ready this time and he closes his throat, spits out the bubbling water leaking down his lungs. A bolt of air sticks in his throat—suspending him in a long, still moment between life and death before he gags, struggling for air he doesn't even want any more. His life flashes past him like a fast-moving film. Sinking. Falling. Dying.

*It's OK, Dad. I don't care.*

They swing him back up the second he goes under, the sudden movement shooting his body back into place with a violent thump to his chest. Blood rushes from his head to his heart. Fists pound his belly to bring the water up again as he vomits the racking pain in his head, wringing himself inside out. A sudden wave of air tears his chest from his body as the plank wobbles.

Gasping for air, on it goes, this hell on earth, only this time, the moment Khalid begins coming round, he gives in and holds up a shaking finger to show he's had enough.

"I did it," he whispers, voice red raw from coughing. With a sharp pain at the back of his nose, his naked body falls to the slippery floor the moment the straps are undone. The suited man looms over him with half a grin on his ugly face. A grin that Khalid reaches for with a blue, trembling fist. Waggling his hand with the serious intention of punching his smile out, his teeth too. But then he falls, cracking his forehead on the wet floor.

"Bring him through," the man says to the guards, barely noticing the twisted body floundering and crying in watery sick next to the drain. Khalid trembles, the blood from his head running down his face as he gasps and gasps for air. The pain is so deep and sharp, all he can do is wipe his weeping eyes with a damp wrist and give up on everything, on life, on the whole of mankind.

The guards do their best to dress Khalid while holding on

to his shivering body. One clutches his small waist with an elbow, while the other pulls up the prison overalls.

"You only lasted ten seconds. The last guy did twenty," one of them sneers.

There's no towel to dry him, wipe the blood from his head or clear his waterlogged ears. What animal is worth a towel when he's been deemed a dangerous terrorist?

Once the shackles are safely in place, they drag Khalid next door, throw him into a chair and tie his feet to rings bolted on the floor. Sitting opposite him, on the other side of the black table, his torturer curls his thin lips.

"Let me go now," Khalid begs, but the man smiles.

*He's smiling*, Khalid thinks. *How can he smile?* Spitting more water from his lungs, breathing rapidly while doing his best not to choke, he tries to swallow normally even though his throat hurts, his nose aches, his eyes feel raw and he wouldn't mind dying.

"These are the crimes you've confessed to in the presence of four witnesses. Read them before signing and make the changes you want." He pushes the pages towards Khalid, along with a pen.

Khalid tries to breathe but his throat snaps shut, his mind spins and his eyes feel sprinkled with sand. Then, finding a last tiny drop of dignity and pride, instead of crying he pulls himself up and says in a state of breathless shock, "How come this is already printed?"

Narrowing his eyes, the man pauses before running a chubby thumb over his bottom lip. A steely look begins creeping over his face again and Khalid gets the message.

"Sign these, then you can go home."

*You can go home.* Finally, the words he's waited so long to hear. Quickly, Khalid signs all eight pages, his sore, streaming eyes barely able to focus on the words swimming in front of him.

Back in the cell, it seems that having him sign the confession after drowning him isn't quite enough for them. The lights are still on, blazing down as always, and it's colder than ever, the air-conditioning unit on full. The green light's blinking on and off for no reason, as it always does. *Is this what they call home, then? This cell?*

Khalid is unable to think of anything but killing that ugly guy. Anger boils inside him, feeding on itself until it overtakes every other desire, even the desire to see his family again. His mind feels sharper than he can ever remember. How many seconds did he last? The guy said ten. Ten short seconds and it was over, but it felt like half an hour. In that time Khalid saw his whole life flash before him. Saw Niamh in the library, saw himself playing football down the park, scoring a goal and discussing a new game plan for the match against Heywood. He saw himself arguing with Mum, walking behind Dad down the road—pretending he wasn't with him because he felt ashamed. How can you see all that in just ten seconds and decide to die—say goodbye to your life and then let go in that short amount of time? As well as relive everything you've ever done wrong. See the faces of everyone you've ever hurt. How?

And now they have a bulletproof confession proving he's a dangerous terrorist, an enemy of the world, and no one cares.

Why did he let them do that? How pathetic is he? Tony Banda would have stopped them somehow. Look at what happened when that center half knocked him over in their first match against Bolton. Tony yelled like mad for a minute, but then he went charging down the field to score their only goal and nobody knew until afterwards he'd broken his big toe. Exactly how Tony would have stopped these maniacs, Khalid doesn't know, but he's certain he would have lasted longer than ten short seconds. Much longer than that. While he gave his life away for a breath of air he doesn't even want. He feels ashamed of caving in so quickly. Totally weak and useless, incapable of lasting more than ten seconds, while the guy before him lasted twice as long.

Then the weirdness of this thought suddenly brings Khalid to his senses. The guy's an idiot, a fool for lasting twenty seconds. He's not a hero or someone to look up to. He was just another guy, a Muslim like him, being drowned. He simply suffered for longer. And why did the guard tell him he managed twenty seconds? To make Khalid feel like a coward, that's why. And why should he believe him anyway? If Khalid told people about the attempt to drown him, would they believe him? Apart from the cut and bump on his forehead, there are no marks on his body. Nothing to prove anyone was trying to kill him.

The air-conditioning unit rattles for a second, then continues humming. Khalid curls into a ball on the mat and shades his eyes by burying his head in his arm, thinking that not only did they drown him, but they've left him with a burning anger that has no outlet. All he can do is grind his teeth in hatred. As he slips back into delirium, one of his little sister's paintings flashes through his mind the moment before he falls asleep. The light bulb blazes overhead. Unrelenting as always. The smell of burning dust and the memory of a watery hell never far away.

## SLEEP

Staying put, getting up—neither choice is a good one when every part of Khalid's thin body aches. Hatred and guilt scrabble like ferrets at his brain. Guilt at the thought of his stupidity. If only he hadn't done that. His tired mind haunts the life he once knew for a memory that might bring him comfort.

Any reason to go on living.

All night long, under the constant bright lights, the picture at the front of Khalid's mind is the painting by Gul. A picture stuck to the fridge at home in Rochdale. His stomach churns when he remembers the green sun, the orange sea and the mad red grass. Everything was painted the wrong color, including the blue dog, but that's why it keeps going round his head. The memory of the odd colors adds to his feeling of being locked out of anything normal. Little Gul's painting is a reminder of something ordinary to hang on to—even if the orange sea gets brighter and weirder every time it rolls through his head. Anything's better than remembering that moment—his hand on the pen . . .

If he can close his brain down for a bit, then maybe he can forget. Perhaps if the guards stay away for a while . . .

One sleepless hour later, they barge in to wake him again. Yank him from the mat and haul him around until his eyes stay open. Yelling obscenities in his ears to stop him passing out. As if they haven't got what they wanted by now. Then, as the aroma of a sickly lemon aftershave fills Khalid's nose, the back of his throat tightens.

A pink cat begins pawing his face. Or is it a man with pink hands squeezing his cheeks for fun? They win. Khalid stares at the soldier and his tinted glasses. Recording every detail of his bright, shiny face for posterity, because once they see he's fully awake, they'll leave him alone. And they do—for a bit. Leaving him with nothing but the sound of his heart thumping louder than the air conditioner.

Sinking to the mat, he passes out. Fast asleep in seconds. Asleep until a total madness starts up out there: dogs barking, plane engines roaring, men yelling orders at the tops of their voices. Don't say they're planning on doing more water tricks now? But the noises—they're new, aren't they?

Khalid focuses, listening carefully as the noise suddenly changes to a tinny banging.

"NO. NO." Two guards barge in, shackles swinging from the stocky one's arms. Khalid blinks. Not really taking them in. Vaguely recognizing them as two of the five men who'd woken him through the night.

The one with the strong lemon-smelling aftershave shouts, "Get up!" Yanking Khalid from the mat.

The psycho one with tiny fish eyes says, "You've got thirty seconds to eat this."

A peanut butter sandwich presses into Khalid's face, along

with a plastic bottle of water. Only half here, Khalid stumbles. They catch him under the arms and slam him angrily against the cell wall, pinning his shoulders back with their fists. Their roughness suggests Khalid has the strength to resist them. After days without sleep, he can barely stay upright, let alone escape. He's almost unconscious. The guards messing with him like this is beyond crazy—they really are insane. Without tasting anything, Khalid gorges on the cardboard-like sandwich. Peanut butter sticks to his teeth and he dribbles, croaking down warm, plastic-tasting water.

Barely able to swallow more than a teaspoonful at a time, Khalid says, half smiling, "What, no Coca-Cola?"

"That's it." The stocky soldier knocks the bottle from his hand. "Jackass." The blue plastic dreamily double-bounces before rolling on the steel floor. Water slips between Khalid's toes and the smell of the guy's aftershave hangs over him like a smashed-up lemon tree, and all he wants to do is sink to the floor and close his eyes forever and ever.

First they kit him out in an orange suit, then they twist his arms together. One sneers at Khalid's skinny arms and wrists as he clicks the cuffs tightly shut, then they attach the handcuffs to a middle chain they fix around his waist. At that point Khalid's head flops to his chest and he drops fast asleep. Moving quickly, they lock his ankles to the waist chain. The cold, heavy metal catches his cuts and bruises by surprise, bringing him round for a moment with the fear they're going to drown him again.

"Too loose, mate!" Khalid mutters, awake again. But they don't laugh. They never laugh.

"Bye-bye!" A guard pulls a black hood over Khalid's head. The sudden darkness is a shock after days of dazzling bright lights, a weird relief until a sickening loss of balance comes over him as they lead him down the corridor, staggering all over the place. His bare feet kicking together with sharp toenails.

"Guantanamo!" someone whispers as they pass. Bringing Khalid to—for a moment—before he shuts his eyes again. It's OK, he's going home. They said he could go home. He signed the papers to go home.

The sound of dragging feet and clanking chains pierces the midday heat. The sun beats down like boiling tar on Khalid's masked head. He can sense other people nearby. Three? Or maybe a hundred? He's going a long way away. England? Yes. Why else the sound of so much sudden movement and the horrible smell of petrol?

"Hey, dude, get them over here!" a soldier screams.

Someone shoves earmuffs on Khalid. The world goes suddenly quiet. Leaving him bent and gasping, on his knees in the searing heat like a captured, half-dead dog. Breathing in the smell of soldiers' socks and desert boots.

Maybe he is going to Guantanamo. But they said he could go home if he signed.

After a few minutes, Khalid's yanked up again. Step by step, they shuffle him along the ramp of the plane—up hot, ridged metal that seems to go on forever and burns his curling toes, shackles cutting into his ankles.

The moment his aching bones hit the plane floor, Khalid knows he's going to be sick. But nothing comes up. Just the same dizzy, nauseous feeling he's kept down for hours. One part of his brain watches himself fall to pieces, while the other no longer cares about anything and just wants to sleep.

The drone of the engine grows louder.

Khalid tries pushing the earmuffs off his sore ears. Cuffs rub his wrists raw as he pushes and pushes, elbows in the air. The hot, plastic smell of the mask turns his guts over. A terrible desperation spreads through him as he twists and wriggles the earmuffs farther off his head. But they spring back and he has to wait a while before bending his head and trying again. This time he succeeds in freeing his sore lobes for a few minutes. That's better. Now his ears aren't hurting, he can close his eyes and go to sleep.

"Allah hears and knows all things," a prisoner says over and over again.

*Shut up.* Khalid wishes the guy would shut up, that all of them would stop praying and groaning, because he feels nothing for anyone. Not even the tiniest spark of concern or compassion for any of them any more. No way are all these hooded men going to Britain.

"Camp Delta, what a stupid name!" Khalid remembers laughing when Wade told him about it. He actually laughed. Not realizing they were going to warm him up for the journey by leaving him alone in a brightly lit cell for days. Days where he wasn't allowed to sleep or talk to anyone before they tried to drown him. Which brings it all back to him.

Brings back the thing he's trying hard not to think about or admit. Submitting finally to the memory of something the suited man said before they hauled him on the plank.

"You spoke in a secret code when online?"

"No, it was normal computer chat," Khalid had replied. "We were playing a stupid game."

"Who's 'we all'?"

"Us gamers."

Khalid mutters, "Gamers. Gamers."

He forces himself to remember being stripped naked and thrown backwards on the plank. Tilted back. Feet in the air.

"This procedure will continue until you confess your part in the worldwide bombing campaign you planned with known accomplices."

"Known accomplices." The expression haunts Khalid's every waking hour.

Remembering every detail. The cloth smelling of old bandages smothering his face. Water clogging his nose and throat until he gagged. Coughing and spluttering for air. All the time, someone shouting, "Tell us what your plans were and we'll stop." But they didn't and he couldn't, because he had no idea what they meant. Khalid closes his eyes but the man next to him is still muttering and his mind's still spinning. Racing and racing with question after question.

What plans were they thinking of? Khalid's suddenly wide awake. What was really going on in that guy's mind? And then the suspicion he's been burying for a while rises to the surface again.

Did Tariq have something to do with this?

How else do they know so much about the fact he'd been on the computer? Did he really betray him? His own cousin? Had he been talking to Abdullah, the aunties' neighbor in

Karachi? He'd found Abdullah on the computer. He knew Khalid had been playing a game. Did he know it was Tariq's game? Do they know each other? Were there other people involved in this that he hadn't considered? Abdullah said his brother and his sister's husband used the aunties' computer. Did they have something to do with this? Either way, Khalid's thoughts keep returning to Tariq. He's the link. The other gamers didn't know where he was, but Tariq did. The thought sticks in Khalid's throat. It's obvious: he's trusted him way too much since they began messaging. After all, what does Khalid really know about Tariq? They've never even met, so why should he expect anything of him? Apart from the fact they were family, they didn't have anything special in common.

One after the other, he'd signed all those pages because of him. Signing them with a nicer pen this time. A black shiny one. When he glanced at the names on the pages, though, he hadn't recognized any of them. Not that Khalid looked closely —he was still choking. Half dead. Shivering, at the time.

Now he wishes he'd paid more attention. Perhaps Tariq's name was there—in some form or other.

All the gamers used pseudo names that they changed regularly. Names like Tariq Van Dam. TVD for short. One guy called himself Purple Pizza before changing it to DungHill. Another was Verminate before becoming Boss X. Khalid still has no idea what their real names are, apart from Tariq's.

Thinking back to that second after they whisked the black pen away, he remembers a feeling of absolute peace spreading over him. Realizing they had no need to hurt him ever again.

It was worth lying for. Worth it for that moment's peace. It doesn't feel worth it now.

Now the regret he feels is driving him crazy. Why can't I just sleep? Why can't I stop thinking and thinking?

As he rocks back and forth, the relentless drone of the plane's engine bores into him until he hears and cares about nothing but getting the truth from Tariq once and for all. Settling the frantic feeling in his stomach for a few hours by imagining Tariq admitting his part in Khalid's abduction. But what was all that about Afghanistan when they questioned him in Karachi? Where was his passport? Abdullah, the neighbor and random people at home, like Nasir, the shopkeeper in Rochdale, were they members of al-Qaeda? Jim, who helped him look for Dad, what about him? What about Dad? Anyone he's ever met?

Angry. So angry. There are so many people he'd like to destroy. Their faces go round and round his head, the layers of fury expanding as they circle his brain.

Yelling, "HOW DARE YOU DROWN ME?" But the sound comes out weaker than an abandoned kitten whining for food.

Exhausted, Khalid's heart slows to normal for a few seconds. Allowing him to breathe more easily, unleashing the desire to sleep again. His eyes open and close in a dreamy spin.

Clutching at hope, Khalid imagines he's going home to England, to Mum and Dad and his little sisters, and a life of shops with milk and newspapers. Chocolate and lottery tickets. Ordinary things. But the deafening plane engine roars into action and it doesn't feel like it's taking him home. Or anywhere nice.

A sudden, dense heat smelling of petrol overtakes the trapped desert air inside the plane. Khalid can't help gasping. Since they tried to drown him he's been continually gasping for air. Unsure it's really there—sucking it up in case it's his last breath.

The inside of the mask dampens with sweat from his dripping forehead, the salt sharpening his swollen lips. All Khalid can do is waggle his head to keep the drips from his eyes. The hot uncomfortable earmuffs cling to the sticky mask. The available choices are simple: either put up with the din of the engine or suffer the pain of the earmuffs and get some peace. Either way he can't sleep. His eyes won't stay closed.

Khalid maneuvers the earmuffs back slightly using his shoulder. By mistake he moves the mask round to reveal a hole in the plastic which he can clearly see out of.

His eyes land on a soldier with fat, freckly arms. His big hands are attached to a silver camera and he's taking pictures for fun. *Flash*. *Flash*. Anger flares up inside Khalid again. He can't believe anyone would do that for kicks. Maybe he wants photos to sell to the newspapers back home. Either way, each click is another hammer blow to Khalid's heart.

*Who do they think they are, these guys?* Khalid fumes.

It sparks a memory of the time they'd been studying the Spanish Inquisition in school with Mr. Tagg and he'd got them all worked up about the subject of torture. Everyone began arguing. Loads of kids said it was a good way to get information from evil people, but in the end Jacinda Parker, who lives over the music shop, got them all thinking differently.

"It's a stupid way of finding anything out. Whenever my brother twists my arm up my back, it hurts so bad I say anything he wants me to just to get him to stop. So what's the point in torturing someone if all you get is lies?"

None of it adds up for Khalid. If only he could stop all this stuff going round his head. His mind returning from the sight of Jacinda Parker and her horrible brother, Josh, and their nice two-story flat over the yellow-painted music shop, to his sore arms and aching head. To the raw feeling in his throat and itchy eyes. To the thought of Tariq turning him in.

He thinks about Guantanamo Bay again. If he's really going there. Wasn't it a place for members of al-Qaeda?

Someone had said Guantanamo was the worst of the worst, but Khalid hadn't really listened. He half thought they were making the stories up. He doesn't even know why it's in Cuba and not America.

*Surely they won't take a kid like me there?*

The thought makes him catch his breath, and when he comes to breathe out he gasps for air again. Defeated. Totally shattered. His mind begins searching for that place deep inside where peace happens. Where nice memories are stored. Eyes wide open, he begins wanting. Wanting his mum. Wanting his dad. Wanting his annoying little sisters. Wanting his friends, Mikael, Holgy, Nico and Tony, and a longed-for kickabout in the park.

Drifting back to Rochdale, he's walking through the town center wondering what the old mill town used to look like before they covered up most of the River Roch that flows underneath the main street. The nice old buildings that are still there with the best town hall in the universe. A majestic building with a beautiful wooden staircase and wallpaper by William Morris, who, the art teacher, Mrs. Dowling, says was a genius.

Then there're the cheap lunches they do in the town hall for retired people. Khalid helped out, along with two others from school, during Help the Aged Week last year. For three pounds they get a three-course, home-cooked meal in a lovely room with William Morris wallpaper. How good's that?

Rochdale is a nice place to live. Plus Khalid's house is only a ten-minute walk from the Odeon cinema.

Now his mind's right there on the football terraces, shouting for Rochdale to win—at their away matches especially. Seeing the town with its—he's not quite sure how many exactly, but definitely more than six—mosques. Each of them floats past his eyes. Mixed with people who are Muslims, Hindus, Christians, Jews, Buddhists, Rastas. Plus loads of people who don't believe in anything. Others who sometimes believe but never go anywhere near the mosques, temples, churches and synagogues. And plenty more believe whatever makes them feel good. Then there're those who hate everything. Who just get angry and spew up any old crap. All of them live side by side in Rochdale. His Rochdale. Khalid likes that.

As the plane taxies to the runway, Khalid's totally back there. Down the park, playing football. Skidding on the grass. Racing his shadow up the line. Trying to avoid Adnan, who looks like Jesus and tackles too hard. Delivering a perfect corner kick into their penalty area, with Mac cheering him on.

Dad's words at the back of his mind: "At the age of sixteen, son, you must decide what kind of man you want to be."

Now his best friend is this anger that won't go away.

Khalid had told them the same thing over and over again. He'd given them his address. His doctor's name. The name of all his Rochdale schoolteachers, including his favorite, Mr. Tagg. Plus the details of his post-office savings account with the sixty-one pounds and eighteen pence that took him five months to save.

Over and over again they'd asked him the same questions.

Perhaps they'd confused him with someone else. With more than two million hits on the Internet when he googled his name, Khalid Ahmed, he knows they've got the wrong one even if they don't.

What more could he do to prove his innocence? But they don't want to believe him. Khalid even told them about the money Dad and his friends had collected to help the refugees in Albania. Two planeloads of food, plus medicine, clothes, blankets and tents. The local paper said the mayor was "immensely impressed with the efforts of the Muslim community in raising substantial funds for the refugees."

"Cut it!" The soldier had kicked the chair from under Khalid to stop him talking about the mayor. As if he'd made the story up. Punching him in the stomach for no reason. The heartbreak was that they didn't care about the truth. Why else leave him half conscious on the floor to rot?

*Funny*, Khalid thinks, remembering that feeling of absolute shock. *I'm not even that interested in religion. Any religion. Not even my own Muslim religion.* His family is relaxed about it, though. Dad's always telling him he'll work it out

169

for himself before too long. Allah, the bountiful, will happily wait for him.

*Dad. Come back to me, Dad.*

The reality of the mess he's in suddenly comes back to Khalid. Unimaginable fury bubbles in him again and he smiles at the thought of taking revenge. Eight months ago they kidnapped him for committing the unholy crime of being in the wrong place at the wrong time and one day he'll get these maniacs, tip them upside down and shove water down their noses until they drown. Only he'll leave them to drown. Yes, do the whole world a favor and finish them off.

With that satisfying thought, Khalid finally lets go, closes his eyes and sleeps.

# 16

## GUANTANAMO

This time no one disturbs Khalid until they land and another kind of hell begins.

The strange smell of the sea greets Khalid as he leaves the plane, finally free of his hood and earmuffs. But this definitely isn't home sweet home. The bright sun throws dark shadows on the ramp that follow him down—a warm breeze in his face. The unexpected sound of birds brings with it a sticky heat that covers his body in a sudden sweat, reminding him of an old school trip to Blackpool on the hottest day of the year. He had been thrilled at the thought of the bus journey with Niamh close by.

And there it is, that day, flashing through his mind again . . .

Khalid was feeling great after Rochdale's win on Saturday and he pushed himself forward to say hi, hoping to swing his arm round Niamh's shoulders. Trying to make his stumbling into her look accidental. Ready to glance back at Holgy with an accusing look if it all went wrong. Ready to say it was Holgy who pushed him into Niamh's side.

Then, somehow, dorky Gilly got in between them. She grabbed Khalid's hand and, squeezing it tightly for a second with cold fingers, began licking her lips and fluttering her eyelashes to tease him even more. Holgy pretended not to notice his mate crumple and flush as Niamh scrambled red-faced on to the coach, hurrying to the back row.

The sound of their squealing told Khalid her friends were having the last laugh. Thankfully, Holgy and Nico were on hand to make him feel better.

"Nice one, Kal!" Holgy nudged him.

"Next time, move in closer." Nico winked.

As if he ever would after that.

But later Niamh waved a chocolate-covered fork at him while they had lunch in a cafe near the pier. Beckoning him over, then sliding up in the booth to give him room. Her mates squashing to the end so Mikael could sit there too.

"Ow," Niamh yelled as Mikael stamped on her foot in his rush to grab the vacant space next to her. He dumped his plate of steaming pasta on the smooth table and dug in as if he hadn't eaten for a week.

"Sorry," Khalid apologized for him, standing there like a fool at the end of the table, more embarrassed than ever. Nico shook his head at Mikael for ruining what could have been a truly romantic moment.

"What? What did I do?" Mikael said, wide-eyed, his mouth crammed with chunks of pasta dripping in tomato sauce.

"You nicked his place, you moron!" Niamh laughed. Making them all laugh.

"Doesn't matter," Khalid said.

"Doesn't matter!" Gilly echoed.

Khalid's still half smiling at the memory as the sound of a

barking voice snaps him back to reality and he's shoved down on to his knees.

"Welcome to Guantanamo Bay Prison. You're now the property of the US Marine Corps. Heads down!" Soldiers with black dogs walk along the lines of kneeling men. Khalid lowers his head, but not until he's taken a peek at the nightmare that is Guantanamo Bay. *Those lying bastards!* A bleached-out expanse surrounded by high fences topped with rolls of razor wire two meters high and watchtowers draped in American flags at either end.

To his right all he can see is scrubby rough ground with patches of thin grass and a heap of masonry with lines of stones and sand marking it out. In the distance, more fences. A tinkling sound like wind chimes starts up in the huge rolls of rusty wire reaching for the sky. Khalid gazes at the hot earth, thinking, *This place has wind chimes? How come?*

Then, like a scene from a film, an iguana darts in front of the poker-faced marine who's busy shouting orders—yelling at men who are unable to do anything but listen while they bake to death in the blazing sun.

Khalid wonders how mad it would be to break open a packet of Doritos. Listen to a bit of hip-hop. Look up the word "maniac" on Google. Watch *The Simpsons* on TV. The kind of stuff he does when he gets home from school. The kind of stuff his mates are probably doing right now. While all the time a vulture circles in the sky above him and the warmth of the sun tickles the stubble on his head. A dazzling, silvery light in his eyes makes it hard to focus on those dusty desert boots for a moment longer.

From the tone of the marine's voice, it's obvious they don't tolerate time-wasters here. This place is far more serious than Kandahar, built to contain highly trained assassins, security threats, enemies of America. The atmosphere grows ever more threatening as the marines march up and down, giving each of them the evil eye.

It's not often that Khalid can look at his life from a distance. But, instantly, he can see himself clearly for once. He's another meaningless bent orange shape dropped into some weird world game, the sun fixing him here on this lump of tarmac like a dart in his back. He's nothing but an orange heap for soldiers to toss around because they think he's a terrorist who wants to blow up cities. Think he hates the West, even though he lives there and doesn't know anything about weapons of mass destruction or bombs or buildings crashing to the ground in New York.

"Where's your evidence, then?" Khalid mutters to himself. Eyes closed, he whimpers like a baby. "Where? You got it all from stupid little me, that's where."

Soon they lead Khalid inside a long building done out like the prisons he's seen in films, with rows of locked, diamond-shaped wire doors. A sign spells out CAMP DELTA. The soldiers pause to force him inside one of the small kennels.

"Stand closer, 256," a man drawls with a strong Southern accent as he clicks the lock.

Khalid shuffles towards the metal door, which has two oblong holes, with flaps top and bottom. Holes the size of three plastic lunch boxes, side by side.

"Closer to the flaps," the drawling voice shouts again.

"Stand with your wrists and ankles to the beany holes," another shouts.

Khalid obeys and the guard unties his wrist and ankle shackles through the door holes that he thinks are the beany holes, with great caution, which makes Khalid smile at the sheer silliness of it all. Why can't they undo the chains outside the cell? Why this stupid, over-the-top arrangement of holes in the door? Do they think he might escape if they removed them beforehand? Khalid can just see himself breaking out by ducking their bullets, charging from the building and across the hot ground while men in watchtowers train their guns on him, only to make the superhuman effort of climbing ten meters of barbed wire and diving into the sea and swimming to safety. His mates would crack up if they could see these soldiers undoing the chains through these stupid holes.

After the metal flaps are raised to cover the holes, the sound of slamming echoes down the lines until all the prisoners are done and the thundering boots march away.

A small room with a plastic bed with round corners built into the wall greets Khalid when he turns. Thin foam mattress on top. Two blue blankets at either end. A copy of the Qur'an in English. One pair of white flip-flops. Two white towels. Wash cloth. Soap. Shampoo. Toothpaste. Bottle of water. Two buckets this time.

And so another routine begins. Breakfast on a plastic tray: a box of cereal, white roll. Bottle of water. Sometimes sloppy scrambled eggs and overdone peas. Maybe an orange.

For lunch: a piece of tough meat, some form of potato,

usually canned and half mashed with sweetcorn or turnip. Peanuts. Water. Sometimes a packet of raisins.

The dinner menu remains unaltered for the next two days: tasteless white rice, hard red beans, revolting gray fish. Bread. Water. On Friday, a banana.

Khalid doesn't understand how food can be this disgusting and tasteless. He knows some pathetic effort has been made to keep to the halal diet, but anyone with half a brain could have come up with something better than this.

After two days, he's determined never to eat any of the vile bread rolls again. If he gets a choice, that is. The motto here being "eat or starve," he chews his way through the slice of white bread with the satisfaction of someone about to throw up. Convincing himself things will change soon. Or so he hopes, because they can't get any worse. He's already nearly died and is now slowly going out of his mind.

Since he arrived in Guantanamo, Khalid hasn't really seen anyone. Just the food trolley man and the soldiers. The only sounds that keep him company day and night are terrifying screams from the other end of the building and then someone who coughs and coughs—he doesn't know which is worse. Plus the constant slamming of metal flaps gives him a headache, like a pneumatic drill in the side of his skull.

The only good thing is that he's slept most of the time since he arrived. And he's getting used to his mind blanking, wandering off in odd directions after so much humiliation and pain. The sensation of drowning still catches him out when he becomes aware he's swallowing for no reason, or sometimes just breathing hard, but he's getting used to that now and it doesn't scare him as much any more.

Just lately, though, he's been picturing his face on the news. A mugshot of a convicted terrorist who's hated by everyone. Even his mates. Seeing Niamh snarl at herself for once smiling and flirting with him, while her friend Gilly says, "I never liked that loser."

The other thing is, unless Khalid's busy hating himself, he doesn't feel fully here. Making up scenes like this is the only thing that stops him from thinking about what they did. From going out of his mind blaming himself for being so stupid. It's so much easier conjuring up horror movies with him in the leading role than it is watching himself staring at the empty walls, too wrecked to hold his head up straight. At least it seems that way until he begins confusing the dreams with reality and starts believing the dramas in his mind are actually happening.

More than a few times he's woken up and been surprised to find David Beckham, Niamh or Nico standing in front of him. Shocked to see them there instead of the small bed, white towels, toilet bucket on the floor. The familiar sound of someone screaming nearby seems to make his visitors smile.

Khalid has a feeling of dread he might join in and smile with them, slowly believing the noise of approaching boots might be a fantasy too and he's really somewhere else, somewhere he doesn't know, and the wasted, patchy, not-here feeling only subsides when the soldier yells something ridiculous. "You Taliban guys don't know how lucky you are! If you were in Afghanistan now you'd all be dead. Thank God for the US of

A." Making it clear to Khalid that the soldier has no idea how nice dying would be. The upbeat, insulting tone of his cheery voice tears him apart bit by bit.

No one cares. They don't care about him. Nobody does. If only he hadn't signed those papers. They said he could go home, the liars. If they'd let him sleep, things would have been different. Then he might not have signed his own prison sentence. Reminding himself he was pretty much mentally and physically dead the moment his hand picked up the pen doesn't help. He can't forgive himself. Neither will Nico and the rest of his mates. Niamh hates him now, he knows it. His mum and dad. Aadab and Gul. Everyone does all over the world.

He'll never be sure of himself again. How will he know who he is after this?

On and on, the day before they tried to drown him, they held up those pictures of children killed in 9/11. Photos of women jumping from the towers. Flashing them up as if their deaths were Khalid's fault. Wearing him down until his nerves were completely shattered. Until he started believing maybe it was all his fault. In the end, he signed the papers and what happened? They shut him up here.

Does anyone even know where he is? He doubts it. Arms folded, Khalid sits on the bed and stares at the wall. At the blank space with pockmarks and dead flies he knows so well. The smell of his own body in the warm room, the sound of his own breathing and the thudding of boots make him think his whole life has been a gigantic mistake.

Then one day . . .

"Get up, you," the guard says. "You never get up!"

His bad breath adds to the whiff of cold battered meat from the plastic tray he's passing through.

"Sorry to put a crimp in your day but Britain cooled out —whupped the United Nations. Blair's with us. Europe's a bunch of cry-babies." He laughs, then pauses a moment to work out which inmate nearby is reciting a verse from the Qur'an. The melancholy voice calling to Mecca.

Ignoring him, the guard turns back to Khalid to gloat.

"We gonna kick your butts," he adds. "You ain't going nowhere now, man. Tony Blair—with his decision—he clean done y'all in."

"What decision?" Khalid drops the tray on the bed and, glancing back at the sneering face pressed to his fence, he's surprised to see the guard's big popping nostrils are flaring with excitement.

"Britain's with us—at war in Iraq!" Shouting so loud, someone in the camp responds by translating the news into various different languages. Soon it's passed on, until eventually everyone knows what's happening. People run to the doors, kicking and banging to show how they feel, yelling and screaming in their own languages. Fury travels along the rows of cells like a crashing, unstoppable flood. The nearest thing to a riot Khalid's ever experienced.

Guards respond by racing up the lines and leveling automatic machine guns at the detainees. Ready to fire at the drop of a hat. Khalid's overwhelmed by the news Britain along with America are at war in Iraq and not just Afghanistan. Why? No one's more surprised than him. Suppose he never gets out now? The guard said so, didn't he? What else has changed out there that he doesn't know about?

Khalid loses his grip on the door, letting his hands fall to his side like lead weights. Emotionally frail, he wanders the few steps to the bed. Collapsing in a feeble heap. The constant banging and yelling have broken down the flimsy layer of protection he hoped would keep his mind together today.

The violence is so horribly real to Khalid, he can't help brooding on the hatred he feels growing in the world and the problems the war will bring to his family—for Muslims everywhere. He knows Dad would go out of his way to complete the Muslim duty of *zakat*—acts of charity to help people in need during the war in Iraq. But where is he now?

Eventually the banging and kicking die down and a pitiful whine starts up somewhere beyond him. Out there. Outside this field of right and wrong. The familiar, high-pitched, grating cry of someone who Khalid knows is being harmed. Bringing it all back to him . . .

## SWEAT

Day follows day. Weeks and months pass by and nothing changes. Time stretches for Khalid. Sometimes the hours between breakfast and lunch feel longer than a day at school. He remembers the school day going so slowly. Often, by the time the bell went, he couldn't recall what happened that morning, it felt like so long ago. Then, at other times, the minutes shrink. He finishes the tasteless cereal and two seconds later the lunch tray clatters the flap and all he's been thinking about is the TV program he once saw about an Olympic diver. The guy explained how he has two and a half seconds between jumping off the board, doing two perfect spins and hitting the water, and in that short time he must rectify any awkward position he finds himself in. Deciding instantly while he falls to straighten his back or lower his arms.

How is that possible in two and a half seconds? In the time it takes for Khalid to say his own name?

Khalid wakes covered in sweat, perspiration running down his neck. The two-and-a-half-second dive is still on his mind. How can anyone plan what they are going to do in that amount of time? Suffering a slight headache, dry mouth, he glances at the air-conditioning unit bolted high on the wall behind him, wondering why the green light is off.

Now there's a spider on the grill. Tiny quivering legs climb slowly inside the unit. Perhaps that's the reason it's not working. Don't they check them? What do they do all day, these soldiers?

He places a sticky hand on his chest and the orange uniform feels wet. Hot pools of sweat are forming on his damp skin.

With no chance of release from the dense heat, Khalid lies on his side. Keeping as still as possible, he breathes gently to bring his temperature down. Concentrating on each breath until he can bear to reach for the half-empty bottle of water on the floor at the end of the bed.

Then a peculiar faintness passes over Khalid as he tries to sit up. His head's worse, hurting badly now. His fingers feel weaker than jelly when he tries to unscrew the tight blue lid from the bottle.

After a swig of warm water, he senses a metal clamp tightening around his forehead. Forcing him to make a superhuman effort to focus on putting the bottle down without knocking it over. But when Khalid lifts his chin, the gray room swivels round ominously. Rising, swerving, moving in hills across his eyes. Flashing round to nuzzle the back of his head. Then pulsing and pulsing before coming back in a sickly rush.

Eyes popping, a broken man jumps ogre-like from the gray walls. Reaching for his throat from the pit of a nightmare. Arms wide.

A booming sound shoots from Khalid's mouth with a

heart-rending roar. Hands tear at his screwed-up face and he bashes the back of his head on the wall. Numbing his brain. The pain is a welcome relief as he thumps and thumps his head, suffering the kind of torment only a prisoner knows. Locked out, not in. Not here, not there. Not human at all. The only reminder he's real is the ache, the sharp pain, again and again. The moving walls hold whatever's left—together—for as long as the pain throbs and throbs. But are they walls?

When the air-conditioning light suddenly twinkles green, the walls fall back to steady the room. Khalid widens his eyes, sweat dripping from every pore. Forehead throbbing. Has he been going mental for minutes and hours or days and weeks? What month is it? Did he hear someone saying "Happy Christmas"? Or did he imagine it? Without a clock or a calendar, he can't tell. Plus, the ceiling lights—are they getting brighter? Or is he imagining the increasing glare?

Groaning with pain, he begins flicking through the pages for the passages in the Qur'an he's come to know well, turning quickly to the blessing of Moses. Hoping to find clues about how to deal with the pain that's eating away at his guts. The holy book is his only link to outside help of any kind. Praying he'll learn to become a better person and not the bitter, angry guy he turns into whenever he thinks of his cousin. Tariq's never far from his mind. All Tariq ever talked about was himself and where he'd been and that stupid game. By the time the dinner trolley comes squeaking down the corridor, Khalid has been driven almost crazy by the memory of how devoted he'd been to his cousin.

"Yes, cuz. No, cuz. Two bags full, you're so clever, cuz."

Why didn't he just tell him to get lost? All those times he'd crept downstairs when everyone was asleep. Nights that Khalid had wasted telling Tariq how brilliant *Bomber One* was going to be. And it wasn't, no way, it was just OK. But why, oh why, did Khalid care if *Bomber One* was going to be great or not? Why did he care so much about how Tariq felt about himself?

Sickened by the idea of Tariq's smiling face bearing down on him, to get the thought of Tariq out of his mind, he escapes in other ways too. By the time the trolley stops outside he's shocked to see perfect tooth marks sharply outlined on his arm. He's been biting himself. Why the trauma comes out this way, he doesn't know, but lately it has.

Khalid doesn't notice the twinges of pain on his arm because today his fractured mind can only locate the many pictures Tariq had e-mailed of himself. All of them were digital photos of Tariq with his friends pulling mad faces. One with his dad and three brothers, lucky him, grinning at the camera as if everything in their family is perfect.

For a second, Khalid thinks he hears a car door opening and closing, but it's only a dinner tray snapping into place.

Khalid glances at the gristly meat, boiled tomatoes and ball of undercooked rice and goes for the small banana first, before rubbing hard and trying to make the red tooth marks on his arm disappear.

A sudden surge of energy comes over him now.

His stomach feels better—yes. His heartbeat's slower—yes. But the passage in the Qur'an he wants to read is still swimming in front of his eyes. The unchanging words are spinning in groups of three or four. The shapes jump out to confuse him, linked as they are without meaning to his previous, less shadowy brain.

Spreading white rice with the plastic spoon on the lumps of gray meat to disguise the gristle, Khalid's half tempted to tip the lot on the floor.

Fading away into something beyond sleep for an hour or two after he's eaten, he joins up the dots on the wall to make a giraffe shape with a rabbity ear. Then he eyes the eight gravy marks on the floor to see if the distance between two is smaller or larger than another two. Sometimes he counts the footsteps going up and down the row. Over and over again. Now and then he loses track, often when his fingers settle on the weird ridges of skin between his smallest toes. Is it night-time? Or morning? Did he eat breakfast today? Or did they forget to bring it?

Waking up to trace the red scratches on his face, Khalid catches sight of the spider speeding to the door and breathes a sigh of relief.

Perhaps he's slept too long. Weeks, for all he knows. Only learning it's early morning when the call to prayer wakes him up. For a while, Khalid imagines daylight breaking outside.

An unexpected feeling of peace spreads over him at the memory of being outside in the sunshine. Hoping, by concentrating on this, the last of the wooziness in his head will fade away. When did he last go out? He can't remember.

But he mustn't lie here forever . . .

Grabbing at the walls, Khalid stumbles to the door, banging and kicking. Someone shouts his number: "256!"

The metal flap's unlocked, snapping open. Slamming against the wire. Khalid punches the corridor through the beany hole, yelling and swearing.

Two minutes later, they come for him, attaching the shackles with nifty hands. Khalid raises his bruised head.

"Thanks!" he says. Feeling a strange pleasure at the sight of ordinary human beings instead of the dark things flowing through his mind. Even though they're guards, he's suddenly grateful to them.

"Get up," one guard says, shackling him tight. The word "up" takes on a nice meaning that was never intended. And why? Where's he going now?

It's good for Khalid to walk. As he goes down the corridor, he realizes he's OK. He's just been hallucinating bad things. Good things too. Knowing the dark dreams, strange fantasies of Niamh and David Beckham, might have damaged his ability to tell what's real and what's imagined. But by creating bad feelings, he's stopped himself from dying inside, and even though they have seen him through the long wait, the pressure on his brain when he wakes up is still too much to bear. That's why he tries to bang it away on the wall.

*At least I know it now*, Khalid thinks to himself, *and I'm not going to let them win.*

At the same time, he realizes this awareness might just save his life. He makes an effort to take in his surroundings. Grounding himself by staring at the soldiers' laced-up black boots—which are highly polished but have dusty creases. Stopping high above the ankles, they look almost girly, those big boots, with those jungly combat trousers that are a bit like the combats Niamh sometimes wears.

Another reason to concentrate on the here and now is because it keeps the demons at bay and might just prevent the nightmares from returning. David Beckham can take a hike. Too much is at stake. Madness, for a start.

Gray linoleum, Khalid notes, as they reach the end of a long white corridor, past cells so enclosed by wire it's impossible to make out the faces of the men inside. *There are people here a lot worse than me*, Khalid realizes, as he sees a man desperately banging the wire with his bleeding head. His fetid wound the size of a cup.

He's led outside and his senses are assaulted by the rapid whistling of a nearby bird, dazzling sunshine, countless shadows. He's almost blinded by the sudden piercing light. He was here a few days ago. Wasn't he? Heart pounding, Khalid's led over uneven ground to a wooden shelter. Watching his shadow shuffle along beside him, a whiff of disinfectant hits him, followed by the sound of running water. The smell reminds him of the routine. His shadow overtakes him as they round a corner to arrive at the row of basic showers. Khalid likes the showers now. He hated them at first, but he likes them now.

Armfuls of shackles and chains just to walk him to the showers? Yeah, Khalid always smiles at that.

Two prisoners try to hide their nakedness, as they do every time the guards herd them under rusty shower heads that release the thinnest trickle of water. Khalid hurries to undress, used to the routine, while others hide their embarrassment with their faces in the crook of their arm. Doing their best not to look at anyone.

The birdsong disappears as Khalid throws his head under the cold stream of water. Closing his eyes for a moment to catch the feeling of sunshine on his bare skin. The square of hard soap smells of vanilla ice cream and is pretty useless, but the tingling, refreshing sensation of rubbing his wet face makes Khalid feel alert and clean. Much less like the sweating maniac he was before and more like the kid who once scored two goals in the Rochdale Junior League quarter-finals.

When Khalid opens his eyes he stares straight into the kindly face of Masud, the necklace-seller from Cairo whom they beat with a pipe and he met in the dark room in Karachi all that time ago.

But Khalid's not going there again. Oh no, not right now. Not while he's enjoying being outside under the shower. No matter how good it feels to imagine Masud in the shower next to him, he knows it might as well be David Beckham.

"Khalid, you are here? For why?" the vision whispers.

*For why?* The words pierce Khalid's brain for a moment. Prodding it to come up with an answer. But he can't if he doesn't know why. Know anything. Especially why the water is calling his name.

"Khalid. Khalid." Trickling his name—the water. Am I upside down? About to drown?

Stumbling forward, Khalid catches his big toe on a stone.

"Khalid! Take your hands from your face. Look at me. Look."

Instantly, Khalid opens his eyes, balancing himself by staring into the man's face.

"Masud. It's really you?" Shocked to recognize his friend from Karachi is actually standing there, cleaning his large ears with a corner of yellow soap.

"This I'm learning—they're bringing young people to Guantanamo? I'm not understanding. You can see me now?"

Nodding, Khalid steadies his breathing, deciding to believe his eyes as he takes in Masud's gaunt, clean-shaven face. Then he catches sight of the soldiers moving slowly to the end of the row to gossip, thinking the prisoners are too ashamed of communal washing to communicate with each other right now.

"I've been, like, weirding out in my cell," he tells Masud. "Too much time to think. I was, like, in Kand—Kand—Kandahar, as well."

"Kandahar? You?" Masud's shocked. "Me, they taking me from Karachi to Morocco. Hang me from wall for long time."

Khalid turns white as Masud explains how, instead of a pipe, they beat him with a strap attached to a wooden handle. Cracked his ribs. Kept him in an underground room in a shuttered house in the middle of nowhere. How one man held a gun to his chest for an hour and promised to kill him, saying his wife was already dead.

"That man, you see him." Masud points to a wiry man being led away. "Him went to Jordan. They have blind him one eye. Americans having many prisons like this all over world."

Taking care to hide his shock from a passing guard, Khalid whispers, "How do they get away with it? Where are the police?" Shrinking at the memory of his own abuse. Afraid they'll come for him again if he talks about the drowning, the sound of his own voice mixed with the noise of the trickling water tips his brain too close to the surface of his other self for Khalid's liking. For mentioning, yet.

Wiping water from his big, dark eyes, Masud continues, "This I'm knowing for sure is against the law they set in Geneva. Certainly. No one here has received a trial. They cannot keep a child like you on your own. This is cruel torture. What camp are you?"

"Delta Skelta." Khalid gestures to the nearest gray building.

"They take you for exercise from that camp? What happen your head? Bruises there you have. You arm. You must stop hurting you arm. Stop biting."

"I can't!"

"Khalid, no do this hurt to yourself. Stop. Ask for lawyers. For help. Shout for paper to write letters," Masud says quickly before the soldier hurries in their direction after getting suspicious of their friendly gestures.

Khalid turns his face away and blinks, trying hard to mix his tears with the veil of cold water running down his face.

"And sign everything. Say, 'Yes, Bin Laden he very good friend.' Agree all suggestion. Don't let this happen, Khalid. Take no pride in holding against threats. Pray, Khalid. Pray and learn. I learning better English. Me practice good," Masud shouts as they drag him off, dripping wet, to get dressed. "Remember, they will have to account to God for this one day."

A soldier forces Khalid to step away from the muddy water to make room for another man, head bowed, clutching a rag to wash himself with.

*That guy needs his toenails cutting,* Khalid notices while bending down to pull up the orange suit. But the harsh color suddenly smacks Khalid in the face, too bright in the shimmering sunshine for his sad, crying eyes to absorb. His fingers won't stop shaking and his body's trembling and suddenly he can't breathe.

*I did sign everything, Masud,* he thinks, *and look where I am now.*

"Did you catch the baseball game on TV last night?" a soldier asks his mate. His gun on Khalid's every awkward move, until he's shackled tight.

And all Khalid can think is, *How many seconds did that take?*

# 18

## EVERY SHRED

Khalid wakes up one morning to a new sound. The sound of music. Rap music throbbing in his ears. Drowning out the call to prayer. Drowning out the early-morning noises of the base he's become so familiar with.

Sparking the memory of the sound of house, techno and hip-hop booming from the old speakers in Nico's bedroom, black foam pads peeling from the corners. Khalid's suddenly back there, wide awake. Himself again. Clear in his head for a while. Recalling both of them singing, jumping along to the driving beat, rapping about life in mean streets that were way cooler than Rochdale. Hearts on fire, hands in the air—the delicious smell of fish and chips drifting up from the kitchen. In the ghetto—yeah. Khalid's just getting into the rapping when it stops. Ending as suddenly as it started. Making him think it's a trial run for something. An experiment to test the loudspeakers?

Khalid smiles, remembering a time when Nico wrote a rap of his own called "Hey Leona." It was rubbish. Nico was a good singer but he had too much confidence. Believing the moment he wrote it he was going to be the best in the world, he even entered a rap battle online, where one of the real rappers said it was the worst thing he'd ever heard in his whole life. And everyone, all the people logged on to the site to hear them battle it out, agreed.

The next day Nico bought a trumpet in the school jumble sale, even though it had a massive dent down one side. But Nico didn't mind. The rest of them did, though, Khalid especially. Every conversation after that was interrupted by a deafening blast from the old thing.

Khalid looks again and again at his life, as though he's searching through an old photo album for the millionth time. Days and weeks pass by with him revisiting incidents and events he hadn't thought anything of at the time. Always yearning to be back there, pushing the play button on Nico's CD player, looking at his collection of *Star Wars* figures on the windowsill, the poster of Eminem on the wall. It hurts so much sometimes it makes him want to end it all.

He really wishes he'd had a girlfriend. That Niamh had put her arms around him just once. He imagines being married to her and living in a nice big house with a flat-screen TV and music piped into every room. They'd have kids who were brilliant at football and clever as well, and that makes him feel good—for a bit.

With a sudden bout of pins and needles in his right leg, Khalid sits up, totally cross with himself for not yet being able to talk to girls in the way he should.

"First look her in the eye," Tony said. "Then give her a compliment, say something nice—I like your shoes. Girls have a thing about shoes. Say that, or nice coat. Anything you can think of to make her smile. Then lay a hand on her shoulder, know what I mean?" But Khalid finds all this stuff harder than it sounds. Although he likes to give the impression he's all right with girls, in actual fact he's just as awkward and lacking in confidence as Holgy, who blushes whenever a girl gives him the once-over.

Khalid's mind traces and retraces every reaction to every girl who's ever looked his way—who's ever passed him in the street and caused him to turn round. Like the first time he met Niamh in the library last year.

She joined the school a year ago when she was fourteen, having moved to the area with her family from Ireland. At first everyone sort of ignored her—she was just the new girl and she seemed nice and that, but so what? It was only when the GCSE art students put some of their work up in the library that Khalid became aware of her.

He'd wandered in there with Tony to hand back the books he'd borrowed for his English essay and couldn't help noticing the pictures on the walls. There was one of a doorway leaking blood from the handle that caught his eye first, then a pencil drawing of Mrs. Warren, the headmistress, which looked just like her.

"Here, look at this one," Tony called, dragging Khalid's attention to a painting of a filthy swimming pool with a stag beetle floating in it.

"Erghh, disgusting!" They were about to go when Khalid noticed a painting of a green grassy field with a single yellow buttercup in the middle. There was something so still and beautiful about it, he found it impossible to look away. He could almost smell the damp grass just by standing there.

He can almost smell it now.

"'The Last Buttercup' by who? Who Reilly? Is that Nim or Neem or what?" Khalid read out the title.

"It's pronounced 'Neeve.' The new girl, you know?" Tony said. "Bit of a boring picture, though—I told you girls love shoes. They love flowers too for some reason."

But Khalid carried on staring, impressed by how real the painting looked. What he didn't know was that Niamh was leaning on the table right behind him, watching his reaction.

"You coming, mate?" Tony said. "We'll be late for math."

"Yeah, yeah." Khalid turned round and fell straight into Niamh's green eyes. A bolt of electricity passed between them. It did. He can remember that feeling even now. It hypnotized him for what felt like ages, it was so full on. From that moment, wherever she was—sauntering down the corridor, chatting to her mates at the school gates, leaning on the classroom door—he could pick her out without even trying. A sharp buzzy feeling always told him exactly where she was in a crowd. If only he'd plucked up the courage to talk to her in the library. If only he hadn't gone all shy and walked away. And even though he's spoken to her many times since, he can't help regretting the wasted opportunity from way back then.

More fragile than he realizes, Khalid pitches forward and back, unable to keep still. Helplessly trapped by the rocking movement of his body, he can't believe how little fun he's had in his life. He's never been to an all-night party, had a real kiss or scored any girls, and while his friends are probably getting loads of action at home in Rochdale he's still stuck here in this kennel on his own. The imagined picture of playing Spin the Bottle with Niamh mixes with other terrible images of small children being blown up—burning hope and fear into his mind at the same time.

Then a few guys start yelling and soldiers begin storming into cell after cell.

"On your knees!" they yell, shackles swinging.

Khalid is ready on the floor, head bowed when they get to him. And, like before, they push him outside and along the hard, scrubby ground to another section of Camp Delta. Into another building and another room that resembles the last one in every detail except it has a room off to one side. A cell with its own private interrogation room and a door that opens to reveal a black table with two people sitting behind it.

Khalid's locked in, thinking, *Oh, so that's the way they're doing it now.* Recognizing them as the cold American woman from Karachi and the guy who stood behind her, saying hardly anything, while she and the posh English guy questioned him about being in Afghanistan. But this time, excited by running into Masud, knowing he didn't imagine him, Khalid decides not to be fazed by them. Not this time, no.

As the soldier attaches the chain from Khalid's left ankle to the bolt on the floor, pulling up a black chair for him directly opposite them, he holds his head high. Ready for them.

"Pakistan last time, wasn't it?" the woman says pointedly. "We've been looking at your confession again. Have you got anything to add?"

"Yeah, I'm really Bin Laden!" Instantly Khalid wishes he hadn't joked with her. By the look on her face, she's not in the mood to be messed with.

"You were part of an Internet plot to bomb various cities. It says so here in your signed statement. So now will you tell us the order of the planned bombings?" She bites her lip impatiently.

"I want a lawyer," Khalid says.

"A lawyer? I'm a lawyer, you can talk to me." She smiles patiently. "The name's Angela. This is Bruce. You remember."

"You're not a lawyer!"

"Yes, I am."

"No. No." A rare moment of sanity returns to Khalid as he looks into Angela's hard little face. A much-needed shot of confidence suddenly gives him strength. "I want to write to my family. You're not allowed to treat me like this. Where's the judge who found me guilty, then? Go on, where, you tell me? I haven't had any exercise. No education. Nothing. Well? I'm going to get you all back for this."

Bruce interjects now. "Come on now, we know you. We know exactly what your intentions are." He's sneering at Khalid's pathetic attempt to stand up for himself by shouting his mouth off.

"How? You don't know me. My intentions? What exams was I taking, then? Answer that! You can't, can you, because you're idiots. Nothing but creeped-up worms. Ask me how I know that. Go on, ask me!"

"We have a document signed by you which proves you and your accomplices plotted online to bomb a number of cities throughout the Western world. We intend to find out which city you planned to bomb first," Angela says.

"Yeah, but I made it all up. I take it all back. You locked

me up on my own, trying to make me crazy. Well, hard luck. Stopping me from sleeping. Not letting me get letters, or see a lawyer, or get any help. You're going to get in trouble for trying to kill me! You wait."

"You were friends with known members of al-Qaeda. We have photos." Bruce remains unfazed. "Plus members in England who have recently been arrested."

"What? What members in England?"

"We're not going to give you that information. We want the details of the movements and conversations you had with these people," Angela adds.

"But I don't know who they are!" Khalid shouts.

"You will tell us what you know about al-Qaeda!" Bruce says menacingly. "If not now, then tomorrow or the next day. I hope you'll think about how your actions are harming innocent people."

"Innocent people? I'm the innocent one here and you'll go to hell for this," Khalid warns in the same tone of voice Bruce is using. "There are millions of Khalid Ahmeds on the Internet. You've got the wrong one. What's wrong with you?"

"We know there are many members of al-Qaeda with your name. We have details of your involvement with the Taliban from other detainees in Afghanistan and here in Guantanamo."

"I don't know anyone here except for . . ." Khalid stops himself from mentioning Masud, unsure how the information will be judged.

"Except for whom?" Angela stares blankly ahead. "Perhaps you're thinking of Ahmad Siddique? Msrah Shia-Agil? Kamal Sadat? All known members of al-Qaeda?"

"That's total crap!" Then suddenly a flash of inspiration tells Khalid what's going on here. "Wait, I get it. You made these guys I've never heard of say they know me, sign papers, like you made me sign, and yeah, then you've got something on me. That's what you do, isn't it?"

"You're imagining things." Bruce frowns, glancing at Angela for agreement before calling the guards. Interrogation over, they untie his ankle from the bolt on the floor, but only after Angela and Bruce have left by their own secret door. Angela's heels clicking quickly down the corridor.

Over the next few weeks, Khalid's brought next door for questioning many times. Sometimes by Angela or Bruce, sometimes by another man who claims his name is Joe and the woman he's with is called Sal. Each time now he's given a chair before their insane questions begin.

"What would you do if you knew someone was planning a suicide attack?" Joe asks him.

"I have no idea," Khalid murmurs.

"Come on now, you must have friends who talk about this stuff?" he says.

"No," Khalid says. "Do you?"

"Why not trust us for once and tell us what you know?" He doesn't seem to notice how tired and thirsty Khalid's becoming.

"Leave me alone," Khalid begs.

"As soon as you give us some answers you can go."

Khalid scoffs. "Yeah, right. I've heard that one before. Liars."

Joe goes on and on trying to break him. As if the constant repetition will nudge his brain into remembering something.

Khalid never knows when the questioning will end and when they'll take him back to his cell. Soon realizing how pointless his answers are when all that happens is they come right back, asking the same things over again, until he can almost predict what's coming next.

Tired of sitting in the hard chair without a sip of water, Khalid trains his mind not to listen. Their voices drone on regardless. Although somewhere, deep inside, he knows even these terrible sessions are helping him to reclaim some part of his mind and his memory. Anchoring him to reality for short periods of time. Even just giving him the chance to sit in a chair. Look at different walls. Real shoes instead of boots. The smell of mildew and warm plastic in his nose instead of stale bread, rotten fish and warm water.

The following day, they up the pressure. No chair this time. Now Khalid's lying face down in the middle of the concrete floor. Arms out, his wrist shackles tied to a rusty iron ring. His chin is hard on the floor, while a man with gray hair and gray skin, smelling of cigarette smoke and lounging in a black chair, points a large spotlight at Khalid's face.

A tall, stocky woman in a navy suit stands behind him with arms folded, tapping two long red nails on her elbow. Her silver bangles clink and clank like keys.

The sound is broken by a sudden groan from Khalid.

Pain shoots up his arms as he wriggles his hands nearer to the ring bolted to the floor to try and ease the pain. Fully aware as he stares at the ring that it's a chain within a chain. Inside a locked cell. Inside a guarded prison camp circled by rows of high, curling razor wire. Its perimeter patrolled by soldiers carrying guns loaded with bullets, guarding a prison that's part of a base. A base situated at the tip of an island, in the middle of two oceans. Protected by water on one side and landmines on the other.

The dot on the floor is him, a sixteen-year-old boy. A boy who's looking at himself from every angle. Looking down on himself. Looking up from below. From underneath, then behind and in front. Backwards and forwards, images flash through his brain. Nothing but thin air covers his bones. His lungs. His heart. He can see his own dusty breath sweeping from his mouth.

Mirrors of light bounce from him like laser beams.

"Tell us the name of the fifth accomplice."

"Number five!" Three seconds. Khalid counts. That took three seconds to say: Num–ber–five. Yep, three.

"Admit your role in helping him!"

"Let me go. Let me go." Was that six seconds? Six words—could be five seconds, because the words are short.

Soon the door opens and the man leaves. The American woman is joined by another American man, around forty years old, who looks friendly. Getting Khalid's hopes up for a second. But after whispering to the woman, he turns to Khalid.

"What other international cities were you planning on bombing?"

"Burnley. Barnsley. Bolton. Accrington. Todmorden. Over

there. Yeah, Tod. Tod." How many seconds was that? Khalid breaks out in a fit of hysterical laughter. So hysterical, he can't stop. Annoying the man and woman so much they leave the room to the soldiers. Soldiers who kick and beat him. Anxious for their pound of flesh to get them through the day. The force of their anger is outside anything Khalid knows and he can't be bothered to count the number of kicks they give him.

And there are other times. When they won't give him water. When they push him against the wall to stub out their cigarettes on his arms. But when he laughs they stop. Giving up for a while—at least on him.

Khalid loses himself by pressing his face to the floor. Numbed by the light burning into his face, consumed by the desire to lick dirt from the cold concrete floor. The feeling he didn't really see Masud begins haunting his bleak, staring eyes once more.

Were Masud's eyelashes really that long and feathery when he saw him in Karachi? Or was the room too dark to notice them at the time? Khalid had been in pain, his eyes swollen from the beating when they kidnapped him, but still that face—it looked like Masud's. Now the chatter in his mind's suspended by the memory of the bleak room with the rough coir matting. The scruffy, handcuffed man whose swollen face was covered in bruises, sitting cross-legged on the floor. A strange, calm dignity about him. Yes, that was Masud, with the graying hair and beard. He mixed him up with the guy in the shower. That guy sounded like him. His head and face were bare but still he looked nothing like Masud, hair or no hair. It wasn't him. How could it be?

"What was the name of the fifth accomplice?" A voice interrupts his thoughts.

"I don't know," Khalid says.

"You don't know?" The man leans in to the spotlight.

"There wasn't anyone," Khalid sighs. Out of energy.

"No one at all?" he asks.

"Please let me go. Let me out," Khalid wails. "My arms hurt."

# 19

## THE JINN

Gazing at the lights, staring into the black hole that keeps flashing up the new imaginary face of Masud, Khalid hears the sounds of Ramadan start up again. Hungry men refuse breakfast. Later on refusing lunch and even dinner if it's brought before the sun goes down.

Praying for help. Praying for peace. Always praying, and it sounds nice.

Too weak to join in, Khalid's finding it hard to get up and go to the loo this morning, even though his bladder is full. And it's not just due to guilt because of Ramadan and the thought of a billion Muslims around the world who are fasting and praying while he's lying here doing nothing. It's because he knows another, even more dangerous thing is happening to his brain.

It started when he did or didn't see Masud in the showers. Now the jinn—the genies—have begun calling his name. Just as Masud had done. Or he thinks he might have done. Khalid can't quite remember why. Khalid met one before in the room in Karachi while he stared at that rug. Didn't a genie take him away then on a flying carpet? Back home to his family and friends.

"Khalid, Khalid." The voices grow louder and louder, then soften slightly when the ceiling lights dim. And when the voices drop, the world goes backwards. Khalid gets up from the bed and walks up and down to stop everything moving the wrong way, pacing the room to remind himself of his body. The shooting pain across one shoulder tells him he was bolted to the floor a short time ago and forces him to straighten his spine and rub his neck. How long ago was that?

A deep well of fear and worry adds to the feeling he's been a dimwit most of his life. Then suddenly he's aware of himself sweating and panicking. Standing stock still in the middle of the cell for no reason.

Listening.

Knowing whenever a sound stops out there, like when a soldier clunks to the end of the row and the name-calling finishes. Finishes. A hum starts up where the echo of the boots was before. A hum that rings and rings even though there's no proper noise behind it. Not even the voice calling his name. Then, when it goes quiet, Khalid can see a white space filling out in front of him, even though he knows he's imagining it.

He falls on the bed. Head in his hands. But the worse thing is, when the white space comes, it spreads everywhere. He can't stop himself sinking into it. That's why he wets himself from fear.

The warmth a pleasant feeling for a second until the smell hits him.

*No point getting up now.* Khalid shakes his head at himself. Shocked and half pleased at the same time. Shocked he's lost control of his bladder. Half pleased because the sensation brings him round and, the second he knows where he is, the white noise goes away.

Feeling better for a while. But not better enough to do anything, like pray or think. Especially not think about his family and what he's supposed to be doing for Ramadan.

This morning, when they brought the plastic tray for breakfast, he was still staring at it when they brought the next tray for lunch.

"What's up, man? This place stinks. Why you ain't touched your oats?" The smiling black guard stares at the tray. His voice soon changes to a gentle whisper. "Now come on, you gotta have something!" In the end, it's the dark, syrupy color of his eyes that brings Khalid back.

"I, um, I, yeah," the only thing Khalid manages to spit out. Part of him believing he's skipped breakfast because of Ramadan, while another part wonders how he completely missed hearing the soldier. Maybe he didn't shout his number this morning. Maybe he didn't fall on the bed when he went sweaty. Maybe he stood in the middle of the room for hours. He got up from the bed just now—didn't he?

The thought troubles him.

"Now, you eat this up, you hear me? I'll be back in ten and I wanna see this grub gone."

Khalid nods, pretending not to be a bumbling idiot. Then he takes a deep breath, thinking, *He'll be back in ten and I have to eat this up, otherwise they'll* . . . He doesn't know what will happen if he doesn't eat the cold canned potatoes, one after the other. Then the peas, one after the other. Then the . . . it looks like fish, but it smells like stinking cabbage. He'll be back in ten and then—what?

The rancid smell of urine overpowers Khalid as he stands with the tray in his hand in front of the hole, waiting. Waiting for the guard to come back.

Only he doesn't come back in ten. He doesn't come back in fifteen or twenty. The man only said that to get Khalid to eat up.

So Khalid stands there, tray in hand. Waiting for the man to come back. Refusing to sink into the white space or listen to the voices until after—yes, after the sound of footsteps disappears down the corridor. Refusing to believe in the white space that he's already in. Seeing it over there. Not here, next to his shadow.

When the prayers begin from every corner of the camp, Khalid's mind starts up for a second with the thought that maybe they've given him the wrong number.

Rubbing his forehead with his free hand, he bursts into tears.

His number is 256 and he knows now they've given it to someone else, because no one's called his number for a long time. So something must have happened. They used to call his number for showers. A soldier would shout, "256! 256!" Khalid would know then they were coming for him. Then it all stopped. Or did it?

"256!" Khalid yells to remind them, just as the beany hole slams open and another man, not the one with the kind eyes, grabs the tray.

"You're stinking the place out!" he barks at him. The beany

hole snaps shut. Khalid listens to black boots march on. Holes banging open and shut, on and on down the corridor. The sound of plastic trays clattering on the trolley. Then it all stops and the smell of urine takes over.

Suddenly the air conditioner starts up, blowing out freezing-cold air. Khalid moves back to the small bed, covering his shoulders with the blue blankets. Placing a white towel on his head, he sinks into the white space that opens up after the last of the prayers die away. Unable to resist anymore.

His empty brown eyes rest on the empty gray floor. There are only a few gravy stains and dead flies and his bare feet, but a less earthly realm takes over the moment he closes his eyes and makes space for the jinn, the genie man with the purple hat and big wide grin who slides him into his playground. Others come too, trailing behind Khalid, yes, behind him, if he meets their gaze. Shivering. Shivering. There's no need to run when the jinn come calling, because they live in a world where all Khalid's thoughts are acted out right in front of him. Some have wings, others have swords. Some have unfathomable powers. One has a wife by his side. Another has an army dressed in black.

You never know with the jinn.

Anything can happen with them.

Only when he hears the air conditioner click off does Khalid blink himself back to sitting on the bed. The blue blankets are on his shoulders. White towel on his head. Watching the jinn fall down.

"Go on, take everything with you," Khalid says. Leaving him with only the ash-colored walls, plus the sound of someone being dragged past the door, shackles scraping the floor. And then the unbroken noise of a man screaming, which has been going on for hours and is beginning to make Khalid feel he should join in.

There's something strangely soothing about the thought of screaming his head off. Anyway, it's better than listening to the yelling. That gets on his nerves. His mind becomes a flickering video camera, recording the screamer's pain, hunger, desperation. He can see him pacing the room, banging his head on the wall, biting his arm. Waiting for something to happen to break the monotony of wondering how everything went wrong. Of wondering how anyone can spend their time making other people unhappy. Kicking their heads in for saying the wrong thing. Smiling at the wrong time. Being other, not like, separate—them—they—demons—Muslims—insurgents—enemy combatants—extremists—terrorists—whatever. It's one big scam. And then go home and have a chicken dinner in front of the TV.

"Watch it, or we'll hang you up by the wrists to a wall. Be careful, dude, or we'll pour water down your face until you drown. No mistake, we're the good guys. We don't hit our kids but we're happy to kick you about. Next one, please."

More crap. How can you fight for peace? Peace doesn't understand war. Khalid shakes his head angrily. Why don't they get it?

"War doesn't work, you jackasses!" Khalid screams. Screaming high and wide until his throat rattles and throbs. The word "they" comes back to him in a flash of inspiration.

The word "you" cracks his spine like a mugger's fist, making him jump out of his skin. Then Khalid sees—there is no "they"—there is no "you." Bin Laden and al-Qaeda are just as bad. Look at the killing they've done and the hatred they've spread, because in the end there's just "us"—just "us." He stops yelling. Stops banging the door and falls back on the bed to wonder at the powers of the jinn.

The blue blankets are in a heap on the floor. The white towel is on the bed. The gray walls, though, are in the right place in front of his eyes.

Any minute now it will be dinnertime. Khalid can always tell when it's dinnertime. By now he knows the noises that come before the sound of the trolley wheels hitching up on the concrete to begin the round.

First there's the guards marching up and down twice in two minutes instead of once every three minutes. Sixty seconds— more than just a number—Khalid's counted them out a billion times. The slamming begins, getting nearer as the holes open and shut, and this time Khalid's ready for them. He's hungry now and he's hoping it might be sweetcorn and chicken lumps in a half-cold tomato sauce, because that's the only meal he can eat without wanting to gag. And the bananas are always nice. Even the ones with the black skins are much tastier than any of the food on the tray.

Khalid's mouth begins to water as the metal flap of the hole next to him slams shut. Arms ready to grab the tray. A whiff of putrid sardines lands on him but, hey, there's a sprig of parsley on top. No banana today, though. Chewing the parsley, he lines his mouth with the sharp taste before bracing himself for the slices of gray-sided fish in yellow gloop. Swallowing it anyway and saving the wrinkled peas for after, he pushes the four canned potatoes to one side.

At least the screaming guy has shut up for a bit. All he can hear is the sound of lots of plastic spoons scraping the last peas from the plastic trays, echoing down the row.

That's it for another day, until the volunteer prisoners come to slop out the rooms. One of them, Shafi, sometimes whispers to him from the Qur'an. Yesterday he said, "They claim that He has kinship with the jinn, yet the jinn know they will also be brought before him."

Khalid likes it when Shafi comes. With big, mad eyes, he looks something like 50 Cent but he doesn't rap. Khalid wishes he would rap, but no, his head is somewhere else entirely. Quoting from the Qur'an is his thing.

Soon it's slop-out time again and the door's unlocked. Two men point their guns at Khalid in case he goes crazy, like the man last week who rammed himself in the stomach with the mop handle. Keeping it there in a frenzied grip, sniveling and yelling until the soldiers dragged him away. Shafi had calmly carried on, going about his business without the mop, and washed the floor by hand with the man's white towel, he said.

"Two men they keeeksh." Shafi draws his fingers across his neck like a knife.

Khalid gasps, nodding, "They killed themselves?"

"Yes. Also five they going starving death. Nearly killed," Shafi says. "Don't do this."

"No, I won't." Khalid feels sorry for Shafi, because he's not quite right in the head. Not quite here. A good reminder you have to keep your feet on the ground in this place or the jinn will take over.

Shafi stares at the bucket. Looks at Khalid. Rolls his eyes a bit. Then whispers, "Signs are in the power of God alone!"

"What signs?" Khalid says, watching Shafi dunk the dirty mop in the dirty water.

"Signs." Shafi runs off with dripping mop and filthy bucket, leaving Khalid thinking about signs, wondering if rainbows are signs, because he used to like rainbows whenever they appeared in Rochdale—which wasn't often.

The expressions on the faces of the watching soldiers are ones of utter boredom until Shafi comes back with a bucket of clean soapy water, when they nod to him, then chat to each other in low voices.

"Eight more days and I get to go home," the first soldier says, scraping around for something to talk about.

"Twelve for me if you don't count today," his mate answers.

A foul smell of disinfectant drifts suddenly from the corner of the cell. Shafi pads off. The beany hole slams shut, leaving Khalid alone again, always at the mercy of these small interludes to provide a few minutes' company, entertainment and food for thought.

And sometimes his thoughts settle down. Settle down to ordinary things.

This time it's rainbows occupying his mind, plus the science of the color spectrum they learned in primary school, remembering the colors from the rhyme they were taught: "Richard of York Gave Battle in Vain." Red, orange, yellow, green, blue, indigo, violet. Rainbows are signs of the power of good, he decides. Bored enough to try and see good in whatever's left in his brain, he battles hard to come up with something else. But nothing wraps itself around him like the vision of the last rainbow he saw over the oak trees in the park.

He'd just spotted the perfect semicircle of radiant color over the high branches and when he turns round, there—tipping backwards on the bench—is Niamh, with her hair in a twist on top of her head. She smiles up at him. Did she smile up at him? Now she does. The biggest smile in the world. Her perfect face, beautiful mouth, made him feel like a million dollars for the rest of the week. A million dollars until the smell of disinfectant evaporates and the smell of urine returns.

Her face fades suddenly with the fatal realization she's not here. Curling up on the bed like a baby, Khalid reaches for the blue blankets to cover himself. Pulling the white towel over his face to stop the jinn from bothering him.

# 20

# EXERCISE

After six days of yelling and screaming, shouting at himself, listening to the silences and the pauses between them, things improve slightly when the library man, Will, comes with a cardboard box of old Reader's Digest condensed books.

"Any books, man?"

"Books?" Khalid can't see them at first. Where are they?

"Yep, books." Will smirks. "You want them?"

Khalid nods in the belief they're not actually being poked through the hole at him. "Yes." He carefully squeezes the word out and three small books tumble to the floor. Will's soft footsteps stroll away. Khalid listens to him saying the same thing to each man as he saunters from cell to cell.

Then, flicking open a yellowing book, Khalid puts it to his nose to smell the dusty pages and runs his fingers over the smooth covers. He uses them as playthings by lining them up in a tidy row on his pillow, then stacks them on the floor to enjoy the small footstool they provide. He even tries to walk up and down with a book on his head.

Over the next few days, Khalid reads the three condensed

stories in each book over and over again to himself until the characters become his friends.

"Come out, you Dam Busters. I know where you are. You want the rest of this bread roll, Atticus Finch? Well, too bad."

Everyone, prisoners and soldiers, sigh with relief at the sound of relative normality coming from Khalid's cell, and Khalid sighs, because the words spark a tiny flame of pleasure in his broken heart and mind. Bit by bit the white noise shrinks and the characters in the stories take over. Khalid finds himself poring over the words and thinking about the passages he's read for hours and hours, and some of the emptiness he feels dies away because the books become his family.

Until . . .

"Time to go," the guard yells just as Khalid opens *To Kill a Mockingbird* for the fourth time. It was one of the books on his English GCSE list but they hadn't read it before he left.

"Not now," Khalid says, but the door swings open and a bunch of tinkling shackles catch his eye. Forced to drop the book on the floor, Khalid's desperate to have the story back in his lap. Desperate for the special feeling of peace reading brings him, but the guards clamp his wrists and ankles tight and seem to enjoy leading him outside the moment the rain starts. They walk him through endless small puddles on the path towards the building next to Camp Delta and all Khalid can see is the face of Boo Radley in the reflections in the water.

The waves of hissing, cold rain do their best to stretch the cracks in Khalid's flip-flops to the limit. He slips and slides past the limp wet American flag hanging from the pole and is transported to another time, the 1930s, and another place, a small town in Alabama, and Scout, the six-year-old girl, and her brother, Jem, and the story waiting for him on the floor of his cell.

Where are the showers? Khalid's not sure. Everything looks different in the rain. There are no shadows for a start and a tingling freshness fills the air when, like magic, the rain suddenly stops. There's a smell of damp earth underfoot and, reaching the line of showers and their weak trickle of watery disinfectant, he's already soaked to the skin and aware this is going to be a pain in the neck.

Looking around routinely to see if any of the men are as young as him, Khalid glances briefly from one to the other. No one seems to be under the age of twenty.

Unless that man over there with his back to him is younger than he looks? Khalid tries not to stare. It's bad enough he's looking at all. Instead, he concentrates on washing his feet for a moment, but the smell of soap makes his nose tingle and he starts sneezing.

"Time's up, 256," someone shouts. But he's only half washed. Why is he ordering him to get dressed when he's covered in suds? The next man steps hurriedly under the trickle to take Khalid's place. A man who requires not one but two guns on him. Why two, when everyone else has one?

Khalid glances at him: a tall man with a firm, quiet look. There's nothing to mark him out from the crowd apart from a disfigured left hand with stunted fingers the size of a child's. He's standing proudly even though he's naked, so Khalid reckons he's someone important. The kind of bloke who holds his own in every situation, no matter what. His natural stance is dignified, almost regal, while Khalid knows his own is more like a beggar these days. Lost. Pathetic. Weedy.

Suddenly feeling worse, Khalid turns away embarrassed. Cross with himself for staring, even though he was only trying to work out why the man warranted two guns pointed at him. Maybe he's a suicide bomber or a real terrorist? A leader of some crazy group? Whatever he is, he stands out from the crowd.

Without warning, instead of going back to the cells, they march Khalid with dried soapy skin to a new recreation area which is nothing but a large open cage in the middle of a concrete yard. A yard surrounded by razor wire, enclosed by wire fencing, open to blossomy clouds and smelling of rain. They undo the shackles and lock the wire door.

Khalid stares at the shimmering wet concrete space which is about twenty steps wide. He's never been here before, although he's been in the camp for, he thinks, about—how long is it? They brought him here autumn 2002, he knows that much. He was fifteen then. The festival of Eid came and went without any celebrations and Tony Blair joined Bush and went to war in Iraq. When was that? Ages ago. He was sixteen at some point, March 11, although he doesn't know exactly when that was, because no one told him it was his birthday. And now, with Ramadan over, it's nearly December, so he's been here about a year. At this rate he'll be an old man and in a coffin before he gets out. Before he can run and jump and yell and do all the stuff he used to do without anyone making a fuss.

The thought makes his heart sink.

He walks to the end of the fenced yard, testing out his new-found space, and the sun suddenly peeps out from behind a sparkling spider's web criss-crossing the wire. The gray clouds part and a wide-open soft blue sky opens up. In that moment the vast space takes Khalid out of the yard and into the source of a bigger, deeper blue that's more blue than anything he's ever seen. So perfect a sight he can almost touch it.

A sudden whiff of wet grass lingers for a moment as Khalid imagines hours of walking round here, gazing at the light, and his heart skips a beat at the deep, sudden peace breathing fresh air gives him.

Two minutes later, the sound of padding footsteps breaks his trance. Khalid widens his eyes as the guards bring two men through the gate. Both are as surprised as Khalid to be here. Their shackles are undone and, smiling from ear to ear, the men gaze round the yard as if it's a football stadium or something.

For a minute, Khalid's annoyed. Why did they have to come? He was enjoying having the place to himself.

The guards lock them in and wander off to one side. Leaving the three of them staring at each other, all wondering if they're allowed to talk or not. Unaware what the rules are and bewildered by the sudden freedom to move about as they like.

"*As-salaamu alaikum.*" The black guy speaks first.

"*Wa alaikum as-salaam,*" Khalid and the smaller man quickly answer.

Luckily, the first guy also speaks English.

"My name's Ali Abaza. I come from Ghana but live in

Saudi Arabia most of my life."

"I'm British," Khalid replies. "I'm sixteen."

Ali widens his smile to show off a row of perfect sugar-white teeth. "Only sixteen?"

"Yeah, the name's Khalid Ahmed."

"Balendra Varshab," the smaller guy butts in. "Bengal, Bengal." Unable to understand a word of English, he nods while repeating his name and country until eventually Khalid turns away. Then Balendra walks a few steps to the end of the wire and lies down on his back. Arms behind his head, he does a few sit-ups. The sudden panting and thudding are an unwelcome addition to Ali and Khalid's conversation as they pace the perimeter of the fence.

Eyes on the ground, talking non-stop, Ali quickly explains he's twenty-seven and was working as a lawyer when they picked him up for questioning. Because he speaks four or five languages and has traveled in the West as well as the Middle East, he aroused their suspicions after 9/11. A devout Muslim, he was accused of helping fundamentalists and Islamists working on dirty bombs. Men they refused to name.

"How can I defend myself when I don't know what I'm accused of? Tittle-tattle, gossip, lies, that is what has brought me here. If I told you what they did to me in Bagram you would weep." Ali shakes his head with the same disbelief that Masud, the necklace-seller, had shown.

Khalid watches him choke back his anger, running his hands across his shaved head, back and forth as if it's hurting.

"Are there other kids here?" Khalid says at last.

Ali thinks for a moment. "A young boy was on the same

plane as mine from the camp in Bagram. He was no more than twelve years. Another one I saw being taken for interrogation in Saudi. He was also younger than you. At that time his mouth was bleeding. He had his hands over his eyes because his face was covered with bruises. All he did to deserve that was "pretend" to be sick when they played the American national anthem one morning. A guard told me that himself. And he said it turned out the boy was actually sick." Ali sighs. "I studied hard for a better life. I had my eye on getting married. Now my life has changed forever."

Khalid wants to tell him he's not the only one. "Where are the 9/11 bombers, then?" he asks instead. "Someone here must be a terrorist. Where are they?"

"I wish I knew the answer to that. Let me tell you this, Khalid: I was researching an important subject which I know implicated me in some way. Learning about the many secret prisons all over the world. Guantanamo Bay is the famous one, but there are many more. They are everywhere. They employ torture as many have done throughout history to gather information and I will tell you, being a lawyer, this subject of human rights is the closest thing to my heart."

From the corner of the compound, Balendra sits up suddenly. His forehead is dripping wet and he pats his head, then his heart to calm down, congratulating himself on so much exercise by muttering rapidly. The soapy smell of his sweat drifts towards them. Ali stands rigidly beside Khalid, staring into the distance. Staring out beyond the fence. Beyond the soldiers watching them from the whitewashed wall, past the concrete and rolls of barbed wire, beyond the sky of Cuba and the sea, to his large office on the second floor of a small block in Saudi Arabia.

"My office is crammed with books of every kind. Books about King Solomon's Temple, the Roman Empire, the Islamic court of Cordoba, the Torah, Greek theology, poetry, architecture, art," Ali says.

Khalid imagines the huge room with books on the desk, on the chair, stacked everywhere on the floor. The sun peeps down on his silent shadow as Ali travels back there in his mind.

"The world learned about chivalry and brotherhood from Islam." He pauses to make sure Khalid has heard this great truth. Only when Khalid nods, does Ali continue talking.

"A great tradition of learning was spread across Europe during the Dark Ages by Islam, which not only tolerated every other religion but allowed them to flourish. The major religions lived side by side under Islamic kindness. Remember this was at a time when Jews were being hounded to death by Christian Europe."

Uplifted by Ali's knowledge, Khalid's heart begins pounding with fear. Fear they're going to be interrupted at any moment, if not by Balendra then by the guards. One of whom stretches his shoulders, glancing at Ali, who's deep in thought.

"At that time the Islamic court in Cordoba in Spain was packed with poets, artists, philosophers, mathematicians, while the rest of Europe, including the aristocracy, could barely read. They were too busy persecuting non-Christians," Ali says.

"Cordoba, I've heard of that," Khalid says quickly, to show Ali he's not as stupid or as crazy as he looks.

"Islam is not a medieval culture, like they pretend in the

West. Evidence of its sophistication can be found in every library in the world. And the basis of that well-documented sophistication is Islam's tolerance of other religions and other cultures."

"Yeah, but what about the war with Israel? The stonings, the beheadings and stuff?" Khalid asks. "The way women are treated? Forcing them to wear the hijab?"

"These things have nothing to do with the rich Islamic culture that still exists." Ali frowns.

"Yeah, but how come it's happening?" Khalid has to make the point, because he sometimes has a lot of trouble understanding this stuff himself.

"Let me tell you, for hundreds of years Muslims and Jews lived in peace. The Ottoman Empire was torn apart after the First World War, when it was divided between different countries. The imperialists drew lines on maps without thought to the people who had lived there for thousands of years. New states were formed, countries with new names like Iraq. Suddenly Kurds, Sunni and Shiite Muslims were made to live together where before they occupied different cities and had their own systems of government. Divide and rule, you have heard this term?"

"Yeah, yeah, my history teacher told us about that! Divide the people so they fight each other and then you can rule them when the country is in chaos. That's what happened with the British Empire, wasn't it?" Khalid says. Pleased he's able to act as if his brain is still working in front of someone as clever as Ali.

"Yes, and many other empires. For eighty years politicians have divided the Muslim from his Jewish neighbor and brother.

And now from his Christian brother. Unification and peace are the only things worth fighting for. Any act you commit with anger, hatred, aggression, unkindness in your heart that hurts another human being of whatever religion is not an act of tolerance—so cannot be considered. Not for any reason."

"But the stonings and stuff are done by Muslims. Maybe they don't feel any anger or unkindness when they're doing it?" Khalid says.

"This behavior has been learned from history. Politics and culture must not be confused with religion. This issue is not a religious one. Let us not forget, Khalid, at this moment, as we speak, men and women in America are being sentenced to death. They are being killed day after day, year after year without end. These deaths are taking place because of their laws, in their country. Do you blame Christianity for this, or those who make the laws? Perhaps you blame the people? Or those who are paid to execute? Many think it is correct for these executions to happen. Why do they believe this?"

"It's political, right. OK, then. Nah, I don't believe in the death penalty for any crime." Khalid's mind spins from so much information and talk.

"Oxford and Cambridge universities in your country, England, were modeled on the Muslim seats of learning in Spain. Prejudice has worn us down, but we will rise again as the noble, peace-loving religion that we have been throughout time. We are not demons."

"But the bombings and that?" Khalid wonders what Ali's going to come out with next.

"Any person who commits an act of terrorism violates the

laws of Islam," Ali says.

Khalid's confused, wondering how to reply, when suddenly Balendra's beside them, smiling. Breathing forcefully, he grabs his hips to steady himself.

Ali turns, happily smiling back, white teeth sparkling like pearls.

A familiar noise of squeaking boots forces them to glance at the fence, where two soldiers are approaching. Keys at the ready.

There they are, the same as all the others. Middle height, medium build, brown-haired, slightly stocky soldiers. Leather gun straps making a rubbing sound on their shoulders as they walk. An overdose of strong aftershave disguises the smell of their sweating skin.

"Take note from the Qur'an, Khalid. 'God is not so weak as to need a protector.'" Ali's led away, his perfect shadow beside him.

Khalid catches sight of his own shadow. Straightening himself to alter it, he glances up to see the clouds closing in again. A vulture flaps overhead while he wonders at the things Ali's told him. Realizing he knows nothing about anything. Now the lights are on concerning the history of Islam and how misunderstood the subject is—even in his own mind— several arguments start up in Khalid's brain.

Arguments where he takes both sides, sees both sides, defends both sides. Pointing his finger at his friends if they disagree.

At anyone who'll listen.

His mind burns with imaginary people who agree with the death penalty. He argues with himself until he becomes exhausted. At the same time, he wonders where his brain has been all these years while he's been playing football down the park, gaming on the computer, thinking about Niamh. He'd ignored the important things in life and regrets not listening to what Dad tried to teach him.

Caught in a roller-coaster of strong emotions that fling him from wall to wall. From sanity to craziness, with nothing in between. The chat with Ali has added more complications to the whirl of activity in his head. Only the books Khalid's been reading can take him out of himself and back to a more solid, reliable world. Beginning, middle and end. Where the problems belong to someone else and everything about them is more interesting and easier to understand than what's happening to him.

# 21

# HAIR

This morning, Khalid lies on the bed, hands tracing the itchy grid of dark stubble covering his head. Tired. So tired. Tired of thinking about Ali and his clever brain while his own twisted mind is caked with moss. And scared. Scared that any day now they'll shave him again.

"I haven't got lice!" Khalid shouts. No answer. There's only the sound of padding footsteps heading away from him. Are they afraid that if they don't cut and shave them some ugly monster will grow on their heads and do them in? Or maybe the shaved heads make it easier to tell who are the detainees and who are the soldiers, as if the orange uniforms aren't enough. Or, more likely, they do it to make them feel less like men and more like laboratory mice.

The library man, Will, came yesterday with two more yellowing Reader's Digest condensed books and a copy of *National Geographic* magazine. But it's not enough. Khalid had read both books and the *National Geographic* from cover to cover by this morning. He's read the article about Sri Lankan elephants twice and even found time to glance at the Qur'an again.

What's he going to do for the rest of the week until Will comes back?

"Please can I have more books?" he asked the female guard at breakfast time.

"Buddy, you've had your books," she says.

"Yeah, but I've read them. Can you maybe give mine to someone who's read theirs? Swap them over?"

"You bet your sweet bippy you've read 'em," she crows. "What else have you got going on? Nada! Hey, relax. Chill, man. I'll maybe see what I can do."

"Thanks very, very much." Khalid gives her a wild, smarmy, begging look for luck and she says, "Oh, you guys—some nerve!"

It was worth a try.

Now he's waiting for two things today. The head shaving, which he thinks is more than a week overdue, and, hopefully, a couple of new books to read, deciding it'll be great if the shaving comes first, because afterwards he'll have the new books to look forward to.

Yeah, the barber will loosen his collar so a few sharp hairs drift down his spine to irritate him, like he always does. Khalid expects to be butchered by him yet again. Whereas, if the books come first, he'll be sad and fed up knowing he can't enjoy them until he's been cut to shreds by the shaver. Maybe even find he's read them before, which will make him feel even worse. Knowing then he's got nothing to look forward to.

It's all so complicated.

Khalid goes over the timeline of the day's expected events so fully, his heart starts racing, while his neck begins itching from imaginary stubble. Hope soon fades of a simple solution when breakfast arrives, but no barber or books. Not even a shower, which he badly needs.

Between avoiding the scary pictures at the back of his mind and waiting for the barber and books, his heart's beating faster, pounding hard with worry and waiting. He's getting himself more and more worked up and the sweat pouring over him is making the waiting worse. The air conditioner has gone off at the hottest time of the day and, being on the kind of timer only Einstein could figure out, there's no chance it will start working right now.

Lunch has come and gone before footsteps come to a halt outside his door and someone shouts, "256—barber!" Goosebumps break out on Khalid's neck at the sound of the loud voice. He knew it. Knew it was barber day today! As long as the books don't come while he's there, all will be cool.

Khalid jumps up, arms at his side, waiting for the door to click, bang and thump open. He lifts his hands for the shackles to be tied. Hurrying the guard in his mind so he can get the whole shaving thing over with and be back here for the new books that he prays will come later. He was right about the hair, wasn't he?

The moment the guard leads his dragging shape into the corridor, Khalid notices the linoleum's been washed. Usually there're tiny bits of dirt and dust in the crevices between the bubble-like shapes but today there's none. Then he realizes the last time they took him out for a shower was before lunch and maybe they don't sweep the corridor until later. Khalid tries to remember the sound of sweeping after lunch.

Did they sweep the floor without him noticing?

He promises himself he'll listen more carefully tomorrow, to see whether the sweeping routine has changed from early evening to early afternoon.

He knows tracking these changes is pathetic but it's something concrete to latch on to—as well as something he can congratulate himself about when he works out the new routine. Occasionally he even thinks he can read the guards' minds.

This one, for instance, look at him. He's not as tall as Khalid and his thick, meaty neck throbs, the large vein pulsing as he walks. His dead eyes stare straight ahead. Khalid guesses he's wondering whether to have a second helping of chips with his steak for dinner. It occurs to him that this soldier looks more brain-dead than most.

Khalid steps into the sunshine and once again the same delicious blue sky greets him, but with no hint of rain in the thin clouds. Quickly, he takes in the full force of the shimmering light on the pale earth and a beautiful, sparkling spider's web swinging from a truck mirror.

Light reflects light until his head is pulled down again by the weight of the waist chain it's connected to. He finds it easier, though less entertaining, to follow the flickers of sunshine passing over the guard's black boots. The sound of hammering in the distance tells him yet another fence is being erected.

A group of soldiers drop cardboard boxes beside the door of a shed. More soldiers patrol the fence with squeaking boots as Khalid's led past an open truck smelling of bananas.

In the distance, more trucks, more bland buildings. More impossible-to-see-through fences. More rocks. The sunshine quietly points Khalid's eyes to the lizard on the wall of the open building. Its pale body is a perfect match for the spotted, uneven concrete it's glued to and the sight makes Khalid smile.

Several men stand hunched and bowed in a line, guards at each side. A fleeting glance of recognition passes between Khalid and the man just arriving behind him. It's Ali Abaza from the recreation ground. Khalid shuffles round, twisting his head slightly to get a better look. He expands and then relaxes his chest to make the abrupt movement look more natural to the guard standing right next to him.

Ali lifts his head, nodding quickly. A horde of unspoken thoughts and feelings pass between them. The snap message from Ali's eyes tells Khalid things are worse than they were and he wishes he could explain what's been happening. Khalid nods politely, as best he can.

Just then the guard shoves Khalid forward, blocking the gap between them. The whining sound of the electric razor cuts off his thoughts with the more pressing threat he'll be next. The wordless conversation is sadly over.

The noise of the clippers and a faint breeze distract Khalid from the sight of men's shadows lined up beside them. The shapes merge with the guns and soldiers' boots and there's not a breath of energy between the men and their shadows. Everyone's as dead as dead can be.

The strange sound of loud breathing and the whiff of burning hair confuse Khalid for a moment as he's pushed down on the stool. Quickly, he catches sight of a wide face beaming with pleasure as the man slices into his scalp with pink hands. Beside Khalid is a small wooden table with a bucket of water for rinsing the blades and a silvery tin box with spare batteries and a face shaver with three cutters. A tin box Khalid's never noticed before.

The chrome clippers begin whizzing and spinning to cut him open in a hundred places and the razor threatens to slit his ears and gouge his eyes out if he moves a muscle. Preventing Khalid from catching anyone else's eye with an elbow in his shoulder blade, the barber nudges him. But when Khalid's head is forced down, then sideways for the barber to clip his neck, he catches his own eyes clearly reflected in the shiny surface of the tin box. Tripping him into the sight of an unknown skinny face covered in stubble, black eyes staring out like someone mad.

The more he looks, the more shocked he is by the hugeness of his chin. Did it always look like that? With a swift flick, his head is turned and the reflection disappears. The glinting blades flash past his forehead.

This one's enjoying slashing Khalid's temples to pieces. Prodding his ears out of the way. Slicing his scalp as if he's trying to lift it off. So aware of his power, he gives a little laugh when he slides into an eyebrow and Khalid recoils, only for the barber to grab his chin and push his forehead back with thumping fists. Khalid can do nothing but tense up, gritting his teeth.

A drop of blood dribbles down his face and slips over his lips.

The barber jerks Khalid's head swiftly, one more time, to finish off his low hairline, sending itchy hair flying down his back. Scraping his skin so hard, red weals form on every part of his sore, dry head and neck.

For as long as Khalid can remember, a visit to Robbie the barber in Rochdale was a quick, pleasant non-event. After asking what he wants, the barber does the cut with a smile and a few fast, gentle strokes. Maybe a kind word about his thick hair and the new aftershave he's wearing as he softly brushes loose hairs from Khalid's neck before shaking the clippers for the next guy to take his place.

This barber flings the chrome clippers in the tin box and replaces them with a black battery-powered shaver. He has no use for creams, soaps or brushes. There's nothing to ease the attack on the teenage hair on Khalid's face as the shaver is applied with the same vengeance as the clippers.

Khalid had never been shaved by anyone else until this prison ordeal began. At home in Rochdale he'd started shaving a couple of times a week when he was fourteen and he was always careful not to cut himself. This shaving feels like another abuse. Three blades thump into his cheek, mangling his chin to pulp.

At last it's over. Khalid's back in his cell. Shivering. Sore. Miserable. The blasts of ice from the air conditioner are turning the room into a fridge. Wrapping himself in blankets and a towel, he crouches on the bed, feeling sad and empty, going through the process of trying to keep warm when actually he doesn't care.

Was that really his face? Khalid runs his hand over his chin.

It's not that big, is it? Chins don't change shape, do they? How come his face is so long and skinny? He knows he used to look better than that. Or maybe he looks peculiar because the tin's not a proper mirror and that's why the reflection is odd.

Struggling to settle his mind, Khalid gazes at the spots of blood on the white towel hanging from his shoulders, then gently explores the bumps and dents in his skull for the secret place where three prickly hairs escaped the clippers. He wiggles the ends, sharp as needles, with the tip of a finger.

Dinner comes and goes. Still no books.

"You bet your sweet bippy. Thanks for nothing," Khalid says, echoing the words of the female guard from this morning. Listening to footsteps fading down the corridor with a faint clack, he knows they're hers. Doing his best not to stew, or lose his mind because of the lack of fairness or order in his life, he rests his sore head on his hands. Without a pillow, his neck aches. His back aches.

The smell of the thin foam mattress reminds him of the smell of little Gul's dolls. Pressing his nose in the damp scent until he turns on his back to stare at the ceiling, Khalid finds the strength to join in the prayers before he falls asleep.

During the night he wakes up several times with red eyes to look out suddenly as if he's seen a ghost. He closes them slowly only after he's checked every inch of the tiny cell. Even his flip-flops. And all the time there's a shaft of cold air blowing on his bleeding head.

What would Dad say about the picture at the front of his brain that won't go away? Probably tell him his life's wasting away and his big dreams have come down to a park bench and a pretty girl. Sounds about right. She flashes up a lot, Niamh. As if she'll look at him twice when he gets out of here. As if she ever did. Anyway, who cares? She probably hates Muslims. Everyone else seems to. Why not her?

She was in his mind just then, but Khalid can't remember why she ran away—leaving him devastated by the sight of her disappearing back. Wavy hair flying. Oh yeah, he tried to—never mind—that was it. He would never try—not in real life. Not in a million years. No way would he tell Dad about that. And, if by some miracle he did, then Dad would frown, yeah.

"Tell the young what not to do and they will forget the not and go out and do whatever you told them not to," he once said to Mum when Aadab was being naughty. Khalid smiles at the memory of Mum chasing Aadab round the kitchen. Chairs scraping the floor, Aadab screaming her head off and giggling at the same time, the bowl of oranges on the table in danger of sliding right off and crashing to the floor. It was so long ago, he can hardly remember what his sisters look like. What the kitchen looks like.

Khalid turns on his side, moving closer to the wall, not prepared to think about Niamh or his family any more. Setting them aside, because toying with pleasant memories just leaves him more upset, frustrated and exhausted than before. Forcing himself instead to listen to the last clunking of the doors along the row being checked to make sure they're locked tight. Then to the sound of his heart.

He knows the books help keep the voices at bay. Make the white space go away. What will he do if they don't bring him more soon?

And he did see Ali. There's no doubt in Khalid's mind he was there at the barber's. But he'll never be certain he really saw Masud.

The air conditioner starts buzzing out even colder air, chilling Khalid to the bone. Turning the thin mattress icy.

# 22

## NEWS

Khalid wakes up, puts a hand over his mouth and listens to the sound of vomiting. At first he thinks it's coming from inside his own head. But—there it is again. Wondering what the guy's chucking up when the breakfast trolley hasn't even come yet. As suddenly as it starts, the sound of vomiting stops and Khalid turns over. For the last three days he's been keeping track of the days by scratching a mark on the wall just below his bed. He heard the guard yesterday say, "Happy holidays, Rusty." So Khalid knows it's holiday time, but is it Easter? July? Or what?

It could still be December for all he knows. It's a little cooler in the mornings than it was a week ago and although there are no winters here, the last time he went for a shower the crisp blue sky reminded him of a day with a sky just like this. When was that? It was December then. So it's probably January again. When was Eid? When everyone shouted to each other across the wires? Ages ago? Or just recently? When did they bring this lot of books? Was it five days ago or yesterday?

Khalid wishes he'd started making the marks when he did

know what time of year it was. Now all he has to go on are a few scratches that tell him another day is over. Today he decides to find out what the date is when breakfast comes. He needs to know the precise date all of a sudden or he'll have to keep pacing the room. The sudden clacking of trays forces him to run to the door, rehearsing the question in as few words as possible.

"What's the date?" Or, "What's the date today?" That'll do it—practicing out loud so he's totally prepared for his first human contact of the morning. Patiently, he waits to catch the guard's attention.

A simple thing, today's date is something he once took for granted, had easy access to on a daily basis. Could find out in a flash. Now this stuff is a stranger to him. If the guard chooses not to answer there's nothing Khalid can do.

In a jiffy, the white tray's shoved through the hole faster than usual.

"What's the date today?" Khalid quickly says, grabbing it.

The guard ignores him and moves on.

"What's the date?" Khalid yells. Blitzed by the sound of clacking trays, spoons and plodding feet, the trolley relentlessly thunders up the linoleum away from him, Khalid yelling, "WHAT'S THE BLEEDIN' DATE?" If only he had answered. If only—then today would be different. The day would have started with a victory instead of yet another failure. Now the question will go round his head all day long. His chance of standing firm on the cell floor is gone.

"What's the date? What's the date? What's the date?" Like a mantra. Stifled as he is into repeating the question he woke up

237

with—all day. Getting an answer is his only chance of moving on to another phase of thinking.

"What's the date? What's the date?"

Saddled with saying the same words over and over again, Khalid's childlike insistence begins to drive everyone on the row insane until someone shouts from the cell next to him, "It's the day after yesterday, you dorkhead!"

You dorkhead? *You dorkhead?* Only one person in the universe calls Khalid a dorkhead. Disbelief takes over as he grips the wire.

"Tariq?" Rattling the fence with all his might, Khalid yells, "You're the dorkhead, cuz!"

"Keep your voice down," a soldier shouts. "It's January first, 2004."

"DON'T CALL ME A DORKHEAD AGAIN!" Khalid yells.

"I told you to shut it!" a guard warns.

Silence. No other voice rings out.

Khalid leans in to the wire. Nothing but a concrete wall lies between them but there isn't a sound. Just the rumble of a shackled man moving past with cringing steps. The muscular shapes of soldiers go by, hurrying him along, leaving the smell of men and rubber boots behind for Khalid to block out.

"Tariq? Is that you?" Khalid whispers to a broken link in the fence. "Tariq. Tariq."

His hands fall from his mouth as he walks backwards to the bed. Unsure he's heard right.

Someone shouted "dorkhead." Didn't they? The name

didn't sound inside him. It was out there for sure. Or was it? Then it comes to him, he might have said it. That's how it happened. Khalid said it himself, because the moment he heard the date—he . . . Or did someone shout the date afterwards? No, no. Or maybe yes. Today might even be . . . what was he thinking? Thinking Tariq is the other side of the concrete wall. How could it be him? Right here, next to him? Why won't he answer?

"TAREEEK!"

"Cut it out, pal," a woman gently calls. Buying him a moment's peace before his mind speeds backwards.

It's her—leaning forward—on the bed. Niamh, tut-tutting. Her long, wavy hair cascades from the fist she clutches to her head. Anchoring Khalid to the dream, she'll stay forever—or at least until Tariq calls him a dorkhead once more. Won't that be cool? He can introduce them to each other.

But Tariq's not here and neither is Niamh. What about that? Khalid's suddenly wrapped in a shudder of pain so strong, he punches the wall to plug his fury.

"Stop that, pal," the voice says again. Covering him in a wave of calm, unexpected sweetness that forces Khalid to listen carefully in case she calls him pal one more time.

"You don't wanna make things any worse than they are," she says, with pretty light brown eyes.

*Don't I?* Khalid wonders, shocked by the sudden sight of his swollen knuckles. Quickly he stuffs his hand in his mouth before turning round slowly to see a pretty woman in her early twenties with a reddish ponytail, nice smile and perfect teeth standing in front of him.

Amazed by the sight, the smell of expensive perfume drifting towards him.

"My name's Lee-Andy. I got here a few days ago from my home town, which is a long way from here, near the North Carolina line. Guess you don't know where that is. Too bad. Want some chocolate?"

Khalid blinks and manages to nod as she hands him a thin brown wrapper. The more she smiles, the weirder he feels. His eyes widen with shock at the present she's given him.

"Let me do that for you. Your hands look pretty sore." Lee-Andy cracks open the wrapper while he watches in amazement. Is that chocolate smell hiding the fact the bar's laced with poison?

"See ya." Lee-Andy nods. The throbbing pain in Khalid's hand spreads quickly up his arm as she turns to leave.

"You forgot to say 'Happy New Year,'" Khalid says.

"Oh my, that's terrible. Didn't know you guys cared about that stuff." From the tone of her voice, Khalid believes her. The rhythm of her ordinary, everyday kindness takes him by surprise, shocking him more than the gift of chocolate.

"That's OK. Do you know what the man's name is in the cell next door?" he asks.

"I don't, but I can find out for you." She smiles apologetically. "I'm back here at seven in the morning. Now you stop yelling and hurting your hands or they'll take you somewhere you don't wanna go. You hear me?"

Yep, he hears her all right. The second she's gone, Khalid sits on the bed and nibbles the chocolate to make sure it's real. Taking his time to roll each morsel round his mouth and breathe in the sweet smell, he savors the perfection of the rich, smooth taste that spreads over his tongue like honey.

He's almost halfway through the little bar when he pulls himself up. Wrapping the remaining squares under his pillow to save for later, he remembers how much he's taken this taste for granted in the past. Seeing himself munching Fruit and Nut bars, Twix, Flakes, Kit Kats, Galaxy, Bounties, on his way to and from school, without any real appreciation for the amazing pleasure of every mouthful.

When night comes, the ceiling lights dim slightly and Khalid finally forgets his painful hands. Distancing himself from the noise of someone coughing somewhere and the men calling goodnight to each other in Pashtu and Urdu across the doors, he hears only the high-pitched, squeaky voice of the man he thought was Tariq, who is loudly, too loudly, joining in.

Listening hard for a sign that might tell him who he is, Khalid knows deep down it can't be Tariq. It's highly unlikely they'd put him next door. And anyway, how much can Khalid learn from a strange voice like that? A voice that reminds him of the irritating short beeps of a reversing truck.

Khalid unfolds the empty chocolate wrapper and presses it flat to his nose. That was nice of her to give him the chocolate. Sniffing the silvery paper hard to stop himself from thinking about Tariq. Not even the memory of his new friend, Lee-Andy, and her small act of kindness, which was a hundred times more uplifting than she will ever know, can alter the deep-seated hatred and contempt he feels for his cousin.

*

The next morning when he wakes up Khalid doesn't feel quite as stupid as he did yesterday. Today he has one small thing to look forward to—a conversation with Lee-Andy, who might just bring him another chocolate bar and tell him Tariq's not the man in the cell next door.

After morning prayers, his back to the wire, Khalid waits for the soldier who's bound to peer in as he walks past, draw closer, pause, then march on. When he's gone, ignoring the bursting anticipation in his guts, Khalid bangs his elbows on the door, whispering, "You're the dorkhead. Not me!" His whole life surges into this present moment as he listens for an answer.

"Quiet, he's coming back," the voice squeaks. Khalid listens to the sound of heavy boots striding purposefully towards them. But the dim-witted soldier appears to see nothing more than the image Khalid gives him of a young man standing with his head bowed. Staring at the floor. Fingers gripping the wire. Probably waiting for breakfast. The squeaky voice starts half singing, no doubt to give the impression he's praying, until the soldier clumps off, then mutters, "Khalid? Is that you? It's me, cuz."

"Shut up," Khalid says, tears streaming down his face.

"When did you get picked up? They picked us all up on the same day, I'm guessing," Tariq says.

"Us all?" Khalid asks, daring to believe it really is his cousin.

"Yeah, all the gamers. I heard about the Australian guy in Islamabad when they took me there. Almost killed him, the bastards. It's best you don't ask me about his injuries. A guard

242

told me what happened. I bribed him, I'm not ashamed to say, with my gold watch. From my understanding it was that gamer who did us in. He said we planned to bomb the Houses of Parliament and the White House. Can you believe this?"

"NOOOOO!" Khalid yells, fury rising. The distant sound of footsteps thudding towards him with armfuls of shackles echoes through the clawing noise coming out of his mouth.

"YOU were the one who set up the links. Only YOU had everyone's real names and locations. That's why you didn't answer me yesterday."

"Shush! How could I answer you yesterday? I didn't know it was you. Even when you called me cuz I never imagined it was you." Tariq pauses for a moment as if to remember. "How can you accuse me?"

"Liar," Khalid mutters.

"What? It wasn't until that female soldier said you were asking for my name and she said yours was Khalid that I got it. The guards were listening to you going crazy, and you are completely crazy if you really believe I did something wrong. Now they're—"

"No. No." The door smashes open. Two guards walk Khalid backwards into the wall. Causing him to float out of himself as he knocks his elbows and head on the concrete. Forcing him into the orange suit, the shackles clicking quickly into place like latches. Then they cart him off to a thunder of rap music which blasts suddenly from the single loudspeaker in the corridor to shut the rest of them up as breakfast's served.

Shocked by their sudden anger, Khalid struggles as they

lead him down the row. One or two men bang their doors and shout to show support, but the noise is lost in the breezy rap beat throbbing in his ears. His head is dragged down by the waist chain and the back of his neck starts aching. A new sharp pain pricks his shoulder. As he shuffles along this white linoleum there seems never to have been a time when he hasn't felt the whole world is against him. That someone's out to get him. There's a plot to slice up his life and destroy it bit by bit because they hate his guts.

The guard beside him is in too much of a hurry, impatiently pushing Khalid outside and across the hard earth. A hot fist on his shoulder, Khalid pauses for a moment to take a breath and stare at the sunlight glancing from the chains like silver bullets across the ground. A light so bright it hypnotizes him for a second.

"We ain't got all day," the guard warns.

A hundred small pattering steps later—Khalid counts each one—they arrive at a building he's been to several times before. A building that smells of hard-boiled eggs.

A door opens. The shackles clink like a handful of coins as they undo them and Khalid looks up to see a room without a bed, or blanket, or water, or toilet, or windows, or lights, or air conditioning. But there is a new black loudspeaker high on the wall that blasts out the same loud, simple rock song over and over again until Khalid screams at the walls for release.

They played that rap music at breakfast ages ago, now it's rock music before lunch. What new thing are they up to?

But this time it's not so enjoyable. The unbearably loud, thumping bass hammers his head. Chews his eardrums to pieces. It's not long before Khalid feels he's going totally insane. Sitting on the floor with his knees under his chin and hands on his ears, he screams and begs for the noise to stop as it drives him back to that crazy place inside his head. Tariq. White noise. The jinn. Again.

# 23

## LEE-ANDY

Now and then, over the next few days, Khalid thinks he hears Tariq calling his name. His cousin's high-pitched voice cuts through him like a knife while he lies there bent double on the bed, head buried in his arms. The throbbing pain in his ear makes him feel like he's just been thumped by a stray cricket ball.

"For me it was a game. Just a game," Khalid whimpers, breathing in a whiff of bad breath on the back of his hand when he jams it in his left ear, which is badly damaged from being blasted by the relentless, pounding rock music in the isolation room. The pain spreads down the side of his face to his neck and is the reason why he can't sit up to eat the pasta shells in cold tomato sauce, which is turning to solid red glue in front of his eyes.

The tray smells of tin for some reason. Not plastic.

Yesterday, after he was brought back to his cell, Lee-Andy gave him an aspirin. She told him the guy in the next cell is called Tariq and apologized for not coming before but she had to work someone else's shift in another block because the timetable had been marked out wrongly. "Sorry!"

Today he's in too much pain to care whether Tariq's calling his name or even if he's dead or alive. Feeling worse with every passing hour, Khalid hasn't seen Lee-Andy at all and it's nearly dinnertime. Where are the bloody aspirins? There's no point in yelling for help. They'll just take him back to the isolation room and leave him there again.

Lee-Andy is his only hope.

The dinner trolley comes and goes without Khalid getting up from the bed to take the tray being offered to him. The guard doesn't care either way and whistles a silly tune as he slides it back on the metal shelf.

"No water?" the trolley man asks before passing on, unanswered. "Your choice, dude!"

Luckily, Lee-Andy hasn't forgotten Khalid. When she undoes the door to flood his cell with her lovely perfume, he twists round, spaced out, to face her.

"Eee–gad! Back in two seconds!"

Wherever she went, whoever she told, whatever she did, a miracle happens. Two guards rush to help Khalid, who's clutching his head and groaning on the floor. Helping him up, they take him outside, unshackled for the first time, across the sun-baked concourse to a building he's never seen before. Their footsteps patter away down the smooth white corridor of a hospital Khalid's shocked to discover actually exists. Then he's led through to a small ward smelling of bleach that contains three other men.

One of the men has yellow tubes down his nose that make him gasp and cough every few seconds. Another is covered in wounds that resemble leprosy sores. While the last man, with

247

sunken cheeks and a deathly pallor, is unconscious on the bed with a drip in his arm.

The guards wait beside Khalid, who moans while trying to remain upright on the bed, not daring to lie down. A military doctor, no more than thirty years old, with deep-set dark eyes and a tight mouth, eventually appears with a nurse.

Abruptly, he tips Khalid's chin to one side and presses a cold instrument into his ear. Then bends down to look without any introduction.

"Infections spread from the hands. You mustn't put your fingers in your ears. Not that bad. No reason to keep him here."

He nods to the nurse. "When you're ready." And writes a prescription for antibiotics.

"It was that crappy rock song that did my ears in," Khalid mutters.

The doctor laughs. "You must have been listening to the wrong stuff!"

A smile passes between them for a second. In the midst of which the half-dead man with the drip in his arm sits bolt upright and gazes round the room. Then sighs as if remembering something and crashes back on his pillow. The whole thing reminds Khalid of a scene from a hospital sitcom on TV.

Not long after, Khalid's given a glass of water and three pills, one of which is a strong painkiller. Strong enough to allow him to feel almost human by the time he lies down on the narrow bed in his cell.

Facing the stark wall, Khalid rubs the side of his face, not daring to touch his ear after what the doctor said. Slowly, he massages the skin front and back, hoping to ease the pain that's lurking behind the soreness. He can't help worrying they'll forget to give him the next dose of painkillers before he goes to sleep.

"Khalid, Khalid." He hears Tariq call his name but he doesn't answer.

This time the demons who stalk him have to step back a few paces, because Khalid has something else, apart from his cousin, to think about as he drifts off.

It was the sight of the man in the hospital with yellow tubes forcing food down his nostrils who'd got to him the most— the rattling gasps he made between breaths as he lay dying, blood on the pillow. There was no one beside him to hold his hand. In fact, Khalid noticed, the doctor didn't even glance at him when he hurried to the door, which makes him think something's not right here.

Why did they bother to pay attention to his little ear infection? He'd been in far worse states before and never had any help or been taken to the hospital. The only reason that makes sense is there's more to Lee-Andy's intervention than he realized. Were they using her to spy on them by putting Tariq in the next cell? Was that the reason for the chocolate bar? To gain his trust? Well, it worked, if only for a while. But now he's on to her. Tariq would be too, once Khalid found a way to tell him.

Once upon a time, if ever Khalid fell out with a friend, they would just move on one day. Continue chatting as if nothing had happened. And that would be that. Like when the bell went on the last day of term and everyone started rampaging in the corridors. Yelling their heads off. Foaming at the mouth. Pushing each other out of the way to get out first.

They were in second year, Khalid remembers, and he was trapped by the rush on the concrete stairs with Pete, Nico and Holgy, who turned from good friends to screaming morons in five easy strokes by somehow agreeing to push Khalid aggressively down the steep stairs. Laughing and shouting, they became more determined to get him to the bottom in less than three seconds the more Khalid tried to stall them. Tried to stop them by desperately reaching for the railings and elbowing them off. All of them thundering down like a herd of wild elephants.

The floor began rearing up, was right in Khalid's eyes as, pushing and shoving, the pace increased and Holgy let go suddenly, leaving him to fall the last few steps, where he landed on his shoulder with a crack. Fracturing it, the idiots. The pain was so bad he yelled for Allah in front of everyone.

After the X-ray, they gave Khalid a pink spongy sling which he wore for six whole weeks and he avoided Holgy for a good few days because he was still angry with him. Of course he hadn't turned any of them in to the principal—they're mates, aren't they? Then, when he turned up at the park on Saturday evening, Holgy started chatting about Rochdale's 2–1 win, and that was the end of it.

Not quite the same problem Khalid has with Tariq, he knows. The small chance he'll forgive him just because he doesn't have the energy to continue hating him begins to form in Khalid's mind. Hadn't he decided a long time ago to give up hurting and to forgive those who'd hurt him because he couldn't bear to inflict or suffer any more pain? He's seen too much of it. And now, the first chance he gets, he turns away and somehow can't turn back.

"Khalid. Answer me." Tariq's irritating voice feels more grating than ever and Khalid is suddenly consumed by fury. Ignoring him, hands on his head, he listens angrily to the sound of Tariq slapping the door with his flip-flops. Then silence. Khalid lies back on the bed and hears Tariq whisper, "They snatched me from my house."

Khalid sits up but he doesn't answer.

"I bet it was the same day as you," Tariq adds.

"What?" Khalid jerks forward in shock as the door rattles open and Lee-Andy barges in with a handful of pills and a glass of water. Her ponytail swinging from side to side.

"How ya feeling now?"

Khalid mumbles a thank-you and gazes at her unblinking hazel eyes for a sign she's more than an ordinary soldier. He gulps down the pills while staring at her face.

She looks away, glancing at the floor. Did her hand shake just now?

"Guess those will see you through till morning." Lee-Andy grins.

"Yeah, maybe. Is Masud in the next cell?"

"Masud? No, his name's still Tariq."

"Tariq? You sure?" Khalid says.

"Yes, pal."

"Just checking," Khalid mutters.

"That's all?" Unable to return her winning smile, Khalid

nods and turns away. Anxious for her to leave so he can talk to his cousin again.

Lee-Andy's not happy with Khalid's response and surprises him by leaning her side onto the wall next to him, arms folded, as if they are on the same football team and about to share a Coke after winning a game.

Khalid jumps up. Terrified.

"Whoa!" Lee-Andy jerks forward from the wall, hand raised. "Just being friendly, buddy. No reason to freak out. Just wanted to see if you're OK."

Lee-Andy shakes her head to protest her innocence, hurrying shamefaced to the door. "Sorry again."

Khalid is barely able to breathe straight until she's gone. Her suffocating perfume in his nose, he listens for the sound of her fast steps padding away before grabbing his heart to hold it in place. Thankful she's gone. Then, taking a minute to collect himself before pressing his nose to the wire, he speaks to the cousin he's never met.

"Can you hear me?"

"Yes, yes," Tariq answers quickly. "I've been waiting for days for you. It wasn't me. I didn't do anything."

"They captured us because of the game, don't say they didn't," Khalid says.

"Yes. For them it was a dangerous plot to destroy the West. Someone, I don't know who it was, told them that. Maybe the new Saudi player. Then they tracked the locations of our computers. They held me in Bagram for over a year. I hope you made up a good story. I convinced them weapons of mass destruction were in my teacher's cowshed."

With the sound of approaching footsteps, Tariq pauses. Soon Lee-Andy reappears, waves to him, then nods. Standing with her back towards them. Legs astride, arms folded, taking up as much space between their cells as her slim frame will allow, she obviously means to stay there.

Khalid wonders what on earth she's playing at.

"Thought I'd waste some time here before I go for lunch," she mutters. "I'll cover for you, so you can talk."

"What?" Tariq and Khalid both ask at once.

"You go ahead." Lee-Andy swishes her ponytail. "I'll stand here for a while. Don't worry, I won't listen. Nobody will come down the line with me here."

Khalid doesn't care if she does listen. He's got nothing to hide.

"Erm, thanks," Tariq says. "What were you saying, cuz?"

"Is this OK?" Khalid asks.

"Sure, talk. Don't mind me," Lee-Andy answers.

"I still can't work out why they picked me up," Khalid begins slowly, not sure Lee-Andy will believe what he's about to say but glad he finally has someone in authority who might listen.

"I dunno, but I think they thought I was dangerous because they had a photo of me at a demonstration in Karachi. But I just got caught up in the crowd on my way to look for Dad. And I bet one of the aunties' neighbors got money for making up lies about me," Khalid says. "When did they come to the conclusion about the game, I'd like to know? There's so many things I'd like an answer to. I know when they got my confession, which was just a bunch of lies I made up to stop them killing me, they really went mental. Don't you think it's weird they've put us next to each other?"

"After so much time, over a year since they brought me here? No. No. This is the result of stupidity. Not weird anything, I'm certain. I said your father is a fund-raiser for extremists. I lied to stop them beating and driving me to insanity. Told them many lies about everyone. I'm asking for your forgiveness, cuz."

"You said that about my dad? You snake. I knew it, you creep."

At this, Lee-Andy turns round for a second. "OK, I'm going now. Cool it, you guys, or you'll be in trouble."

Tariq ignores her while Khalid doesn't care whether anyone hears them or not.

"At least I admit it to your face," Tariq says. "They beat worse from me. I'm sorry!"

"Get lost, scumbag," Khalid whispers. "Don't you ever speak to me again."

An empty, cavernous silence fills the space between them all of a sudden. Khalid retreats four paces to the corner of his cell. Head in his hands. Heart thumping with rage. Trying his best to hide from the shapes leaping from the swelling walls.

On the floor now, back pressed hard against the bed, half dazed. His eyes dart round him as if he's seeing terrible things. Eventually, Lee-Andy interrupts.

"Hey, pal. Don't mess up. You look like you're going crazy. Do this for me, will you? Snap your fingers in front of your eyes to stop rolling that horror movie in your mind. If you don't make plans to stop them, they'll keep on growing."

How does she know what he's seeing?

Khalid does as he's told. Snapping his fingers a few times. Her words spark an unexpected light which, along with his snapping fingers, causes the walls to fall back to their rightful place. The jinn to shrink. The plank to straighten. Water jug to smash.

Khalid turns his head to smile at her.

"Good job. Wish I had some orange juice to give you." Lee-Andy walks away with a bounce in her step. More snapping fingers start up close by. The new rhythm is a pleasant addition to Khalid's own snap-snapping, his own personal rap beat.

"Good night, cuz," Tariq whispers. "You heard her. She's right. Don't mess up. There's too much reason to cry after what's happened to us both. If we give in, we're finished. No life will come to us again. We must find some dignity to see us through."

"Dignity? Piss off." Khalid can't believe the rubbish Tariq's coming out with. But then he hears him too and deep down inside knows he's right. Whatever Tariq said about Dad wasn't meant to be said. It was another last-ditch attempt to stop the pain. Something he understands only too well.

Next day, the sound of plastic spoons echoes down the row. Voices rise every time a disgusting lump of green fish is placed on the tongue.

Khalid's eaten the banana. That's all. He can't face anything else. Leaning on the wire door, he stares at the light, eyes hurting. Standing where he is, doing nothing but listening. With a stillness in his heart he hasn't felt for a long time.

"I could have died," Tariq whispers. "But that would have ended the lives of my mother and father and I could not do that. I had a deep feeling I had betrayed them. I died then in a way. I do admit I had a friend who was, I suppose, an extremist. He hated the West for its materialism and lack of belief in God. Yes. Yes. I admit that. But does that make me an evil person because I knew him? Someone whose head must be slammed against walls day after day? So evil they must burn my arms with cigarettes? Does that make me bad because I had a friend like that?"

Khalid is startled by the sadness in his cousin's voice and a rare feeling of gratitude and happiness spills over him despite almost two years of desperation. Listening to Tariq talk about his depression, his deepest worries, his pain, Khalid feels as if he's talking to someone he's never known. Tariq never spoke about his feelings before and now he never stops.

Day after day, Khalid hangs on the wire door waiting for Tariq to speak. A beggar waiting for the small crumbs of comfort his squeaking voice brings.

"Actually, if I'd known then what I know now I wouldn't have called the game *Bomber One*," Tariq says. "I was stupid. I didn't realize someone would add up two and two and make one million and ten. For certain, the world has gone mad. Yes. Yes."

Over the next week, Khalid learns just how insane the world has become. Tariq fills him in on what's been happening since they were captured. Helped by the fact he speaks several languages, including some Arabic, Tariq has managed to pick up plenty of information from the guards in Islamabad and Bagram, as well as from other detainees. His ability to understand politics and make sense of scraps of conversations means he has a lot to explain. A lover of facts, he's keen to share the details.

"In March 2003 more than a million people marched in London against Tony Blair's decision to go to war in Iraq. Ten million people marched all over the world, but I ask you, since when do politicians take notice of these things?"

"Dunno!" Khalid realizes his brain has shrunk to nothing as he listens to Tariq's larger mind expand on anything and everything. Strangely, the more Tariq talks, the more he doesn't feel the need to respond. It's just that Tariq's got this habit of making him feel not very smart, stupid even. With Ali it was different—he was older and so experienced—but Tariq is only two years older than him.

Like now, for instance, Khalid listens to Tariq greet the guard who's passing him breakfast.

"Hi, Marvin. How you doing today? How's the wife and kids? Everything all right back home in Oklahoma, is it?"

"Yeah, bud, thanks for the inquiry. Appreciate your kindness." Marvin laughs heartily as he moves to pass Khalid his tray. Khalid eyes the stocky guard with distrust. Unable to pretend they're friends. Unable to behave like Tariq and forget even for a second that this man's his jailer and he's an innocent prisoner. Why act like they're friends when they're not? It's just fake.

"He's not going to do you any favors. Why be nice to him?" Khalid says.

"Hah," Tariq laughs. "If you understood how much easier

these small human exchanges have made my life you wouldn't say that, cuz. I am practicing English and, of course, I am gathering much information about other places from people like him. For example, did you know Oklahoma is home to sixty-seven American Indian tribes who were forced into relocating there after they were driven from their homes? I found this out from him. And Marvin was the one who helped get me moved from Camp Echo, which is far worse than Camp Delta. Plus he gave me a new toothbrush. And he told me the corn in Oklahoma is as high as an elephant's eye. One day I will go there and see it."

By the time Tariq finishes, Khalid feels like going on hunger strike. Who cares about Oklahoma? How come Tariq's got a new toothbrush? What kind of toothbrush? Unable to admit his own prison toothbrush that fits on a ring on his finger has only a few bristles left because he can't get a word in edgewise. Not that going on hunger strike is a joke, as Tariq goes on to explain.

"When I first came here, in February 2003, many men went on hunger strike. It lasted for a long time," Tariq begins. "They tried to cover it up. For a while no one would admit what was happening, but I could see the food coming back uneaten. Plus a Turkish man who had been tortured so much he could hardly stand straight told me every day the latest news."

"Why didn't I know about this?" Khalid asks.

"Probably because you were lost in your own world, cuz. That's what prison does to people. You become more dead than alive. What is there to notice when you stop existing? Nothing. No. No. They say I am a good prisoner now—high compliant is what they call me."

"High compliant?" Khalid remembers overhearing a guard use the phrase.

"Seventy-one days the hunger strike went on," Tariq continues. "The military ended it by force-feeding. You might know this is not legal. It was a non-violent protest but they pushed tubes down their noses to feed them against their will. One guard said the hunger strike proves we are evil."

There are so many things Khalid doesn't know, suddenly remembering the sight of the man in hospital with yellow tubes down his nose. So that's what they were doing. Force-feeding him. Maybe that was why the doctor took no notice of him.

"Under the Geneva Convention, prisoners have the right to grow flowers. Did you know that?" Tariq says. "It's just one of the many things we haven't been able to do in Guantanamo."

"Why would I want to grow flowers?" Khalid smiles. "That's so lame." His mind drifts back to the small front garden in Oswestry Road and the rows of purple, white and yellow flowers that appear outside the living-room window each summer. He can see himself lying on the sofa watching TV, with long green leaves poking their tips at him in the breeze.

"It would be nice to have the choice," Tariq says. "And do you know the words "enemy combatants" have been invented to deny us the status given to prisoners of war?"

"Yeah?" Khalid replies, still shocked by things like this, even though it doesn't really surprise him.

"But the worst thing is," Tariq tells him, "millions of people around the world have objected to us being here, writing letters about abuse and no fair trials, except now a military tribunal where they have their own rules."

"Why haven't I had a military tribunal?" Khalid finally interrupts.

"This is not the law of the land they keep in these tribunals. No jury is there." Tariq sighs.

If Khalid had known all this earlier, he might have felt better.

"Make no mistake, this tribunal would find us guilty!" Tariq says.

"How come?"

"You told me you signed the papers. I signed the papers. The fact we signed after being tortured means nothing. We are guilty now to them," he says.

A couple of minutes later, when Khalid hears guards clanking shackles and pushing Tariq's door open, he leans closer to the wire. This is his first chance to see Tariq instead of just hear him.

He presses his body tight, hands spread high, gripping the wire to take in every bit of his cousin when he finally appears. Marvin's chunky shape is there first—standing to one side to usher Tariq out. An overpowering smell of vanilla soap drifts from his shirt pocket, which is crammed with the stuff.

"Shower time, buddy," Khalid hears him tell Tariq.

"You bet it is," Tariq says in a strange accent which isn't quite American.

Marvin lays a hand on Tariq's shoulder to lead him the other way, but not before Khalid, who's flat against the fence, shouts, "Hey, I want a new toothbrush. Marvin. Marvin."

"Later, man." Marvin smiles.

Tariq half turns towards him. Recognizing his classic features from the online picture next to his name, Khalid notices he's taller and slimmer than he had imagined. In profile, he reminds him a bit of Mum. "Hi." Khalid gets another brief glimpse when at last his cousin manages to twist his head right back from the heavy middle chain pulling his neck down. The second their eyes meet, Tariq's big, black, warm eyes make everything else fall away, burrowing straight to the core of Khalid's soul. Suddenly his whole family had come home to him.

The moment Tariq's gone, Khalid sinks to the floor. Sobbing. Head in his hands. Overwhelmed by his first meeting with the cousin he used to adore. Touched by a friendly smile that he knows is genuine. By his chained hands and feet. By his shaved head and face. By his shuffling away, obviously deeply moved by the powerful emotion that passed between them.

Khalid recognizes between sobs that since they found each other this place has changed. Even when he hated him, just knowing he was there brought him comfort. Someone. Something. Some future to look forward to. Plus, he brought him a precious link to his family and the outside world that he could tap into at any time.

No matter what has happened, Tariq has explained so much and led Khalid from the dark side of his mind. Suddenly, he sees it's not enough to forget. It will only be enough if he can recognize the steps he's taken to get to this point and decide not to allow this experience to poison his life. For that reason, he has no choice but to forgive Tariq. For once. For always.

And now he's actually met his cousin, he's made so weirdly happy all of a sudden by the thought he might see him again when he returns from the shower, Khalid finally forgives himself for hating him, for misjudging him and—yes—wanting to hurt him.

Breaking free from the stranglehold of so much anger and blame, Khalid wipes away the last of his tears. Shaking his head to rid himself of the memory of the different kinds of hell he's lived through. Shaking it so hard he doesn't, at first, hear Lee-Andy's quick steps coming towards him.

"Just come to say good-bye, pal," she says.

"Why?" Khalid quickly comes to the conclusion she's OK, now it's too late.

"Politics, I guess. Who knows what goes on in their minds? I sure don't."

"Me neither." Khalid smiles.

"How's the ear doing?" Wrinkling her nose, she places her hands on her hips.

"Better!"

Lee-Andy looks him in the eye for a second and Khalid catches the disappointment she feels at having to go.

"You don't want to leave?"

"No way. What's the use in pushing paper? But that's how it rolls." The feeling that their odd, short relationship has helped him surfaces in Khalid's mind. She was obviously so bored out of her brains here she decided to talk to him and maybe that's helped her in some way too.

"I'm snapping my fingers in front of my eyes all the time," he mutters, instead of the deeply felt thank-you he'd like to give her

"Don't forget to keep doing it."

"I'll try," Khalid says.

"Probably won't see you any time soon. Stay cool, pal." She turns away.

"Yeah." Khalid sighs. Pleased by her genuine regret. I mean, now he has Tariq close by, why should he care what happens to her? But he does, because she's been kind to him, and besides, he'll never forget how delicious that chocolate bar tasted. In a way her concern has helped him to forgive Tariq. She didn't care that they knew each other from before. She stood nearby, letting them talk, and no, he doesn't really believe she was spying on them. Lee-Andy allowed them to chat for no other reason other than she thought it would help him.

The idea that she's going alarms him for a second until she swings her reddish ponytail, smiles briefly, then rushes off, but this time the door shuts with a certainty which feels lighter than it's ever done before. Lee-Andy has gone but Khalid is coming back to himself. Even the movie in his head of the girlfriendless hell he's endured here—that just rose up in front of him—is shrinking back. Aware of how his brain is creating the sudden feeling of a lifetime's future loneliness by flashing up pictures of all the girls he's ever liked, he can't help going right back to the beginning, to the girl in elementary school whose bag he once carried to the gym.

"Bye, hugs 'n' kisses," eleven-year-old Ariella whispered in his ear before Khalid had time to catch his breath. Throwing open the door to times when girls are people to like instead of ignore.

Realizing he has the power to change his feelings by

deciding what pictures he allows in his mind, a rare feeling of peace rises in Khalid. Ariella's gone, and so have all the others, probably Niamh too. If only he'd told her just once that he liked her.

Rubbing his face, Khalid finally admits to himself, yeah, Lee-Andy, he fancied her a bit. So what? At least it proves he's not quite dead inside, and anyway, she is the only attractive female he's seen for a long time.

The sound of slow, plodding footsteps forces Khalid to turn quickly to grab the door. Desperately tweaking the fence to try and part the strong wire, all he can see is a ruddy-necked, chunky soldier standing with his back to him. Legs apart, completely blocking Tariq from view.

"Get out of the way," Khalid mutters. But Marvin doesn't move. Instead he slowly edges Tariq into the cell, but even though Khalid can't see him, a wave of pleasure passes over him as he breathes in the smell of vanilla soap coming from Marvin's still-bulging pocket. Tariq's returned and knowing that makes him smile.

# HARRY

Khalid doesn't get the chance to tell Tariq how he feels because none of it matters anymore. Anyway, there's nothing to explain because his cousin carries on as if everything has always been fine between them. Now that they've joined forces, they keep each other going and are making up for lost time as good friends.

Later that week, after lunch, Marvin and another guard arrive for Khalid with an armful of shackles and unlock the door.

"Hey, Marvin," Tariq calls from next door, but they haven't come for him today.

"Not now, bud," Marvin replies, his low tone of voice giving Khalid the impression Marvin's on serious business right now. What, he can't imagine. Marvin's giving no clues away as he and the other guard enter the cell. His shirt pockets are flat. No smell of vanilla soap today, just the faint whiff of cigarettes, so Khalid knows he's not going for a shower. Plus he went for exercise yesterday, so unless everything's changed he won't be going again until the day after tomorrow.

Marvin's an expert with shackles, fastening them not too tightly. Smiling broadly to show he means no harm.

"Where we going?" Khalid asks, shuffling behind, trying to keep up with him.

"You'll soon find out," Marvin says solemnly, leaving Khalid in the dark as they cross the yard and walk round the corner to enter a small building. This place smells of white paint; it's cleaner and brighter than the others. The long, low building has small windows in the roof that throw patches of sunlight on the immaculate concrete floor.

Marvin flings open the door to a small room with a black desk and two chairs.

Khalid's first thought when he sees the two floor bolts is, *Oh yeah, another interrogation room*, but seconds later a man who looks like a teacher comes in and he changes his mind.

"Hi, Khalid, I'm your new lawyer. Name's Harry Peterson."

"Eh?" No one has called him Khalid in that way for the last two years. Looking him up and down as the guard undoes the wrist shackles and motions him to the chair to bolt his ankles to the floor, he's sure he misheard him.

"What did you say, man?" It comes as a huge surprise to hear words like that from anyone, let alone this guy, Harry, who has a big, gentle face and fair, scruffy hair. "You're my lawyer?"

"Yes," Harry says. Khalid takes in the loose, navy shirt, the same beige corduroy trousers that Mr. Tagg always wears. He looks old-fashioned, way uncool. Plus he nods all the time, but he smells of a nice aftershave that reminds Khalid of one he used to wear at home.

266

"Yes, I'm your lawyer."

"Pardon?" Khalid almost chokes he's so shocked, which makes Harry laugh.

"Here. This has been a long time coming, I'm afraid." Harry hands over a white envelope addressed to him here in Guantanamo Bay. His first letter. Trembling, Khalid tries to settle the wave of surprise and excitement that's bubbling in his stomach.

"That's my dad's writing."

"Yes, it is." Harry lowers his eyes out of respect for Khalid, whose sweating fingers fumble awkwardly with the corner, which is stuck down tight. The ordinary, small, delicate task is an ordeal for him. He hasn't even tied a shoelace in the last two years. Sighing heavily, he taps a knee with the envelope for a moment before mentally snapping his fingers in front of his eyes and starting over. This time he gently peels back the obviously glued and messy re-stuck edge with a fingertip, slowly working along it until it tears. Pulling each slice back until the neatly folded letter appears inside. With a badly trembling hand, he rustles the thin sheet from its sleeve and opens it carefully to read the letter in silence. Doing his best to hold in his emotions, he's unable to stop the odd tear racing down his face.

Meanwhile, Harry is busy shuffling papers, trying to give him the space to take in the sudden, amazing news that Dad's fine.

"I'm sorry it's taken so long to get to see you," he says when Khalid folds the letter away. "Your family is well and sends you their deepest love." Harry explains he's spent months

267

attempting to get the Americans to follow the due process of law by giving Khalid access to a lawyer and family and friends.

Khalid drops his eyes. He doesn't want to talk about anything—not yet. A few minutes' silence passes before Khalid says, "What are they accusing me of?"

"Well, the trouble is you signed a confession, albeit under duress, and they're using that to detain you indefinitely. I have to be honest—this might take a while, Khalid. There's a paranoia out there about people they refer to as evil terrorists that's difficult to dispel."

All this is too much for Khalid. It's the first conversation he's had with an Englishman who looks and talks like one of his teachers and probably went to university and all that. Plus he speaks so properly and friendly, it sounds weird. But at least he doesn't talk down to him. Feeling suddenly grateful for the last few weeks spent chatting to Tariq, Khalid realizes he's not as out of his depth as he would have been before.

"The fact you were picked up when you were just fifteen might work in your favor." Harry frowns, nodding slowly.

"How come? It hasn't so far."

At this, Harry laughs. "I know. It took us a while to find you. Your dad traveled all over Pakistan looking for you, refusing to go home to Rochdale until he discovered what had happened. When he returned to England they confiscated the family computer and hauled him in for days of questioning but were unable to find anything."

Harry goes on to tell him what's been happening in the past two years. The various bombings in India, Turkey, Indonesia, Bali, the Philippines. The capture of Saddam Hussein. Most of which is lost on Khalid, because he can't bear the thought that anyone might think he was involved in something as terrible as the events Harry describes. The fact there's a small window behind Harry through which Khalid can see a truck going past distracts him for a moment from fully imagining the pain these people have suffered.

Harry seems to think with his fingers; he keeps patting his open laptop while trying to reassure Khalid that everything will be OK. Then he clicks his short nails together when he explains how long it took to get permission from the American government to visit him here.

All the while, the letter from Dad is safely folded in Khalid's shaking hand and its words pierce him with pleasure as Harry talks.

"Is there anything you want to know?"

"Don't suppose you have Rochdale's soccer results by any chance?" Khalid asks.

With a long, deep laugh, Harry throws his head back and flicks his forehead with two fingers. "Why didn't I think to find that out? Your dad told me you're an avid fan. I'll do my best to get that information for you as soon as I can. Don't worry, Khalid, one day all this will be over and you can go back to your normal life, even though it might not feel normal for quite a while!" Looking him straight in the eye, Harry frowns. "Are you OK?"

"Not really!" He guesses Harry's trying to tell how this conversation, the letter and his time here are affecting Khalid, and by the way Harry's pursing his lips right now, maybe he's wondering whether Khalid's all right mentally.

When they come to take Khalid away, Harry glances at the floor, clearly emotional but doing his best to hide it.

"I'll be back tomorrow to take a statement about everything," he says.

"About how they tortured me?" Khalid says loudly for the guards' benefit.

"Anything and everything." Harry smiles to give him confidence and keep him going until then.

As soon as Khalid's back in his cell, the flap in the metal and wire door slams open with an earth-shattering bang. Dropping the letter on the bed, Khalid moves quickly to take the plastic tray smelling of rotten fish from the soldier outside. Hardly bothering to glance at the bread roll and ball of rice, the foul-smelling fish in runny tomato sauce, he rests the tray on the floor, ignoring Tariq's whispers as he rushes to read Dad's letter again.

My dear, dear son,

So much sadness that you are knowing nothing about has been in all our hearts since you are gone. My heart is breaking in two as I write this letter. Everything in my life comes to nothing when I count the days since I last saw you in Karachi. Now we have found out where you are we are doing everything in our power to get you home. We will not stop until you are with us again. This you can be sure of, son. Don't worry. I will make certain of it.

First I will tell you what happen to me in Karachi. It is a long story but I know you must be thinking of this many times. Perhaps you been imagining I'm not in this world any more. So I tell you about it so you don't worry. I was walking down the street when a bike came into me there. Knocking me to my feet. A young man took me inside his house and offered me tea. I'm thinking this is kind and of course I was still in shock because actually my leg was painful and I was feeling dizzy at the same time. But something bad he put in the tea and then he robbed me and locked me in the basement. This is sounding like a film, no? But it is true. Every bit.

There I remained for three days until the man returned. He was most shocked to find me still alive. He freaks out, as you would say, then he runs off. Extremely weak and ill, I manage to make it up the steps and then it's too much for me and I pass right out. For how long I'm there, son, I'm not certain, but when I wake up I'm at home in my sisters' house. Luckily, a neighbor went by and when he glances down on the steps for no reason he recognizes me. Everyone was knowing I'm missing from the house. Almost dead I am. Then, son, when they brought me home and brought me back to life, Fatima says by feeding me her special spicy chicken curry, I eventually got myself better again for you. Only informing me when I was well enough to sit up that you had gone missing soon after me. I looked down every street for you. I walked and walked until I became sick from worry. I could not eat. I could not sleep. None of us could. Your poor mum, every day she cries and cries.

Now we don't understand anything about why you are there. Nobody tells us anything at all. It was only much later when ███████████████████████████ who is a friend of a policeman, who was talking to his wife about a boy called Khalid who was held in Karachi at that time, that we were able to put the numbers together. That was after we ████████████████████████████
████████████

Choking back tears, Khalid holds the letter up to the light in an effort to see what's written under the black crossing-out, but no words are visible. How dare they wreck Dad's letter? Staring at the clear, round writing, Khalid fixes on the certainty that, yes, Dad wrote this—to him. The loving words force him to climb back into all the things that have happened since he last saw him. All the horrible cruel things. But now he knows Dad's alive, he'll never care again if anyone tries to hurt him. He'll never care if anyone likes him or doesn't think he's special. Nothing matters except his dad's safe, he's alive and he's out there fighting for him, and so are all his family.

"Where did you go, cuz?" Once more, Tariq whispers from the corner of the cell next door, anxiously pleading for a quick answer. "Cuz?"

"A lawyer called Harry came from England to see me."

"WHAT? Why?" Tariq's shocked.

"He brought me a letter from my dad. He's fine and Harry's going to help me." Khalid still can't quite believe it himself.

"Why all of a sudden, though?" Tariq asks. "What happened to bring him here?"

"I dunno," Khalid says. "I think they had to let the lawyer in when they found out how old I was. Or maybe they read all my letters and saw I was innocent. Or maybe Lee-Andy helped me and loads of lawyers are coming here. Who knows? Perhaps they're closing the place down and letting everyone out."

"That would be cool," Tariq says, a bit deflated. "Can you ask him if he'll help me?"

"Yeah, course. Didn't have time today, but sure I'll ask for you. He'll help you if he can, I promise."

"Thank you, cuz. Thanks!" Tariq sounds thrilled at the idea of an English lawyer helping him.


Barely able to sleep, bleary-eyed and weak from all the excitement, Khalid's in a state of disbelief when morning comes and the call to prayer sounds across the camp.

Stumbling to wash himself quickly, Khalid unrolls the white towel and faces the wall to join the hundreds of prisoners looking towards Mecca. Only this time as he prays Khalid gives thanks for his family, for Tariq and Harry and for the chance that, one day, he might go home. A thought he gave up on a long, long time ago.

Soon after breakfast, when the smell of stale bread has left the cell, a weird and wonderful thing happens as Marvin tells Khalid, "Time for your visit." Like those words are normal around here.

"Already?" Khalid's standing in no time.

"Good luck," Tariq whispers. Which gives Khalid another chance to pause in front of his door and wink and smile, as they always do, but today his head's so full of questions, he wishes he'd taken the time to write them down and he barely notices Tariq.

Luckily, Khalid remembers a few.

"When can you get me out of here?"

"I wish I could answer that." Harry sighs, scraping the metal chair closer to the table. A whiff of shampoo from his freshly washed hair fills the short distance between them.

"Parts of my letter from Dad were blacked out—how is he? And Mum? And my sisters?"

"I didn't get to talk to him until the end of last year for the first time. Since then I've seen them many times. At first they were greatly disturbed by your disappearance, fearing they'd never see you again, but now your dad is back at work in the restaurant and your mum at the school, which is helping them cope much better than they were. The Muslim community and many others in Rochdale have rallied round your family to fight for your release. I can't tell you how excited they all were by my coming here to see you. Aadab and Gul send you hugs and kisses, as they all do."

Khalid lowers his eyes in an effort to stop himself from breaking down completely.

"Why did it take you so long to come and see me?" he whispers.

"It took a great deal of legal wrangling to get permission to visit Guantanamo," Harry says, moving on quickly to explain that international law, including the Geneva Convention, requires certain conditions that still haven't been met here. Including the one that child prisoners must be separated from adults and receive education while in detention.

"But I haven't had any education!" Khalid says, wiping his tears.

"I know." Harry shakes his head. "But US federal law has similar requirements, so you should have been receiving something."

"This is all rubbish now, unless I can sue them." Khalid likes this idea.

"Well, it seems they've only just accepted you're seventeen."

"Seventeen, yeah. I'm seventeen. I didn't really care the other day when I figured it was my birthday but hearing you say it feels weird. They have to let me go now that they know I'm young?"

"You'd think so. But you signed a confession saying you planned with a number of accomplices to bomb various cities around the world," Harry says.

"But it was a game. We weren't gonna really do that. I was stupid to sign it." Khalid still hates the part of him that gave in.

"Yes, it was an innocent computer game, and there's nothing stupid about you from what I've heard. Can you tell me what happened, Khalid?" Harry clicks his laptop open, ready to record his story.

From now on, Khalid wants to be seen as honest and sincere, brave, forgiving and kind, so he thinks hard. Knowing once his words are taken down, they're written in stone and he never wants to be caught out again.

"I didn't even read the confession after I signed it," Khalid begins. "They gave me loads of copies, about eight pages, I think. I should have read them. I only pretended to read them. They had the stuff printed out, ready for me to sign when they dragged me from the room after trying to drown me. That was after loads of times they took me for questioning . . . interrogation, I mean. They left me on the floor without any water or anything to eat. Like about the fourth time I thought I was gonna keep being taken there until I said what they wanted me to. And I was right. Some of the guards, it wasn't their fault. One gave me some chewing gum and another gave me some chocolate and tried to help me. But the others, the ones in Afghanistan, they tried to—they pushed me upside down on a plank to drown me. That's why I signed."

Harry stops tap-tapping the shiny white keyboard for a second.

"Do you want to tell me about that?"

"No. Yeah. But not right now, or I might start crying."

"If it makes you feel any better, Khalid, there are other young people here, some as young as twelve, who are in a worse situation than you. I don't know their full names yet, but I'm trying to track down their families, who live in various places in the Middle East. In my experience, you did the right thing by stopping the torture."

"How can they do this? That's the bit I can't understand, man." Khalid sighs, gazing at the glowing white logo of Harry's laptop. Still slightly stunned by his caring attitude.

"That's the bit I'm trying to understand too." Harry smiles, fully understanding Khalid's weary glances.

"They tied me to a ring on the floor like I was a cow or something and put the air conditioner on until it was freezing. I was shaking and they kept blasting me with the same questions. Saying stuff like, 'Just admit your part in the plot and we'll let you go,' until I was gonzo. They kept me awake for days until I was so wasted, man, I wanted to, like, chuck up. I didn't know what the hell was happening and there was no one to talk to. Once I needed to take a leak and they wouldn't even untie me."

"Thank heavens you got through it," Harry says.

Finally, Khalid smiles. "Yeah, I ain't weak no more. Or stupid."

276

"No." Harry nods. "Many people haven't made it through. Isolation is a tough thing to deal with. There were two suicides last week in Camp Echo."

"Does anyone care about them, though?" Khalid asks.

"People do, Khalid. They do," Harry says. "We must remember that once we divide the world into good and bad, then we have to join one camp or the other, and, as you've found out, life's a bit more complex than that."

"I know," Khalid says.

"Right now it's important to collect the evidence to close this place down," Harry says firmly.

"Yeah, and they said they knew me from the demonstration in Karachi where someone was killed and they have a photo of me next to some guy they're after."

"Yes, it's in the confession. I must say when I read that, I laughed, because the man next to you in the photo, we found out, is an Afghan doctor who agreed to attend the demonstration in case there were casualties. If you look closely you can just see the black doctor's bag under his arm." Harry nods. "He's disappeared."

It dawns on Khalid that Harry might just help him get out of this hellhole.

"So where are all these maniac terrorists, then?"

"That's a good question, Khalid. No doubt there are some, and that's why we have courts of law to decide who's guilty and who's innocent. From now on, what I can say is that you must be taken for exercise each day and given access to other prisoners, plus some form of education. Is there anything I can bring you next time I come?"

"When will that be?"

"Soon, I hope," Harry says.

"How about bringing me my coursework and schoolbooks? Yeah, big laugh that would be, wouldn't it? I should be working on A-levels now, not bloody GCSEs. Too late. Forget it. Who cares?"

"I'll see what I can do." Harry scrapes the chair back and carefully folds the laptop under his arm.

"Maybe some sweets. More letters. Any more books by that Harper Lee guy and yeah, books, loads of books."

Khalid's sorry to see Harry go. He's a nice guy. He likes his soft voice and restless, jittery hands.

"You've read *To Kill a Mockingbird*? It's one of my favorite books!" Harry smiles.

"It was in one of those old Reader's Digest things," Khalid explains.

"Ah, I see." A smile spreads over Harry's face. "Like you, I thought Harper Lee was a man's name when I first came across it. But I'm sorry to have to tell you, that's the only book *she* ever wrote. Pity, isn't it?"

"It's written by a woman? Wow. Shame there's no more of them. I really like that story."

"Now, what I'm going to do, Khalid, is try and get you some more books and perhaps even a teacher."

"Thanks." Khalid smiles.

Then the door slides back right on cue, as if someone's been listening the whole time. The guards quickly unlock the restraints bolting Khalid's ankles to the floor and lead him away.

It's only when he's back in the cell that Khalid wishes he'd asked Harry to bring him some of that lane cake that Harper Lee mentions. Coming up with plenty of other things he wanted to say as he sits on the bed to think things over.

"Khalid, what happened?" Tariq whispers again.

"Give me a couple of minutes," Khalid says, anxious to go through everything himself first. It's not until he's said the last prayers of the day that he moves to spread his hands on the wire mesh door to fill Tariq in on Harry's visit.

"So what did you tell him about me?" is the first thing Tariq asks.

"Yeah. Yeah, let me think!" Khalid kicks himself for forgetting to mention Tariq. *What's wrong with me? How could I forget?* So much for kindness.

"Sorry, Tariq, I forgot. I'll do it next time. It went right out of my head," Khalid humbly admits.

"No problem, cuz. You always were a dorkhead. Don't let me down next time, eh?" Tariq says.

"On my mum's life, I promise I won't, man." The muscles in Khalid's face tighten as he tries to smile. "My hand's on my heart, you know that?"

"Yeah, brother, mine is too."

## ECHOES

Ten days later and Harry still hasn't returned to see Khalid, who's growing increasingly anxious to tell him about Tariq. No word arrives, leaving him cross and angry, more ashamed than ever for forgetting to mention his cousin. The only easy thing about the situation is that Tariq doesn't pester Khalid about anything, not even his lack of help.

A postcard has arrived for Khalid since he last saw Harry, a picture of Rochdale Town Hall from Mum and Dad, via the Red Cross. A postcard that reminds him they're doing all they can to get him home. They leave out the precise details, because even they know by now that the military reads the mail first before deciding whether to pass it on. The old-fashioned card is a welcome link with home and Khalid places it on his bed and gazes at it all day. Once he even held the card out through the hole for Tariq to see and even he agreed that the town hall is an "impressive building."

Khalid had given up writing letters a long time ago. He never received a reply so what was the point? But now, every day, he writes and writes to whomever he can think of, always mentioning Tariq. Some letters he gives to the Red Cross man to deliver, but now and then he passes one to the soldiers, knowing everything's seen by them anyway. Whether they're mailed on afterwards is anyone's guess. Tariq says they aren't—they're destroyed.

All the same, Khalid is sure some must get through. Either way he's left in limbo, waiting each day for a reply. But no letter, card or lawyer ever arrives for his cousin, and he feels bad about this, even though Tariq manages to hide his feelings.

"I'm certain my family is thinking I am dead until Uncle—your dad—tells them about you. Then they will cry, 'Ah, so this is what might be the case with Tariq. It is possible he is alive in the same place. We must keep up with this idea.'"

"Something will happen soon," Khalid tries to reassure him.

"Of that I have no doubt," Tariq says. "What, though? All we can do is trust in Allah."

Thanks to Tariq, Khalid now speaks a little Arabic. His cousin's endless patience has helped him learn the prayers. When dawn breaks, at midday, mid-afternoon, after sunset and at nightfall, Khalid and Tariq unroll white towels kept clean for this reason and, facing Mecca, pray to Allah.

A feeling of peaceful connection soon descends on Khalid and he realizes that the religion he once ignored and avoided because he thought it was uncool has become a major source of comfort, giving him something to turn to. A reason to forgive himself for all the hurt he's caused in his life to his mum and dad, to his sisters, to random teachers, and the rest. And when he remembers everyone who's ever hurt him, he never wants to feel that pain or inflict it on anyone else again. Day after day of going through each incident and forgiving himself and others has brought its own deep peace. Plus he's learned the true value that small things—a piece of chewing gum or a bar of chocolate—can bring. Acts of kindness he will never forget.

Whenever the call to prayer begins and he turns to the back wall, round, long notes echo from Khalid's throat as if he's been doing this all his life. The sudden rise in tempo makes him feel blissed out as he pauses mid-flow to lower his voice for a moment before a longer, higher note starts up. Singing so high nearly takes his breath away. He carefully draws out each *n-nnnn-n* and *mmm-m-m* and breathing *r-rr-r-rrr* into the gray walls, while sudden *kk-k* sounds smack the humid air, creating a chemical reaction in his veins that feels like heaven is coming his way.

A few minutes later Khalid rolls up his towel and places it at the end of the bed, ready for the next prayers. He sits down to share a moment's silence with every person in the camp—prisoner and jailer alike. Whether they know it or not, they are all embracing peace for peace's sake. A feeling of calm instead of the pain, bitterness and rage this prison has created. So it's doubly unexpected when two guards come to take Khalid away.

"You're being transferred to another block," the big lump of a guard announces. "Get your things."

"No!" Khalid panics. "I'm staying here!"

"Dude, move yourself. That's an order," he says with a wide, laughing face.

Jumping up to collect Dad's letter and the postcard, Khalid grabs his library book and turns back to pick up his copy of the Qur'an, plus the new toothbrush Marvin brought after Tariq had a word with him. Imagining if he leaves anything behind, it will stay here forever. Not that Khalid has much else to gather up apart from a few sheets of paper and the blue pen the man from the Red Cross dished out yesterday.

Soon Khalid's dressed in the orange suit. Hooded. Then the shackles are ratcheted tight. The chains drag as the door shuts behind him.

"They're moving me, Tariq!" he shouts, knowing it's not worth whispering now.

"I heard. Don't worry, cuz. Goodbye," Tariq answers softly.

Shocked by the sudden intake of his cousin's breath, a terrible feeling of loneliness and isolation overpowers Khalid as he clunks and stumbles, hooded and despairing, past Tariq's door.

"I won't forget you!" Khalid yells. Broken in two by the sudden realization that he doesn't know when they'll see each other again.

Emptier than he's ever felt before, Khalid's led to what he thinks must be a van. A van so hot the smell makes him feel faint. Leaning forward on the hard seat to stop himself from passing out, he is aware of a new, rock-hard ache of frustration stirring in his scrawny stomach.

The van pulls away slowly, traveling for a short while before stopping. The guards remove Khalid's hood to reveal a face drowning in sweat mixed with a veil of tears. Leading him from the van, one guard starts hiccuping as they arrive at an area crammed with wire cages full of men.

Rows of cages with bundles of men confront Khalid. Only

this time they are all talking at once through thick mesh walls. Everyone turns to greet Khalid by shouting, "*Salaam*." Slightly smaller than the previous kennel, the second to last cage is Khalid's new cell. Covered in criss-crosses of sunshine, it's open to the sky and the patch of blue gives Khalid the strange feeling of hot metal on his head. A small compensation for the constant chatter in Pashtu and Farsi that surrounds him, which he can't understand. Everyone here is older and livelier than him and, more importantly, none of them is his cousin.

Harry must have asked for Khalid to be moved out of isolation, not realizing he's far more alone here, surrounded by men he doesn't know, than he was in the cell next to Tariq. Wishing desperately he'd remembered to mention him, Khalid sits in the corner, holding his knees. He peers through the wire at the men on either side of him and the man opposite, who's quite clearly staring back. Khalid ignores him.

A guard wanders by with cups of sunshine reflected on his black boots. Each perfect circle slips like a gold coin to the pale earth as he walks, bringing a moment's magic to the dreary scene. Every so often the man to Khalid's right looks at him and mutters what sound like a few kind words, if only he could understand them.

There's a more relaxed feeling here. Remarkably, men are not shouted at for talking to each other, and many chat openly with the guards. Others seem to enjoy waving to each other for no reason. But none of it brings Khalid any comfort. He can't understand their arguments but many seem to be about the Qur'an because they turn pages to point at certain passages then hold the holy book close to their hearts. Khalid watches them but the pent-up emotion he feels for forgetting to mention Tariq to Harry dominates his brain. Contorted by the agony, Khalid starts sinking again and drifts in and out of the constant chatter in his mind.

Only this time there are too many distractions.

After watching the faceless man to his left hang his sheet on the wire mesh to give himself privacy when he uses the toilet, Khalid gets his nerve up to go to the loo, washing himself in the small bucket of water next to it.

It's hard to describe how much this constant racket is getting on his nerves. Resting his chin on his knees, he gazes at the splashes of diamond-shaped light on the steel floor and wishes the jinn would take him back to his old cell.

In early evening, a vulture flies overhead. Then another before the sun sinks in the sky. When the call to prayer comes, Khalid stands up and stretches, walks around the cage, before the man opposite waves at him to unroll his towel. The hollow clatter of a guard's rifle being moved round his body distracts Khalid for a moment before he does what he's been waiting for. Gets down and prays at last.

The voice broadcasting the call to prayer across the camp sounds much nearer and louder than ever before and soon his echoing prayers are whisked away into the darkening sky. A sky Tariq cannot see.

First thing the next morning, to Khalid's surprise, he's taken for interrogation again. His ankles are tied to the rings cemented on the floor and a familiar sinking feeling sets in. Two military-looking men in casual white shirts and beige trousers smile, pretending to be his friends. The one who's nearest starts the whole thing off.

"*Harry Potter*, have you read that yet?"

"I've been learning Farsi. Fascinating culture. Do you know anything about it?" the other man asks.

They try a bit of chit-chat, but Khalid's been through this too many times by now. Finally, they fire the questions they want to ask at him.

"What do you know about al-Qaeda?"

"Who have you spoken to from al-Qaeda?"

"I'm not saying anything about anything without my lawyer here," is all Khalid will say, aware he's talking like a character from some TV legal drama.

The first man sighs. "You do want to protect your family? When you help us, we'll help you."

"I've got nothing to say to you liars. I'm going to sue you for millions of dollars when I get out of here," Khalid threatens them instead. Feeling good about himself until the thin one leans in angrily, pink nostrils flaring.

Then he takes his hands out of his pockets and folds his arms to show he means business, so Khalid shifts in his seat to show he means business too. "I've got a lawyer now." And slowly whistles. Whistling like he's never whistled before, making it impossible for them to continue. A small payback for all the hours they haven't listened to him, a small payback for causing his family so much distress.

Eventually the guards take Khalid back to his cage and this time he feels he really has, at last, got one over on them. His confidence grows at a rate of knots at the thought. Tariq would be proud of him. If only he could tell him, or at least get a message to him.

Over the next few days Khalid's taken for interrogation several times. He soon works out that's the reason they've moved him here. But just like the last time, the interrogators soon learn they're getting nowhere. While Khalid becomes an expert at half whistling, half singing, tapping his feet to every beat he knows. Starting with Eminem and 50 Cent. He hopes the Americans know the words, because every pissed-off expression he spots on their faces makes him think of his dad. Now his dad knows he's here and so do loads of other people; it makes Khalid feel he's protected and gives him the confidence to stand up to them.

This morning, trying hard to disguise how angry he's getting, one interrogator calls the guards after only two minutes of Khalid being in the room.

"Yeah, get fed up with me, because I'm so fed up with you," he tells them as they take him away.

Back in the cage, Khalid sits on the floor under a shifting line of passing clouds to write a long letter to Mr. Tagg. Imagining him reading and sympathizing with every word Khalid writes, an exquisite feeling of rightness pumps up his desire to tell the world how he feels, to explain what his life here has been like.

*Hearing some real rap now would just round things off,* Khalid thinks, smiling. But no event here is a harmless one and soon the familiar feeling he's going to have to pay for his rude behavior starts pressing down on him. As the long hours draw out and the last prayers end, he begins to lose faith in the idea he'll ever get out of here. What are they waiting for now? What is Harry doing?

When night falls, the men begin calling goodnight to each other in many languages and Khalid starts to worry they'll come for him again before morning. The sound of barking dogs being walked the length of the perimeter fence adds to his restlessness. As he closes his eyes, arguing the toss with himself as he always does these days before finally drifting off to sleep, a damp, rotting smell creeps over him. Reminding him of the two frogs Aadab once ran in with from the garden, holding the croaking things up to his nose.

"Say hello to them. Go on!" she begged.

"Ergh—they stink. Get them out of here," Khalid said, and she burst into tears. At the time he didn't much care, but now the memory of her sweet little face crumpled up and crying breaks his heart in two.

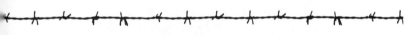

## HOT SHOTS

Khalid thinks the worst when the heavy-built guard with eyes like moons stops outside his cage before the first prayers are called, rattling keys. His hair, still damp from an early shower, smells strongly of almonds and he seems in a bad mood.

"Your head's covered in baby hair, dude," he says.

"Done for, am I? How sad." Khalid rubs the thin clumps of hair on his head to check they're still growing. "What's up, then, eh?"

"You get your things," he adds. "And cut it."

"You're moving me back. Great!" Khalid grabs his sheets of paper and pen, unsent scribbles, postcard and precious letter from Dad. Then his Qur'an, quickly checking the cage for anything he might have missed. Oh yeah, his flip-flops.

"We ain't got all day." The guard tries to hurry him up, without any luck.

"Hang on, what did I do with my flat-screen TV and iPod?" So glad to get out of there, Khalid's larking around, busy pulling apart the diamond-shaped wire to prove he's left nothing behind. One man starts waving and laughing at his antics.

It's only when they're outside the cage that Khalid, his arms full of papers, begins to realize something strange is going on.

"You forgot the shackles," he tells the guard. "You're going to get into trouble now."

"Is that right?" He smiles.

Walking normally is something Khalid's only done inside his cell or that time he went to the hospital because of his ear. Unable to do more than three and a half unrestrained steps in all from one end of his cell to the other since he came here, he's pigeon-toed now.

Khalid manages to nod goodbye to each man as he goes past with his small steps, walking weirdly like an old man. They greet him with affectionate *salaams* and questions in various languages, wondering where he's going without his chains. The same thought occurs to Khalid, but all he can do is wave and try to concentrate on not tripping over as he's led to a nearby block, put in a small room and left there.

"Hey, there's no water in here!" Khalid yells as the guard clicks the lock shut. The sound of heavy boots fades away, leaving him with nothing to do but sit on the blue chair, his stuff in his lap, and wait for someone to come.

With no air conditioning, the room is hot and sticky. Khalid stares at the desk and chair opposite him and listens to the sound of a door opening and closing. More footsteps. Trucks starting up outside. Dogs barking. The call to prayer begins. Surely they're not going to leave him here for much longer without water? The more he thinks about it, the more convinced he becomes that he's been brought here because

Harry has demanded to see him. And if he has been told to bring his stuff, they must be taking him to another block afterwards. Maybe they're playing another psychological game with him. All Khalid knows is he's thirsty. There's been no breakfast or lunch and the chair he's sitting on is made of rough, itchy material that feels like carpet. The next time he hears footsteps, Khalid jumps up to bang on the door.

"Hey, where's my water? Where's my water?"

The door opens at last. A female soldier with deep-set dark eyes passes him a warm plastic bottle and then an amazing thing happens. She nods, saying, "Sorry, you should have been given this earlier this morning!"

Unbelievable.

Khalid is so flabbergasted, he takes the bottle and just stands there staring at her. No one has ever, ever, ever said sorry to him since he was kidnapped. Except for Lee-Andy, of course. That one time, yeah.

When the door closes and he sits down to drink, Khalid also realizes, for the first time, that he might, just might be getting this special treatment because he's got a lawyer to hear his complaints.

It's past midnight when two guards come to take him away. One scoops up his Qur'an, papers and pen, the other clicks the shackles into place with unnecessary force. Khalid's eaten nothing since yesterday and he's feeling dizzy from the heat, so he doesn't care where he's going, but he's shocked they've taken all this trouble merely to walk him ten paces down the corridor to a room similar to the one he's just left.

Only this time two hot-shot American military men in smart uniform are waiting for him.

"I'm Major Donaldson. This is Major Leeth," says the first man, holding out a palm to introduce the more important-looking man standing beside him. Both eye Khalid as if he's another nuisance they can't wait to get rid of, while the guard at the door watches his every move.

"We're here to tell you, number 256 . . ." Major Donaldson pauses.

Khalid shivers. *What? What?*

"You're," Major Leeth butts in, "yes, you're going home!"

"What?" Khalid swoons, going hot and cold at the same time. Overwhelmed as the length and breadth of Rochdale flashes before his eyes. Is this for real?

"You'll be given a bag for your things. Follow the guard." Major Donaldson nods.

"That's all you've got to say?" Khalid narrows his eyes. "That's the lamest thing I've ever heard." This idiot is clearly a robot. He's no use as a major, that's for sure. "How come you're letting me go all of a sudden? Are they going to put me in prison in England? Go on, tell me!"

"Let's just say you're no longer considered a threat," Major Donaldson replies.

"You're the threat, mate, not me. I'm going to sue you for all of this. Just so you know," Khalid says.

"I think you'll find you were never arrested," Major Leeth tells him, smirking.

"No, that's right, I was kidnapped, wasn't I? You suckers better apologize for torturing me."

At this, the guard grabs his shoulder to push him outside.

"Wait. I need to say goodbye to someone first," Khalid begs. "Please can I?"

"Take him directly to the exit gate." Major Donaldson hands the guard a sealed brown envelope and closes the door.

"Thanks for nothing!" Khalid yells, elbowing the guard away. Two years' worth of anger in his eyes.

"Hey, man," the guard says, trying to calm him down, not quite understanding. He raises his eyebrows. "Be OK, you'll see."

"Yeah, if they're telling the truth." A number of conflicting emotions pass through Khalid as they walk out of the building. What are they up to now? Where's he going? How's he going to get home? Will anyone believe him? The idea of no longer being bound by shackles, barbed wire, soldiers, feels too frightening to imagine. Free? What does that mean?

Day after day he'd pictured being back in Rochdale—at home with his family and friends, at college, with Niamh even —but he'd never actually imagined walking out of here one day.

"I don't know where to go. I haven't got any money." Khalid shudders.

"You're not done yet." The guard smiles. "Don't worry."

"Look, will you do me a favor?"

This time the guard eyes him suspiciously. "Depends what you want."

"Find number 372. Tell him about me going. Say I won't stop trying until he's free too. Will you do that for me, man?" Khalid begs, desperate to let Tariq know what's happening.

"Sure, no problem." The guard eyes the dark clouds scudding across the black body of the night sky, anxious to avoid Khalid's gaze. A wall of distrust divides them as they walk across the floodlit base, making dusty footprints on the path. Past concrete buildings and soldiers going about their business. Along a row of parked-up trucks and barking dogs, razor wire rattling in the breeze, then a sudden flap of wings from a bird overhead.

The smell of binned sausages outside the kitchen quarters as they pass by reminds Khalid of the kebab shop at home on Roland Road. He salivates suddenly at the thought of lamb doner being sliced from a vertical cone into pita bread with tomatoes, lettuce, onions and chilli sauce.

Sparking the memory of Mikael at the counter, shouting, "I love you. I love you," to a fistful of oozing bread and Tony Banda with his hand out for his special vegetarian order of chips, tomatoes and Cheddar cheese in pita bread with chilli sauce *and* mayonnaise.

"Leave some of that mayo for me," Nico warns.

Half crazy with nerves, a hungry hollow feeling in the pit of his stomach, Khalid follows the soldier inside another building, where three men wait for him. And before anything happens the shackles are unclicked and dropped on the floor. One man fingerprints him, the other hands him a navy T-shirt, socks and jeans. The last guy points to four pairs of blue sneakers on the table.

Without a word, Khalid's fitted with old-man, high-waisted jeans and a baggy T-shirt. Clothes more suited to a chunky American than a skinny kid. The sudden whiff of denim makes Khalid think of the pile of clean folded clothes Mum lays on his bed each week. Every time he used to pull a face at her for coming in without knocking. He'll never do that again. He imagines being at home in the kitchen, being helpful, extra nice and respectful as he breathes in cinnamon and cloves from the apple tart she's made before going off to work. When she pulls up the hood of her white rainproof jacket, he's going to rush to find the umbrella for her and open the door to her smile.

He's going to get up early to clean Dad's shoes and surprise him by twisting the lid back evenly on the Kiwi polish. Tell him, "It's OK, Dad, when I'm rich I'll look after you. No worries."

He'll be grateful to walk his sisters to school instead of complaining it'll make him late. And he'll tell Holgy he's the best footballer out of all of them, which he is.

But then Khalid's worst fears are confirmed when another soldier turns up with new shackles hanging from his arms.

"What are these for?"

"Security," the guard says. "Won't be for long!"

A shattering feeling of relief builds up inside Khalid as they throw a hood on his head and usher him into a vehicle waiting outside. Finally, he's leaving Guantanamo Bay after what feels like thirty years.

And Niamh, what can he do for her?

For a start he can tell her he loved her buttercup painting. That it was way better than anything else and when he stood in the library looking at it he lost all sense of time—he was right there in the long grass. A rush of pure, vibrating pleasure suddenly shoots from Khalid's stomach to his throat. Yeah, there're so many nice things he's going to do. He can't wait.

Khalid doesn't know where they are taking him this time but he's back in the vehicle and smelling the night air and the whiff of petrol as they drive for a while and then stop. He listens to the sound of soldiers opening metal gates and the vehicle driving off. When it stops next time, he's moved to a boat. A large boat, Khalid thinks by the easy feeling he gets from speeding across the water. Before long they are back on land. Soon he's shuffled out and the shackles are undone and the hood's whipped off for the last time.

Staring at the military plane, Khalid says a quiet thank-you to the thousands of stars in the Cuban night sky and says a silent prayer for the men who are still there. For a moment he hears the patter of rain as he's guided to the plane. A soldier hands him a white plastic bag with his Qur'an, letter, postcard, sheets of paper and pen. No goodbye. No good wishes. Nothing but a soldier directing him. Gun at the ready.

On board, Khalid's surprised to see lots more people. A few police and men in plain suits. Then there's the guy he saw in Karachi. That bloke with the posh voice. Other guys who nod and smile as he walks past. And what looks like another newly released detainee: T-shirt half off, he's reading the *Daily Mirror* and quickly working his way through a packet of salt and vinegar crisps.

"Khalid . . . finally, at last." Harry jumps out of his seat to greet him, grinning from ear to ear.

"Hiya." A bit dazed from lack of sleep and starving hungry, Khalid sits next to him.

"Did you ever believe you'd be going home?"

"No way. Thanks for everything," Khalid says, tears welling in his eyes again.

"No, no. Thank your family and friends when you get home. Rochdale is a good place, you know? That whole community has been fighting to get you back. Your dad got up a petition and thousands of people have signed. The *Rochdale Evening News* took up the case. You're famous! Want these?" Harry hands Khalid a packet of cheese crackers and a bottle of water.

"Thanks."

He hasn't eaten anything since yesterday and taking his time to enjoy each mouthful, the extraordinary feeling he's going home slowly flows through his body until the certainty can no longer be denied. But not only does Khalid find this Rochdale stuff hard to believe; it seems incredible that from now on people will think he's special, though not for anything positive, just for spending time in that prison.

Roaring to the end of the runway, the plane finally takes off.

That's it—the nightmare's really over. But before Khalid gets the chance to absorb the fact of his freedom, Harry has another surprise.

"I almost forgot!" Bending down to riffle through the bulging black briefcase stowed carefully under the seat in front, he finds the package he's looking for.

"Ah, yes, here they are." He hands Khalid three bright

envelopes held together by an elastic band. "From your family."

The first one Khalid opens has a huge red number 17 on the front and the words "Happy Birthday." The others are handmade cards of birds and flowers from Aadab and Gul.

"Happy birthday for three weeks ago," Harry says.

"Yeah, March eleventh. Seems so long ago now. Thanks."

"Hundreds of people have sent cards," Harry says. "Your mum's keeping them for you."

"Really?"

"Yes." Harry laughs. "A belated happy birthday from me too. Why didn't I get you a present? Wait a minute. Excuse me?" Harry calls to the soldier on duty. "Any chance of a couple of fresh orange juices?"

Clinking small plastic glasses to celebrate his seventeenth birthday, Khalid catches up on the family news he's missed from the letter inside the huge blue football card from Mum and Dad. The news of his Uncle Amir's death, plus details of the small flat the aunties have moved to in Karachi. How Aadab has started a gymnastics class at the sports club and Gul is enjoying swimming after refusing to go anywhere near the water. And how Mum's the first person in the family to pass her driving test. Loads of things that make Khalid smile.

Harry then fills him in on the War on Terror, plus the Madrid train bombings three weeks ago and stories of the renditions, all the handing over of prisoners which Khalid has been part of.

In some ways Harry's more excited than he is. But then Khalid guesses he's had a good night's sleep, unlike him.

"I made a few notes for you about what's been happening with Guantanamo Bay. Here—take a look. It's pretty shocking stuff."

Khalid glances down the page, reading about the widespread criticism of the military tribunals called "kangaroo courts" by a British Lord Justice. Reading the section on juveniles with growing disgust.

In January 2004 a Pentagon spokesperson told a BBC journalist that after the release of three Afghans aged eleven to fifteen, no other juveniles remain in Guantanamo.

"Yeah, well, I was still there," Khalid says, pointing this bit out to Harry.

He nods. "A report from the charity Reprieve says many more juveniles have been held at the base and none have been given a fair trial and found guilty."

Khalid hands the whole thing back. "I can't take any more in at the moment."

"No, of course," Harry says.

Then a policeman walks along the aisle and pauses for a moment to give Khalid a warm smile. Khalid shrinks back, half expecting him to shout. But the man does nothing more than hold out a small plastic bottle of water, saying, "Enjoy the journey. Want anything else?"

"Yeah, I mean no. No, thanks." Khalid turns to Harry, eager to ask the long-awaited question that's just popped into his mind. "My cousin Tariq Waji Hachem is still in Guantanamo. He's only two years older than me. Can you help him?"

Immediately, Harry looks concerned. "Your father mentioned him several times. We've been unable to get confirmation from the authorities that Tariq's being held there."

Slowly and in great detail Khalid tells his cousin's story, which, in many respects, is identical to his own, explaining how Tariq was abducted from his home while playing *Bomber One* on his computer and was taken for questioning in Islamabad before being carted off to be tortured into giving a confession, which he later retracted. The moment he's finished giving him Tariq's details, Khalid sinks back in the seat, suddenly tired.

"Now we have your testimony, it's going to be easier to help him," Harry says. "But you look tired. Perhaps we'll leave everything else until later. I haven't even told you what's going to happen next, have I?"

"Just two more things before I pass out," Khalid says. "That woman in Karachi said they had my passport."

"Impossible. Your dad took your passport when he first went to the police, then to the newspapers—everywhere—to prove you were missing." Harry grins. "I remember the rare light-hearted smile your dad gave me when he showed me your passport photo. He said it was one of the few you liked and you wouldn't mind him showing it to anyone. What was the other thing?"

"I need the loo."

Harry laughs. "No need to tell me. It's the far door on the right."

Anxious at the thought of walking past so many policemen, Khalid almost decides to wait, but Harry gives him an encouraging glance which helps him take his first unaccompanied steps since his ordeal began. But as Khalid stumbles into the aisle, the policeman the other side of him jumps up to escort him, and stands waiting outside the door to walk him back. Forcing Khalid to realize this whole thing is not quite over yet.

Sadly, there's no mirror in the loo. Just a basic chrome toilet and sink. He was hoping to see himself—see how bad he looks.

Once back in his seat, smelling of the sweet coconut soap he'd found in the sink, Khalid asks, "Will they ever close that Guantanamo hellhole down?"

"One day, Khalid, one day. But the trouble is, they don't know what to do with the men there. Many of them are stateless refugees with no place to go."

The idea that some of those men have no home kicks Khalid in the guts. He'd spent so long being consumed by his own problems, living in his own sad little world, that he hadn't given much thought to anyone else. At least he has a country, a home and family, mates even. In that moment, Khalid feels very, very grateful to have everything that matters.

# TOUCHDOWN

The wing flaps flick up, waking Khalid from a delicious long sleep. His head's been twisted sideways on his shoulder for what must have been hours and he's paying for it now that he tries to sit straight, hands on his aching neck. Through the window he catches sight of an astonishing maze of gray clouds. Clouds that go on forever without a hint of blue.

The noises coming from the galley kitchen sound like bones cracking until someone laughs instead of screams and Khalid breathes in the pleasant smell of warm bread rolls.

"Feel any better?" Harry smiles.

"Yeah, just starving," Khalid says.

"Well, that didn't take long." Harry nods at the steel trolley making its way towards them and before long the trays soon slot into place. One fresh bread roll, a golden square of butter, curly omelette and a portion of baked beans. The best meal of his whole life. He swallows everything so quickly, Harry pushes his tray towards him.

"Have mine too. I'm not in the least bit hungry."

"Thanks, mate." Aware that Harry is totally enjoying watching him eat with his elbows in the air, grunting happily after each mouthful and licking his lips at another small chocolate croissant, which he saves until last, Khalid scoffs the lot and sits back to rub his stomach.

"What now?"

"Well, I'm afraid you won't be going directly home. We land at RAF Northolt." Harry pauses for a moment to scratch his chin. "There are a few formalities to be dealt with first. More interviews, that sort of thing. Plus someone will talk to you about adapting to real life after your ordeal. It will take a few days and then you'll be going home."

"How many days?" Khalid had imagined the plane was going to land in Manchester, not RAF Northolt—somewhere else in England.

"Three or four days. A week at the most," Harry says. "Nothing to worry about. You'll be given a comfortable room this time—with a bathroom."

"What about my family?" he asks. *Aadab and Gul? How tall are they now?* Khalid suddenly wonders. Do they want him back? Aren't their lives better without him? He wasn't that nice to them before. Would they be pleased to see him again?

"They'll have to wait until you're brought home, Khalid. But they know you're on your way. Everyone does. You can use my phone to talk to them when we land."

"I was looking forward to seeing my mates and that," Khalid says as the seat-belt sign flashes on and the plane begins its descent.

"It won't be long, I promise," Harry reassures him.

Home. England. This is England. As he looks out of the

window to watch the plane coming in, endless gray clouds burst with hard, cold rain and Khalid feels an overpowering sense of peace just gazing at the lush green fields, busy roads and small houses below. But the moment they land a plain-clothed policeman in a navy suit boards the plane and walks towards him.

"Just a formality," Harry whispers as the man bends over Khalid to quietly tell him, "I am placing you under arrest under the Prevention of Terrorism Act." A policeman quickly handcuffs him before they move on to do the same to the other man who has been released.

"This happened with the last three men who came back. Nothing to worry about," Harry says. "I'll see you later." But Khalid's stomach turns over—what with all the food, the sight of England after two years away and being so close to home, and now this.

Within minutes, he's led to the doors of a black van that's driven on to the plane through the open back. A driving wind forces heavy rain up the cold tunnel, chilling Khalid to the bone. The other prisoner begins shivering uncontrollably as they're ushered on to the van's hard seats and the doors slam shut.

"What a pisser, eh? After all that shite we've been through, we end up freezing to death in the back of a bloody police van. My name's Ashwin Al-Asmari and I'm from Birmingham. The guy on the plane said we have to go through this because the Americans are watching us. So what? Let 'em have an eyeful, I say."

"Quiet in the back, please!" one of the policemen shouts.

Ashwin pulls a face and starts coughing.

"You were that guy—the one who was coughing all night in Camp Delta," Khalid whispers.

"They wouldn't give me my right medication. Said I was pretending to have asthma. I practically died in there."

"Quiet down!" the policeman demands.

It's the last Khalid sees of Ashwin after they are led quickly from the van through pouring rain into a long, gray building. A drooping cobweb catches Khalid's eye as it swings from the door in a cold draught of English spring air that smells crisp and fresh and suddenly full of hope.

Ashwin's taken to one room, Khalid to another one farther down the corridor. A room larger than his living room at home, with a proper-size single bed in the corner. A pile of new old-man clothes and a new Qur'an, newspapers, crisps, water. Not quite as good as a hotel room but a hundred times more comfortable than the cell he's been used to. The police escort smiles.

"You might want to dry off—take a shower and get changed," he says. "Your lawyer will be here soon. Would you like a hot drink? We have everything."

"Yeah, tea. No, wait, hot chocolate please, with two sugars."

Khalid's relieved to see the back of him. Two minutes later, he's staring at his face from all sides in the bathroom mirror. Eyeing his body from all angles. Surprised to see he doesn't look anything like he thought he did. His face seems gentler than he remembers it. Sadder. His chin *is* bigger than it was, he's sure of that. And his shoulders are rounder than they were. His neck seems to poke forward and definitely isn't as straight as it used to be either. But apart from that he decides he's still basically good-looking, even though he's grown so much taller. Standing with his back to the door, he tries to measure his height with a hand over his head, then looks back with surprise at the distance it is from the floor.

"Yeah, that's way over six feet," Khalid says out loud. "Probably six feet three."

After luxuriating under waterfalls of steaming-hot water, then changing into clean clothes, Khalid begins to feel almost human. By the time there's a knock on the door, he's ready to face the world. But when Harry bursts in grinning, offering him a flash silver mobile, and says, "Your dad's on the phone!" Khalid freezes in shock.

"Dad! Dad!" Khalid grabs the mobile. Holding it close, he turns away from Harry as Dad's soft, gentle voice passes through him in a wave of longed-for pure pleasure.

"I'm fine. I've just had a lovely shower, Dad." Sitting on the bed, Khalid sinks into his voice, into the warmth of his home in Rochdale, with the sound of his sisters kicking up a fuss in the background.

"I know, Dad. They didn't tell me either. It's a shock for me too. Are you OK? Dad, don't cry. You'll make me cry. Yeah, put Mum on. Me too, Mum. Don't. Now everyone's crying. Hi, Aadab. No, I know you're not going to cry. You're too grown up, yeah, course. You sound a lot older. Hareema's your new best friend? She sounds nice. Gul, I love you too. What new bike?"

Over the next twenty-four hours, Khalid is fingerprinted and questioned briefly by two men he assumes are the police.

"Name? Address? What date did you travel to Karachi in Pakistan? Where did you go while you were there?" All the usual stuff, but this time there's no mention of a demonstration, or a computer game, or accomplices, or anything else. Plus they write down the answers. When they ask Khalid to explain his abduction, they act like they are listening and write that down too. The whole thing feels like a conversation to Khalid and not like an interrogation.

Several times Khalid speaks to his family, mostly just saying, "Yes, I'm fine. No honestly, I'm all right. It'll be OK." While they do most of the talking, telling him about the efforts made by the people of Rochdale, charities like Reprieve, the Islamic Human Rights Commission, Guantanamo Human Rights Campaign, Amnesty International, and many other groups who have been working hard to get him released.

The next morning a policeman escorts Khalid along the corridor to another room with comfy armchairs, a small kitchen and a gray table.

"Take a seat," he says, as if it's a place the soldiers use at break times to read the papers and relax. Khalid glances at the coffee machine bubbling on the worktop beside the sink. For a moment the sight of the beige froth fascinates him and the policeman smiles.

"Would you like some?"

"Er . . ." Khalid hesitates as the door opens and another man rushes in who looks like an office worker in gray trousers and white shirt, a pile of blue folders under his arm.

"Sorry to keep you waiting. I'm Professor Wolfson. My job is to help you settle back into normal life as soon as possible."

"When can I go home?" Khalid asks.

"Tomorrow probably," says Professor Wolfson, smiling. "Let's see now. Yes." He drops the blue folders on the coffee table and looks Khalid straight in the eye. "Good. I think we'll have one to start." He gestures to the policeman, who moves towards the kitchen area.

Khalid quickly nods an answer to the question in his raised eyebrows. "Hardly any milk please."

"After an ordeal like yours," the professor says, "most people experience a number of problems. We'll talk about them one by one and see how we get on, shall we?"

"Yeah, sure." Khalid thinks this will be easy, and hearing he's likely to be going home tomorrow makes him anxious to please the nice professor and get this over with as soon as possible.

"Even simple things like the sound of people talking at once might prove hard to deal with at first," he begins.

"Yeah, I get that. It might feel weird." Khalid pulls a face as he sips the mug of almost black coffee, shocked by the bitterness of the taste. Did he really used to drink it like this? Urgh!

"Not just weird," the professor says. "You might experience a physical reaction and feel faint. Want to run away from the noise of their voices. Just remember that every reaction you have to anything is absolutely normal and is to be expected in this type of situation."

"I don't think I'll wanna run away!" Khalid reckons the professor's overreacting slightly. I mean, he doesn't look that crazy, does he?

"You might shrink from ordinary affection from your family simply because you're not used to it. A hand on a shoulder might feel threatening all of a sudden."

"Yeah, I can maybe see that," Khalid admits. But bit by bit, as Professor Wolfson talks him through a typical day at home and how he might react to ordinary things like going out on his own to the shops for the first time, Khalid realizes he's going to have a lot to deal with when he gets back. Sparking the sudden memory of his trip to Nasir's grocery shop all that time ago without a worry in the world. Unaware of passing cars, of people, of anything much but the thoughts inside his head. Remembering cutting through the cul-de-sac on his way to the park.

"What if I suddenly bump into someone I don't know? Will it scare me?" Khalid's suddenly frightened he won't be able to cope with anything. Not his parents. His friends. Being out on his own.

"It might do, but you can prepare yourself for that by thinking about it beforehand," the professor says patiently, and slowly talks him through every eventuality.

Khalid's still worrying about things when he's led out to another exercise yard where two policemen stand waiting on either side of the locked gate. This time the exercise yard is a huge, windswept, rain-drenched field, marked by high metal fences that are impossible to see through.

It takes Khalid quite a while to walk round the edge with his hands in his pockets; his white sneakers make a squelching sound as he marches as fast as he can. Quickening his step after the first full circuit to include a sudden fast header, then the kick of an imaginary ball. Then a jump and a run to become the speediest footballer on the field, racing down the line faster and faster to score an amazing goal. Followed by a leap in the air, fists punching the sky, head shaking, Khalid lets out a spine-tingling "YES! YES!" He's going home.

## HOME

Many things are on Khalid's mind as Harry's old Fiat turns into Oswestry Road. For a start, the sound of heavy traffic in the distance is much louder than he remembers.

A red Mini Cooper races past with four teenagers inside. One of whom he vaguely recognizes. Martin Weeks? Nah, it can't be him. His curly black hair was never that wild, or was it? The worrying thought bangs into Khalid suddenly that he might not recognize any of his mates. How much have they changed over the last two years? Will they still want to be his friend or will they hate him? Do any of them believe he's guilty? Or will they pretend everything's cool but talk about him behind his back as if he's a terrorist? The thought of them behaving like that makes him feel slightly sick. A tight feeling spreads down his throat at the idea of coping without them.

As the car pulls up outside his house, Khalid's surprised to see Mac's garden next door is full of new orange and yellow flowers that are growing over the adjoining low wall. There's a new metal gate and his beige curtains are neatly tied back, white nets shaking enough to suggest Mac's whole family are watching Khalid arrive—which makes him smile. He waves at the window, knowing they can see. Knowing Mac won't ever treat him differently from the way he's always done. He's not that kind of bloke.

"There's no side to Mac," Dad always says.

Khalid's house looks exactly the same. The same narrow concrete path with patches of grass growing over it. The same white-painted front door with two empty bottles of milk on the step. A new pink bike left on its side.

His homecoming—an event he's imagined for so long—is here at last. But a weird feeling of remoteness descends on Khalid, a strange detachment from what he knows is about to happen.

A few of the neighbors rush out to stand at their gates and watch as Khalid and Harry go up the short path. Within seconds the door swings open and Aadab . . . no, an older Gul races up the path first and jumps into Khalid's arms. Followed by a much taller and lankier Aadab, glossy hair almost down to her waist. Then Mum in a smart navy skirt and long-sleeved white blouse, with her arms open wide, cries unashamedly as she walks towards him, but Aadab and Gul are in the way and she stops when they meet on the path. Mum reaches for his shoulders, weeping, but doesn't hug Khalid because as a family they don't do public displays of affection, which is why Dad's standing awkwardly back. Pretending to keep the door from slamming shut as he proudly watches Khalid walk up the path at last. Everyone begins talking at once. Smiling and nodding with quivering lips and damp eyes. The neighbors avidly watching their every move.

Lowering his head, hand over his mouth, Harry follows Khalid inside. Everyone chatters at once as the door closes on the whole family, who are crammed together in an emotional heap in the narrow hall.

Aadab and Gul tug at his jeans for attention.

"I can't breathe," Khalid says, disentangling Mum's wet face from his neck. Unused to being touched in a way that isn't violent for the past two years, he feels smothered. Trapped. Claustrophobic all of a sudden.

"Let him be for a little while." Dad takes Khalid's elbow and leads him into the kitchen, brown leather shoes squeaking.

But even that small gesture feels strange to Khalid, who fights it by saying, "Thanks, Dad. New shoes?"

"Yes. I bought them especially to welcome you home, but the color isn't quite right with these trousers. What do you think?"

"I think they're the best shoes you've ever had, Dad." Khalid's eyes well up.

"They don't match properly. I should have taken them back. But compared to the state of your muddy sneakers, Khalid, they are very good."

Then Khalid does something he hasn't done for quite a few years. He takes Dad's round, smiling face in his hands and kisses him right on the nose.

For a moment Dad looks shocked, but then he laughs. "Always you found my nose funny," he says.

"I still do." Khalid grins.

Once tea and the big, sugary welcome-home cake have been demolished, Harry prepares to leave.

"Here, you nearly forgot this, Khalid." He hands him the white plastic bag he left Guantanamo with and it falls open to reveal the Qur'an, the letter, the postcard and papers, the few things he'd owned in that terrible place. And for a moment he's back there on the bed, head in his hands, waiting for the dinner trolley to come down the row, and he trembles—the kitchen moves away from him . . .

"Khalid," Dad calls. "Khalid."

"Eh?" He blinks for a moment, suddenly aware he's gripping the table. No, he's here, at home. The ache inside dies and a feeling of hope takes its place.

They all scrape back their chairs and follow Harry out to see him off. At the door, Khalid shakes Harry's hand and nods in the same way he does. At that moment the neighbors start running down their paths again to have a good look and everyone waves and waves until Harry's car disappears from sight down the long road.

Khalid is the first to turn back inside to stare at the heap of mail from well-wishers addressed to him that is stacked in neat piles on the hall floor. He's about to open one of the cards when he's shocked to hear his name come from the crackling TV in the living room. The news is on and his face is spread large across the screen. The family crowd round to cheer when the newsreader says he's returned home to Rochdale.

It's all a bit much for Khalid, who feels an urgent need to get away from everyone and climbs over the sofa to make his escape.

"No, leave him," Dad tells Aadab, who darts to block the door.

A sulky expression crosses her face. "We've been waiting ages for him to come back—he has to talk to us some more."

"I said let him go. Khalid's tired out now, can't you see?"

"Yeah, tired." Khalid nods, quickly making his excuses. He only begins to feel more like himself when he sits on the pale blue duvet of his strangely chunky-feeling bed. The Rochdale Football Club league table from 2002 is still stuck to the wall opposite. His football boots are on the red carpet beside the white chest of drawers, blue cap on top where he left it. Feeling weirdly absent from this house, this room, he suddenly thinks of Tariq and the remaining 600 men locked in Guantanamo Bay while he sits here in comfort, the bedroom door wide open for him to walk through whenever he likes. The kitchen's full of cake, biscuits, Cheddar cheese, crisps and orange juice he can get whenever he wants. Khalid's mouth waters at the thought of real home-made curry for dinner later and the taste of nicely cooked rice and naan bread, even though his stomach is full to bursting from so much cake.

A car whizzes past the window. The sun casts a shadow across the neat and tidy room before sinking behind a distant row of houses. It's not until the smell of boiling rice drifts up from the kitchen that Khalid finally accepts he's home to stay. A thought both wonderful and unbelievable at the same time.

Then there's all the people knocking on the door, day and night. The local imams, Muslim leaders, journalists, friends and neighbors—even the guy who owns the restaurant where Dad works. Their constant voices, welcomes and polite inquiries cause exhaustion and pounding headaches for Khalid.

"Please, Dad, tell them I've had enough! I don't know what to say to them." But Dad's too polite, though sometimes he keeps them on the doorstep for so long they get bored and leave.

Some days are harder to get through than others, because Khalid's finding it difficult to sleep. He keeps waking up to pictures of high razor wire and the sound of screaming, and gets up to pace the bedroom. The window and door are always wide open, but he's afraid to look up in case he's back there, hurting. And all the time he's trying to pluck up courage to go and see his mates and he's desperate to bump into Niamh and see her pretty face again. Khalid's sad that none of them have come round, until he remembers they always meet at the park or the shops. Not since primary school has anyone knocked for him, and anyway, they usually meet at Nico's house, because his mum and dad are always out. Deep down he knows they're waiting for him to make the first move and that's what scares him the most.

It takes two more days before Khalid finds the nerve to get up in the middle of the night and go downstairs. He's been avoiding going downstairs at night and, feeling slightly chilly, he pulls on a black hoodie over the white T-shirt and red boxers he's slept in, listening for a moment to the sound of Dad snoring in the room next door.

The only sound in the kitchen is the hum of the fridge and for a long time Khalid stands at the door, staring at the dense, black square on the table in the corner, wondering if he has the nerve to turn the computer on.

With one click and ping, the screen splutters into action, lighting up faster than Khalid remembers. Hitting the search engine to bring up his e-mails, he's shocked to find several hundred people have sent him a message.

But the name he wants to see—Niamh—isn't there.

"Come round when you're up to it, mate," Nico says. "I tried to see you yesterday but there was a nutter blocking your gate asking me my name, so I scarpered."

"Hey, bad man, you's cool," Holgy says.

Glancing down the list, Khalid sees there are a few nasty ones from kids he knows mixed in with the nice messages.

"You don't deserve to come home, you terrorist bastard. I hope you rot in hell."

Khalid tenses suddenly. His stomach muscles tighten, his throat turns dry and a wave of nausea comes over him. An imaginary mirror rises in his mind to reflect back the picture of a gloomy cupboard, with Khalid jumping up from playing *Bomber One* to go to the loo. Heading back with a smile on his face, his jeans half zipped, then the sound of someone in the hall . . . the sound he thought might be Dad. But men in black walk him backwards, force him into the kitchen, where they wave a gun at his face.

"NO!" Khalid yells, falling out of the chair, head in his hands with the sound of feet rushing towards him.

"Son. Son." Warm hands clasp his shoulder and bring Khalid into warm arms and the soft cotton smell of Dad. Standing there in his beige pajamas, Dad weeps along with him. Holding him close like a baby.

"They—those men . . ." Khalid sobs. "They came from nowhere. They beat me up and threw me in a truck. They just took me."

"I know, son. I know."

After a while, when Khalid quiets down, they talk and talk about the prison, what happened, about football and girls and his hopes and dreams, until the morning light peeps through the kitchen window and the deathly fear that's been keeping him awake leaves him for a bit.

Late afternoon the next day, Khalid's out of the house in baggy black jeans with a new mobile in his pocket. Settling the queasy feeling inside with a hand on his stomach, he checks he's up to it before turning right, then second left. Cutting through the cul-de-sac to the park, he imagines Nico and the rest of them are already there and a few of the steroid heads are beating each other to a pulp beside the tennis courts. Maybe Niamh and her friends are down by the far gate smoking their cigarettes and sharing a couple of those disgusting alcopops that girls seem to like.

Running as fast as he can past the kids on the swings, Khalid races towards the benches under the oak trees, then stops suddenly to see the bushes have all been cut back. The broken benches have been replaced with brand-new green ones. All the bird poo, flattened Pringles tubes and beer cans have gone. Even some of the oak branches have sadly been lopped off, opening their secret place to the wide sky and noisy road behind.

A couple of schoolkids he vaguely recognizes, who've grown uglier and ruder than Khalid remembers, saunter past smoking cigarettes. It's not until they're way past him that one calls out, "Thought you were dead, Kal, mate."

"Better not bomb anything round here or yer soon will be," his mate says, laughing.

Without answering, Khalid hurries in the opposite direction, out of the park gate towards Nico's house.

Finding himself unable to cross the busy road, he stands for a moment, suddenly hypnotized by the sight and sound of cars rumbling past. A whooshing sensation flows through his head as he sees the traffic lights change from red and amber to green, then amber to red again. And the roar of buses and lorries thundering past his face, spitting dirt over his new sneakers, while the sickly smell of deep-frying fish leaks from the chip shop behind him. He can't breathe. He's going to faint.

"Is that you, Kal? Hiya, mate. HIYA!" Wide-eyed and suddenly there in front of him, Holgy pulls him away from the traffic and he's grinning and grinning. Taller than Khalid now, he's got a crazy line of hair round his chin, joining up to crazy sideburns.

"How you doing, Kal? Your face is everywhere. I keep saying, 'I know him, he's an old mate of mine.'"

"I'm a bit all over the place." Khalid lowers his eyes, shaking. Trying his best not to faint.

"Well, you would be, wouldn't you?" Holgy sighs and presses the button to cross the road.

"What you up to, then?" Khalid breathes out.

"I'm down the sixth-form college. They let you dress how you like," Holgy says brightly. "You ought to come and scope it out."

"But I haven't got any GCSEs, have I, Holgy?" Khalid says.

319

"So what? There's two old ladies there doing A-levels and they haven't got any GCSEs either. Anyhows, you've got a pretty good excuse, eh, Kal? By the way, me name's Eshan now. No one, like, calls me Holgy any more. I'm too old for that hologram rubbish now."

"Sure, Eshan, no problem." Khalid nods, feeling a little better. *I sometimes felt like a hologram inside that prison*, he thinks.

They cross the road together and Eshan fills him in on everyone.

"Mikael's moved to Australia with his family. He got eleven GCSEs, eight As—did best of the lot of us. Like we didn't know that was gonna happen, eh?"

"And Tony?" Khalid asks.

"Tony Banda left school once he were sixteen for his apprenticeship with British Gas. He was made up—it was all he ever wanted, remember?"

"No." Khalid doesn't remember that at all.

"Well, it's true. He stopped playing football when he broke his leg, and after you went missing, the team fell apart," Eshan says. "And, you won't believe this, he's still going out with Lexy."

"Really? Lucky bloke! How about Nico?" Khalid says, not daring to ask him about Niamh.

"Nico's still at school. His mam wouldn't let him go to sixth-form college, said he'd never do any work if he got there. She's probably right. He did about as well as me—seven GCSEs, mostly As and Cs—not bad, not brilliant. But then we didn't exactly push ourselves, did we?"

Arriving outside Nico's terraced house, Eshan says, "Good to see you again, Kal. Come over any time. We missed you, mate. It wasn't the same after you disappeared."

"What about, er . . .? Have you seen—um . . . No, never mind. See ya later, yeah?"

"Bye." Eshan walks backwards down the road, doing crazy rapping gestures with his fingers, shouting, "East is East!"

Khalid stands for ages outside Nico's door before walking up the path to knock for him, but there's no one in and he sets out for home sad and disappointed. Wondering if he ought to go via the road leading to the school on the off chance he might bump into Mr. Tagg. Then he can find out what forms he needs to apply for college or whether you have to be an old lady to get in without any exam certificates.

But when Khalid arrives home there's a surprise waiting for him. As if he's read his mind, Mr. Tagg's in the kitchen talking to Dad and puffing a cigarette out of the window.

"Welcome home, Khalid." The scruffy, wild-haired history teacher in jeans, red shirt and brown leather jacket stubs the cigarette out on the chipped blue plate Dad's given him.

"Thanks." Khalid looks at his teacher standing there by the sink, nodding and smiling, genuinely pleased to see him, and becomes embarrassed, self-conscious and shy—suddenly fifteen again with no idea what to say.

"I kept the letter you sent me." Taking a worn page of scribbled writing from his jeans pocket, Mr. Tagg hands it to him and Khalid's eyes dart down the page, shocked to see the letter had actually reached him, immediately recognizing the words and sentences from that day in his tiny cell. The strange sensation of reading it again speeds him back to the darkness and distress that caused him to write it. When at last Khalid glances away from the crumpled page, he catches the concerned look on Dad's face and pulls himself together by faking a huge smile.

"Thanks. I was thinking of asking you about sixth-form college," Khalid says with a gulp. "I want to get my exams."

"I'll be more than happy to help," Mr. Tagg says, nodding.

"Great. I suppose it won't be easy, though," Khalid guesses.

"I'll have a word with the principal. Can't see why there would be a problem. Unforeseen circumstances and all that."

"Yeah. OK, well . . . er, thanks!" Now Khalid's really smiling.

"And thank you very much on behalf of my family, Mr. Tagg," Dad chimes in.

Sitting back down to finish his large mug of tea, Mr. Tagg looks thoughtful for a second.

"My pleasure. There's only one thing I ask, Khalid. Will you come and help me do an assembly on that awful place you've been? There's a lot of anti-Muslim feeling building at the moment and we want to keep the school and Rochdale free from that kind of sentiment."

"Yeah. Why not?" Khalid grins. "I'm up for it."

"We hate terrorists as much as you do," Dad agrees.

It's not until two days later that Khalid catches up with Nico, who's running to get through the school gates before the bell goes, rap music spilling from his earpieces. Khalid can't quite make out the words but Nico's clearly enjoying the strong bass beat.

"Hey!" Khalid jumps in front of him. Overwhelmed by the wideness of Nico's shocked smile as he rips the plugs from his ears, tries to lift his old mate Khalid in the air. But Khalid's too tall for him now and they both crack up.

"Kal. Kal. Kal." Nico makes do with bouncing him round for all to see. "Mam said to stay away until you'd settled back in. How's it been, me old matey?" Finally he lets him go.

"You're about to find out—I'm doing the assembly with Mr. Tagg this morning!" Khalid laughs.

"Aw no, his assemblies go on for hours. Do you have to?" Nico sighs, grinning from ear to ear.

## ASSEMBLY

"And now, this fine young man, Khalid Ahmed, who's been to hell and back in the last two years, has agreed to read out the letter he sent me from his cell in Guantanamo Bay. It was the only one among the many letters he wrote to me that arrived here for me to read. As you know, Guantanamo Bay is situated on the south-east corner of the island of Cuba . . ."

A group of teachers behind him shift in their chairs. Some with drooping, tired faces and untidy hair look half asleep, while others with eager eyes and polished shoes lean forward to listen.

Finally, Mr. Tagg stops talking and nods for Khalid to get up from the seat at the side of the stage, which causes him to stop fiddling with his shirt cuffs and break out in a nervous sweat.

Scraping his chair back, Khalid looks down at the sea of faces watching him walk towards the microphone, the letter in his hand. Breathing heavily, heart thumping faster the closer he gets, Khalid becomes irritated with himself for shaking so much as he grabs the microphone. Seeing most of the kids he used to play football with all looking up at him now as if he's a hero, thinking because they know him they understand what he's been through, Khalid is suddenly put off. And all the time he's scanning the crowd for Niamh's pretty face, longing for it to jump out at him. To see her is all he wants now, her brown, wavy hair flicking up from her neck. The memory of her smile hypnotizes Khalid for a second, blanking his mind completely. Now, two long years later, someone who looks a bit like her is smiling up at him from the front row and he knows she means nothing by it because she isn't Niamh.

Mr. Tagg rushes to the microphone to cover for him while Khalid's heart and mind are lost in the memory of Niamh's pretty face—an image that has helped him make it to this point.

"Ahem. One. Two. Yes, it's fine. Go ahead, Khalid. Go on, lad. Speak."

Then Nico, in the back row, suddenly cheers. Everyone turns to look at him, which makes Khalid laugh and gives him a moment's pause before he starts.

"Dear Mr. Tagg," Khalid begins shyly, voice trembling. "I thought I'd let you know why I didn't finish my history coursework." A raucous laugh rises from the hall resulting in a sudden burst of confidence. The second the noise dies down, Khalid clears his throat and lays into the letter again.

"It's a bit of a long story and beggars can't be choosers, as the man said. I asked my dad to fill you in about all the lies they've made up about me here so I won't go into that now. But I know one thing—even if I am an evil person that doesn't mean someone has the right to try and drown me by hanging me upside down and pouring water down my nose.

They've beaten me. They've kicked me. They've bolted me to the floor like an animal. They've kept me awake night after night. Almost burst my eardrums with loud music. Some are suffering worse things than me, they've been badly damaged in so many ways you don't want to know, and my cousin Tariq is here too. They've put the finger on me for no reason is what I'm saying and I'll never understand why."

A rumble of murmuring and spate of shuffling fill the hall as kids twist in their seats to catch every word. Shock, horror, disbelief passes over their surprised faces while Khalid takes a quick breath before continuing.

"Hurt is hurt. Harm is harm. Bullying is bullying. What everyone wants is the same thing—kindness. I'd like to see more kindness when I get out of here, because I'm sick of hearing about bombs and seeing pictures of people dying and terrorists doing this and that. I'm just a kid who wants to get A-levels and go to uni and make something of himself. I don't want to hang around waiting for someone to give me anything, but I do want to see the snow blowing over Rochdale again and get a game of footy going down the park with my mates. That's something I dream about every day locked up in Guantanamo. I hope you can help me get started again one day, that's if they ever let me go.

"I know one day, Mr. Tagg, you will ask me what I've learned. Well, if I could advise anyone out there, I'd say the only way to prevent violence is to stop being violent, stop thinking nasty thoughts about other people. Stop hurting other people. Stop lying and cheating. How come the world doesn't get that? One day I'd like to go to Mount Snowdon in Wales or to the Lake District or out walking in one of those pretty villages with nice stone cottages in the Dales. I'd love to have that freedom. But you know what? I haven't got the nerve to go there because people might stare at me and the woman in the shop will maybe get her husband to serve me because she's scared.

"There're woods and streams and fields and nice places in England my family have never seen because people are so suspicious of anyone who looks different. When people do that, I shrink up, trying not to look like a wacko. I hide my face by pretending to find a shop or pavement that's interesting.

"I'm writing this because I would never have the nerve to say this stuff to your face. Yeah, and sorry about not having spell-check and that to do this properly. Bet you a million pounds this won't get to you at the school anyway. By the way, you ought really to stop smoking. I've seen you light up two cigarettes before you get to the main road.

"I've been a regular blatherer, I know. Sorry. I just want to get back and stop in my house, eat some decent food and see my mates. I suppose the main thing I've learned is that hatred changes nothing. It just adds to the hatred that's already there. The person who's hated has the choice to ignore it, while the hater is always overtaken by his violent feelings. So who's the loser? It's the person who hurts every time, who lies and cheats, and I'm never going to be like that, because then I'll have learned nothing.

"Yours sincerely,

"Khalid Ahmed (10G) (from two years ago)"

The minute he finishes, the hall erupts with cheering and

clapping. Nico starts whistling, then shouting, "Close down GUAN-TAN-AMO!" And then another burst of cheering, clapping, whistling and foot-stomping breaks out. Rocking the school hall until everyone joins in. Even a few of the staff.

"Close down GUAN-TAN-AMO!" The sound hits the roof, bouncing off the walls as Khalid returns to his seat. Shaking. Mr. Tagg anxiously flaps his hands to calm them, while proudly nodding at his former student.

"Well read, Khalid. Well done. Thank you!" But his voice is drowned out by another burst of stamping feet.

"Words aren't enough," Khalid whispers. Tired of everyone getting high on their own righteousness. Refusing to allow his heart to swell in case he starts sinking. In case he starts forgetting how to let go. Something no one else in the room will ever understand. How can he be blown away by the sound of their chanting? Their words are too far outside the hell he suffered.

Leaving the stage with Mr. Tagg's arm round his shoulder, Khalid catches sight of a pretty girl smiling at him. A picture that lights up his mind for many days to come.

Hour by hour, Khalid jumps back into ordinary sounds. The crackling TV. Humming washing machine. Aadab singing. Chit-chat in the kitchen. Back into ordinary colors: green socks, red cars, Mum's purple cardigan on the chair.

Back into light and shade from the living-room windows and lamps that turn on and off. Mobile phones. Ordinary pleasures like a fridge full of food. And ice trays. Taps with water available at any time. Shops with chocolate and lottery tickets. And every dinnertime the kitchen smells of fresh food made with love.

Khalid walks through Rochdale not as he used to do—like someone who belongs there, head high, hoodie hanging off his shoulders—but like a dignified shy young man in black jeans and blue T-shirt who looks at the pavement more than he should. Nervous he'll trip over or bump into someone or, even worse, get shouted at.

Today Khalid takes the time to stare at the new laundromat that occupies the space where Nasir's greengrocer's shop used to be. He digs his hands in his pockets, sparking the memory of standing there wet through after helping that female jogger get her phone back from the steroid heads. How Nasir had offered to give him his old fleece jacket and warned him about what was happening in Pakistan.

Where is he, Nasir?

Now, instead of cabbages and grapefruits and the sound of rain on a green canvas roof, all Khalid can hear is the swish of soapy washing machines. He watches a blue plastic basket of clothes being filled by a factory woman in white overalls who waves at him suddenly, then waddles to the door.

"Thought it were you, lad. Recognized you from telly and the *Rochdale Evening News*. They want shooting, that lot, after what they did. You don't look owt like a terrorist, any fool can see that. Bloody 'ellfire."

"Thanks." Khalid shuffles from foot to foot. "Don't suppose you know what happened to the bloke who used to have the greengrocer's here?"

"Yeah, lad, I do." She grins. "It were a while ago someone put a petrol bomb through his letter-box and almost burned the place down. Lucky the bloke and his family were out.

They were at the hospital because the wife's friend was ill. He moved out the area soon after. Some say they went back to Pakistan. Poor devils."

Khalid nods and walks away, deeply saddened. Nasir's kind face stays at the front of his mind as he heads down to the high street to see what else has changed, before pausing at the newsagent's on the corner to buy some chocolate. Khalid takes his place in the queue behind a teenage girl with long hair and a pierced eyebrow. Dressed in short skirt and thigh-high boots, she throws three magazines on the counter. Adding chewing gum and a packet of Pontefract cakes as an afterthought.

"Just a minute, I've got the exact money here—somewhere." Scrabbling noisily in her deep leather bag, she brings up a handful of coins and a bent cigarette.

Fascinated by the tattoo of a chain around her arm, Khalid doesn't at first notice the sudden whiff of sweet perfume behind him.

"Hiya, Kal. Didn't you see me?" Niamh taps him on the shoulder. "I was in the pet shop next door looking at the parakeets when you went past."

Stunned, Khalid freezes. All the color drains from his face. Wearing white cut-offs and a yellow sparkly jumper, Niamh looks nothing like she used to. Her hair's cut short in a bob and she's overdone the gold eyeshadow a bit. He remembers her face quite differently. She's pretty but not in the amazing way he thought she was. Now she's too skinny and he'd never noticed how fake her smile was before.

"You were great in assembly," Niamh says. "Wasn't it cool when everyone started shouting? I was like, hey, Kal deserves this. Gilly was like, 'But he must have done something bad, otherwise why did he end up there?'"

Khalid gazes at her face. At her pale green eyes. At her fluttering eyelashes and smudged mascara. At the pink lips he's dreamed of kissing over and over again.

"You OK, Kal?" she asks.

Khalid trembles. "I, um. I was . . ."

Stuffing the magazines into her expanding leather bag, the tattooed girl gawps at him, then Niamh, before hurrying past.

"What do you want, lad?" the newsagent asks, staring at Khalid's tranced-out face as if there's a strong possibility he's going to remain frozen like that, blocking up the counter forever. In the end, Niamh takes his arm.

"Come on, Kal, let's get out of here."

Together they cross the road, with the foul smell of exhaust fumes in his face.

"Anyway, as I was saying, we all tore into Gilly because she said that about you." Niamh smiles. "And I went off her soon after, because she tried to snog my boyfriend. Can you believe it? Some friend she turned out to be."

Boyfriend? Did she say boyfriend? Khalid's arm shoots forward. He grabs a black railing to steady himself. The roar of cars dies away. A deadly hush falls on him.

"I think you need to sit down." Niamh frowns. "There's a bench over there."

At that moment an empty black bin bag catches a puff of wind and blows past them down the street. Cars roar past once more and Khalid remembers he's here at home in Rochdale.

Not dreaming. Niamh takes his elbow and leads him to the bench outside the pharmacy.

"Sit down. What's on your mind, Kal? You look ill all of a sudden," she says.

"Nothing," Khalid says. But then something deep inside him remembers all the hours he spent wishing he'd said things to Niamh when he had the chance. And now he does. But the words won't come.

"What is it? You can tell me," Niamh says.

"Well, s'ppose I was thinking, yeah?" Khalid starts.

"And . . ." Niamh nods. "Go on."

"Well, er . . . I guess I, yes, I always liked your buttercup painting and, er, I like you. Always have done." He can feel his face blushing slightly, but he doesn't care. He's said it now.

"Aw, thanks. I really like you too, Kal, so that's great, isn't it?" Not taking the hint at all. "If I wasn't going out with Josh Parker, I'd so def be into you. So I would."

The hammer blow to his heart lands so hard and fast, Khalid doubles up in pain, coughing.

"You *are* in a bad way." She grabs his arm. "Do you want me to go in the pharmacy and get something?"

"No. I just got a tickle in my throat. No problem." Clutching his chest, Khalid points to the sports shop. "I'm going in there. Need another cap. Worn this one to death to hide my hair growing out."

"Let's see . . ." Niamh watches him hesitate for a moment before revealing his crazily stumpy black hair.

"It's not so bad, Kal."

"Too right. Thanks. Later." He jumps up to duck quickly

inside the shop's glass doors and, holding a palm up to make sure she doesn't follow, waves her away. Khalid walks over to a rack of red and black caps, shaking his head with disbelief.

Niamh's going out with that total idiot Josh Parker?

The guy who lost them the league match against Burnley because he can't even kick a ball straight? How can she like him? Didn't his sister, Jacinda, tell the whole class he twists her arm so badly she says anything to make him stop? Anyone going out with that loser needs to get their head examined. Fast. About to try on a cool black cap because the spotty shop assistant is watching his every move, Khalid loses track of himself—of the shop, the cap in his hand and the gormless assistant.

An overpowering weakness forces Khalid to perch on the edge of the gray display board before he passes out. Lifting his right hand, he tries to click his fingers. Click them in front of his eyes. But he's shaking all over. His hand won't keep still and he can't breathe. A streak of sunshine on the edge of a gold kit bag catches his eye and two plump jinn dart out from the flickering light with big smiles and sugar-white teeth. Khalid's throat tightens and sweat pours from him. He's in such a state of panic he doesn't notice Nadim and Sabeeh, his old friends from primary school, on their way home from the mosque. Khalid doesn't see Nadim running his eyes over the new half-zip shirts and black-and-white sneakers in the window, then suddenly stare in more closely and beckon his mate to take a look at Khalid, trembling and shivering. Two shop assistants standing warily close by.

Moving as one through the glass doors to get to him, "Khalid!" Nadim and Sabeeh shout.

"We'll look after him," Sabeeh says, nodding to the shop guys, while Nadim bends low to gently take Khalid's shaking hands from his damp forehead. Shocked by the fear in his wild popping eyes, he pats his shoulder.

"Hey, Khalid. You're OK, mate. We'll take you home."

But Khalid doesn't answer. He can barely walk straight.

# 30

## GUL

Today sunshine streams through the open kitchen window. The sound of heavy traffic can be heard zooming down Oswestry Road because the short cut to town has been closed due to roadworks. Not that Khalid minds. Resting an elbow on the kitchen table, he's chewing a blue pen and wondering what else to tell Tariq after scrawling two pages of news that he doubts he'll ever see.

He's already told him about reading his letter to Mr. Tagg in front of the whole school and the amazing reaction of all the kids. Plus how he's continually stopped by people he doesn't know and everyone expects him to say something, anything, to account for his time in Guantanamo Bay. He's running out of ideas.

Surely they must realize he would rather forget about the place and talk about Rochdale's latest win. Fed up with the thought that the subject will never go away, which hits Khalid harder each time he sits down to write to his cousin. He quickly rushes through the description of the lame bunch of kids from yesterday.

"There's that terrorist who tried to blow up London," one

of them shouted, sending a shiver of fear and rage up Khalid's spine.

If only everything would calm down, he might be able to get on with his life. Get through another day without having a panic attack and being overcome by despair at the years he's missed out on.

Then seeing Niamh. Learning she's going out with Josh Parker of all people. No wonder Khalid needed help getting home that day. He'd built her up into some perfect beauty who loved him—who was going to fall into his arms the moment she saw him. Out of desperation mostly. And she'll never know how just the thought of her kept him going. Still keeps him going, though not in the same way as before. Now when he pictures her face, he sees her as she actually is: a nice girl, not a pin-up fantasy or some kind of savior at all. Someone whose eyes and smile used to light up many lonely hours, and he'll always be thankful to her for that.

Looking around the kitchen for inspiration at the polished knives in the correct slots of the wooden knife holder. At the blue striped dishcloth folded neatly on the metal drainer. Bar of pink soap in the new see-through plastic dish. Everything in the kitchen makes Khalid smile. Mum, in her favorite navy-blue dress, stops sprinkling nutmeg, salt and pepper on the plate of chicken breasts to smile back.

Opposite him, Gul, with glossy hair fanning over her shoulders, arms everywhere, draws a picture of someone else's street. Khalid writes to Tariq about her racing to finish coloring the birds in the sky before the dinner plates and cutlery clatter down and how stumps of wax crayons are rolling like marbles across the table. Snap-snapping to the floor as she wildly shades the horse in the field brown, the grass green, the houses the same yellow as the summer sun.

The sound of falling crayons brings back the powerful noise of clacking food trays and the picture of Tariq staring at the air conditioner. Alone. Bent double on the bed, hoping for the sound of footsteps that might bring him someone to talk to while he waits for the call to prayer to sound across the block. Another brutal twenty-four hours of nothingness stretching out in front of him without any idea when it'll end. Without anything to look forward to now that Khalid's not there.

"Gul, can I have that drawing to send to Tariq?" Khalid asks. "I've run out of things to say and you know he once had a sister called Radhwa the same age as you."

"I remember." Gul smiles. "But he can't have my picture."

"Did he ever mention Radhwa to you?" Mum turns to face him suddenly.

"No. Never. But he always liked hearing about Aadab and Gul."

"Such a shame." Mum shakes her head. "I can't help wondering what part Tariq played in this whole mess."

"MUM! You don't even know him or anyone he used to chat with. He just invented a silly game that someone decided was dangerous. He's stuck there right now, as innocent as I was."

"I understand everything, you know that, Khalid. I feel sad for Tariq. For what happened. But those things he said about your father, they can't be forgiven."

"Mum, don't judge him unless you know all the facts, OK?

I made that mistake," Khalid says. But seeing he's made her feel guilty, he attempts to cheer her up. "Any chance you can make fluffy chips to have with the curry?'

Her face softens into a smile. "Yes. Plenty of potatoes in the cupboard, son. How happy it makes me saying "son" to you. Yes. My son is here with us once more."

"Don't get soppy again. You promised you wouldn't."

"Soppy? Me? Not me, son. Never."

Khalid grins as his attention turns to the swirl of orange smoke Gul's adding to her picture.

"Gul, don't wreck it with that horrible orange color."

"Why not?" A silly grin is plastered across her face.

"I don't like the color, that's all." Khalid frowns at Gul. Concerned because Mum's hiding her tears by looking for something in the highest cupboard and he doesn't want Gul to see her crying.

*There's not much more I can tell you, cuz,* Khalid writes quickly. *I don't think that feeling of total misery will ever really go away. Soon, I promise, you'll get home. But whenever I start to think of that prison, I stop and remind myself how kind most people are in the world. Did I tell you Mac, my nice neighbor, is going to teach me to drive his car? For free. How cool is that?*

The front door clicks. Khalid listens for his dad to pause in the hall to hang up his brown zip jacket. He comes in, his face full of warmth and happiness when he sees Khalid.

"Hi, Dad, did you see that poster for the oriental rug sale on Saturday up the road?" Khalid asks.

Before answering, Dad smiles and quietly slips off his

brown shoes to reveal ribbed gray socks, then empties his pocket of nutmeg cake wrapped in wrinkly tin foil on to the kitchen table.

"Yes, it starts at ten in the morning and goes on the whole day." He scrapes the chair back and sits down.

"Well, we're going. Don't look so surprised. Just think of it as a little act of kindness on my part."

"Oh, I will, I will." Dad laughs.

Mum, Aadab and Gul join in too.

There's nowhere in the world Khalid would rather be than right here . . .

Spying his dad's new shoes on the floor reminds him of something. "Dad, give us your shoes. You've got dirt all over them. A right mess they are." He darts to the cupboard under the sink to take out the cardboard box.

His dad stares at him, amused, as Khalid unfolds a sheet of newspaper on the floor and sits cross-legged. He lays the cloth and brushes neatly side by side on the paper, just as he's seen his dad do so many times. Carefully, he opens the tin of dark-brown Kiwi polish and pats at it with the brush. Then, fist in the shoe, he spreads the polish evenly, working it into the leather one section at a time. Focusing hard on polishing the rims of the sole, before starting on the toe to patiently bring up the shine. In the middle of all this hard work he breathes in the lovely smell of sizzling chicken cooked with toasted almonds and couscous, and a small fire lights up not only in Khalid's eyes and stomach, but also in his heart.

Dad looks on with approval and Khalid knows this small act

of kindness means more to him than he could ever imagine.

Then, for that moment, as he sits on the kitchen floor cleaning Dad's shoes, some of the sadness in Khalid's heart lifts and the past collapses into a little burst of happiness. The kind of happiness that a loving family brings.

# Afterword

The fact that has struck me hardest about Guantanamo Bay is the number of juveniles who were brought there, as many as sixty in a total population of some 780. And not just "juveniles"—but kids.

These kids include Mohammed el Gharani from Chad, one of Reprieve's clients, who had never even been to Afghanistan until the US paid a bounty to his captors and took him there. US Intelligence thought Mohammed was in his mid-twenties: despite years of interrogation, it had not been discovered that he was only fourteen years old and had gone to Pakistan simply to learn about computers. US District Judge Richard Leon later determined that he was innocent of any wrongdoing, and he was released after more than seven years in captivity.

Mohammed was innocent and should have been in school. Yet he learned the lessons of adolescence in a maximum security prison, in cells with those reputed to be the most dangerous of terrorists.

Sadly, it's happening elsewhere. Now a similar situation is occurring in the US detention center in Bagram Air Force base in Afghanistan, where a kid called Hamidullah was himself just 14 when he was first detained. At Reprieve, we're working to defend his rights and the rights of other prisoners. As a nation, we cannot expect the world to embrace democracy and the rule of law unless we respect it ourselves.

—Clive Stafford Smith
Founder and Director, Reprieve
March 7, 2011

*For more about Reprieve's work regarding Guantanamo Bay, please visit www.reprieve.org.uk.*

# GUANTANAMO BAY TIMELINE*

**2001**

September 11, 2001 — Operatives of Al-Qaeda, an international terrorist group, attack the World Trade Center and the Pentagon.

October 7, 2001 — The war in Afghanistan begins. The US military targets the Taliban, the ruling militia in Afghanistan, which refuses to hand over Al-Qaeda leader Osama bin Laden.

December 2001 — Osama bin Laden escapes from Afghanistan.

**2002**

January 11, 2002 — Twenty suspected terrorists are detained at Camp X-Ray at Guantanamo Bay. They are the first detainees to arrive.

January 17, 2002 — The US military allows the Red Cross to establish permanent residence at the Guantanamo Bay prison.

January 18, 2002 — President George W. Bush declares that Guantanamo Bay detainees are not protected under the Geneva Conventions, which require that certain rights are given to prisoners of war.

February 27, 2002 — Detainees go on a hunger strike to protest a rule against wearing turbans, which are a common part of Muslim religious life and are often used during prayer.

April 25, 2002 — Camp Delta is built to house 410 prisoners.

(continued on next page)

**2003**

April 23, 2003 — The US military admits that children sixteen and younger, many of whom have been held for a year, are among the detainees. Three boys from Afghanistan, ages thirteen to fifteen, are among the inmates and are held in a dedicated juvenile facility; they are released in 2004.

May 9, 2003 — Guantanamo Bay prison reaches 680 detainees, the most it has held at one time.

October 9, 2003 — The Red Cross says there is "deterioration in the psychological health of a large number of detainees."

**2004**

October 16, 2004 — According to the *New York Times*, detainee abuse is more pervasive than the Pentagon has let on.

**2006**

February 15, 2006 — A report from the United Nations recommends the closure of Guantanamo Bay prison.

May 28, 2006 — According to London lawyers, dozens of children as young as fourteen years old have been sent to Guantanamo Bay prison, and they estimate that more than sixty detainees were under eighteen when they were captured.

June 29, 2006 — The US Supreme Court rules Guantanamo Bay detainees are protected under the Geneva Conventions.

**2007**

February 7, 2007 — According to a Pentagon inquiry, there is no evidence of abuse at the Guantanamo Bay prison.

**2009**

January 14, 2009

A senior Bush administration official releases a public statement detailing the torture of one of the Guantanamo Bay detainees.

January 22, 2009

President Barack Obama issues executive orders to close Guantanamo Bay within one year, to ban CIA interrogation techniques that might be considered torture, and to review the prison's detention policies.

**2011**

January 22, 2011

Two years after President Obama's executive order to close Guantanamo Bay, the prison remains open with 174 prisoners. Many have called for its closure, including General Colin Powell, General David Petraeus, and General Wesley Clark of the US armed forces; former FBI Director William Sessions; and Defense Secretary Robert Gates.

April 25, 2011

Leaked classified documents reveal that more than a hundred detainees at Guantanamo have been innocent or low-risk inmates, including cases where officials were aware of their status.

May 1, 2011

Osama bin Laden is killed by US forces in Abbottabad, Pakistan, during a covert operation authorized by President Obama.

May 3, 2011

When asked whether the information leading to Bin Laden was obtained by waterboarding, a controversial interrogation technique, Deputy National Security Advisor John Brennan replies, "Not to my knowledge."

*For sources, please see last page.

## *Guantanamo Boy*
## Synopsis and Discussion Questions

by Michael Robinson, award-winning
high school social studies teacher

# SYNOPSIS

The book begins six months after the events of 9/11 in
Rochdale, a large city near Manchester, England. Khalid is an
average fifteen-year-old student at Rochdale High who enjoys
hanging out with his friends, watching and playing soccer,
and playing video games on the family computer. His father is
originally from Pakistan, and his mother is from Turkey. The
family is Muslim, but his mother does not wear the Islamic
veil, and the family only occasionally says Friday prayers.
The family goes on a vacation to Pakistan to visit and help
Khalid's father's sisters move to a better house. Once there,
Khalid's father goes missing, and Khalid goes to search for
him. While looking for his father on the streets of Karachi,
Khalid becomes part of a street demonstration. Unable to
find his father, Khalid returns home, where shortly thereafter
several men storm into the house and take Khalid prisoner.

Over the course of the next two years, Khalid is taken from Pakistan to Afghanistan and finally to Guantanamo Bay. He is questioned relentlessly about being involved in terrorism and undergoes tremendous mental and physical torture. With the help of his family, community, and his lawyer, Khalid is released from Guantanamo Bay shortly after his seventeenth birthday and allowed to go home to England where he is finally free to live his life. This is a story of injustice, survival, and courage. Khalid was your typical average boy in almost every way, but after surviving two years of imprisonment, torture, conditions of near insanity, and severe loneliness, Khalid shows how the human spirit can overcome and survive the worst situations imaginable, proving he is anything but average.

## THEME DISCUSSION

Use the following questions and prompts relating to the overall themes in *Guantanamo Boy* as a basis for discussion of the book.

## Family

- How does one's family influence the choices that one makes?
- Discuss how one relies on his/her family for help, support, and guidance.

## Prison and Punishment

- What is the purpose of a prison?
- Discuss if the punishments found in the book are effective and appropriate.
- Discuss if torture should be used to obtain information from someone.

## Terrorism

- Define terrorism and a terrorist act.
- Discuss what types of terrorist acts have occurred in the United States and other countries around the world.
- Discuss how countries should respond to terrorist acts against its people.

## Governments

- What is the role of a government?
- How do governments protect and provide security for their people?
- Discuss how a country can balance a person's rights and still provide the security that is needed.

## Religion

- Define religion and discuss the role it plays in society. How do religions affect a person's way of living?
- Discuss how the world's two largest religions (Christianity and Islam) are similar and different. What about other religions, such as Judaism, Hinduism, and Buddhism?

# CHAPTER DISCUSSION QUESTIONS AND PROMPTS

The following pages contain discussion questions and prompts using direct quotes from each of the book's thirty chapters.

## Chapter 1: Game

p. 4: *"Six months after 9/11 and the world is getting madder by the day,"* [Khalid's father] *says from suddenly behind him.*

> How did the world change, especially in the United States, after 9/11?

p. 4–5: Khalid's father to Khalid: *"Things will get worse before they get better," Dad says. "A man came into the restaurant today, pointed his finger at the waiter and said, "You better watch your step round here, mate.' Can you believe it? The boy hasn't done anything wrong. Nothing except wear the shalwar kameez. That's it."*

> What is a shalwar kameez?
>
> Discuss the meaning of racial profiling and how it applies in this example.

p. 11: Khalid on his mother: *Mum has never worn the veil and neither did her mother in Turkey, where she was brought up.*

> What is the veil?
>
> Why would Muslim women wear the veil? Why would they not wear it?

**Chapter 2: Blood's Thicker Than Water**

p. 25-26: *Khalid reads the message written in large black words on his flapping white T-shirt:* SMALL-MINDED FLAG-WAVING XENOPHOBE. *Eh? Khalid stops for a second to wonder at the meaning of the word "xenophobe."*

What is xenophobia? Give an example.

p. 28: Nasir to Khalid: *"I'm thinking you must be careful, lad. My wife's family have plenty of friends who live there and they say the Americans are paying people big bucks to report anyone suspicious to them."*

What is the danger in paying for information?

**Chapter 3: Karachi**

p. 40: *[Khalid] logs on to his e-mail and discovers that Tariq's game—Bomber One—is ready. A whizz-kid friend of his in Lahore has helped to finish the program and download it. Tariq's sent him instructions on how to set up his profile so they can all play together soon.*

Discuss what type of game *Bomber One* is. What kinds of computer and video games are popular? Explain.

**Chapter 4: Missing**

p. 47: Khalid finds himself part of a demonstration in Karachi: *The throng of men is growing by the second. Khalid stops. Turns to go back and find another route to avoid this chaos. But he gets caught in a sudden wave of men surging from a side alley. Pulling him forward in a lawless mass of anger that reminds him of getting caught in the rivers of fans coming out of Old Trafford after Manchester United have lost a game.*

Why was it dangerous for Khalid to become involved in the demonstration?

p. 50: *Jim shakes his head. "Everybody from a Muslim country is seen as a threat to the USA right now."*

Discuss why Jim makes the statement above.

p. 52: *"Will you have to marry a Muslim girl?" Niamh asked. "I can marry who I like," [Khalid had] said. Not wanting to get into this. Thinking, Should I tell her if she isn't a Muslim she can convert? Loads do.*

Discuss why it would be important for a Muslim to marry a person who is also Muslim?

How does this quote relate to other religions such as Christianity, Judaism, Hinduism, etc.?

## Chapter 5: Easter

p. 62: *Blocking the hallway is a gang of fierce-looking men dressed in dark shalwar kameez . . . Confused by the image, [Khalid] staggers, bumping backwards into the wall. Arms up to stop them getting nearer. Too shocked and terrified to react as they shoulder him to the kitchen and close the door before pushing him to his knees and waving a gun at him as if he's a violent criminal. Then vice-like hands clamp his mouth tight until they plaster it with duct tape. No chance to wonder what the hell is going on, let alone scream out loud.*

Discuss what Khalid may be thinking as this terrifying abduction is taking place.

p. 63: *Paralyzed by fear, Khalid wonders desperately where they are taking him. Who are they? Why him? What for? Questions he can't even speak out loud.*

Discuss what we know about Khalid and the events of the day that may have contributed to his being kidnapped.

Discuss the following statement: Khalid was innocent. How can this happen to an innocent person?

## Chapter 6: Power

p. 67: *"This is Karachi, not England," [Khalid's interrogator] says. "You don't have any legal rights here. Tell us what you know and you can go home."*

What rights does Khalid not have while he is in Pakistan?

Discuss what human rights have been violated.

p. 76: *"Do I look like a terrorist?" [Khalid] says aloud, totally confused by the whole thing. His thoughts scatter to consider every possibility.*

Discuss Khalid's question, "Do I look like a terrorist?"

What (if any) characteristics do terrorists have?

## Chapter 7: Bread

p. 84: *Khalid stares into his invisible future and sees nothing worth living for . . .*

Explain why Khalid has given up on his future.

## Chapter 8: Masud

p. 91: Masud to Khalid: *"Americans looking everywhere, all time for Bin Laden . . ."*

Who is Bin Laden? What is he responsible for?

Discuss why Americans are looking for Bin Laden.

p. 92: Masud to Khalid: *"They accuse me of being enemy combatant."*

Define enemy combatant.

Why is this term used?

p. 94: *The one thing [Khalid] wishes he could change right now is the religion he was born into.*

Discuss why Khalid would want to change his religion.

### Chapter 9: To Kandahar

p. 95: *[Khalid] curls into a ball on the floor and cries. He'd always thought of himself as strong . . .*

> Discuss if anyone would be able to be "strong" if they had to go through what Khalid goes through.

### Chapter 10: Processing

p. 101: Khalid reacts to the shaving of the prisoners' beards: *It ignites a terrible anger in Khalid, who knows the shaving of the man's beard—an important part of his Muslim identity—is the final insult for him.*

> Discuss why a man's beard would be an important part of his Muslim identity.

p. 104–5: *[Khalid is mad] at the Americans for seeing them as just that: Muslims. Dangerous foreigners whom they can't even tell apart. Angry too at the Muslim religion for getting him into this mess. He once heard a newsreader say it was the fastest-growing religion in the world. Khalid remembers wishing the media wouldn't say stuff like that. People don't want to hear those facts, and he doesn't particularly want to be lumped together with loads of people he doesn't know, Muslim or not. And Muslims aren't all the same, just like Christians aren't all the same. He's Khalid—himself, not a result of any religion. He hasn't even done anything with his life yet.*

> What stereotypes exist about Muslims?
>
> Explain how Muslims are not all the same.

### Chapter 11: Red Cross

p. 120: A Red Cross worker approaches Khalid with a question: *"I'm with the Red Cross. Do you want to write a letter to anyone?" "A letter?" It's the first time Khalid's thought about it.*

*"Just one letter? Can't I do more?" "However many you want!"*
*The soldier opens the cell and hands Khalid three pieces of paper*
*and a black pen. Plus a cup which holds a card with a number.*
*His is 256.*

> Why was a member of the Red Cross allowed to speak
> with Khalid?
>
> Why is Khalid referred to by a number instead of by his
> name?
>
> Define dehumanization. Is Khalid being referred to as a
> number an example of dehumanization?

## Chapter 12: Wade

p. 129: Khalid's reaction when being allowed to see the sky:
*Khalid gazes at the sky as if for the first time and the sudden,*
*searing light makes him feel drunk as anything. It's so wonderful*
*and perfect . . .*

> What ordinary things would you miss if they were taken
> from you?

p. 132: Khalid on his solitary confinement: *It's a room Khalid gets*
*to know well, because every single half-hour over the next three*
*days the soldiers barge in to wake him. He fades in and out of*
*the most disturbed sleep ever conceived as his mind wanders to*
*thoughts and images he had no idea were even stored there.*

> How is this an example of torture?
>
> Is torture an effective way to find out important information
> from someone who does not want to cooperate?

## Chapter 13: Lights

p. 139: *. . . If [Khalid] can close his brain down for a bit, then*
*maybe he can forget? Perhaps if the guards stay away, he can fall*
*into a long, timeless sleep instead of the half-hour here and there*

*before another bitter wake-up . . .*

Why did the guards not allow Khalid to sleep?

p. 145: *Footsteps down the corridor sound inside a mind of shadows so dark, [Khalid] can hardly remember what day it is anymore . . .*

How did Khalid survive the torture?

**Chapter 14: Water Tricks**

p. 150: *Eyes closed, [Khalid's captors'] hands pressing down on his shoulders, Khalid hears the jug being filled with water at high velocity. A cloth lands on his face. More hands hold it down, so that he breathes in the smell of gauze bandages, and at the same time a trickle of cold water pours through the cloth and down his nose and mouth.*

Explain if this is an example of torture.

What is the purpose of this type of interrogation?

p. 152: *The suited man to Khalid: "This procedure will continue until you confess your part in the worldwide bombing campaign you planned with known accomplices," the man says firmly.*

Discuss why Khalid would confess to doing things he never did.

Do you think there would be people who might think Khalid is guilty even if they are aware of how the confession was obtained?

Discuss the consequences of his signed confession.

**Chapter 15: Sleep**

p. 167: On torture: *"It's a stupid way of finding anything out. Whenever my brother twists my arm up my back, it hurts so bad I say anything he wants me to just to get him to stop. So what's the point in torturing someone if all you get is lies?"*

    Answer Khalid's question: "So what's the point in torturing someone if all you get is lies?"

## Chapter 16: Guantanamo

p. 176: *Since he arrived in Guantanamo, Khalid hasn't really seen anyone. Just the food trolley man and the soldiers. The only sounds that keep him company day and night are terrifying screams from the other end of the building and then someone who coughs and coughs—he doesn't know which is worse. Plus the constant slamming of metal flaps gives him a headache, like a pneumatic drill in the side of his skull.*

    Discuss what it would be like if you had to go months with almost no contact with other people.

## Chapter 17: Sweat

p. 190: Masud to Khalid on his imprisonment: *"This I'm knowing for sure is against the law they set in Geneva. Certainly. No one here has received a trial. They cannot keep a child like you on your own. This is cruel torture."*

    What were the laws that were set at Geneva?

    What has happened to Khalid that could be against the law?

## Chapter 18: Every Shred

p. 197: *"I want a lawyer," Khalid says.*

    Discuss why and how Khalid can be held for this amount of time without access to a lawyer.

    Why has Khalid not had a trial?

    Discuss the demands Khalid is making, and explain if these are valid demands.

p. 198: An interrogator to Khalid: *"You will tell us what you know about al-Qaeda!"* Bruce says menacingly. *"If not now, then tomorrow or the next day. I hope you'll think about how your actions are harming innocent people."*

Define irony.

Discuss how the statement made by Bruce is ironic.

## Chapter 19: The Jinn

p. 204: *. . . Khalid hears the sounds of Ramadan start up again.*

What is Ramadan?

Discuss how fulfilling Ramadan is difficult for the Muslim prisoners.

## Chapter 20: Exercise

p. 221: Ali to Khalid: *"Islam is not a medieval culture . . ."*

Discuss how the culture of Islam is relevant in modern-times.

Why would someone assume that Islam is a "medieval culture"?

## Chapter 21: Hair

p. 232: Khalid after seeing his face in a mirror while getting his hair cut: *Was that really his face?*

Describe how Khalid reacts to seeing his face.

## Chapter 22: News

p. 241: *[Khalid feels] deep-seated hatred and contempt . . . for his cousin.*

Explain why Khalid has feelings of hatred toward his cousin.

Are these feelings justified?

### Chapter 23: Lee-Andy

p. 254: Tariq to Khalid: *"I said your father is a fund-raiser for extremists. I lied to stop them beating and driving me to insanity. Told them many lies about everyone. I'm asking for your forgiveness, cuz."*

> Discuss if Khalid should forgive Tariq for his lies against his father.

### Chapter 24: Harry

p. 266: *"Hi, Khalid, I'm your new lawyer. Name's Harry Peterson."*

> Describe how Khalid might feel when he realizes that he finally has a lawyer.

> Discuss who is supporting Khalid's release.

p. 275: *From now on, Khalid wants to be seen as honest and sincere, brave, forgiving and kind, so he thinks hard. Knowing once his words are taken down, they're written in stone and he never wants to be caught out again.*

> Discuss if Khalid has been brave since he was kidnapped.

### Chapter 25: Echoes

p. 281: *[The] religion [Khalid] once ignored and avoided because he thought it was uncool has become a major source of comfort, giving him something to turn to.*

> Discuss how religion has become an important part of Khalid's life.

> Discuss how and/or if religion can help people when they are in desperate situations.

### Chapter 26: Hot Shots

p. 292: *"I'm going to sue you for all of this. Just so you know,"*

*Khalid says. "I think you'll find you were never arrested," Major Leeth tells him, smirking. "No, that's right, I was kidnapped, wasn't I? You suckers better apologize for torturing me."*

Discuss what the major means when he tells Khalid that he was never arrested.

Discuss what type of compensation (if any) Khalid should receive for being kidnapped.

p. 297: *But not only does Khalid find this Rochdale stuff hard to believe; it seems incredible that from now on people will think he's special, though not for anything positive, just for spending time in that prison.*

Explain why Khalid is not excited about being seen as special.

### Chapter 27: Touchdown

p. 306: *"Your dad's on the phone!" Khalid freezes in shock. "Dad! Dad!" Khalid grabs the mobile. Holding it close, he turns away from Harry as Dad's soft, gentle voice passes through him in a wave of longed-for pure pleasure.*

Discuss what Khalid and his father would talk about on the phone after not seeing one another for two years.

What would you talk about with your family?

p. 307: *"Sorry to keep you waiting. I'm Professor Wolfson. My job is to help you settle back into normal life as soon as possible."*

Give examples of the difficulties Khalid might have adjusting to normal life.

### Chapter 28: Home

p. 315: *Then there's all the people knocking on the door, day and night. The local imams, Muslim leaders, journalists, friends and neighbors—even the guy who owns the restaurant where Dad works. Their constant voices, welcomes, and polite inquiries cause exhaustion and pounding headaches for Khalid.*

Discuss how Khalid reacts to all of the attention.

How would you react in his situation?

p. 322: Mr. Tagg to Khalid: *"There's only one thing I ask, Khalid. Will you come and help me do an assembly on that awful place you've been? There's a lot of anti-Muslim feeling building at the moment and we want to keep the school and Rochdale free from that kind of sentiment."*

Explain why it could be difficult for Khalid to tell about what happened to him while imprisoned.

### Chapter 29: Assembly

p. 326: Khalid on preventing violence: *" . . . I'd say the only way to prevent violence is to stop being violent, stop thinking nasty thoughts about other people. Stop hurting other people. Stop lying and cheating. How come the world doesn't get that?"*

Explain if you agree with what Khalid says about preventing violence.

### Chapter 30: Gul

p. 338: Khalid's letter to Tariq: There's not much more I can tell you, cuz, *Khalid writes quickly.* I don't think that feeling of total misery will ever really go away. Soon, I promise, you'll get home.

Discuss the possibility of Khalid's cousin being released.

p. 340: *. . . Khalid's heart lifts and the past collapses into a little burst of happiness. The kind of happiness that a loving family brings.*

Discuss how this statement means more to Khalid at seventeen than it did when he was fifteen.

## SOURCES FOR TIMELINE

www.cfr.org/publication/20018/us_war_in_afghanistan.html
projects.washingtonpost.com/guantanamo/timeline/
www.npr.org/templates/story/story.php?storyId=4715995
www.guardian.co.uk/uk/2007/dec/19/politics.terrorism
www.guardian.co.uk/world/2003/apr/23/usa
www.guardian.co.uk/world/2003/apr/24/usa.afghanistan
www.abc.net.au/am/content/2010/s2979501.htm
news.bbc.co.uk/2/hi/americas/3172617.stm
www.independent.co.uk/news/world/americas/the-children-of-guantanamo-bay-480059.html
news.yahoo.com/s/afp/20110425/ts_alt_afp/usattacksguantanamowikileaks_20110425091947
www.businessinsider.com/bin-laden-death-torture-waterboarding-obama-2011-5

U.S.A.

● Guantanamo Bay, Cuba